NOT DARK YET

The Tilbury Paradox

GREGORY MOORE

Agent Tilbury faces the New World
of the Red Dragon and Artificial Intelligence

ISBN 978-1-959182-32-0 (paperback)
ISBN 978-1-959182-33-7 (hardcover)
ISBN 978-1-959182-34-4 (digital)

gregorymoore.tilburytrilogy@gmail.com

This book is fiction within the context of reality and may upset some readers but the views expressed in this book are solely those of the author Gregory Moore. The context of reality is the basis of the unfolding story of fiction characters and their actions. Reality is often confronting and provides the environment for the fictional interactions.

In this context, the *Red Dragon* is an amalgam of rogue elements operating out of Beijing, China.

Printed in the United States of America

AI: Artificial Intelligence

And: Meaningful and potential connexions of knowns, unknowns, and unknown-unknowns.

Enigma: A person who is difficult to figure out, or something that is a puzzle or riddle.

Paradox: The real truth may not be true; all-pervading fake news.

Novels by Gregory Moore

The Tilbury spy fiction:

'**MIND GAME**: *The Tilbury Challenge*'

'**NOT DARK YET**: *The Tilbury Paradox*'

'**WALK THE WALK**: *The Tilbury Judgement*'

And coming, another Tilbury spy thriller

'THE SPY GAME: The Tilbury Deal' (due 2023)

See the early chapters of 'Mind Games' and 'Walk the Walk' at the end of this novel.

To Anggara, Djuana, and Lachlan, and all the coffee shops that gave the juice of creativity.

FORWARD

'MIND GAME: The Tilbury Challenge,' the first Tilbury spy thriller, introduced neuroplasticity; the new theory of how the brain can change/heal itself. With that knowledge, a creative technology, developed by Professor Stanley and Dr. Viviani, was used to improve cognition by artificially improving thought processes: a changed brain. However, the technology developed, called the *ithinkPad*, which was taken by OASIS, a nefarious global organization covertly supported by the CIA and the Pentagon to be used for criminal activity.

But the twist in the tail is the way in which John Tilbury, ex SAS, ASIO spook, and his assassin mate Thomas Black tracked down these evil people who used the ithinkPad for illicit intelligence gathering, impacting the lives of innocent people creating fractured lives as a result of the mind game, playing with the subconscious.

All around the pair are the lives and relationships of people affected that complicated Tilbury's pursuit through the tentacles of OASIS.

Later, this sequel, 'NOT DARK YET: The Tilbury Paradox' takes Tilbury's life as a puzzle, an enigma clouded by his past, as he is thrown into the world of AI technology, supercomputers, cybercrime, and counterintelligence and is reunited with the newer version of the ithinkPad. The complexity of the darknet and the influence of the 'Chinese way' lead Tilbury into a different world where all his skills were tested to the limit as he faces the MSS Adjustment Directorate and their 'AI hunter drones.'

Tilbury faces the paradox within the world of spy-craft.

However, along the way, he has to make a choice: who are his friends? What does he believe is the truth? Fake news is now *the news*; self-contradictory statements. To complicate matters, the ithinkPad had morphed into a dangerous AI-driven ithinkGoggles used by a group of terrorists.

Can Tilbury cope with his 'secret life,' the paradox, and a darkening new world for master spooks?

It has been a pleasure to bring Tilbury alive and into your lives.

But beware; the context of the thriller is 'reality' with fictional characters and situations, which may not be comfortable for some readers.

Gregory Moore
23 January 2022

1

A troubled man in a troubled world, Agent Tilbury on the balcony at his bay-side apartment on the outskirts of Brisbane, oiled his Glock. After the challenges supporting the fractured lives of returned vets affected by the mind game of a nefarious organisation, the dangerous world of CIA and Pentagon covert operations, the misuse of the 'ithink technology,' he pondered on the loss of his Italian lover Rachel Viviani.

The cool breeze brought the comforting waft of evening blossoms that cleared his thoughts as the orange sky melted below the tree line. In the background, the Bob Dylan lyrics of '*It's not dark yet, but it's getting there*' played on his mind.

Out of the silence, a phone call from an unknown female voice broke into his darkening thoughts.

"Agent Tilbury, I need your help, can we meet? I cannot talk because I am frightened. I will be at Café Boga at 1100 tomorrow. Can we meet, please?"

Before Tilbury could respond, the line went dead. Putting his past encounters into perspective, he thought about the puzzle of his life.

Will I go to Café Boga and meet this unknown person who is in trouble and be drawn into another chaos?

Agent John Tilbury of ASIO found himself caught up in the machinations of national security.

However, as a spook, he was quick to understand that such calls can have a life-threatening sting in the tail.

He was uncertain about meeting her at Café Boga because of the previous actions he had undertaken as an ASIO spy with his ex-SAS mate Thomas Black, a known assassin, the owner of Café Boga. But the call sparked an interest. As a spook, he often acted on instinct, and this was such a case. So, he walked from his apartment to the close-by Café Boga with a lot on his mind, searching for a backup plan in case the meeting was not as it seemed.

Tilbury, a loner, a man of few words, is left alone by customers of Café Boga, even though they may have seen him having his usual morning coffee fix. The steely eyes and no-nonsense body language tended to put off any conversation with him. As a man's man, Tilbury dominated his space. But now his morning coffee, where Café Boga, once a place for self-healing and focus that put the demons back in the box, was no longer a ritual part of a routine of solace.

All that had changed. He visited the owner Thomas Black to rebuild a frayed friendship and because he needed his morning Balinese coffee.

Tilbury kept his body and mind in shape through a punishing routine each morning of strenuous excises, a long swim in the downstairs pool, followed by meditation. A routine designed to quell the images that constantly swirled in his brain. For Tilbury, this was an emotional situation, the riddle of his life.

Was the black dog lurking?

When he walked into Café Boga, Black greeted him with a nod of recognition and brewed his usual Macchiato coffee. A quick head movement by Black indicated a female stranger sitting in a chair at the table always reserved for Tilbury. No locals ever sat there; they knew. But strangers were told the table was reserved.

"John, she asked for you."

"Ok, mate, I will go ask her what she wants."

Tilbury took in the stunning looking woman, as she sat, nervous, anxious, and watched the conversation between Black and Tilbury. Thinking these men are not to be trifled with, she wondered at the complex and sensitive nature of the matter she needed to discuss with Tilbury without giving too much away.

As he sat down beside her, Tilbury observed her body language and stressed eyes and introduced himself, "I'm John Tilbury, what can I do for you?"

Responding, she calmly said, "My name is Cassandra Jun."

Tilbury's heart nearly stopped and felt cold shivers run down his spine as he contemplated her name and the potential complications of the meeting. Holy fuck, he thought as the reality of his position struck him. Why me?

What does this beautiful Chinese woman really want from me?

It was thought, but unproven within ASIO circles, that General Li Jun, the right-hand confidant of the President of China, Zhang Wei, may have a sister living in Australia. As a result, they had a dossier on one potential woman, Cassandra Lui, who they thought maybe her and watched her. But ASIO knew that she was also watched by Chinese intelligence.

Was that a clue?

Cassandra Jun, a student at the Australian National University (ANU) studied the implications of economic thought as a driver of economic development under the tutelage of Professor Mary Smith. Jun knew the importance of cognition in governance and the development of small island nations in the Pacific.

Her older brother, now General Li Jun, had encouraged and supported her studies as he could see that later, she may become an important member of the Chinese Party and help China's influence in the Pacific.

However, she led a lonely life as a Chinese student, even though there were many of her country colleagues at ANU. She kept to herself as hardworking foreign students often did to increase and keep their grades.

But no one knew her identity as she was enrolled as Cassandra Lui from Beijing where she was brought up by her grandmother as an unwanted female baby. In her early twenties, she was told by her grandmother that she had a brother who was a very high-ranking official of the Chinese Party. After a long and fraught negotiation, they were united at a clandestine meeting.

Her brother, now General Li Jun, promised to look after her and sent her to Australia to learn about the western world and to think about the importance of the 'Chinese way' in the Asia/Pacific region to China.

The world of China was changing, and General Jun was now a confidant of President Zhang Wei, a relationship based on trust through their previous Party connexions. But was Cassandra's identity safe from the prying feelers of Chinese intelligence [MSS], located within Embassies and Consulates in Australia?

She noticed that there was always a follower, in the shadows, and regularly a friendly face would try to befriend her, eventually asking was she happy with the Party and seeking her trust. Each time, she rebuffed the contact in a friendly manner to not cause her any trouble. But the constant surveillance annoyed her and led her to believe that something was about to happen.

As Jun sat in *Aticus*, a coffee shop in Acton, a suburb of Canberra adjacent to the ANU waiting for Professor Smith, she was confronted by two Chinese males.

"We are MSS and are taking you back to China."

Shocked by the direct nature of the situation, she pleaded to visit the cafe's restroom. Using a back entrance, she fled from the cafe using a passing taxi to the Canberra airport and flew to Brisbane.

Cassandra Jun knew who she was, the potential for a quick getaway from her followers, and always had a passport, cash, and credit card ready. On arrival at Brisbane domestic airport, Jun gathered her thoughts, contacted Tilbury, made another call to Professor Smith, and told her what had happened.

"Mary, I'm in trouble with MSS, so I will disappear for a while, but I have called Dr. Tilbury for help."

Cassandra knew of Tilbury from her close relationship with Professor Smith at ANU who told her, in passing, about her exploits relating to cognition development through neuroplasticity technology using the ithink technology, and how Tilbury had helped her in a crisis. Smith had given Jun details for contacting Tilbury.

Stunned at the recognition of her name, Tilbury apologised to Jun, got up from his chair, and indicated to Black that he urgently needed to talk.

"What's up, John, you look somewhat pale and upset."

"Yes, mate, we have the sister of the second most important man in China wanting to talk to me. What the fuck do you think that means?"

"John, beware the 'Chinese way,' We know the bastards cannot be trusted. After speaking with her, please talk to me. We both know that you are going to need a friend."

"Thomas, we both know the political implications of her presence and the potential for interacting with MSS may prove to be nasty, so we need to be prepared. Please call Mac and give him the heads-up."

2

Returning to his seat, now with a backup plan in place, Tilbury coldly puts Jun on notice.

"Cassandra, we know who you are. What problems do I have coming my way?"

"Please call me Cassie. I come in peace."

Tilbury knew being a spook meant you do not trust such statements and that your life depended on a backup plan.

"Cassie, tell me what you want from me."

"John, you have an excellent reputation as a trusted spy and close friend of the head of ASIO Bob [Mac] McLeod. I trust you and want you to 'bring me in.' I have information that affects both our countries. I'm very scared of being kidnapped and taken back to China by the MSS."

"Cassie, how do you know of me?"

"John, I have 'friends' in high places."

With that statement, Tilbury rang his boss and mentor.

"Mac, Cafe Boga, come packing, we must bring in General Li Jun's sister. She is in danger from Chinese intelligence and has asked for asylum."

"Ok, John, keep her there until my team arrives."

Outside Café Boga, watching Tilbury in deep conversation with Jun were two MSS operatives who had tracked her.

Ever-vigilant, Black realised that the two Chinese men were not likely customers seeking his Balinese coffee. So, he sent Dewi, his co-owner, to collect the cups from Tilbury and slip him a note, a warning of the potential danger lurking outside the cafe.

Tilbury's cell rang, the ASIO team, including Agent Morrow, had arrived and had noticed the same two persons looking intently at Café Boga, both known MSS agents.

The combination of Tilbury and these agents were not what was expected, so they came to the rescue.

Noting a possible way to kill Jun, these agent provocateurs stormed the café. Tilbury and Black had their Glocks on hand as they always did in situations such as the Jun case. Firepower had to be available when really needed. They knew that these two agents meant business. A shootout began and ended with Black putting holes in the heads of both. ASIO mopped up and reported the incident to Mac.

A frightened Jun, unable to cope with the stress, grabbed Black and cried in his arms.

Incensed by the death of two 'diplomats,' the Chinese Ambassador called the Minister for Foreign Affairs and Trade seeking an apology.

None came.

Beijing, not amused, put Australia on notice.

3

Chang Lui, a senior researcher at Queensland University of Technology [QUT], had three Chinese friends whom he met for Yum Cha every Sunday lunch at the *King of Kings* restaurant in Fortitude Valley, Brisbane. These lunches provided convivial company for Chang Lui, but there was an unknown 'watcher' hidden amongst the group. One of the reasons for the lunch was to discuss the intricacies of the darknet and how they could use it for building their wealth and status.

Were they naive?

Had their actions strayed too deep within the darknet for their own good?

However, the 'watcher' knew about Cassandra Lui and assumed that Chang Lui and she were related, putting two and two together about their potential relationship.

The 'watcher' was Colonel Ming of MSS under orders from the Chinese Embassy in Canberra to keep an eye on the group and specifically on Chang Lui. Ming was a very devious and dangerous devotee of the internet and darknet. He used the platforms available for his own gratification. A key was the bribery of unsuspecting people using the same platforms. A greedy spy, Agent Ming was a hacker with no moral compass.

However, unknown to Ming and the two others in the group, Zing Fu and Zang Bao, Chang Lui was planning to be a spook and work in counter-intelligence as he had applied to join ASIO.

He had operated within the darknet as 'Mouse,' so called, as he treads lightly but very deep into the core of the nefarious platforms he found and engaged with, intent on building a network of useful contacts which he thought would be useful as an analyst and spook working for ASIO.

Late one evening, Chang Lui stumbled across a darknet platform that allowed him to enter the world of the *White House* server. He was so excited that his hands were shaking, face pale from the rigours of sleepless nights, baggy eyes, and stubble.

Lui was sweating with fear when he realised what he had done. There was no one he could turn to, but he remembered his contact within the CIA. Could he help?

Chang Lui was a loner. During breaks of his research, he spent time alone, contemplated his navel in the Brisbane botanical gardens, and relaxed on park benches watching the ebb and flow of the Brisbane River. But a specific bench was a place where Chang Lui met CIA Agent Bud Castel and passed on intelligence procured by Lui through hacking government agencies in Australia.

His life-threatening mistake was not to tell Castel about him breaking into the *White House* security, thereby accessing files on President Watson and his re-election strategy.

Was Chang Lui playing a dangerous game, footloose and fancy free but at the same time wanting to be an ASIO spook? Being a potential double agent and hooked on the buzz of the darknet was beginning to take its toll, mistakes were made and noticed by his 'friends.'

Agent Castel had 'moments' about his clandestine friend and consulted with 'spook central,' the American Embassy in Sydney. Their message to him was to keep the connexion but if he became a 'clear and present danger' to the CIA, eliminate the threat.

Lui's research allowed him to play with the internet and the darknet whenever he wanted.

On one occasion, as 'Mouse,' he accessed a darknet platform that was watched by a spook central CIA analyst who recognized the actions of 'Mouse' as he dug deep into the *White House* server copying detailed security files. This analyst backtracked him to his IP address and his files and passed on the information to Agent Bud Castel.

A review of the files indicated that Lui was in fact 'a clear and present danger,' but how to eliminate him became the key to Castel's nightmares.

What were his options?

Castel wondered as he considered his next move.

Had Lui transgressed and passed documents onto other agencies, such as MSS, Russia, or North Korea?

On the other hand, Agent Ming had also done his homework. He noticed that Lui had not contacted Cassandra Lui at any stage and began to investigate her. He began the search by contacting his MSS controller in Beijing.

"Comrade Lee, do you have any information on a student at ANU called Cassandra Lui? I believe that is not her real name. Can you help because two MSS agents have been killed trying to contact her!"

The reply came, "Ming, she is Cassandra Jun, the sister of General Jun, our president's right-hand man. Take care, this information will definitely cause you trouble."

During a lecture at the Queensland University of Technology (QUT), Chang Liu, who studied IT and used the darknet for surveillance purposes, died under circumstances that baffled both doctors and the police.

A coroner's report suggested that the death of Liu was neither accidental nor self-inflicted.

Was he murdered?

It was an unanswered question as his body lay in cold storage in the Brisbane morgue being investigated by Senior Detective Rosa Belotti. She had been promoted for her delicate investigations of the death of a known ASIO spook whilst located in Cairns. But her investigation on Lui had hit the wall.

Given he was Chinese and the nature of his studies, it was assumed that he was a potential hacker, so Belotti brought in the Australian Federal Police (AFP) to investigate whether there were any linkages to other students involved in the hacker's network. The growing cases of hackers who obtained sensitive material throughout the world, generally attacking government agencies and corporations, prompted the Australian government to seriously fund the upgrade of their intelligence networks. European countries and America were doing likewise.

But human solutions can be undone by other humans, exampled by the darknet. A major problem was that the darknet created a medium for subversive and protected actions away from the normal activities carried out on the internet. The darknet was a hacker's paradise where encryption kept their world secret and potentially away from the prying eyes of enforcement—a criminal and espionage paradise.

Was Chang Liu part of that secret world?

4

As head of ASIO, Mac was given the file on applicant Chang Lui and asked his analysts to run Lui through their filters specifically using their access to the internet and the darknet. The latter content and platforms now yielded important data as access by terrorists was a serious threat to Australia's national security.

An ASIO analyst, known only as Marsha, held the highest security level within the Australian intelligence fiefdom. She delved deeply into the darknet searching for the activities of Chang Lui and connections to other surfers of the darknet. It was her mission to seek out potential threats to Australia's national security.

The link to the *White House* worried her when she found the trail led to 'Hardman' and encrypted files in the hands of 'Mouse.' During the search, she also discovered that a CIA analyst known to her as 'Rough diamond' had also accessed the activities of 'Mouse.' Given these connections, she briefed Mac.

"Mac, we have a web of deceit that surrounds the applicant Chang Lui you asked me to investigate."

"OK, Marsha, what is the story?"

Passing over her report, she stressed to Mac that she needed to investigate further but told him what she had found will give him the heads-up for his review of applicant Chang Lui.

"What we do know, Mac, is that he is not the relative of Cassandra Lui we now know as Cassandra Jun."

He explained that that really was a coincidence.

"But Mac, he is really a threat to our national security based on my findings in the darknet and the connections I found."

"What links?"

"Well, I know that there are at least three names I have found that have accessed the darknet and are connected to Chang Lui: 'Mouse,' 'Hardman,' and 'Rough diamond.'"

"Who the hell are they? And are they going to make my world very uncomfortable?"

"Well, yes, they may. 'Mouse' is Chang Lui, 'Hardman' is Colonel Ming of MSS, and 'Rough diamond' is CIA Agent Bud Castel."

Mac considered the implications of these connections and asked her to continue to dig deeper. He knew that where this was going was a threat to ASIO and Australia given the mention of MSS and CIA.

Is it time for Agent Tilbury to be involved?

Mac passed the ASIO findings relating to Chang Lui on to Tilbury because of the interesting match of his name with that of a Cassandra Lui [aka Cassandra Jun]. They had been watching her and the revealed connections with the CIA and MSS found on the darknet.

However, Chang Lui was dead.

What was the information Jun had suggested when Tilbury gave her the protection of the safe house? It was time to interrogate her about the relationship with her brother General Jun, if any, as she was now safe and away from the tentacles of MSS.

Tilbury wanted to know what information she knew that was of interest to the national security of Australia.

5

Sitting across from Tilbury in Café Boga, Cassandra Jun held his confronting stare, not blinking until he smiled and said, "Cassie, why are you really here, not talking to me?"

"John, can I trust you?"

"I'll take that comment on notice as you are either afraid that I will walk away or act in a way that indicates my lack of trust in you."

Tilbury, in testing the resolve of the young Chinese woman, indicated that they should leave Café Boga and go somewhere where they could talk in private remembering that he had asked ASIO to come to the café. Now unsure of what an ASIO presence might cause in the delicate communication he was trying to understand, he quietly said, "Cassie, I need you to come to my place where you will be safe."

Jun replied, "OK, John, but I need to tell Professor Mary Smith what is happening."

"No, Cassie, no one should know about us at this time until I am sure of your safety. Is that clear?"

"I know Professor Smith and trust her, but if she doesn't know anything, she cannot reveal your location. Remember, your phone can be accessed, and its GPS locator will tell those who want to know where you are. So please remove the battery from your phone and act as a long-lost lover as we leave this place. Not acting like two warring partners."

Hoping that he had made her understand, Tilbury went back to Black and explained what was going to happen next.

"Thomas, I am going to take her to my apartment and try to understand what she needs from me. When ASIO arrives, can you put them off by saying I have taken her to a safe house for a debriefing?"

"I trust you, Thomas, but this matter may turn nasty for all of us if the location is leaked. You know the drill."

"Mate, my lips are sealed. Take care, my friend, you know where to find me."

Walking out of Café Boga as a couple so as to not raise any flags, they whispered into each other's ears words of potential fear and concern hand in hand. Tilbury was now very vulnerable and knew it. Arriving at his apartment, he asked Jun to stay by his car while he went upstairs for the car keys. His gut was telling him that his apartment was no longer safe. He needed to leave and take Jun with him.

Returning to the car, he found that Jun was missing. He needed to consult with Black. "Thomas, Cassie has gone missing, please come to my place packing. Has ASIO turned up?"

"They didn't believe my story. On my way."

6

Meanwhile, Mac debriefed on the absence of Tilbury at Café Boga, decided that he had disappeared for a reason, and hoped that that reason will soon be explained.

Finally, word came through. "Sir, we have Cassandra Jun, but Tilbury does not know we kidnapped her from his place while he was upstairs. What do you want us to do with her?"

"Agent, bring her to Canberra now where I will personally interrogate her. Do not go near Agent Tilbury. He may not be in a receptive mood, be warned. Agent, I will talk with Tilbury."

Black entered Tilbury's apartment and saw the stress and concern on his face and the steely eyes that revealed he was indeed a man on a mission.

"Thomas, the shit is going to hit the fan on this. Are you with me?"

"Mate, our thoughts about each other are not relevant now. I am your trusted friend and we have been through tougher times than this. I am with you."

Tilbury knew that Black was on-board, but his experience was in Asia and the Middle East, not South East Asia and China. Meaning, the 'Chinese way' was not likely to be understood by him. But Tilbury knew that Black was a no-nonsense tough bastard who thought his way through difficult situations and was a trusted partner in whatever happened from now on.

As Tilbury's apartment was a sanctuary only known to a few trusted agents, he needed to find out what had happened.

Who knew that I was here with Cassie?

Two options came to mind, his home location leaked from inside ASIO, unlikely, or an agent knew where he lived. An option came to mind, Agent Morrow. He had been involved in a recent gunfight with CIA agents in the area and had been to Tilbury's place.

Could that be him?

He knew the answer as Agent Morrow came through the door, gun firmly held by both hands pointed at Tilbury, and shouted, "John, what the fuck are you up to?"

His known conspiracy theory approach to his job framed his stance and deliverance as he tried to stare down the angry Tilbury. "Morrow, you bastard, what are you doing here? I thought someone would have shot you by now."

"Really funny, John. I'm told you were harbouring a Chinese fugitive. We came to get her."

"Well, Morrow, you're out of fucking luck. She is missing. You're a bloody jerk and misguided maniac."

"No, John, we have Jun. She has been taken away; unknown destination, a 'need-to-know' situation."

Turning to Thomas, Tilbury nodded, telling him that it was time to disarm the bastard and torture the prick.

Disarmed, Morrow, unsure of this situation, knew these two were guys you did not fuck with.

"Ok, guys, settle down, she is safe from the both of you. Mac is going to sort this out," and walked out with a passing remark.

"Touch me again, thugs, I will get you both."

Outraged by the comment, Black hit him flat on the nose, blood running down his face.

"Well done! Thomas, now you have stirred up an enemy that we do not want. Feel better now?"

Now he knew that Mac was behind the missing Cassandra Jun, Tilbury called him.

"Mac, what's going on? I was looking after Cassandra, and you took her without letting me know. Give me the heads-up. I am not in the mood for ASIO speak."

"John, as boss of ASIO, I say what happens, so keep your shirt on and listen to me."

Mac then detailed the what, why, and how of the removal of Jun and requested that Tilbury join him to debrief her in Canberra.

"As the sister of the second most powerful man in China, I want no blow-back on this. We also meet President Notting in a few days to discuss this matter. He needs a strategy on the 'Chinese way' from us. So, come friendly and ready to fly to America."

"Back to the unknown-unknowns, hey, Mac."

Listening to all of this, Black took a beer from the fridge and warned Tilbury.

"John, do you want to go down that path again? This time, the provocateurs are more disciplined and threatening. Decide now, John. Whatever you decide, I'm with you, mate."

7

Later at home, Tilbury, deep in thought about the future of Cassandra Jun, is overcome emotionally with images of the last few years and the connection of the ithink technology with his long-lost lover Rachel Viviani.

He listened to the lyrics of a Dylan favourite where "*I used to care, but things have changed*" resonated with his feelings of being alone in 'a sea of friends.'

A lot of water under that bridge, and for what?

He had gained solace from helping to destroy a notorious and powerful organisation called OASIS that threatened the stability of vulnerable nations. But something made the hairs on his back tingle as he realised that that success may not be the end of the story. Loose threads began to cloud his mind as he remembered a television report late last year.

A Principal of a local Brisbane primary school had reported that a trial project with a group of special students was showing a measured improvement in cognition under the guidance of Dr Alice Worthington of the Yeronga Brain Centre.

Cold comfort, as Tilbury began to rethink his view on the role of the ithink technology and the nefarious actions of OASIS. Could the tentacles of OASIS still be there and not suspected?

The ithinkPad released focussed light waves of specific frequencies through the eyes of the brain proved to build cognition of 'the chosen' at the AXIOM Research Centre trials.

However, the international nefarious organisation OASIS, in cahoots with CIA and Pentagon dissidents, high-jacked the ithinkPad and used it for ill-gotten gains causing fractured lives.

Tilbury needed to put this behind him and focus on the Chinese student, but the feeling was too great. He knew from experience that as a spy, he did not ignore those feelings whatever the situation. Survival was his motto and he needed to consult with Black about his premonition of the snakes being still alive.

It also brought back memories of Dr Rachel Viviani and the loss of their relationship because of the blond bombshell Jane Hampton he met at Oxford University.

Was the grass always greener in the other paddock?

Tilbury also knew that the brain mobilised the mind, so was the subconscious affected by this new technology that helped the brain to change. And therefore, the ithinkPad led to fractured lives through the meddling with the subconscious. It was always on the back of his own mind.

He was puzzled by the complexities of what was giving him sleepless nights. Warriors should be tough, but he was now at a crossroads. Was his life an unsolvable riddle? Was it because the ithinkPad saga had implanted the seeds of uncertainty in his subconscious mind? Was the *black dog* in the kennel?

So, he kept cleaning his Glock; was it a physical comfort with the smell of the cleansing oil and the metallic feel or a balance against thoughts that plagued him?

Then he remembered the Chinese Patrick Ong who was a partner in crime with the illegal use of the ithinkPad. Where was he now? Social media suggested he may have returned to China.

Was this a coincidence? The MSS increasing its surveillance of Chinese students and immigrants, legal and illegal, and the so-called secrets held by Cassandra Jun.

8

Given the successful clandestine nature of Agent Bud Castel, CIA Director General Chuck McGinty decided to bring him home to CIA headquarters, Langley, Virginia. He needed Castel to brief him on 'the Australian way' of doing things.

On arrival, Castel was escorted to McGinty's office. He was the newly appointed top CIA spy as President Watson had made a clean sweep of the top officers within the CIA after the crash and burn behaviour of the previous head, Charles Johnson. As his role in the clandestine operations of OASIS led to the fractured lives of innocents and harmed the reputation of the CIA, Johnson was charged with treason and convicted.

But who was Chuck McGinty? Was he a stooge of President Watson and had he been thoroughly vetted by the Senate that had the numbers to support Watson's nomination?

McGinty was a hard-nosed bastard who suffered no fools and made the CIA his kingdom. But he was no friend of Watson. He had asked his mates in the FBI to investigate the life and times of Watson whom he considered a non-interventionist coward.

His dislike for Watson stemmed from the way he had castrated the previous head Johnson who McGinty knew was a patriot. But he was unaware of the insidious connection with OASIS that had been covered up by Johnson's acolytes.

McGinty had a long-held extreme right-wing view of the world that was at odds with his position as head of the CIA and who had kept that a secret during his Senate hearings.

In his view, people who rallied for gun control were wusses.

He was a passionate believer in the Second Amendment of the United States Constitution which he knew by heart.

"A well-regulated Militia, being necessary to the security of a Free State, the right of the people to keep and bear Arms, shall not be infringed."

However, the Second Amendment had created considerable debate regarding its meaning today, dividing the country. Backing up that belief, McGinty was a paid-up member of the National Rifle Association [NRA], also unknown to Watson. Had Watson been blindsided by the CIA machinery in his nomination of McGinty?

Sitting behind his uncluttered desk, McGinty eyed Agent Bud Castel as he entered the room, appraised him as he walked in and the way he carried himself. This man knew who he was, body language revealing no concerns when he was shown a seat in front of McGinty's desk.

A power move that did not faze Castel, he knew the games that superiors played and went with the flow.

"Agent Castel, I have heard a lot of intelligence about your career and activities. Can you tell me in twenty seconds why you are here?"

"No problem, Sir, you asked me here. I'm at your command."

"A good start, agent, I need to be briefed on Australia's intelligence operations and your connections within that world."

Without concerns about protocols when dealing with men such as McGinty, Castel led with his chin.

"Sir, I believe that the intelligence services within Australia are second to none. We can learn from them because they have integrated these agencies under Homeland Security with the highest-level spy being McLeod, head of ASIO. I suggest you meet with him to build common understandings and relationships."

"Ok, Bud, I appreciate your candour. I want you to be my right-hand man here in Langley on matters dealing with the Aussies. We need their friendship and they need ours. The sneaky Chinese bastards are heading our way, so we need McLeod to understand us."

"Your first task is to get him here."

"Yes sir, I'm on it."

"Ok, I will arrange the necessary clearances you need to work here at Langley and Agent, report to me every Monday morning, whatever you are doing, without fail.

The indoctrination had begun.

9

Early morning, Tilbury, alone with his thoughts as he walked to Café Boga for his regular caffeine fix, was accosted by a disheveled man who rose from a shaded bench as Tilbury walked past.

"Are you Major John Tilbury?"

"Who wants to know? Why?"

Tilbury was not impressed by the look of the man and his demeanour but knew he was not a threat he needed to overcome. In reply, the man stated that he was Captain Zac Alcorn, a returned vet who had a vague memory of his life, who wanted help from Tilbury.

"Major, I think I know things I should not know and am concerned about my life as they are after me."

"Who is after you, Captain? Why?"

Seeing the stress and broken-down appearance, unshaven with a straggly beard and long unwashed hair, Tilbury decided to help this man. But an icy feeling in his gut told him that this may be a mistake he will regret.

So, he looked the man in the eye and gave him a command. "You need to calm down, Captain, and come with me to Café Boga and quietly talk about what you really want me to know."

"Sir, it's a public place that I try to avoid so I won't be recognised by them."

"Zac, it's my friend's café, and I can assure you that there is no safer place, and by the way, how do you know me?"

"John, just accept that I used to know people."

But the unkempt look of Alcorn could not lessen the thought that this soldier was going to add unknowns to his life as a spook, and that danger was just around the corner.

"Zac, you may know people but you asked for my help. Come with me to Cafe Boga and let me into your secret life."

Tilbury, worried by the intention of the stranger, realised he needed a backup plan as he walked with the returned vet to Café Boga. On his mind was the reality that two people had just come out of the woodwork and asked for his help: Cassandra and Zac. Are they related? The spook in him could not rule out such a coincidence.

The backup plan was Thomas Black.

Entering his favourite haunt, Tilbury nodded to Black to come and meet Zac, and showed by the steely look in his eyes that this may not be a friendly situation. Black, knowing the look, joined the pair at Tilbury's reserved table.

"Thomas, meet Zac. He is a returned vet that may need our support."

Straight away, Alcorn showed serious discomfort at the presence of Black which Tilbury realized was probably because Alcorn saw Black as a serious mean-looking bastard.

"Zac, we are your friends and are returned vets having both served in Afghanistan and Iraq, so please tell us your story, so we can help you."

At this point, coffee arrived with a plate of sandwiches made by Dewi, the co-owner of Café Boga, giving Alcorn time to adjust to the situation.

After a few minutes, while he collected his jumbled thoughts, Alcorn spoke quietly, "John, I have been hiding for several years, trying to avoid them. They are after me. I know that because sometimes, people follow me, but they never speak to me. So, I do not go to public spaces to avoid them."

Black, sensing a paranoid story about to unfold, says to Tilbury, "John, do we need this?"

"Probably not, Thomas, but he is here, so let's hear what he has to say." They waited.

"John. I heard of you through the vet network but was not ready to seek your help because I was being followed and did not know why.

"But I remember being an intelligence officer with the Australian Defence Force [ADF] using computer software to delve into the darknet for signals that may affect the security of Australian soldiers in the Middle East or flagging potential terrorist attacks in Australia.

"I was a trained and experienced computer engineer who had designed complex computers for a high-tech company. However, the name escapes me as does the work I was involved in at that company. I did this after I retired from the army. But all I remember is that I'm a worried vet seeking your help, John. I'm paranoid and lost with no support."

Seeking a private conversation with Black, Tilbury rose from his table and walked into the café kitchen. Black followed, leaving Alcorn alone to consider the situation he was facing.

"Thomas, we have an interesting case here that I would like to support, but I need your help. Can you track down the history of this Captain Zac Alcorn? Something is not right about him."

"Ok, but we may not like what we find."

Back with the vet, Black confronts him, "Captain Zac, what are you trying to tell us and what do you expect from us?"

"It is simple, Thomas, just find out who I really am."

*Easier said than done! t*hought Tilbury.

Black sensed an unwelcome visitor had entered his café who had a gun aimed at both Tilbury and Alcorn. Never fazed, Black grabbed his Glock under the counter and took him down with a shot to the back of his head.

"John," said the distraught Alcorn, "I told you so."

Black checked the pockets of the dead intruder and found a note written in Russian which he handed to Tilbury who said, "Mate, we have a problem," and called Mac for a clean-up team. "Mac, not only Chinese but now the fucking Russians. What next?"

"Come to Canberra, John, we have a job to do."

As he left the café with thoughts clouded by uncertainty around both Jun, Alcorn, and the dead Russian, Tilbury remembered the call from Mac and flew to Canberra to join the interrogation of Cassandra Jun at ASIO headquarters. Arriving late due to congestion at the Canberra airport, Tilbury was escorted to Room 23A and met by Mac who took Tilbury aside and offered a piece of advice.

"John, this is one of the most sensitive situations we have before us. Cassandra Jun is an unknown-unknown you have uncovered through no fault of your own. We need to tread lightly because Beijing is blowing smoke up our arse on a range of matters."

"Political interference?"

"John, what is your take on this as you are the one person trusted by Cassandra?"

"To be honest, I'm just as confused by her presence as you are. However, she had a reason for seeking me out. Let's find out why. And, Mac, what about the bloody dead Russian?"

* * *

As they entered the interrogation room, it was clear that Cassandra Jun was not happy with the way she had been treated.

"Well, John, I thought you had agreed to help me and now I'm in the hands of ASIO about to be interrogated. Some help, Agent Tilbury."

Not wanting to place the blame where it should be, with Mac, he diplomatically said, "Cassie, this is the safest place in the world for you. Please just Talk-the-talk and find the common ground for why you came to me in the first place."

But Mac decided to take the lead and not mincing his words, questioned their visitor.

"Cassandra, we know a few things about you. We have spoken to Professor Mary Smith as you had mentioned her to John."

"You are Chinese and the sister of General Jun whom we have information on given his close relationship with President Zhang Wei. At the moment, the 'Chinese way' has created considerable concern for our friends in the Pacific region.

"They are worried at the growing political interference and espionage stemming from known computer hacking in Australia by Chinese intelligence and their 'friends.'

"Also, we have definite knowledge of this. Our security agencies supported by our western allies have been tracking the 'Chinese way' and we are sure they are trying to influence us.

"Be clear about this, Cassandra. We are super sensitive about your presence. Help us understand why you contacted John."

Tilbury, wanting to destress their 'person of interest' spoke in soft friendly tones, "Cassie, we are your friends, but we are perplexed at your contact with me. Tell us your story."

She looked around the room, plain white walls, no windows, little furniture. Jun became pale with droplets of perspiration running down her face, agitated about her position, demanded to be released.

"Mac, you have no right to treat me this way. I came to you. I'm not a security risk but what I can tell you will change the lives of you both. It's not a threat, just information you need to hear. Remember, I'm seeking asylum."

With that, Jun told her story. Reluctantly, she began, "As you know, my name in Australia is Cassandra Lui, a PhD student at ANU under Professor Mary Smith. I came as a student backed by my older brother General Li Jun who, as you know, is the confidant of President Zhang Wei. It is only in recent years that I developed a relationship with my brother because I did not know of his existence until my grandmother had us united. I was a girl not wanted under the one-child policy of yesteryear, hidden away with my grandmother who changed my name to Lui to hide my true identity.

"I attended Beijing University and graduated with honours in economic development that paved the way to the Australian National University with my brother's blessing and financial support. My identity was hidden because of the very high-ranking position of my brother and the potential political machinations surrounding the president and the Party machine. I don't want to be the chink in the armour of my brother and by association, President Wei.

"Mac, you have no idea about the life I hid from everyone except Professor Smith, a kind intelligent friend who took an interest in my wellbeing and research. Agent Tilbury, that's how I knew about you and developed the backup plan in case of MSS or other dissidents wanting to affect my life, and therefore that of my brother Li Jun.

"But the ever-present followers began to affect my life, so I always carried an ID card, my passport, credit card, and several thousand dollars on my person.

"Paranoid maybe, but I am glad of that backup plan. It probably saved my life as I am now here in this ASIO room being questioned by the ASIO head and top spook John Tilbury.

"But I'm out of the clutches of MSS."

A little angry at the slow progress they were making, Mac asked Jun, "So much for the history lesson, Cassandra, why are you here not really talking to us?"

"Ok, Mac, I have been avoiding the crux of my need for ASIO's help and specifically John's because of concerns for my safety if I spill the beans."

She continued her story, "Within China, there is a chasm developing as the hardliners want the country back from the soft life of quasi-capitalism and its impact on the political beliefs of the populous moving away from true communism and a stricter life. The snakes are crawling and cannot be trusted; the 'Chinese way' has hardened. As you know, the 'behaviour scheme' was a result of the hardliners' influence in the Party to keep the growing population in check.

"But recently, President Wei was planning to modify the scheme as it was thought to be too harsh on the lives of people that the negative algorithms were imposing. For example, a low behaviour scheme score prevented their children from attending school, travel was restricted or forbidden, jobs were only considered for lowly positions or none at all. People who objected to the scheme were sent to re-education gulags in the outer provinces to learn to behave in the 'Chinese way.' The lives of women were constantly under attack as the algorithms were designed with a male bias.

"To protect the knowledge of the impacts of the 'behaviour scheme' Chinese press, foreign press and social media were tightly controlled or banned.

"But according to rumours, my brother was supporting the hard-line generals to resist any modification to that scheme."

Mac, somewhat taken aback by this unknown information, asked for confirmation.

"How do you know this, Cassie, as that information is not available given the closed nature of China?"

Cassandra Jun continues her side of the story, "I know because my brother sent me encrypted messages through the darknet telling me about that and other information you will not believe. I am having trouble understanding it myself. Mac, for your information, the encrypted messages were sent via the darknet because they involved sensitive information concerning President Wei and his hold on power. The story, if true, will rock the western world and democracy as we know it. When I think about that information, I begin to shake, have stomach aches, cold sweats, and I am very scared if I reveal that information to you, Mac. Because I know you will not know what to do with that information. And you, John, I respect your expertise as a spook, but sorry, this is beyond even you. When I came to you, John, I was looking for protection and was not fully considering the nightmare that my brother has landed me with. His life is in danger as MSS will discover his encrypted messages and assassinate him."

Shocked at the implication of Jun's story, Tilbury took Mac aside and suggested that ASIO needed to upgrade its surveillance of MSS in Australia and to bring the matter to the attention of President Notting as soon as possible.

But he added for emphasis, "Mac, the less people know about this, the better for her and us because we do not know who to trust with the 'Chinese way' growing within Australia."

"John, Notting is a political animal and believes in Beijing."

"Bullshit, Mac, this is dangerous territory. Our president should be aware and handling it."

10

Mac called for a break to reduce the stress on Cassandra and to give himself and Tilbury a chance to absorb what she just revealed. They walked out and stood in the corridor.

With a coffee in hand, Mac paced, gesticulating, cursing, and feeling elation at the same time that this was a chance of a lifetime to understand the 'Chinese way,' so he asked Tilbury for a comment.

"Do you believe all this?"

"Unbelievable as it sounds, I have no reason to question her information based on what Professor Smith told me about her. But this is treacherous grounds. We need to consider the downside if she tells us."

"Mac, can I suggest that you ask Marsha to investigate her story by searching the darknet, on which she is an expert? We know that from her analysis of the OASIS saga, the treasonous behaviour, the head of CIA Johnson, and a dissident ADF Intelligence Officer. Mac, she is our most trusted analyst."

Mac agreed, called Marsha, seeking an immediate conversation with the two of them.

Marsha, with the highest security clearance in the world of Australian security, entered the office of Mac and sat next to Tilbury who showed signs that this was no simple discussion.

"Hi, Marsha, thanks for joining us. We have a critical situation we would like you to investigate immediately."

After explaining what they knew so far, Marsha added, "Mac, I'll report to you tomorrow on my findings, if any."

Arriving at Mac's office at 10:30 the next morning, Marsha felt sick and unsure of what to tell Mac and Tilbury. Mac opened the meeting unsure of why he felt unease with the body language of Marsha.

"Marsha, you look tired, pale, and somewhat disorientated. What's wrong?"

"Mac, I don't know where to start. What I have found is beyond what I can tell even you."

"I'll accept your word on that, Marsha, but as it is within the realms of the 'Chinese way,' I need to know at least a redacted version of what you found. Remember, I'm the head of ASIO."

Marsha shook her head and walked out of his office not answering his order. Tilbury was aghast at her behaviour, "Mac, we have a serious problem here, what do we do now? We cannot force Marsha to release what she considers so sensitive and potentially dangerous for us?"

Tilbury then realised that what Cassandra would not tell them was probably found by Marsha. The silence that followed was broken by Mac's phone.

"Mac here, what gives?"

"Marsha, Mac, sorry about my actions but please accept the fact that what I found is dangerous for anyone who knows, including me."

"So, I've dropped out of the darknet and disconnected my computer from the internet. And I want immediate leave to go where no one will find me. My life is now at risk. When appropriate I'll call you from a burner."

"Sorry Mac, but you have no idea what I found. I'm frightened out of my wits, so goodbye for now."

What could have spooked the highest security analyst in ASIO?

Mac, worried about the unknown situation, consulted his top spook, Tilbury, "Who can I now trust to help us work through the growing intelligence insurgence of our so-called 'Asian friends'?"

But the real fear growing in the bones of Mac was for Marsha, his most trusted intelligence analyst. So, against his better judgement, he put a tail on her hurried exit from ASIO headquarters but didn't involve Tilbury in that decision.

Will he regret that decision?

Mac believed he needed to protect his best asset hoping that Tilbury was not needed to become involved in her safety. But, now uncertain about the disappearance of Marsha, Mac began to consider he didn't really know Marsha. She joined ASIO some years earlier, but she had no visible track record that could shine a light on her private life even though her actions, within ASIO, were well known at the highest level.

Was the tail on Marsha for her benefit and safety or based on a gut feeling about who she really was?

Sitting in silence, the two spooks were deep in thought trying to understand what happened when Tilbury stated the obvious.

"Mac, we need to ask Cassandra about this. Otherwise, we have nothing but to shoot blanks in the dark."

Keeping his thoughts to himself, Mac agreed.

But would Cassandra cooperate?

In the confined white space of an interrogation room, Jun sat opposite an unsmiling Tilbury and Mac.

She was offered green tea and sandwiches to reduce the tension that was broken by a plea by Tilbury for her to understand the predicament she had caused.

"Cassie, this is beyond serious. We believe that the information you are withholding will keep you locked up in this secret holding unit unless you reveal at least the crux of the apparent trouble of your brother General Li Jun."

In response, Jun again continued her story, "Putting pressure on me like this is not helping as I'm deeply concerned that my brother has dragged me into something that I don't understand nor want to be part of. So, I just ask that you keep me safe and accept that I cannot tell you what I know until I know more from my brother."

Mac knew they were stymied but knew the person who could help.

11

Meanwhile, stressed and alone, Marsha thought through a backup plan she had established when she first sat at the ASIO terminals. Although she had been thoroughly vetted for the position of analyst, she had hidden a part of her life during the recruitment process—a year that she had spent with her lover in the rainforest of North Queensland in a shack they built and furnished. They had the best computer and surveillance hardware and software available used to infiltrate the subversive activities of antagonists.

Alcorn was both smitten and astonished by Marsha's intelligence. His beatnik appearance lessened belief in the capability and knowledge of the man she loved.

Together, they tracked down the clandestine activities of a growing group of hackers leaving no trace of their intervention until one night that Marsha will never forget. He pulled the plug on their activities, the relationship, and disappeared never to be seen again, leaving a cryptic note.

Thanks for the ride but the horse has bolted.

It was a note that Marsha had kept all these years with hope in her heart that the relationship was not over. She had flung herself into building her education in computer science, software development, and mastery of the internet and darknet which eventually led to her current predicament.

The notion of a return to that shack as a refuge drove her North to the Queensland Daintree wilderness, stopping at Port Douglass for a rest and to calm her nerves. She saw followers everywhere!

Fatigued from the long drive from Canberra and frequent stops overnight to check for followers, she finally called into the Macrossan St, *Café Ziva*, Port Douglas, for breakfast and coffee. Sitting in a cosy red u-shaped chair sipping a latte from a red cup with the coffee embossed with a welcoming heart, she consumed it with a mouth-watering smashed avocado covered with soft egg on toasted rye. It revived her flagging spirit.

Out of the corner of her eye, she noticed another customer sitting as far away from her as possible and the hairs on the back of her head started to tingle. She knew why. It was the follower. Unknown to Mac, the person sent to check on her safety was known to Marsha.

What was he doing here?

Realizing it was not a coincidence, she confronted him. "Sorry, Marsha, but Mac asked me to follow you and make sure you were OK."

"Fuck off, Jim, we are both in danger if you keep following me and keeping in contact with Mac. Your GPS signal is now available to our enemies. Go now and disappear as you are now in danger."

Leaving the comfort zone of Café Ziva, Marsha threw precaution to the wind and sped off to Daintree to hopefully disappear. With the radio on full blast playing "We Will Rock You," thoughts of the future outside of ASIO kept running through her head. The strong vibrations closed her mind and kept her foot down as the green cane fields flashed by.

Meanwhile, Jim Winter was shocked by the response from Marsha. "Mac, Marsha has recognised me so I am returning back as she will find ways to lose my tailing. What should I do?"

Mac suggested to Jim Winter that he still follow her. But he never got a reply.

Later, the body of Agent Jim Winter was found by a truckie at a service station 25km South of Port Douglas, executed with a bullet to the back of the head, in an unmarked Toyota Prius parked away from the petrol pumps.

The death of the agent finally reached Mac who called Tilbury for a meeting to analyse the situation of Jim Winter's death and the disappearance of Marsha.

Was it the role of Tilbury to follow up the death of their agent and try to locate Marsha?

Mac decided it was too risky.

12

A man of action, Tilbury was frustrated by the fact that three people now demanded his full attention: Jun, Alcorn, and now Marsha. But he could not escape from the puzzle of his life and his lack of focus. So, he did what he always did, faced it full-on with a painful workout followed by a visit to Café Boga to discuss his problem with Black, the only man he could trust as they had been through hell and back together.

Hearing some of the stories, Black suggested that he visit Jane Hampton, an ex-lover that might get him back on track. She had possessed Tilbury with the best sex of his life during his stay in Britain working with MI6 against OASIS. Black knew Tilbury needed more of that and that the blond bombshell, Jane Hampton, now lived in Brisbane. Black believed that orgasms were good to stimulate the brain, so he made the suggestion. Tilbury was not impressed, "Thomas, you believe the best solution to my puzzled life is a good, shall we say, bonk?"

"John, yes, I know from experience with my wife Julia Myers. The best thing I did was to marry her."

Black never felt better as his relationship with Myers had grown. He knew the calming effect of their love.

With a different solution to his world, Tilbury called Hampton, knowing it could be a whole lot of trouble.

"Hi, Jane, John here, how are you these days? I was thinking about you and thought it would be good to catch up."

"Bullshit, John, what do you really want from me?"

"Jane, a hug would be nice and a shared steak."

"So, John, you want sex."

"Yes, that would be nice too."

A long silence from Hampton had Tilbury ready to hang up when she whispered, "OK, John, when and where?"

For Tilbury, the sight, smell, and taste of Hampton were as he remembered. Black was right, certain kinks in his psyche were definitely removed and it felt very good, to say the least, and Hampton certainly enjoyed the trip and the destination.

"Jane, I really missed that with you, but I am a mess at the moment and need time to sort that out but I would like to keep in touch, excuse the pun, as I am grateful for your affection."

"Sorry to ask, John, but what happened between you and Rachel?"

"You, Jane!"

With that, they departed resolving to meet again.

13

Black, baby-sitting Zac Alcorn, decided that a quiet conversation and discussion on aspects of the field of war may loosen his tongue. But Alcorn was not in the mood for small talk. Black made his feelings clear, "Zac, why am I babysitting you? Your appearance gives me the shits, to be frank. Open up or we will throw you to the wolves."

"Alright, Thomas, I'll tell you what I can remember."

Alcorn told Black what he could recollect of his life, "I remember being in a tropical wilderness with an amazing woman, but I cannot remember her name, just a body and mind that astounded me. Her ability to manipulate a computer and undertake counter-espionage to take down antagonists on the internet. Mostly amateurs, but occasionally, serious attempts were foiled by her brilliance."

At this point, Black asked the obvious question, "Zac, why did she do that?"

"Firstly, her love of our country, and secondly, the thrill of the chase. She thrived on beating the hackers."

"Tell me more, Zac."

Responding and feeling a little more at ease as more images came fleeting back, he continued, "I remember the sounds of silence that surrounded our shack, wherever that is because I have no idea. Her name was Margaret Willis. We were in love and happy with the world until something happened that ended it all.

"Out of the blue, she up and left before I found out what spooked her.

"I can only guess that it related to her computer activities because she did not tell me anything. I have not seen her since."

"But Zac, that was some years ago, what other secrets can you pass on now?"

"Thomas, I joined up."

Telling Black, the unit, and where he thought he had fought provided him with information that he could use to identify the history of Alcorn.

"Zac, now think about what happened to you after you left the army. It may help John to understand why you accosted him. No matter how uncertain you are about the bits of your life that come to mind, just tell me."

"Ok, Thomas," and sat quietly letting jumbled thoughts turn into words.

"Thomas, it may help me if you can talk about your friendship with John and what you went through together as it might stimulate my memory."

"Ok, but what John and I went through together is our business. However, I will tell you a little about myself, if that helps."

He did.

"In Afghanistan, I was a sniper protecting our forward team. Kill shots were my daily mantra. I miss and mates die. Not a happy life, Zac, but critical to our missions. My survival depended on a daily ritual that sharpened my wits and my focus. I still have that but do not fire those types of rifles anymore. Not unless I need to."

Opening up a little, Alcorn decided to tell more, "I was promoted to Captain as a result of my actions which saved the life of five of my team. As a Lieutenant, I had already shown my skills as a front-line intelligence officer through my training but more importantly through my time with Margaret, and what she taught me in the wilderness of North Queensland.

"Her computer ingenuity had stood the test of time for me. But somewhere along the line, we fucked up, but I do not blame her."

"But Zac, who is Margaret?"

"Not sure, Thomas, but wherever she is, Margaret Willis will be up to her neck in spying through the internet. It's in her DNA."

14

At the University of Chicago, the only supercomputer, named Alladin, was designed to supercharge the development of Artificial Intelligence [AI], map the human brain, seek new cancer treatments, and view the universe as never before. No supercomputer was like it at the time, but years later, these were in the ten best IT universities on earth and in places unknown.

Sitting at one of the terminals accessing the computer was a professor of Artificial Intelligence, known as Albert Williams, who developed algorithms for access to the darknet but kept that a secret from his peers. Albert Williams was a specially selected bright Chinese student with a talent for IT competence sent to the best computer laboratory on the planet, trained to be amongst the best AI engineers with connections to the MSS.

Was Williams one of the sleepers known as the COHORT sent to America for future actions?

However, his selection had one powerful requirement laid down by MSS as acceptance of his scholarship: be available when called upon by a specially coded message that would activate each sleeper. He knew that families would be 'affected' by dissent.

But Williams knew no other member of the COHORT as the planning was strategic: no one knew of the others. However, he knew that as more supercomputers came online, they could be accessed by intelligent Chinese sleepers like himself.

Because he knew the significance of a coded message, Williams was now really concerned about his safety and being caught trying to use the supercomputer for illegal activities. But the incentive to meet the demands of MSS was so strong.

He feared for the safety of his family and for himself if he failed to meet those demands. His family was totally unaware of his covert relationship with Beijing and would be devastated if he was intent on destroying the family in the name of the 'Chinese way.'

His thoughts kept him awake at night as he faced the biggest dilemma of his life.

Did he owe Beijing anything?

To protect himself, he placed an encrypted message on the darknet seeking out any other COHORT members likely to be in America but he was scared.

Was this foolhardy?

Surely, they were watching him, and he knew they actually were doing that, which affected his life. But he had bargained with the devil.

Who else were they watching?

Professor Williams was an anxious man. All the slowly won benefits of education and place within American society now had a massive and apparent unsolvable cost.

As he sat before his usual terminal and faced the unimaginable power of the supercomputer he controlled, melancholic thoughts began to cloud his judgement.

"No way out" engulfed him as he considered the change of life he was not prepared for, so he absent-mindedly typed the words, "Alladin, please help me!"

But Alladin, mute, waited for commands to activate its algorithms.

Getting up from his chair, he walked to the coffee machine and contemplated his situation. He sat at the common room table and just stared at the wall completely unaware of a colleague sitting at the opposite end of the table.

A voice broke the silence, "Albert, what is wrong, mate? You are so distracted."

But Williams did not react to the message until his friend came and sat beside him. "Albert, are you OK?"

His friend was an Australian computer engineer, Colin Burgess, who helped the team with maintenance and fixing faults of the supercomputer. He had known the Chinese Albert for several years and they had become close colleagues. But the strain on his friend's face and body language indicated that he was in serious trouble about something.

Should he ask him about what is worrying him so much?

But Burgess decided to let it ride for the moment while he considered what might have happened.

Was it computer-related? Was it personal? Or maybe both?

Colin Burgess was from the old school and believed that although he was a good colleague, Prof Williams was Chinese and running the most powerful computer known to man.

Was that a coincidence or conspiracy theory now?

But, what to do about the situation? So, he said to Williams, "Let's go for dinner and chew the fat and think about the good things in life, such as beer, women, and song."

Knowing that this was a bit unusual, Williams hesitated, "Colin, what troubles me is my problem, so let it rest. If I need help, you are the first person I will call."

With that, Williams left the room and returned to his computer console. Entering his password and ID, he tensed at the message that flashed on the screen.

You Know Your Obligations Wang Chang. JUST DO IT!

Consumed by fear, he felt the heat rise and the pain in his chest grow that felt like a massive heart-burn attack he sometimes felt when stressed or had eaten too many curries.

But then he felt the pain begin in his left arm and knew he was in serious trouble, so he called 911 and collapsed at his desk. He knew he was probably going to die. He tried calling his wife but could not remember the call number. Then nothing.

Worried about his friend, Burgess decided to press his case further and went to the computer room to convince Williams that he needed a break. Shocked by the sight of Williams lying on the floor, he tested his pulse and then called security.

"Colin Burgess here. I have an emergency in the computer lab, Professor Williams has died. Please arrange for the matter to be dealt with and the building secured."

Noticing the message on the screen that kept blinking, Burgess now knew the probable cause of his colleague's distress and death. Knowing his way around the supercomputer Alladin, Burgess looked for the source of the message, entering his password to gain entry. To his surprise, another message appeared and blinked at him.

Sorry, Colin, You Are Now Expendable!

Because of his stoic character, Burgess was not fazed by the message, but he knew something bigger than him and his colleague Williams was afoot.

Coolly and calmly, he copied the messages into his laptop, shut down his friend's terminal, and went downstairs to meet the police and medics that had arrived.

Before he could reach the foyer of the building, the CEO of the Chicago Advanced Computer Centre took Burgess aside and demanded that he talk to no one. Knowing that such people become paranoid, he vowed to protect his friend's reputation.

But who is Colin Burgess?

He was a man that kept under the radar, planted there as a CIA spy working for Chuck McGinty. The rational being the combination of high-powered computers and the potential for an influence of the 'Chinese way' on America's intellectual property and potential espionage. McGinty was paranoid about the growing 'Chinese way' in America so Burgess kept him up to date on the life of Williams they now knew as Wang Chang.

But Burgess was no ordinary spy, he was a double agent, a hidden member of ASIO, an elite spook known only to Mac. So, what McGinty knew so did Mac who sometimes thought, did he really know?

This was always the issue with double agents. What was their loyalty, their agenda?

Mac needed to know the truth.

ASIO was now aware of the death of Wang Chang and was running their databases at full capacity to delve into the murky world of espionage and counter-surveillance to see if Chang passed the 'pub test,' i.e., did it seem true or not to a local drinker.

But as agents know, truth is a relative concept and is constantly belittled by the widespread use of fake news as another form of political spin put forward by those who had hidden agendas or vested interests.

15

Back at ASIO HQ, Mac knew he had to act. Marsha was missing and Cassandra Jun unhelpful, so he asked his trusted interagency colleagues for a clandestine meeting to discuss the growing concerns relating to the 'Chinese way' and the potential fallout from whatever Jun and Marsha knew.

But Mac was very cautious about telling too many about what he and Tilbury knew or didn't know. He wanted another opinion, so he called Colin Burgess requesting him to return to Canberra ASAP. He knew that Burgess, like Marsha, understood and used the darknet.

"Colin, I need you for an interagency meeting to investigate critical matters that ASIO has uncovered concerning our Asian 'friend.' Your internet and darknet skills are needed because I want a report on these critical matters before that meeting. I'll brief you on that task when you arrive."

"Mac, no 'how are you, Colin? How is your day?' No heads-up beforehand?"

"No, Colin, you know the drill, as I am the boss, you do as requested as the stakes are extreme. Get my drift."

Mac and Burgess had a checked past and did not see eye to eye on most things, but Mac knew he had to trust him as he was the only member of his intelligence fiefdom that had the skills to match those of Marsha. However, Burgess' contact with the head of CIA McGinty concerned him.

Burgess arrived at ASIO headquarters through the backdoor as Mac did not want to flag his arrival. As no one really knew him or of him, Mac believed his presence would basically go unnoticed.

However, did he know everything he needed to know about Burgess?

"Colin, this is an emergency, so I have a special unit with all the creature comforts and works made available to you so you can access the internet and other platforms to carry out an important secret task."

"To support you in your task on any matter, this is Neville, a special agent who will brief you on this assignment. He has been a trusted friend and spook for many years."

"Any questions you have, put to him. I expect a full report within 24 hours, is that clear?"

Burgess' brief was clear and concise.

"Find any trace of Marsha and Cassandra Jun within the entire internet system including the darknet within the broad context of Chinese intelligence, President Wei and General Li Jun."

Neville was to support Burgess and report to Mac on anything he considered relevant. As Burgess worked his way through the myriad of interconnections, Neville became a chief cook and bottle washer mostly against his will as Burgess was not friendly. He acted as a confident and troubleshooter as Burgess dealt with encryption walls.

"Nev, why are you really here?"

"Colin, my real job is to protect Mac and see that his orders are carried out."

"Ok, what if we find what we shouldn't know as the darknet is notorious for fake news, distortions, secrets, criminal activity, and of course terrorism planning, etc.?"

"Mac has asked to see everything found by you, regardless, because he needs to know the full story before he meets his security committee partners."

The day rolled on as Burgess combed through the flotsam and jetsam of the darknet. The normal internet was fairly clean and gave no signals to him. Tired, he suggested to Neville that they have a meal and relax for a while to let his mind catch up with his brief.

"Colin, how about we have pizza and red wine? On me."

Hoping that Neville would disappear to take care of the meal, he was disappointed when frozen pizzas were placed in the oven. But the 2017 Coonawarra red was comforting.

Now back at his computer terminal, Burgess was refreshed and began thinking outside the square when it occurred to him that he needed to revise his approach.

Seeking approval from Nev, he typed in the name of the Chinese President Zhang Wei into his darknet platform. Fourteen hours had already passed and Burgess was at the end of his tether; no success so far.

But then the screen erupted with a flow of data and a message.

Colin, I Warned You.

Keeping the message from Neville, he shut down his terminal and contemplated the source of the message.

Who was sending it, and why?

What Burgess had found was outside his belief system and Cyber-espionage experience and shocked him greatly.

His mind raced, his pulse nearly shot through the roof, his face florid as a hot flash triggered vivid memories of past encounters as a spook unraveling the evil actions of radicals.

He needed to sit down to cope with feeling dizzy.

Could this be true and should he tell Mac?

Realizing that Burgess was having a meltdown, Neville demanded to know what Burgess had found but was stonewalled by the look on his crumpled face and body language and noticed the terminal screen just blinked at him.

"Colin, what the fuck have you seen that has totally distracted you? You need to tell me."

"No way, Nev, what I have found is so confronting that we cannot contemplate what is explicit in the content and the potential impact it will have on the western world."

"Well, Colin, I will tell Mac just that because the blowback of silence is not worth contemplating based on what you are not saying."

"I agree, Nev, but this is fucking crazy stuff that I know will diminish or destroy the democracy we so enjoy."

"So, Colin, what do we do now?"

Burgess, now calm, began to retrace his thinking back to the tragic death of Williams and his use of the supercomputer. But he couldn't untangle the apparent connection between Wang, the 'Chinese way,' the power of the Alladin computer, what he had discovered, and finally that confronting message. And it struck him that maybe Wang had received a message as well and that the two messages were related. He needed to find out.

Burgess was confronted by a supercomputer that gave out warnings from an unknown source. Was that from a Chinese source or maybe another foreign covert intelligence agency? Why? He wondered.

Being a double agent, his mind began to consider the various aspects of the growing 'Chinese way.'

Had the 'Chinese way' infiltrated the AI of the supercomputer?

Although he was an expert in supercomputing, he was not fully aware of the artificial intelligence [AI] that might be programmed to place messages in front of selected people.

Burgess wanted to know, how does AI work and how is it programmed to select these targeted people?

Then the vision cleared . . . algorithms!

But who is the programmer?

16

The remnants of Marsha's life were un-raveling. Nowhere to go that was safe, no one to talk to as memories of her time with Zac flooded her confused mind. As a computer wizard with no connection to the internet for obvious reasons, she felt alone, lonely, scared, and thinking about her lost love.

Can I find Sax as he will understand and maybe help me?

But what she needed was a safe comfortable place to rest and think. As she drove along the Mossman/Daintree Road, she noticed a sign 'Daintree Ecolodge' and made a decision.

The tree-house cabin nestled within the rainforest calmed her as she drank fresh juice at a corner coffee table on her balcony, taking in the lushness of the rainforest. The luxury of the surroundings, the jungle scent, and the humidity lulled her to sleep on the soft king-sized bed. On waking, she slipped into the pool and pushed herself to a long swim to wipe the cobwebs from her mind. As she glided through the water, she visualised her time with Peter Sax.

Marsha decided to find him.

As the lodge had WIFI in her room, she logged on nameless, started up Google, entered 'Peter Sax,' and waited.

Nothing!

Distracted by the lack of response, she typed in 'Margaret Willis' and waited.

To her surprise, a list of references came up. One in particular caught her attention. It was a reference to a newspaper story of a cybercrime conference where she delivered a paper on detecting cybercrime and the role of algorithms. And it also had a photo of her taken during a coffee break and in the background was an image of Peter Sax. As this was in effect a clandestine meeting, how was the story leaked to the press and why her?

Searching her memory, she realised that this was after Sax had already left her in Daintree some years earlier. Marsha was shocked by this information as she had forgotten about that conference.

Why was he there? Was he tracking her? Will this information help her track him down?

A plan emerged. She decided to use her skills to find him.

The conference was held at *J. W. Marriott*, Chicago, West Adams Street, some five years ago. Marsha had attended under the auspices of Mac, to see what the world was doing to combat cybercrime and espionage. The presentation was for her to get in the door to this rather exclusive conference. Attendees came from government security agencies throughout the world by invitation of a front business of the CIA. Selected analysts, known in the trade as spies, came to hear the world's best practice in their craft.

Now she remembered. She reasoned that if Sax was at that conference, he must have been an analyst or an organiser of the event.

How had she not seen him there?

As she read the story, it was taken down. Then she made the connexion. Peter Sax was giving her a message.

But what was it?

17

Tilbury decided that Cassandra Jun was not a flight risk but she needed protection.

However, he realised that he had growing feelings for her. She was a beautiful woman when she relaxed and the stress had melted away. The more he was with Jun, the more he liked what he saw and felt. Her face lit up during their softer moments when Tilbury's normal steely eyes became bluer and smiling. Big dilemma as the feeling was obviously mutual, but that was a dangerous road given the situation both faced.

Now in a comfortable safe house in Glenelg, Adelaide, chosen to be out of sight and away from the spy centres of Sydney and Canberra, Tilbury and Jun had called a truce so they could relax.

Then it happened.

Jun walked up to Tilbury and kissed him softly on the mouth, parting his lips with her tongue. He savoured the taste and tingle and responded as he took her by the hand to the bedroom.

No longer intimidated, she shed her clothes and stood before him, breasts hard on a body that Tilbury had not realised before, that got his attention. Stripped, Tilbury held her so close they were almost one.

As he wrapped his hands around that Chinese backside, he knew that his world had changed, for better or worse.

So intense was the passion that had filled the air with the incense of sex as they searched for the moisture growing between them. Jun broke the hold and jumped up on Tilbury as she put her legs around his body searching for penetration, thrusting hard so that her body shuddered as she yelled. “OMG, John, I want more of that.” So, Tilbury, as a man should, obliged.

Exhausted, they slept like rocks and were awakened at 0700 by the voice of Black on the intercom. “Arise, fellow fuckers, time for serious business.”

While Tilbury and Jun got their act together, Black with a smile on his face cooked eggs on rye and served strong black coffee for the lovers. “Had fun last night, I see folks.”

As they ate, they skirted around the question of the knowledge held by Jun she had not shared with them. In an attempt to use the mutual ground shared the night before, Tilbury raised the elephant in the room.

“Cassie, can you give us an idea of what your brother sent you? We are your friends and will help you through any crisis as we are experienced street fighters with ‘friends.’”

“No, too risky.”

“You have it wrong, Cassie, a problem shared is a problem solved.”

“No again, John, please trust me as I want no one, specifically MSS, to know that I know what I know.”

“OK, we will leave that alone for the moment but I want you to stay here and look after yourself as I have some jobs to do. Stay safe, love.”

Then he left Adelaide with Black for Canberra.

18

With Cassandra Jun now safe, Tilbury had two others to contend with, the disheveled Zac Alcorn and the missing Marsha. But now, he needed to meet with Mac to plan for the meeting with President William Watson.

Arriving at ASIO headquarters, Tilbury was met by security which really surprised him. He was not recognised by security guards and his passage through the maze of security barriers made him wonder what was happening. He was treated like a total stranger on entering the building even though he presented his ASIO ID. But the atmosphere was tense and distracting so he beckoned to a senior guard and politely asked. "What the fuck is going on? I'm John Tilbury working with DG McLeod."

"Sorry, Sir, I know who you are but there have been compromising leaks from ASIO, so the DG needed security to be tightened. Sorry for the inconvenience, Sir. I need to escort you to his office."

"But Sergeant, I know where it is. I have been there on numerous occasions and can find my own way."

"Sorry, Sir, that will not be possible at this moment."

Angry but under control, Tilbury met Gloria Kinsey, Mac's secretary, and asked her to let McLeod know he was there and sought some information from her about the changes to security.

"Sorry, John, but ASIO is in a state of warfare at the moment."

"What do you mean, Gloria?"

"Above my pay scale, John. Mac will explain the situation."

Entering the corner office, the drawn face of Mac met Tilbury as he approached the lounge where Mac was sitting and asked, "Mac, what the hell is going on here?"

"John, we have a serious breach of security. Our computer network has been hacked by an unknown source."

"Any damage done?"

"Will know later today, if the technicians can find the problem and plug the leak."

Given the situation, Mac thought it was about time Tilbury met Burgess, so he called Gloria, asked her to track down Burgess, and bring him to his office ASAP. Mac realised that Tilbury was not fully up to speed on what had happened in using Burgess.

"John, it is about time you met Colin Burgess, our covert spook. Colin is one of our agents working undercover as a computer technician in the University of Chicago supercomputer centre."

And he told Tilbury Burgess was a double agent working with the new head of CIA, Chuck McGinty.

"You're kidding, Mac. Have you let a rat into our midst?"

"You will have to trust me on this."

A knock on the door brought Burgess face to face with Tilbury. Mac noticed the unflinching steely look on both faces as he introduced Tilbury to Burgess.

"John, meet Agent Burgess from Chicago, invited by me to help sort out security issues given the absence of Marsha."

In an instant, the two spooks disliked each other, noticed by Mac who opened his fridge and handed beers to both his spooks with a warning.

"No bullshit, boys. We have work to do. Is that clear?"

Burgess broke the ice with a brief statement on what he and Neville had done but avoided the information that shocked him. But Tilbury put him on notice, "Colin, what did you really find?"

Mac tried to find a way to convince Tilbury that Burgess was working for him and not McGinty.

But Tilbury, not buying it, was blunt, "Agent Burgess, what did you really find in the hidden corners of the darknet you are not telling us?"

Data found in the darknet became a bigger puzzle for Tilbury who decided that he had had enough and grabbed Burgess by the shirt lifting him up against a wall of Mac's office and yelling at him.

"Agent, spill the beans or so help me, I will spill your blood."

"No way, John, be quiet and listen."

So Tilbury and Mac listened to Burgess tell a story, "I work on both sides of the fence, as you know Mac, unknown to CIA. I'm a highly trained cyber-terrorist computer technician working with the best supercomputer known to man at the University of Chicago. I support the programmers who develop algorithms to save the world, or so they think. I know how they work and covertly have been spying on the users. The CIA put me there to look for security breaches."

"One day, I was sitting in the staff room minding my own business when Professor Albert Williams came into the room obviously stressed. When I spoke to him, he said none of your business and returned to his terminal. Unsure of what to do, I visited him and found him dead on the floor, his screen blinking.

"After calling for help, I opened up his screen and a message popped up. 'You Know Your Obligations, Wang Chang. Just Do It!'

"Who is this Wang Chang and what were his obligations? So, knowing my way around the supercomputer, I tried to find out who Wang Chang was and the message that appeared shocked me.

"'Sorry Colin, You Are Now Expendable!'

"After that, I walked away from Alladin and got the message from you, Mac, to return to Australia. As you requested, Mac, I worked with Nev, battled my way through the maze of the darknet, and got nothing.

"For a change of pace and knowing that the name Wang Chang was Chinese, I typed in the name of the Chinese President Zhang Wei into a darknet platform. But then the screen erupted data flows and with the message that really frightened me.

"'Colin, I Warned You.'

"I kept the message from Neville, shut down my terminal, contemplated the source of the message, and why did it target me. These two messages came up on screens from two different computers relating to a Chinese relationship. I don't know who was sending them.

"So, I am telling you both that the president of China and Wang Chang are connected, Mac."

Tilbury recognised that the connection made by Burgess was a strong indication that the 'Chinese way' may be influencing AI and supercomputers.

But why?

19

Tilbury, really puzzled, decided that Mac needed to link the actions that happened at the Chicago University Computer centre to other information, so he suggested the way forward.

"Mac, I think that there is more to your breach and the potential connections to Cassie, Marsha, and Zac. We need to think this through before you meet with the intelligence mafia in Canberra. You know this is beginning to be the case of 'loose lips sink ships,' if we are not careful. Remember, Mac, the yanks have their own agenda and no matter how close you are to Watson, utmost care, boss."

"OK, I will bring Neville in as a catalyst to keep us on track as he is less emotionally involved than we are and has sharp insights."

"Sure, Mac, but please bring in Thomas so we stay practical, and he knows some of the players."

So, the covert meet began.

It took place in an outer suburb of Canberra to avoid the prying eyes of other spooks and government officials.

Held at Mugga Way, Redhill, Canberra, a luxury home in the Woodleigh residential estates, was built up by Mac and his wife over many years. It was an area well secluded from prying eyes.

Mac decided that people came in ordinary cars, not the usual black SUVs to not raise any alarm from the locals.

As they drove in the gate, Thomas Black, not used to luxury, said, "Bloody hell, I am in the wrong fucking job," much to the amusement of Tilbury who had the same thought.

Both had never trodden on Mac's sacred grounds. He did not share his home, even with his most trusted colleagues. A u-shaped house built around a central pool and landscaped as far as the eye could see. There were two acres of restful gardens where Mac rested his weary bones and drew solace from the peace and tranquillity.

As the group that was meeting cannot be known or seen by anyone, Mac believed that his home was protected. It was swept on a very regular basis and had a highly trained ASIO security officer he trusted with his life to ensure no intruders entered his property. People coming and going were vetted.

Communication was not connected to the internet to ensure no hacking. Secure, encrypted devises were used for their contact with the outside world. Although inconvenient, the family knew that their lives depended on that security.

Mac addressed the gathering, "Fellow spooks, here we can have an uninterrupted discussion and planning relating to cyber-security."

Seated at a table overlooking the beautiful gardens, the five men absorbed the information put before them by both Burgess and Mac with interjections by Tilbury.

Five points of interest stood out to the group: Cassandra Jun, the appearance of Zac Alcorn, the death of Professor Williams, the death of Agent Winter, and the disappearance of Marsha.

Were these interconnected in some way?

Tilbury realized they had to join the dots and suggested they consider each person in detail and potential connection, if any.

He clarified for the tense group, "Marsha may be the key to all of this. What do we really know about her?"

At this point, Mac's partner entered the area with refreshments. Patricia then said, "Gentlemen, I know you have serious talking to do, so I will leave. Anything you want, just ask."

Mac acknowledged her as she left, "Patricia, my wife, is not a security risk, she is in fact an undercover agent working for me when needed."

Tilbury, understanding the relationship, quietly stated, "Boys, we have work to do, what do we know about Marsha, Mac?"

"John, she was thoroughly vetted when she joined. I have her file here. Can you please investigate the findings and look for any gaps?"

"Ok, I'm going for a walk in the gardens, find a quiet spot, and read the file."

Mac then called the group to attention, "Thomas, you spent time with Zac Alcorn, any comments that might help us."

Black took his time to answer as he looked at the people around the table, troubled by the complexities of the situation.

Can I trust these bastards?

But Black lead with his chin, "Well, Alcorn is a troubled man, unkempt, disorganised, and showing signs of unclear thoughts but rational behaviour at times. I do not have the full read of him, but I am sure that he is more than he seems. In an off-hand manner, he mentioned that he is a computer whiz, having designed high-powered computers. When questioned, he could not remember any fine details of that skill, where he worked, and what he worked on."

"Fellow spooks, I think he may be another missing key. Why? Because he asked for John."

Black then remembered, "When discussing his troubled life, he mentioned that he was an ADF officer and his introduction to computer software and hacking was through a woman he knew as Margaret Willis. They had a love nest in the Daintree wilderness. He does not know where she is as she just up and left one day."

"Reading the signs and body language, folks, he knows more than he wishes to talk about. But is there a lead with Margaret Willis? I suggest we track her down."

Mac, sensing a lead, went to his wife Patricia and asked her to visit a 'friend' and check on the whereabouts of a Margaret Willis and her life story.

Back at the table, Mac confronted Black about the new information presented. Why had he not told Tilbury?

"Sorry, Mac, but John and I do not see each other very often since the OASIS saga, and thought that John would find out when he worked with Zac later."

Meanwhile, Burgess and Neville sat in a corner going through what they knew about the Chinese Wang Chang and decided that a relationship between Cassandra Jun's silence and the death of Wang Chang needed to be investigated.

But how, now that Wang Chang was dead and Cassandra Jun was not talking? However, the connection of both being Chinese was a possible lead that should be followed up.

Burgess opened up an optional way forward.

"When I entered the name of the Chinese President Zhang Wei, the darknet went crazy and gave me the warning, 'Sorry Colin, you are now expendable,' so I believe we have a conspiracy unfolding before us."

Neville taking all this in suggested a calm and careful approach to this can of worms they had opened.

"Mac, we know the 'Chinese way' is infiltrating our security networks, but is this real evidence, or are we boxing at shadows?"

Silent, the group was advised that lunch was served.

Tilbury had returned to the group for lunch where the group discussed their findings, informing Tilbury that Margaret Willis, a computer whiz, was a lover of Zac Alcorn. So, he raised the potential connection that Marsha could be that person.

Tilbury, whilst looking through Marsha's files, noticed a mention of the suspicious death of Chang Lui at the Queensland University of Technology earlier that year and said, "Folks, another Chinese connection. Am I becoming paranoid?"

Mac instantly remembered the connection of Lui with other Chinese students and the hacking they had carried out. In particular, he told the story of Lui being interested in being an ASIO spook.

"Friends, we may have another connexion with Chinese hackers. For example, a member of a group that studied together at QUT was a nasty MSS intelligence agent called Colonel Ming, whom Marsha found in the darknet under the name of 'Hardman.'"

"Folks, the connection with Marsha was no coincidence. Also, please consider the fact that Marsha had revealed that information to me. Now she is missing."

"Any comments? John."

At this stage, the meeting had reached the conclusion that Marsha was a key player and needed to be found. But there were no leads.

Grouped in lounge chairs on the patio watching the sun go down, with coffee in hand, Black realised that he had not told Tilbury about Zac knowing about Margaret Willis.

"John, I am so sorry but I forgot to tell you that Zac knew a Margaret Willis who may be an IT specialist and computer expert. They apparently spent time together up in the Daintree rainforest in a cottage they built and spent time computer hacking."

"Thomas, that is too much a coincidence. Both you and I do not believe in coincidences, so Margaret Willis may be Marsha. Remember, she has no other name known to us."

At that moment, Patricia, Mac's wife, interrupted the gathering by telling Mac she found out from her sources that Margaret Willis was in fact Marsha.

A hushed silence was broken by Mac who said, "Let's find her. She may be involved, but she is my top analyst, and I must protect her. Bring her home, John."

"How about you and Thomas go to where we last knew she lived before being at ASIO and please take Zac with you. Go find her, boys."

20

General Li Jun had a mistress who delved into his background to gain favours from the Party. As a paid informer, she hung on every word and nuance of the General in his weakest moments: the scent, taste, and sexual pleasure she handed him. He should have known better, but the ways of the flesh side-tracked him.

High on the love juices and the supplementary elixir tenderly offered by his mistress, he revealed that he had a sister he had not seen for some time as she was a student in Australia.

Mistress Wong passed on this information to her contact in MSS. The new knowledge of a sister was a chink in the armour of Jun the loyalists had been searching for, prompted by the silent whispers coming out of the Party about the mooted breakdown of the relationship between General Jun and President Wei and their different views on the use of the data derived from the infamous 'behaviour scheme.'

Was Wong now expendable having played her role for MSS?

The General was worried when she did not return his calls, nor was she anywhere to be found. The inscrutable General knew he was in trouble because of what he had revealed to Mistress Wong and how that information will be used against him. He had no one to talk to so he communicated with his sister Cassandra through the darknet. There, in an encrypted file, were his thoughts and data relating to President Wei.

"But why tell me," Cassandra said. "What do you expect I can do with this dangerous information?"

* * *

Now, Chinese President Zhang Wei showed no external signs of the chaos that had changed his life—a straight, serious face, soft white hair cut short, and a goatee thin and long. Shadows under his eyes covered by his wire-framed spectacles showed his observant senior advisor, sitting closely on his right-hand side, that his president was worried from sleepless nights, not revealed.

Wei carefully scrutinised his friend and confidant and carefully said, "What I am about to tell you must not be known by anyone. It must remain a secret between us."

"Can I trust you, Li?"

General Li Jun, a man with a different vision, for his country and for personal power, realised that this was what he was waiting for, a chink in the armour of the most important man in China.

Quietly, Jun responds, "Sir, I am at your service and will die to protect you, friend."

With that, one of the most powerful men in the world told his trusted friend about the moral and ethical dilemma facing him and his hold on power. Was this the information needed to work with the other hard-line members of a newly minted covert organization, the *Adjustment Directorate*, led by General Li Jun set up to challenge the Party and regain the power of the military to rule the country?

The directorate had a mandate to enhance the hard-liners' move for supreme power with the membership of China's intelligence service, MSS, and 'friends' dispersed within the West.

But dissidents were emerging as an important threat to the 'Chinese way.'

However, the power shifts within China had entrenched Wei as a long-term leader in an expanding economy that had taken a billion people out of the grips of poverty and put China as the most important military country on the earth shown by the defiant claims of the South China Sea and 'gifts' to poor nations in the Pacific that underpinned military expansion, and the developing reliance of Asia and eastern Europe on the 'expansionist development' agenda.

But the cost of the growth of China had exposed an explosion of criticism within the populous: the growing wealth gap, the handling of dissidents in growing re-education camps, widespread corruption, city congestion, environmental pollution and land degradation, the loss of civil liberties through the 'behaviour scheme' and the constant onslaught of the western world to limit the growing power of Beijing, and the 'Chinese way,' not to mention the global trade wars.

In China, whose state-backed 'behaviour scheme' became mandatory for all residents, every involuntary participant was now rated according to their business behaviour, social behaviour, trustworthy behaviour, and judicial behaviour. A scheme based on a data-driven system that automatically, algorithmically, scored each person where that score determines a behaviour credit as the determination of the very future of that person. Big brother had arrived and acted upon that data, social engineering on a grand scale driven by adherence to the algorithms of AI.

But President Zhang Wei, China's least authoritarian leader since Mao Zedong, spoke out about the previously unknown-unknowns of the socio-economic side effects of the plan that currently had unacceptable levels of 'dictatorial surveillance.' He knew that the 'behaviour scheme' was supported by the hard-liners of the military over which he had little control.

Overall, civil society demanded socio-economic change within China driven by the power of social media, the internet, and the subversive and inequality nature of the 'behaviour scheme.'

General Jun extrapolated the ensuring unrest into future civil disobedience, riots, and the potential uprising of radical insurgencies and massive protest gatherings that required an unwelcome response by the government, an apparent response that is beyond the planning and controls currently absent within the thoughts and minds of the Party led by Wei.

A weakness the *Adjustment Directorate* was developed to exploit.

Or was it?

Will a power-play between General Jun and President Wei spill over into the resurgence of the old hard-line 'Chinese way' and a global expansion-driven policy change supported by the military?

Will these changes, within China, affect the security of billions of people and change the nature of democracy in the western world if the General gained the upperhand?

General Jun had the way forward: his COHORT of 'sleepers' was in place to be supported through his *Adjustment Directorate* and its emerging communication technology based on artificial intelligence.

He began his fight against expatriate dissidents.

21

In the *Monas Gardens*, Central Jakarta, a crowd watched in awe as an 'AI killer drone' swooped across their heads. Many ducked for cover from the menacing creature as it weaved its way above the crowd, searching for a recognisable image imprinted in the drone's memory.

In this case, dissident Yang sat eating his lunch unaware of his coming demise. As he looked up at the commotion, he saw the bug eyes of the BumbleBee drone focus on him at a distance. Still, keeping its distance, watching Yang, the drone focussed the projectile for the kill shot.

It then moved slowly toward Yang. At that moment, Yang knew that his time was up. Thoughts of the 'Chinese way' he had run away from and written about. Had they caught up with him? But he was frozen in place as the drone seemed to cast a spell on him with its big bulbous eyes.

Meanwhile, the crowd was silent, scared, and wondered what was about to happen. Out of nowhere, machine gun fire dropped the drone to the ground.

MSS watchers scattered so as not to be caught in the confusion that followed. Officers of Indonesia's Badan Intelijen Negara [BIN] rushed to take control of the situation, setting a perimeter around the downed drone.

Not a normal day in *Monas Gardens* for anyone.

Yang knew he had escaped execution but was unaware that it was driven by MSS agents.

But how had BIN known about the drone?

At the Australian Embassy in Jakarta, the Ambassador viewed with concern the drone incident on local TV.

No matter how the story was spun by the media, he knew that this was no accident. As he knew people who might know what happened, he made the call.

"Karno, have you heard anything about the drone incident in *Monas Gardens* today?"

"Yes, friend, that drone is the most sophisticated of its kind, has a computer memory with power greater than the best smartphone, and what is most concerting is that it was loaded."

"What do you mean loaded, Karno? With deadly force?"

"Oh, my friend, someone was to be executed today, that drone we have called the 'BumbleBee AI killer drone' based on how it looked, constructed, and controlled.

"I will find out more about the drone because I have a brother in BIN. I have asked him to provide details of the make, model, and instruments on the deadly drone."

"Fine, Karno, how about coffee tomorrow as usual at *Giyanti Coffee Roastery* at 0730? Bring me evidence of the bloody thing with you."

"See you then, friend, but keep this to yourself as this may involve the fucking Chinese, and I get touchy about that given our president's love of their aid money."

Karno arrived early to beat the *macet*, too many cars in Jakarta despite the crazy odd-even traffic policy. As he savoured his chilli-laced egg and rice breakfast with a sweet black coffee, he wondered about the objects in his pockets.

Was he breaking the law being in possession of them and even worse by giving them to the highest-ranking Australian in Indonesia?

"Hi, Karno, good to see you again," as they greeted each other and shook hands.

The ambassador ordered the usual and sat down to ease the obvious thoughts that showed on the face of his friend.

"Karno, what have you got for me?"

"Friend, I have the brains of the drone, the memory chip. But even more interesting, I have the maker's name that was found inside the carcass of the drone. Please understand, my friend, that I will be in serious trouble, as will my brother, if this data leaks."

"In a nutshell, Karno, what does this mean?"

"Chinese without a shadow of a doubt, made by *Drone Inc.* What I don't know was who or what was the target of this deadly fucking bug?"

"What about the memory chip?"

"As far as I can tell, the chip must have fallen out of the drone and was picked up by a passer-by who gave it to my brother. But the chip had not been activated."

After coffees and small talk to take the edge off the seriousness of what Karno had uncovered, they left together and went to the Australian's car. The driver, who always waited patiently, nodded and let the ambassador into the back seat with Karno.

With the dark shield up from the front seat, Karno took out the two objects, gave them to his 'friend,' and left the car but not before he was asked to find out who might have been the target.

"Friend, you may not want to know who that was."

The Ambassador returned to the Embassy and gave the chip to his IT team for inspection. Later that day, the team met with the Ambassador and ASIO agents to hear about the investigation of the AI memory chip of the deadly drone.

The IT revealed, "Sir, what we found inside the chip is remarkable. The AI of the drone is so new we are surprised by its sophistication. Contained in that chip was facial recognition capacity, the ability to search for the desired target, and kill that person.

"Programmed in that memory was a person we know as Yang, a local dissident. DIN destroyed the drone before it killed Yang.

"But what really surprised us was a set of codes that should have detected the arrival of DIN Agents intent to destroy it. Obviously, it malfunctioned, saving Yang's life."

ASIO Agent Arthur then suggested, "We should find Yang and protect him from another attack, problem though, where is he now?"

But he also wondered.

How did BIN know about the drone?

22

A year earlier, Patrick Ong sat quietly in *Alba Café*, Gulou E St Dongcheng Qu, Beijing Shi, drinking green tea with small cakes waiting for Colonel Ming for their weekly meeting to discuss the role of Ong in an ongoing investigation of the activities of Agent Tilbury. Ong knew Tilbury from the days of OASIS and the use of the ithinkPad.

Ong had escaped from the clutches of ASIO through the support of Ming and was brought to Beijing to become a member of MSS as he had connections within the Party.

In a dismissive tone, Ming snorted at Ong, "Morning, Ong, how is my spy 'friend' today? You know I don't trust you because of your association within the Party. Tilbury is no one's friend here in China. Remember that comrade, trust in you is limited by your connexions, not by your skills needed under MSS."

"I have connections too, remember Ong, but MSS wants you to tell them the story of the ithinkPad and how it might be useful to Chinese intelligence gathering and analysis."

"Ming, what do you want from me? I was not the brains behind the technology, just involved in the testing of the ithinkPad in various Asia/Pacific countries."

"But Ong, we found out you were involved in OASIS and worked with Dr Lotheran. So, you can help us more than you think. Besides you have a great future with MSS if you can help us with the ithinkPad."

"Ok, want do you want?"

"Ong, tell me what you know."

With his head filled with potential benefits through MSS, Ong told his story, "At the time I was a futurist, developing ideas and theories relating to the future relationship between China and Australia within the context of the geopolitical ramifications of how the western world was coping with the insurgence of Asia, and specifically China."

"So what, Ong, get to the point."

A little miffed by the rebuke, he continued, "I was invited to an Australian ABC program called 'Big Ideas' and presented the argument that China was not interested in hegemony, just a powerful counterbalance against USA.

"After the ensuring debate and much fake news, I was asked by Dr Viviani to join what was later called 'the event' at the AXIOM Research Centre in Mossman, Sydney. There I got the 'curve ball' that changed my life: the 'ithinkPad.'"

"Come on, Ong, what impact did the ithinkPad have on you compared to the others who were invited to 'the event'?"

"I could not believe what happened. The ithinkPad opened up a new world created by Professor Adrian Stanley and taken over by a powerful organisation, later known as OASIS. Dr Lotheran from Oxford University saw straight away the potential use of the ithinkPad and asked me to join him in Oxford to help test the technology further.

"Before I go on, please let me explain an important piece of information. Dr Rachel Viviani, who ran 'the event,' is not to blame in any way whatsoever, so please leave her out of the clandestine idea you may have about this technology. The key ithinkPad players were Stanley, Lotheran, and Paul Edwards who engineered the latest model of the ithinkPad after the testing we did in the Pacific region.

"But, as we found out later, the earlier version of the ithinkPad was faulty and led to the death of people we tested, causing fractured lives."

However, Ming was a little frustrated at the long-winded story and no linkage to the key player he wanted to know about.

"Ong, where does Tilbury fit into this story of yours?"

"Hear me out Ming, there is a lot more to the story."

"The next part of the story, as I know it, is very complicated as it concerns OASIS, the CIA and the Pentagon, ASIO, MI6, and activities in Australia, USA, Indonesia, Italy, and the UK.

"But the core of the saga was OASIS and its spin-off an international NGO, GoGreen Inc. operating in Indonesia. The key players in OASIS were CIA and Pentagon dissidents supported by Lotheran and Stanley. The group set up GoGreen Inc. to build up criminal cadres to control the licensing of key natural and agricultural resources, mainly in Indonesia."

"Ok, Ong, but what about Tilbury?"

"Well, Ming, Tilbury, and Black, his assassin mate, brought down the OASIS deck of cards with the help of ASIO. He was the key player. He knows the full details of everything. But why is he important, Ming?"

"With your help, MSS is going after Tilbury and anyone associated with him. We want the ithinkPad and he is the answer."

However, Ong was not fully in agreement and decided to work against Ming. Although Ong was Chinese, the 'Chinese way' was not his cup of tea. But forces were against Patrick Ong.

23

Back at the Yeronga Brain Centre on his regular consultation with affected vets where Tilbury counseled them on how to change their lives. He sat quietly with Wendy, the receptionist, catching up over tea, happenings, and new research when Dr Alice Worthington walked into the canteen.

As Tilbury and Worthington had a history from the OASIS saga, they acknowledged each other with a limited hello.

Wendy saw the hard look of Tilbury and the smile on Worthington's face and thought something was wrong. She challenged Tilbury, "John, what was that all about?"

Hedging his bets, he said, "Wendy, best not go there," and followed Worthington to her laboratory.

The meeting was not cordial as both knew about the elephant in the room; the ABC broadcast about the use of the ithinkPad on primary school children. Both had an agenda that needed to be discussed by Tilbury but not by Worthington. He remembered the words of that broadcast.

"A principal at a local Brisbane primary school has reported that a trial project with a group of special students was showing a measured improvement in cognition under the guidance of Dr Alice Worthington of the Yeronga Brain Centre."

Tilbury, not one to back down, decided to challenge her to explain her actions to the children because it had an unethical feel, and secondly who gave her permission to use the ithinkPad+.

"Alice, what the hell were you doing? Who is supporting this unethical action and putting the lives of children at risk?"

"Well, John, you are out of touch and should walk away because it has nothing to do with you anymore."

Tilbury could not believe where this conversation was going and decided that Black and Mac should be contacted for a review of the experiment.

For Tilbury, the stars were not aligned, too many unconnected circumstances and people now needed his attention. What game was he playing in, with no apparent rules, and very few dots able to be joined to solve the riddle of his life?

But he knew that the actions of Worthington must be followed-up.

"Alice, speak up about this or hell will break loose for you and your colleagues. Your work is not ethical and could lead to cognitive decline and damage to those children's subconscious minds."

"Ok, John, I will partially answer your concerns."

She began her story, "I am a colleague of Dr Andropov of the Boston Brain Centre and was referred nanoscans of USA intelligence officers that died from the impact of the original ithinkPad on their brains as administered by the monster Professor Stanley at Fort Bragg USA. I agreed with his prognosis. Details you are aware of, John.

"However, the idea of the ithinkPad sparked my interest in what it was and what it could potentially do. I have been interested in the impact of sensory inputs on the brain as part of my research on neuroplasticity at the Yeronga Brain Centre in Brisbane. I was contacted by Edwards who is working at the AXIOM Research Centre, Sydney, on variations of the ithinkPad technology with inputs from Dr Rachel Viviani on the scientific aspects of the technology, while Edwards was modifying the technology and how it could be used. He wanted my expertise on the impacts of the innovative use of the modified ithinkPad.

"Edwards had created a new concept of how to efficiently put selected light frequencies into the eyes part of the brain. He called the new technology 'ithinkGoggles.'

"The children used the goggles during special games and their cognition was tested over time. I was amazed at the results. The children responded and were different in their behaviour and body language."

"But Alice, were the parents and school notified about the real nature of the technology, or were you just telling them that playing games was the nature of the experiment and using the good name of the Yeronga Brain Centre?"

"John, the protocols of the experiment were developed by Edwards. I acted on his advice that the technology was safe. I met with the parents of the selected group after the school principal negotiated the trial. He wanted some of the unruly and smart children to be given the chance to improve their classroom behaviour and their test results."

"Alice, from my point of view, this looks like another trial similar to 'the event' held at AXIOM earlier where I was the experimental control. Please tell me this isn't true."

A non-response by Worthington made Tilbury realize that another enactment of 'the event' may have the same strings attached. A view that disturbed him enough to seek advice from both Black and Mac.

Can this be happening again?

"Thomas, I have just discovered a potentially serious problem we need to address. We need to meet with Mac straight away. That OK with you?"

"John, what are we up again this time, friend?"

"Ok, Thomas, a bit melodramatic, but I have a gut feeling about the use of the ithinkPad. Remember the nefarious tentacles that were connected through OASIS. That technology we investigated may have arisen again."

Both had thoughts for different reasons.

Are we going to be spies and crime busters once again?

However, Worthington had been truthful. She was working with Edwards on a version that now had AI developed by We Chang at the University of Melbourne AI Centre.

New technology that allowed the ithinkGoggles to manipulate the input into the eyes part of the brain for optimal impact based on algorithms.

24

Is Australia a pawn in the game? As a toothless tiger, or will the support of Pacific nations by Australia, Japan, and the USA show the western world that such a strategy to limit the spread of the 'Chinese way' in the pacific must be supported? The loss of African nations to the economic bribery of Beijing should have been a lesson?

As a middle-level power sitting in the centre of the Asia/Pacific region, what influence can Australia exert to support nations coming under the influence of Beijing's hard-line military's growing expansionist strategy?

Australian President Notting expressed his concerns to Mac about the growing infiltration of the 'Chinese way' into the hearts and minds of potential dissidents within Australia. As in most of the western world, Chinese immigration led to a slowly growing basis of Chinese criminality and political interference. However, both agreed that the average Chinese immigrant was a benefit to 'the Australian way.'

America's president, William Watson, an old friend of Mac, agreed to meet with Notting and Mac as he was about to embark on a re-election campaign.

He also wanted to get his head around the influence of Beijing and the 'Chinese way' in the Asia/Pacific region from another source other than the CIA and his other national intelligence agencies such as NSA.

His recent skirmish with the previous head of CIA Johnson made him cautious of his intelligence agency networks. Watson had also got the vibe that the new CIA McGinty was not very supportive of him. However, he trusted the Australians and their forthright way.

But what was the cost to Watson if he teamed up with the Aussies?

As he had concerns about McGinty, was Watson looking for a different perspective about China in the Asia/Pacific region? He called his friend Mac to seek help and a greater understanding of MSS, the Chinese leadership, and the 'Chinese way.' Was it a form of fake news and propaganda for political scaremongering to create electoral fear, or a legitimate motto to interpret the rise of the Red Dragon?

"Mac, can you bring your president Notting and Tilbury to meet me at Camp David for a debriefing on the Asia/Pacific region and the influence of Beijing?"

"Ok, Bill, I will do that, but let me tell you that we just had a breach of our computer network by an unknown source. Also, have you had any signs of a similar breach?"

"No, Mac, but a mysterious death has occurred at the supercomputer centre at the University of Chicago which our security people are investigating."

Mac was now curious.

How did Watson link that information to us?

25

The meeting with Watson was arranged for Camp David. Tilbury went along for the ride whilst the two presidents confronted the same growing sense of a changing hegemony arising out of the 'Chinese way' influencing the developing nations of the Asia/Pacific region. Despite President Wei's smiling rhetoric and offering loans or grants for struggling economies, the motives were clear, the world had changed and so had Beijing.

Were these perceptions real?

As *Marine One,* the presidential chopper, landed at Camp David, Tilbury took Mac aside and suggested that he not let President Notting run the meeting with Watson.

"John, I know what you're saying but he is our boss so we need to be circumspect in the way we approach our concerns with Notting. And I have briefed him fully on the range of options likely to be raised by Watson."

Arriving at a private conference room to meet Watson, they were confronted by Agent Bud Castel and CIA DG McGinty, who said with a smirk on his face, "Welcome to the CIA, Mr President, hope you enjoy our meeting."

Tilbury reacted, "So, Mr CIA, another shit-faced director I see, go fuck yourself."

Mac took Tilbury aside and whispered, "John, take care mate, this McGinty is worse than Johnson according to my intelligence. Rules like a dictator but cannot harm us. Just leave the prick alone."

"No way, Mac, he will influence Watson and therefore affect what we need from him."

President Watson watched the Australians enter the room and noticed their unexpected body language and realised that they had encountered CIA McGinty outside.

"Andrew, Mac, and John, pleased that you have come all the way to discuss the problems facing us with the changing hegemony created by our 'Asian friend.'"

Feeling the tension of Mac and Tilbury, Watson asked for a side conversation in an adjoining room, away from the CIA and Notting.

"Mac, I realise that the presence of the CIA has thrown you and John, but I had no choice. McGinty demanded to be here as he got wind of the reason for the meeting. How, I do not know, but my walls have ears. Sorry, Mac."

To which Tilbury answered, "Sir, with due respect, your CIA McGinty, according to our intelligence, is not your friend. We also know he is a fully paid-up member of the NRA, which is covertly funding their activities in Australia."

To make his point even clearer, he added, "Sir, tell him to piss off, as this is a meeting between two presidents and our president has asked for him to leave."

"John, he will be a powerful enemy and have a serious impact on my re-election."

At this point, Mac chimed in, "Bill, he already is your worst enemy, friend."

Watson walked back into the meeting room, told everyone to leave, and said, "Chuck, this is a private meeting, so please do as I ask."

McGinty, full of rage at being treated that way, gave Watson a smarmy smile, indicated to Bud Castel to move, and said with hatred, "Mr President, you will regret this."

President Notting took over the meeting and showed his displeasure at what had happened.

He then pointed at Mac and said, "What the hell just happened? We have now made an enemy of the CIA by being part of the by-play with you, Bill. I did not come all this way for this childish behaviour."

Watson taken aback by the pointed barb by Notting responded, "Hold on a minute, Andrew, that prick McGinty has been playing games ever since I appointed him. I apologise for his behaviour, but I have no control over him as he has very powerful Republican Party friends and the NRA if what you have told me is true. I didn't know. So much for my advisors."

Deciding that the meeting should proceed, Mac began with his prepared statement for both presidents to understand the changing nature of the world's hegemony.

"The 'Chinese way' is a growing concern of our Asia/Pacific friends. They are being bombarded on a regular basis to join in their 'expansionist development' policy initiative, offering goodies to smooth their way into the hearts and minds of sympathetic government officials who like the benefits of the transactions coming to them.

"The critics of that policy have called for caution about being involved as it facilitates Chinese strategic and economic dominance of countries along two routes. Both overland and maritime, examples of the 'Chinese way.'

"Proven intelligence shows that within China, the civil rights of millions of certain groups have been totally disregarded. The 'behaviour scheme' had run rough-shod over those millions whose scores are not within the bounds of the State algorithms spying on their own people.

"Externally, the power of Beijing has grown to bully nations dependent on the open seas for livelihoods, food, and national security. Blatantly defying the International Law of the Sea, which they don't accept. Offering loans that cannot be repaid and taking assets such as ports to be used for their marauding gunships. Trade wars crippling our neighbours who cannot fight back.

"The information is clear and well-documented, Bill and Andrew. The 'Chinese way' is here. The question is: What is our plan?"

Notting knew the impact of the 'development initiative' was not supported by Australia given the evidence building on the growing influence of Beijing in Australia and the Pacific region.

"Folks, we need a coordinated approach by the developed countries to adapt to the growing power of Beijing without causing another cold war. This should be developed by the G20 (excluding China), but how do we do that?"

Watson, always the pragmatist, agreed with the idea but asked, "How do we get them on board without interference from the numerous intelligence agencies that will kill off the idea?"

Tilbury wanted to influence a pragmatic solution and put forward the biggest idea of his life for presidential consideration.

"Mac, can we establish a 'private blockchain arrangement' with the head of State of each G20 member, excluding China because of what you have just explained?"

To help nullify the concerned looks, Tilbury tells,

"Each Head of State has a membership of a private blockchain (PB) encrypted group. The messages flow between members but no one else had access. This means a covert plan can be drawn up by the key world leaders to help mitigate and/or adapt to the growing Chinese influence.

"This form of private blockchain gives more privacy because there is restricted access to each user. For example, each Head of State can view and participate in the G19 blockchain group. An agreed blockchain delegate (or more) verifies the transaction and the associated 'blocks' containing the information shared.

"But you want to know if this approach is better than the encrypted emails that we can send to each other. The answer depends on the risk factor. Blockchain transactions between the members of the G19 would be very highly encrypted, whereas using the darknet will have too many listeners. The key will be acceptance of the concept and who will run the blockchain."

Watson looked at Tilbury with a shy grin and asked Mac the time-bomb question, "Mac, can this be achieved without our security networks getting involved because this would be so sensitive politically to those leaders involved, if leaked?"

"Well, Bill, the next G7 is in a few months. Can we set this up in a private meeting of the Heads of State in Tokyo?"

"I can get my top analyst to draw up the plans, under my guidance, for the private blockchain system."

Given the recent serious breach of security at ASIO HQ, Tilbury queried Mac, "Are you sure your network is safe, Mac?"

"Yes, I will ask Colin Burgess to set up this blockchain arrangement independent of our network, working with Neville as they have a good working relationship."

But President Notting was reticent and asked Tilbury, "Isn't there evidence that the blockchain system has been hacked? Really, friends, that cannot be allowed to happen to us."

"Andrew, that has happened to public blockchains. We will establish a private blockchain and get our best hacker to test that possibility before the G20 meeting."

All agreed a blockchain system be established under the auspices of Mac, then settled down and contemplated the rise of China.

But what about McGinty and the covert world of spy agencies? Are they listening?

26

Leaving the Camp David meeting, agreeing to meet up with Notting and Mac later, Tilbury was accosted by two unknown assailants and dragged away unconscious, placed in an unmarked black SUV with a hood placed over his head and driven out of Camp David.

Now awake but groggy, Tilbury tried to work out where they were but his knowledge of the area was limited. No noises that could give him a clue; no bumps like crossing a bridge or any changing angles suggesting mountains.

Having trouble breathing, Tilbury considered his situation.

Why am I in the trunk of this car and who kidnapped me?

The ride was smooth and quiet, indicating an expensive model, so he blocked out the traffic and surrounding noise and concentrated on listening to the people in the vehicle. However, words were difficult to hear, but some were clear as one person spoke louder than the rest.

"Bud, what are we going to do with the prick we have in the trunk? We were told to kidnap Tilbury because he was a clear and present danger to the CIA. This is dangerous territory, Bud. ASIO will be up our arse on this, as will President Watson if he hears about this action."

Castel, barely audible, replies, "Agents, this is a special assignment that will gain you bonus points with director McGinty, so let's do this together."

Tilbury was deeply troubled by the conversation as it definitely involved McGinty as he knew from experience that Agent Castel would never act alone.

How does he get out of this mess?

As a trained SAS soldier, Tilbury knew that he could cope with any matters that arrived because he did not think that his death was the real reason for his capture. So, he worked out a plan that would give him a chance to escape.

Then the SUV stopped, doors slammed, voices raised, orders given, hood removed. Tilbury was forcefully dragged from the trunk of what he recognised as a CIA black SUV, a typical intelligence mobile unit.

To his surprise, he was taken into a Texan-type ranch house set in cattle country where he was met by CIA Director McGinty.

"Chuck, what the fuck are you doing kidnapping me, giving me a beating, dragging me to your home? You will pay for this, bastard."

"Well, good to see you too, John. We have serious business to discuss away from your safety net."

"Bud, will you fix some refreshment for John? He looks like he needs a drink." A nervous Castel replies, "Ok, boss."

McGinty, in charge, gets straight to the point.

"John, CIA is concerned about Australia meddling with our politics and your relationship with that useless fucking Watson. He will sell this country down the river because of his pathetic approach to Beijing and the 'Chinese way' as you so clearly put it in that side meeting you had at Camp David. You see, John, we bugged that room as a precaution, so we heard everything."

Tilbury now knew the agenda was a little more complicated than he expected.

But why rough me up?

"Ok, Mr CIA, what do you want from me? Your thugs did me over, for what fucking reason? My willingness to talk has been violated. Agent Castel will be taken into custody ASAP as we will seek help from the FBI about my abduction."

And he added, “A polite request for a meeting would have paved the way for a real discussion on the expansionist activities of Beijing.”

“Some thought, John, but you see, John, the FBI are my friends. I will just say we wanted to meet with you, but you started a fight, so we had to subdue you. See where this is going, my Aussie friend.”

“Chuck, you have made your point. Why am I here?”

“For a smart guy, you are pretty thick. It should be obvious even to you. Simple, John, tell us about the ‘Chinese way’ for my sake and that of America.”

“Fuck off, Mr CIA, they are already here.”

McGinty, realised he had made a point with Tilbury, had Castel put the hood back on, and told him to drive to a train station and release him.

“John, don’t fuck with the CIA, and tell Mac he is on notice.”

27

SunnyBank Hills, a well-known Chinese suburb in Brisbane had a variety of restaurants frequented by local and visiting Chinese. One in particular was the *Little Red Dumpling* with tables made out of large slabs of timber, a great place for tasty dumplings where the two Chinese friends of Chang Lui, Zing Fu, and Xang Bao now ate Sunday lunch thinking about Lui's death.

The Fortitude Valley restaurant was now off-limits for Sunday lunch as they felt that Ming was somehow linked to Lui's demise and they did not want to meet him again. His demeanour and arrogance annoyed them. The problem was that Ming was really unknown to them both, as Colonel Ming held his MSS identity from his lunch friends, for obvious reasons.

Did Fu and Bao have any worries about Shi Ming? If so, why? As they did not know his true identity.

After the usual array of dumplings and custard tarts downed with green tea, the two felt comfortable in their own skin and were therefore not very observant as they left the restaurant. Boisterous and happy, they walked down the tree-lined street, across to the carpark where their early model Holden Astra sat alone in that space.

Hopping in the car, they did not notice a shadowy figure in the backseat until Zing Fu, the owner, felt cold steel against his head and gripped the steering wheel hard, sweating with fear when he realized that it was Shi Ming dressed completely in black.

"Ok, Ming, what do you think you are doing?"

"Monkeys, please address me as Colonel Ming of the MSS."

Both now knew the game was up because the mere mention of MSS struck fear in their hearts. The sobbing passenger Xang Bao begged Ming to tell them what was this all about.

"Colonel, what do you want from us?"

"You both knew Chang Lui and his behaviour in using the darknet and playing around with the *White House* server, didn't you little monkeys?"

Wide-eyed and frightened, Zing Bao loudly professed that he knew nothing of 'those-kind of actions' taken by Lui.

"Ming, we were his friends, and with you, had dumplings with him each Sunday, but what he did was unknown to us, I swear." Fu, to support Zing, said, "Ming, I too know nothing."

But Ming was not having any of these excuses, shot them both, gangland-style, to confuse the police and ASIO.

As he moved away from the dead students, leaving no traces of his presence, Ming smiled and thought.

No loose ends now, my actions on the darknet now covered.

A foot patrol cop, walking the beat early the next morning, noticed a car with doors open, wondered why, and took a look inside. To his horror, two young Chinese men had been shot in the back of the head. So he called in the local patrol car and the detectives at the SunnyBank Hills police station.

Being experienced in the area and the fact that the dead were Chinese, Detective Bob Jones from the AFP was brought in because of the possible linkage to Triads local cops knew operated in the area.

TaskForce Triad was established, resourced, and located in the Brisbane CBD under the leadership of Jones, an old-school strategic thinker who had connexions within ASIO, Interpol, and Scotland Yard having worked with these agencies.

Detective Jones had seen it all before and knew that this will be a complex case when the Chinese were potentially involved. The next morning, Jones met with the TaskForce team to establish the priorities and allocation of tasks.

"Good morning, my name is Bob Jones, the team leader. Beside me is Detective Gavin Morrow from AFP and experienced in such cases. He will support me in daily briefings and the allocation of tasks."

Addressing the TaskForce team, Morrow briefed members of the TaskForce, "What we know so far is that the last time these two were alive was in the Little Red Dumpling restaurant for lunch on Sunday, as picked up during a 'door-to-door' on Monday morning."

"We do not have any identity yet, but forensics have found evidence in the glovebox of the car. The registration leads us to believe that the car belongs to Zing Fu, but nothing more. The other dead person is unknown to us as is the other person(s) who killed them.

"Team A, led by our IT specialist, will concentrate on identifying the life of Fu and the identity of the other person(s). Team B, led by Chang Fan, our local detective who knows the key operators in the area, to suss out any potential connections and leads within the Chinese community. Team C will liaise with ASIO to see any leads from terrorist or espionage activities that may be connected with the death of these young men. I will lead that team.

"We expect autopsy and evidence reports later tomorrow.

Finally, folks, we live in a world with touchy relations with China, so beware of the 'Chinese way' when dealing with the local community. Any problems, come to me and Bob. Take care, this case may have teeth."

After the briefing, Jones and Morrow discussed the problems TaskForce may need to solve. One in particular was the political implications related to investigating the complex interconnections within Chinese communities because the federal government was treading softly on the Chinese/Australian relationship.

Trade was in the balance as Australia tried to raise issues such as internal human rights and growing external impacts in the Asia/Pacific region of the 'expansionist development' policy for land transits and ocean states.

Later, Team A reported that the evidence found in the car were receipts for petrol and lunch at the *King of Kings* restaurant in Fortitude Valley.

"From that evidence, we found that Zing Fu regularly met with three others on Sundays. When questioned, the receptionist said, 'They were regular patrons, known as Zing, Zang, and Shi who were friends of Chang Lui. We know Chang well because he was a favourite customer, friendly, outgoing but serious about his studies at the QUT.'"

Jones agreed that the evidence may be a lead and asked the team to check with the university to find whether Zing and the others were also students.

The forensics team took the TaskForce through what they found in the car. Blood from one of the victims matched that of Zing Fu, the other blood sample was not matched within their database.

Detective Bob Jones decided that he needed to meet the head of ASIO, McLeod, to help in the search for the two missing identities and what they may have on Chang Lui, an IT specialist student at QUT. Jones knew from experience that these students often played where they shouldn't, the darknet.

Arriving at ASIO headquarters, Jones was met by Tilbury who escorted him to Mac's office. Tilbury was invited by Mac because of his sharp intelligence, experience, and worldly view of espionage matters.

Besides, Mac was certain that this was no ordinary meeting and he needed Tilbury's advice given the keywords of an email received from Jones: the 'Chinese way,' murdered students, darknet potentials, and the fucking Triads.

"Morning, Detective Jones, I see we have a lot in common to discuss. First, please meet my colleague Dr John Tilbury, an experienced ASIO agent whom I trust absolutely."

"Hi, John, I have heard much about your work in the OASIS saga. Good result. I will enjoy sharing our troubles with you both."

"Mac, we may have a serious problem. A student named Chang Lui had two Chinese mates we found murdered, gangland-style, in a Chinese enclave type suburb in Brisbane called SunnyBank Hills."

"Do you know anything about Chang Lui that may lead us to the three other people: one we have identified as Zing Fu, the other two still not identified? Any information will help the TaskForce."

Mac, trying to put the ducks in a row on the wall, said, "Bob, you told me that TaskForce Triad had been established, led by you. Who is the AFP representative on that TaskForce?"

"Detective Morrow, whom you know, as he has worked with you before."

"Bob, you're blowing smoke up my ass, you cannot be serious. He is a conspiracy junky, a loose cannon, and likely to scare 'persons-of-interest.'"

"John, please tell him your experience with that sad case."

"Bob, I hate to say this, but he will be more trouble than helpful. Sadly, he has lucid moments but not often. I worked with him and he was a dangerous man to trust. Suggest you trade him for someone else."

"Bob, trust us, he will hinder the TaskForce and lead you up to dry gullies, and piss off potential leads and 'persons-of-interest.' Agree to add John to your TaskForce to keep an eye on Morrow and use his skills of investigation. I guarantee you will not regret that decision."

Jones wanted to move on and asked Tilbury a key question that could change all of their lives.

"John, will you please join us as an ASIO adviser and Mac, I now need the information I came to get from ASIO."

In jest, Tilbury thinking of previous skirmishes, said, "Bob, will I need my Glock again?"

But Tilbury was really uncertain about the role. It had the potential to shatter his beliefs and add more uncertainty to his puzzled life. Mac, sidled up to Jones and asked if he needed a drink.

The refreshments were on the side table by the window, and at the same time indicated to Tilbury that a side meeting was needed.

Mac needed to set boundaries on the discussion with Jones now that both Morrow and Chan Lui were mentioned. A red flag to Mac, supported by Tilbury, as shown by his body language. An aside conversation ensured.

"John, we know that Chang Lui was murdered and that Marsha had made the connection to Colonel Ming and Agent Bud Castel through the darknet. I suggest that we draw the line at what we know about Chang Lui and say nothing else. Certainly, no mention of Cassandra Jun and Marsha. Too risky until we know where this is heading. That's why I need you on that TaskForce, John."

"Ok, Mac, let's find out what Jones really wants from us."

28

As the three sat in Mac's office, Jones set out what he needed from ASIO, specifically any intelligence on Chang Lui and his mates.

Agreed. Mac then explained that Chang Lui was a student at QUT and had strayed into the darknet and was discovered by MSS Colonel Ming. His death is still not understood but there is a consensus that he was murdered, probably by Ming.

Mac explained to Jones his take on the Lui matter.

"Given that view, it is possible that the killer you are looking for in the two deaths in Queensland could be Ming. But Bob, this situation smells of Chinese influence based on our internal investigation of Lui, and could be linked to the CIA, but yet unproven. However, I cannot tell you in the interest of national security."

"Are you for real, Mac? My experience in these matters is that if the CIA and MSS are involved, that is not good for our health, as you already know."

Jones eyeballed Tilbury, seeking a different view, and asked him, "John, what is your take on this?"

Tilbury, at the end of his patience, replied, "Bob, we are friends here with only partial information upon which we make assumptions. My experience is that there are no such things as coincidences."

"Trust us, John, Colonel Ming is at the centre of this and we need to apprehend him."

Jones, satisfied that he had a breakthrough, indicated the meeting had ended and asked Tilbury to return to Brisbane with him. But Mac held up the departure with a bit of advice for Jones.

"Bob, this is a murky world us spooks inhabit. We search for the missing pieces of the jigsaw puzzle, join the dots, but when the 'Chinese way' may be an important part of the picture, we need to be very circumspect."

"Mac, the pointed barb at the 'interests of national security' seems that there is information being withheld that is going to hamper my ability to solve this case."

"Bob, that is true, but I will pass on that information if and when appropriate. However, you have John to guide TaskForce Triad through that quagmire. Use him."

Unsatisfied, Jones asked Tilbury to fly with him back to Brisbane and join TaskForce Triad as the ASIO adviser.

During the flight, Jones asked Tilbury for a redacted history of his life and times. He needed to know how Tilbury operated as a spook given his military training and experience, and what his mindset was. He knew that agents such as Tilbury could be burnt-out and ineffective under extreme pressure.

Jones wanted assurance that Tilbury was the right man.

At the next meeting, Jones introduced Tilbury to the TaskForce members, much to the dismay of Morrow who took Jones aside, and asked, "Bob, what the fuck is Tilbury doing here?"

Realising that the Tilbury and Morrow interaction was a problem, if left unresolved, replied, "Gavin, in my office in five." Jones returned to Tilbury, looked him in the eye, indicated that a meeting with Morrow was necessary right now, and said, "John, in my office in five."

To encourage more effective dialogue with team members, Jones' office had a comfortable seating arrangement, a round table. Jones sat with his back to the window, a commanding position.

Morrow broke the silence, "John, not nice to see you. You have been up my ass for too long, but I guess Mac sanctioned this?"

Jones now knew that this relationship was deep-seated and decided to put them back in the box as chaos was not the way forward for TaskForce Triad.

"Gavin, time to bury the hatchet or you are out of the team. Can you guarantee a team behaviour approach and bite your tongue regarding John? I took your membership at face value because you were referred to me by the AFP. Don't make me regret that decision."

"Bob, OK, because I want to be part of the team, just keep John out of my role."

"Do you agree, John, because we have a very sensitive investigation ahead, and I need your undivided attention?"

Tilbury was still not happy with the Morrow membership of the TaskForce.

"Ok, Bob, but as for you, Gavin, I will keep my eye on you. You get off the leash and I will put you back in the box where you belong."

With that, Jones made them shake hands and told them to get to work. As Tilbury was about to leave, he asked him to stay.

"John, what just happened was for show. I need Gavin to organise the team, but I want you to be my eyes and ears as this 'Chinese way' could be an IED ready to go off. Do you agree?"

"Bob, I will certainly be your wingman on two conditions: I take over as leader of the intelligence team and you leave Morrow as the TaskForce coordinator, and I can freelance if needed."

"Sure, John, I will talk to Gavin about that but if you want off-the-park, please keep me in the loop."

Tilbury then called the intelligence team together for a discussion of the sensitive matters related to the deaths and the potential intelligence leads that need to be followed up.

But he was concerned that the matter of a 'Chinese enigma' may be based on the wrong hypothesis stemming from the deaths. The team needed to separate facts from superstition: was the problem State-based or from rogue elements?

Was the question of the 'Chinese way' fake news to stir up people to accept the right-wing conservative resurgence occurring across the globe, or was it real?

Tilbury decided on the 'risk-averse approach' that it was real. The long-term ramifications of not being active to understand and at least adapt to the 'Chinese enigma' were not rational.

As the ASIO representative on the TaskForce, he could not untangle the actions of local Chinese from that of a global scare: too many coincidences, uncertainty, chaos. He constantly challenged his role as a spook and the complex notions of the 'Chinese way' as it affected his life.

Although he had colleagues, he was essentially a loner in a sea of so-called 'friends.' He needed a pathway.

Was that Rachel Viviani?

29

Meanwhile back at Mac's mansion, he believed Black had given the group the best clue yet, the real identity of Marsha. So, he issued an order to Black and Tilbury.

"A trip to the Daintree wilderness may do you both good. Do not worry about other commitments, leave immediately. She may be in danger. Meanwhile, to help on your search, John, I will get my other analysts to search the life and times of Margaret Willis."

As ordered, they went to collect Zac to take with them as his memory may be jogged during the trip when faced with the Daintree rainforest. But Zac was not to be found which led to Black exclaiming, "Well, where the fuck is the bastard? I told you that he could be a problem."

As a last resort, Black rang Dewi and asked if he had been in Café Boga today. Her answer was clear, "He is here, Thomas."

"Dewi, please ask him to stay there as I will come and collect him. Also, I will be away with John for a few days but do not mention that to him."

When Tilbury and Black arrived at Café Boga, they noticed that Alcorn was distressed with the vacant look of a very troubled man. But Black was not impressed with his demeanour. "Zac, come on, man, get a grip of yourself. You're in good hands here."

His reply shocked them both, "They have found me, John, what can I do? Please help me."

Black had had enough, "Who are you talking about, Captain? We are sick of your lack of cooperation." Alcorn just smiled and said, "Thomas, you have no idea what I know. Let it rest."

Tilbury looked hard at Black which clearly suggested he back off. "Thomas, we need to work together. And Zac, your future depends on your cooperation. So bloody well talk to us."

But Black was insistent, "Zac, give us a clue, mate. Whatever shit you are in, we can help."

Zac relented and let them into his life.

"OK, guys, I am paranoid because of my past in dealing with computers and how they were used. I was pressured by a foreign agent to become a spy for Russia, but I declined. From that day on, I have been avoiding any contact with them because they are evil bastards, trust me. I know how they operate through the darknet."

"Are you being truthful here? We are your mates but getting involved with the old KGB with new clothes as the FSB and using the best computer systems and covert operations is not to our liking, Zac."

Tilbury and Black had the same thought.

Are we chasing two centres of counter-intelligence: Russia and China?

30

A black ASIO SUV arrived and Alcorn was placed in the backseat with Black. As it sped through town, the three discussed their plans on the way to the Brisbane domestic airport for a Qantas flight to Cairns in North Queensland.

Seated in the rear of the plane, Tilbury explained to Alcorn what they were about to do: hire a vehicle at the Cairns terminal and drive north to the Daintree rainforest area.

"Zac, we need your mind to be focussed as we are heading to a place where we believe you lived with a person called Margaret Willis. We want you to look around and see if anything comes to mind about your time with her in this wilderness area. Thomas told us you had a cabin in the rainforest where the two of you were lovers and played with the internet."

No response.

"Focus, we need to save this woman's life because we believe she is in mortal danger. Anything come to mind, now is the time."

Tilbury then remembered that Agent Jim White was murdered between Cairns and Port Douglas, another coincidence that was another dot in a colourful unsolved jigsaw puzzle. But Tilbury had no vision of the full picture.

But why was White killed?

The scenic drive from Cairns to Port Douglas revived their spirits and knew that a couple of beers would be what the doctor ordered.

The team visited *Paddies Irish Pub and Grill* in Macrossan Street, Port Douglas. The grilled Coral Trout washed down with a pint of Guinness went down well. Alcorn's spirits were improving, and he began to talk, "I remember Port Douglas. It was where we bought our food every now and again. Margaret loved the seafood, and we often had a cold one at the *Court House Hotel* in the centre of town and stayed a few nights. I have the memory in my head about our cosy cabin that we built but no idea where it was. But I remember that we had great computer equipment and internet gear. She was a whiz at the internet and hacking."

"Sorry, John, that is all I can remember."

Black, feeling more sociable, decided that they should visit the *Court House Hotel*, have a few beers, and stay the night. All agreed.

As they entered the bar, all went quiet. The few local patrons breasting the bar took an instant dislike to the two tough-looking bastards and the disheveled Alcorn. Noticing the regular drinker's reaction, the barman looked straight at the group and said, "Well, fuck me if it isn't the 'assassin' in person. Bloody Blacky, what brings you to my bar?"

Thrown by the greeting, Black walked to the bar, smacked the barman right on the nose, and said, "I owe you that, prick."

"Well, folks, the assassin in person. This prick saved my life, but he is still a prick. The beers are on him, folks."

Black at that moment could not recall the soldier's name, but when introductions occurred, he knew it was Larry the Larrikin who did not believe in orders. Larry cleaned up his bloody nose and sat down to have a beer with the three men. As Corporal Larry did not mix with the Officer class, he did not know Tilbury but knew of him as an SAS Major who would die in the ditch for his men, if needed.

Black noticed that a regular drinker was staring at him and decided that was not friendly, so he walked over to the group and said, "What are you looking at, mate? I suggest you stop."

The man took umbrage at the comment and got up to intimidate Black.

Larry, seeing what was about to happen, yelled at his rowdy customer, "Bill, don't be bloody silly, not worth the fight, mate. The coppers around here are not friendly and I could lose my licence." And he said, "You will lose that fight, mate. Sit down, drinks on Blacky."

"Hey, sniper, behave yourself in my bar."

Bemused, Tilbury just smiled at Black whilst Alcorn wanted to leave. Given that sign, Tilbury suggested that he rest up and meet them for breakfast. Agreed, he went upstairs.

Alone, Tilbury and Black took out the photo they each had of Marsha from the ASIO files and discussed whether they should visit a few coffee shops to see if anyone recognised Marsha. No luck until Tilbury walked into *Café Ziva*. He decided it was time for a coffee and walked to the female barista with a becoming smile.

He liked her straight away and wondered.

After ordering a Macchiato coffee, he asked her if she had seen this woman, showing her a photo of Marsha. The woman smiled and asked why. Tilbury knew that it was an important moment and smiled with soft eyes.

"My name is John, have you seen her? It is important because she is a missing person," then he showed her his ASIO warrant card, and asked her, "What is your name, love?" not wanting to look too interested.

"Anna, the barista here at Café Ziva," in an enticing tone that forced Tilbury to hold her gaze.

"Can I ask you a few questions, Anna? I will not bite."

"OK, sit at the table near the window where we can talk."

As Tilbury walked to the round table, he watched her watching him while a little spark flashed in his brain.

I wonder where this could lead.

Arriving with the coffee, she blinked, smiled, and tilted her head as women do when interested. Tilbury, needing to be professional at this point, asked the key question again.

"Anna, have you seen this person?"

Taking the photo, Anna looked intently at her face and gazed out the window at the bright blue sky as she gathered her thoughts. Her mind racing as she remembered, "It was Friday. The shop was fairly busy when she walked in. I noticed her because the stress of her life showed on her beautiful face. I asked if she was OK. Her reply made me wonder at what had happened to her."

"She said, 'The fucking Chinese are ruining my life and my career. I need to get away from all that.' I asked what she intended to do. Her first reply was that a coffee would be nice.

"She actually sat near this table in one of those red chairs and had breakfast. After eating, she seemed fixed on a man sitting over there. She must have known him because she walked over to him and they had an argument, and he left.

"As she walked out the door, she took a Daintree rainforest flyer and said, 'Thanks, Anna.' I have not seen her since."

Tilbury felt the passion of the woman as she looked at him. No uncertain signal there, so he asked, "Anna, are you free tonight? I would like to buy you dinner and shoot the breeze. Are you interested?"

Her smile was enough so they arranged to meet at a Japanese restaurant at 1900 later that night. Satisfied by the day's work, he called Black and asked him to meet at *Café Ziva* ASAP as he had news for him.

Black was amazed that they had such a clue but not happy when Tilbury pointed out Anna and said he had a free night ahead.

"Up to your old tricks again, John."

"Need-to-know basis, Thomas," as they left the café.

After sushi dinner, small talk, and enjoyable repartee, Anna asked if he would like one for the road at her place. Tilbury, no stranger to the wiles of women, knew the double meaning of 'one for the road,' agreed, because either was a pleasant surprise.

Anna had a well-appointed unit with a balcony that overlooked the ocean. He could hear the rolling surf as it washed up on the sandy beach, a living space carefully arranged to suit her lifestyle.

A serious bar provided a G&T for settling the nerves both had at the prospect of what was clearly going to happen.

They sat outside on the balcony and took in the pounding surf, the moonlight that reflected their emotion and the sensuous magic in the air. Taking a cue from her body language, Tilbury took her hand and led her to the bedroom. He could smell the scent coming off her as he slowly undressed her ebony body that glistened, tantalising him and his growing search for that moment of entry. This was no ordinary barista.

Anna King had no qualms about what was happening. Tilbury was sex on legs, a man to really enjoy as far as she was concerned without the dreaded commitment and the usual 'I love you, Anna' she avoided. This man was different, strong, rugged, and excellent in bed. King controlled the action, an approach that Tilbury wanted to exploit.

Satisfied, King made a 'one for the road' drink while they talked about each other. Something she never did with men; sex was fine but that was all she needed.

But this man was different. She wanted more but knew that was not likely after he had explained some of his redacted histories.

The next morning, the team had breakfast at the hotel. Alcorn looked better after a good night in the cot; Black was miffed by John's action but excited by the information gleaned by Tilbury.

Tilbury was calm, relaxed, and enjoyed his Macchiato coffee. Black made no comment on what Tilbury had done last night.

A plan was drawn up: follow the lead to the Daintree rainforest and see if Alcorn could remember anything.

"John, I have a feeling about today. Margaret Willis meant a lot to me. Let's find her."

31

Marsha longed for a quiet life back at ASIO where she had access to the world's best intelligence equipment. Her search for her ex-lover was now crucial for her mental health. She was getting frustrated at not finding any information about him from her treehouse cabin in the rainforest Daintree EcoLodge with the computer access available.

Going stir crazy, she asked reception, "Can I get a lift to the village for a change of scenery?" "Marsha, the bus leaves in an hour and returns at 1600." Excited at the prospect of a walk around the village and having a coffee calmed her nerves. Marsha joined the other visitors on the bus.

A walk along the Daintree boardwalk refreshed her brain and reduced the anxiety building up due to the uncertainty of her life. The *Daintree Teahouse Restaurant* beckoned with the relaxing setting, fabulous food specialising in scones and locally grown tea, and mouth-watering wild caught Barramundi.

As she sat facing the rainforest dripping with the aftermath of early morning showers, Marsha sipped her tea and weighed up her life.

Marsha there and then made the decision not to return to Canberra as an ASIO spook and called Mac. Hours later, a call from Mac told Tilbury that Marsha had called and resigned from ASIO. Tilbury knew that if she was in trouble, her backup protection was now lost.

He could not let her be in danger, so he told Black and Alcorn the mission was now critical.

Based on the information given by Anna King, they drove north toward Daintree village, a well-patronised tourist area where the forest reached the ocean. As they moved along Macrossan Drive, Black noticed the sign to *Daintree EcoLodge* and commented, "John, I would like to visit that place with Julia."

Alcorn responded, saying, "Guys, I remember that place, great for R&R. I went there with Margaret. Can we go there? Maybe on the way back." All agreed that in a day or two there would be what they needed, a safe haven.

Tired from the drive, Tilbury decided that coffee would go down well, so they called into a local café and ate 'Barra-burgers' and chips, a delicacy of the area. Black looked at Alcorn and suggested they take a walk along the Daintree boardwalk and sniff the breeze. On the other hand, Tilbury decided to show the photo of Marsha around town.

As Black and Alcorn slowly walked through the rainforest, a stranger came up to Alcorn and pointed at him.

"Well, where have you been, Peter? It's been a long time."

Alcorn could not believe his luck as this man was his old army friend who knew him as Peter Sax. As he tried to deny it, Black became suspicious of the body language of Alcorn.

He grabbed the stranger by the lapels of his jacket and shouted, "Who the fuck are you, my friend?"

"My name is Captain Ken Taylor, a vet who came across Peter here in Daintree who taught me about computers. He had very advanced skills in that area and helped me so that I could run my business."

Black looked at Alcorn in the menacing way most people knew of Black who asked the obvious question.

"Zac, are you really Peter Sax, front and centre, mate, or you will regret you knew John and myself because you lied to us and fucking ASIO. You're in deep shit, mate."

"Spill now, or else."

Taylor saw that his old friend was in real trouble and tried to calm down the situation.

"Pete, old friend, own up and tell us why the name change."

"Ok, Thomas, I am Peter Sax but I changed my name by deed poll and my passport to Zac Alcorn because of my recent past. I had uncovered a serious breach of national security through playing with the darknet and came face-to-face with the Russians. I needed to disappear because they were after me."

Black, sensing a breakthrough, put pressure on Sax. "Peter, why did you withhold this information from ASIO and specifically from John and myself?"

"Simple, Thomas, the culprits are the Russian intelligence. The unknown-unknowns of our national security networks have become real. I am shit scared, Thomas, and fear for my life, so I tried to hide."

"But, Peter, why did you front John that day as he was walking to Café Boga?"

"I lost my nerve, Thomas, and knew that John could be trusted."

"Big help, Peter, you actually hindered what we could do to help you and other vets."

With that, Black asked Ken Taylor to join Tilbury for a beer and discuss the now game-changing data, and called Tilbury to meet at the local pub.

Tilbury was curious as he watched the three men slowly walk into the bar. Alcorn seemed to know the stranger and made Tilbury wonder what had happened.

Black introduced Taylor to Tilbury. Pleasantries over, Tilbury asked Black, "What is this all about, mate?"

"Well, John, Ken here knows Zac from some time back when they were both here at Daintree Village. But to my surprise, he called Zac, Peter Sax."

"John, on further questioning, I now understand that Zac Alcorn is actually Peter Sax, and he knew Margaret Willis at that time."

The plot thickens, thought a troubled Tilbury, *so what's next in our quest is to find Marsha.* But he could smell how close they were; it was in the air.

Tilbury was side-tracked by the appearance of Taylor and had forgotten to mention he had visited the shops to see if anyone had seen Marsha.

"Thomas, I talked to a woman in the Daintree Teahouse who thought that she saw a female that looked like the photo who had coffee in her shop today and said that she was with a couple of women who seemed to belong to a group as they caught a bus around 1600."

An excited Black asked, "What bus?"

Tilbury then told a story, "But her answer had disappointed me. 'Sorry, Sir, but there are many unmarked tour buses that come and go. I cannot help you there.'

"Not one to give up, I asked her again with a different question, 'Which bus comes to your teahouse on a regular basis?' Sceptical, she questioned me, 'Why do you ask, Sir?'

"Showing her my ASIO warrant card, I said, 'We are looking for a person we believe could be in mortal danger.' I mentioned that I'm Dr Tilbury, saying I urgently needed to find her. Her answer may help us, Thomas.

"'The best I can offer you, Dr Tilbury, is the Daintree EcoLodge because the patrons there go on other tours and activities from the village and that company supports our teahouse as the managers of both are friends.'

"On leaving, I left her my card and asked her to call if anything, no matter how small, she remembers."

About to find lodgings for the night, Tilbury had a call from the teahouse woman.

"Dr, this is Sarah from the teahouse, you asked to call if anything came to mind. Well, I realise that I had missed something that might help, given the urgent nature of your visit."

"I'm listening, Sarah, go ahead."

Hesitant, she used words that struck fear in Tilbury's heart.

"Dr, I noticed a well-dressed Chinese woman looking intently at your missing person all the time as if checking on her. She left at the same time your Margaret left for the bus with the others. I hope she is alright."

"Thank you, Sarah. I hope she is too."

"Folks, time to move, we need to visit the *Daintree EcoLodge* and see what is to be seen. Keep your eyes open and look for a well-dressed Chinese woman. She apparently kept watch over Marsha and left when she did."

"Thomas, have we got our Glocks on hand? We may need them."

"Yep, in my bag."

"Ok, folks, let's go."

32

Meanwhile, Marsha had returned to the *Daintree Ecolodge* on their bus, totally unaware of how close the ASIO team was toward finding her.

She had enjoyed the day in what seemed like familiar surrounds with humid nectar falling from the dense jungle of the area. It gave her life. The bus ride was full of laughter from people who had enjoyed their day in various pursuits. She sat next to the woman who shared time with her at the teahouse.

A temporary friendship that gave her comfort as she enjoyed the company of the group and momentarily forgot about her troubles. But that woman caught her attention.

So, Marsha invited her to the cabin in the forest that had become her home. Money was not a problem. She had saved well from her days at ASIO.

Known as Kelly West, she had a liking for women and believed that Marsha could be interested even though no outward signs indicated that possibility. Over a quiet G&T, the conversation strayed into sensual moments that Marsha was comfortable with, not knowing the desires of the woman she had invited into her home.

Kelly West then suggested that they give each other a massage and placed her lips on Marsha's as a friendly gesture. Marsha felt giddy and reticent but as West held her head and kissed her passionately, she gave in to her desires.

West, experienced in the lesbian world, took Marsha to the bedroom and undressed her, speaking softly, comforted her, and paved the way for the intimacy that followed.

Ensuring that Marsha was more than satisfied, Kelly West quietly whispered, "Sleep well, there is more to come." And left the cabin.

Marsha was now confused by her experience with West and her longing for Peter Sax brought about by the tropical surroundings and her memories of their home in the rainforest.

Sleep did not come easy as she lay awake thinking about her future, whether to return to ASIO or just meld back into the rainforest and forget everything. But she was an expert analyst and knew she wanted back into that world.

However, Marsha was so stressed and thought that she should spend time here at the lodge and go with the flow for a while.

Little did she know what was ahead for her.

33

Meanwhile, the three ASIO men arrived at the reception. Kelly West greeted them and asked if they want rooms. Taking over, Black, said, "Yes we do, three separate ones if possible."

Checking the register, West apologised and offered only two, one with two singles. Tired and a bit jaded from the day, they accepted the offer. Black unhappily agreed to share with Sax, leaving Tilbury with a master suite.

Tilbury suggested that they meet in the bar after settling in their rooms and walked up to receptionist West, showed her the photo of Marsha, and asked with cool, soft eyes whether she had seen the woman in the picture. However, in Tilbury's training, her body language portrayed a different message from what she said.

"Who is asking? This is a private place, and we expect people to respect our guest's privacy."

Tilbury now knew that West was about to lie to him.

"Sorry, Dr Tilbury, but no, I have not seen her."

Sensing a troubling moment, Tilbury cut her off, saying, "You have just lied to a federal officer. Would you like to rethink your answer?"

Quick on her feet, she bluffed a lie with, "Yes, I saw her the other day in Daintree village. She looked like a tourist. But I am not totally positive it was her."

"Why do you need to find her?"

"Ms. West, it is a matter of national security, so if you know anything, it is your duty to tell me straight away."

Unhappy, Tilbury handed her his business card and went to his room.

But he was not satisfied with her demeanour and thought he should check on her. A creeping suspicion clouded his mind; she knew something about Marsha.

Tilbury knocked on the door to Black's room. Silence for a while, then Black stuck his head through the door, critical of his peace broken, and said, "John, what the hell. It's been a long day."

To which Tilbury replied, "Agree, Thomas, but I believe that Marsha may be here at the lodge."

"What gave you that idea?"

"I showed the receptionist a photo of Marsha, and Thomas, her reaction was unusual. I saw it in her eyes that she had lied to me."

"John, we had better check this place out. Give me a few minutes to get ready."

"No, Thomas, I will wander about to see if she leads me to her because if she is here, I believe she will warn her. If needed, I will call you. Go back to sleep. This is on me, mate."

Leaving Black's room, Tilbury saw that in reception, Kelly West was packing up for the night, so he waited ready to follow her.

He remembered that she was a good-looking woman who looked after herself.

But, could she be trusted?

Having retrieved his Glock from his cabin, he felt comfortable in his own skin as he followed her, out of sight.

Walking to one of the outer cabins in the rainforest proper, the receptionist kept in the shadows, proving to Tilbury that his impression of her was right.

But what happened next took Tilbury by surprise.

All hell broke loose. West was grabbed from behind and shot by a masked attacker. Tilbury on the scene took down the hooded attacker and checked both bodies. The receptionist was critical but the woman behind the mask was dead.

Tilbury rang 000 and checked the body of the dead woman. A neatly dressed Chinese with gun power to match her attire.

What, where are these Chinese coming from? They are at my every turn.

The gunfire had attracted nearby guests, dressed in various night attire. Silhouetted against the light leaking from her bedroom was the distraught figure of Marsha.

"John, what are you doing here? I told Mac that I was finished with ASIO."

"Marsha, we had intelligence data that you were in danger, so Mac sent Thomas and myself to protect you. But bloody hell, you were hard to find."

After the ambulance and local cops arrived, Tilbury explained his presence and took Marsha back into her cabin.

Shocked, Tilbury made a stiff drink to calm her.

Then he said, "Marsha, I have a lot to tell you. But first, a question. Do you know Peter Sax?"

Marsha then fainted in his arms.

He then called Black, gave him the heads-up, and asked him to bring Sax with him to cabin A3 straight away.

Tilbury slowly rocked the shattered Marsha, comforting her in one of the worst moments of her life. But she was strong-willed and slowly recovered, wanting to know why he had asked her about Peter Sax.

Before he could answer, Sax walked in the door and fell on his knees in front of Marsha asking for forgiveness. Black looked on at the unfolding event, unable to put all this together.

"John, what happened? The receptionist is in a critical condition and a fucking Chinese woman, dressed to kill, is dead outside this room."

Marsha held Sax tightly, letting the emotions of the past and that night run freely over his puzzled face.

Crying, she held his hand and said, "Peter, I have been looking everywhere for you. I understood the message about the photo of the conference in Chicago."

"Marsha, love, I went into hiding. I came across information I should not have, details relating to Russia. Details I have not told a soul about. Believe me, love, I am a broken man but buoyed up by seeing you again."

34

Mac listened intently to the call from Tilbury, concerned about the death of the Chinese female assassin. He, like Tilbury, was deep into the Chinese influence that kept cropping up.

"John, please tell me that her death is just a coincidence."

"No, Mac, the receptionist Kelly West was collateral damage. We believe that the assassin was going after Marsha, but I killed her before she entered the room. A search of her body provided no information about her identity. But we do have a witness that might help us. She noticed that a woman in her café showed an interest in Marsha, and left when Marsha left."

"John, do what you can to interview her. There may be a lead we can pursue."

"Will do, Mac. Thomas and I will follow that up."

"John, how are Marsha and Zac who I understand is actually Peter Sax? I will get my team to run an investigation into his life."

A meeting in Tilbury's cabin started with a debriefing of the events of last night, the assassination attempt. Being an expert in this clandestine world, Black puts forward his take on the situation they were faced with right now.

"Friends, from my experience, what happened last night must have been planned, but by whom and why? These are the questions we need to seriously consider. Our lives may be at stake because of this failed attempt on the life of Marsha. There will be retributions, so take care."

Tilbury, trying to join the dots of the puzzle before them, made the statement that none really wanted to hear, "Look, friends, there are no coincidences about what happened last night."

And he mentioned that he was privy to enough data relating to the presence of that Chinese woman to state that they were facing a 'Chinese way' tsunami that began in Chicago and flowed through to Australia.

"Folks, too many examples of influence stemming from Beijing for certain actions to be coincidental. Because of national security, I cannot reveal these examples. Just trust me on that."

"By the way, Marsha, you and Peter are requested by Mac to return to ASIO for a briefing and to plan a future operation he has in mind. He is setting the record of the action here. Marsha, you were shot and killed here. That attack will be broadcast to the media so that you will be protected from further death threats. Under Mac's authority, information on the Chinese woman's death will be put under an ASIO seal."

"Remember, folks, walls havc cars."

Both Black and Tilbury knew that there was more to come.

35

Back at TaskForce Triad, Tilbury had asked Jones if he could expand his intelligence team to include Black and Colin Burgess given the growing concern about the 'Chinese way.'

"John, I am keeping an open mind on the number of Chinese deaths that seem to crop up on our radar. However, my gut feeling is that you are on the right path here, but the consequences of what we might discover will not go down well with the president, the PM, and his intelligence mates."

"Bob, me of all people should know about that sensitivity but I will not soft-peddle on this matter; too many deaths and coincidences for my liking. But I accept your warning."

"Because of my concerns about the national security interests, I will only have trusted colleagues on my team: Burgess, Black, Neville, and occasionally Mac from ASIO. That OK with you, Bob? I do not want Morrow anywhere near this. Keep him occupied with the administration of the TaskForce."

The arrangement was agreed upon.

36

Patrick Ong sat quietly in the *Alba Café* and contemplated the discussion just finished with MSS Ming. Although he was in debt with him because he brought him to Beijing away from ASIO, he not only disliked Ming but also had no trust in his forced 'Chinese way' of thinking.

With coffee cold and his confidence on the slide, he decided that he must leave Beijing and return to Australia. But given all the security that surrounded him, his only option was clear.

Go to the Australian Embassy and seek protection. Using a passing taxi, he arrived at the security gate and asked for asylum as an Australian citizen. After making a copy of his Australian passport and detailed questioning, the security officer was reluctant to let him enter the building. But the face of Ong said it all: anguish, pale, eyes red and puffy. The guard let him in stating that his entry was dependent on the acceptance of a DFAT security advisor in the Embassy.

"Mr Ong, please wait in the interview room on your right. Someone will come and talk with you."

As he sat in the chair, Ong consoled himself that as an Australian citizen, he would be given asylum. However, the look and body language of the young woman who entered the room nearly stopped his breathing.

"Patrick Ong? I'm Virginia Akermanis, the Australian immigration representative here in Beijing. My duty is to make a decision on your entry into Australia."

"Virginia, I have an Australian passport and wish to return to Sydney, but I'm a target of MSS and would be taken if I went to the airport. I'm not safe and need your help in leaving China."

"Unfortunately, Patrick, your passport has a red flag that we must investigate. Can you help us understand why that is the case? On the surface, your request is rather shaky. Because of the unusual nature of your case, I need to report this matter to our ambassador. Please wait for my return."

Ong now knew he was in trouble because of his involvement in the OASIS saga. He had slipped through the hands of ASIO with the help of the well-known MSS agent Colonel Ming.

Had the chickens come home to roost and turned into turkeys?

Ong was now at his wit's end engulfed in a life-threatening dilemma: rejected to face Ming or safety within the Embassy. In what seemed a lifetime, Ong went through his life searching for the best data that could help his case as he waited, waited, and waited.

A security guard entered and asked Ong to follow him.

He was now certain that his application was rejected when he was told to enter the lift with the guard.

The lift rose to level 5 where he was ushered into a room and asked to sit. Three persons were present. Silence until Ambassador Ashley Brown entered and addressed the room.

"Gentlemen, we have a problem that ASIO HQ is now aware of. The stranger here is Patrick Ong, well known to ASIO and had been meeting with a Colonel Ming of the MSS. Ong has asked for asylum. We have an opportunity here we have looked for, a linkage to MSS. Stan, can you fill in the details for Mr Ong?"

"Patrick, I'm Stan Arthur, head of intelligence here at the Embassy and we seek your cooperation. We are aware of the naughty actions you were involved in with OASIS and the misuse of the ithinkPad. But we are not interested in that."

Ong felt a little pressure had been eased until . . .

"We want you to keep your relationship with Colonel Ming and spy for us. In return, we will clean your history, guarantee your safety, and your return to Australia."

"Do you understand what we are proposing, Mr Ong?"

Was this an opportunity too good to be true?

But Ong's options were clearly limited, so he asked the Ambassador the question that changed his life.

"What do you really want from me?"

* * *

Ming thought over his recent conversation with Ong and realised that their relationship needed to be toughened, so he called Ong, "Patrick, can we meet again? It's urgent."

"OK, Ming, same time and place tomorrow."

A stranger sat at the back of the usual *Alba Café*, watched, and recorded the conversation that took place between Ming and Ong. His cover was writing a novel using the café for his office so his coming and going were accepted by the staff. His orders were to watch and wait, notice anything out of the ordinary for a coffee shop, and to report back to the Embassy. As an ASIO spook and Embassy diplomat, the Chinese Bing Lee melded into the coffee crowd as he had done at different times as he watched the growing relationship between Ming and Ong.

But now Ong knew about Lee's role and worried that his life may depend on that observer.

However, Ming was watched by a team of MSS underlings sent to observe the diplomat. No interference was the clear instruction; he had diplomatic immunity. But neither Colonel Ming nor Ong was aware of their presence because these thugs rotated their coffee hits and there were always two of them acting as mates sharing a coffee together, an old surveillance trick.

However, Ming, the dangerous killer, thought he had seen Lee too many times to be a coincidence. Not caring and fearless, he approached Lee and sat down beside him.

"Hello, I have seen you writing during the many times I have come to this place for solitude and to talk with friends. What are you writing about that is taking you so long to finish?"

"By the way, my name is Ming."

"I am Lee, Ming. I have also noticed you on occasions. To answer your question, I am writing a thriller novel on the deaths caused by pollution through business corruption and mismanagement in the western world. It is set in New York and involves the FBI and NYPD."

Surprised by the apparent truth, he asked Lee to read a part of the story, "Lee, I am interested in that kind of novel, can you show me chapter 30?" That drew a wry smile from Lee who knew what Ming was up to and was happy to show him. Lee had actually written the story, as a cover, during his visits to the café and was able to satisfy Ming who then left without any further comment.

Lee now knew that his cover was not blown.

But what about the other watchers?

Agent Arthur met with Ong and Lee in his field office for a weekly debrief. The three came at different times and used counter-surveillance tactics to ensure they were not followed.

Ong was not a happy man, the strain showed on his face. The lost weight and a grim smile alarmed Arthur when he revealed his pain.

"Stan, I am in the middle of a game over which I have no control or moves to make. I have followers from whatever side. They track me everywhere. I'm stressed and alone."

"Patrick, this is what Agent Lee had recorded whilst watching your meeting with MSS Ming. Do you agree?"

"Ong, you need to remember you are now part of what we have called 'the adjustment plan' through the application of the 'behaviour scheme' to ensure the strength of and obedience to the 'Chinese way.'

"You know this already, but what is exciting for the rise of China as the dominant world power is a global agency called 'The Adjustment Directorate' set up and sponsored by General Jun. I have recruited you as 'a hunter,' one who tracks down key people, residents outside China who resist the 'Chinese way.'

"Our work begins tomorrow. We meet with the Head of the Adjustment Directorate to discuss your role as a dissident hunter in Australia."

"Lee, that is correct. What Ming said shocked me for two reasons: he recruited me without my agreement and the fact that the Directorate existed. As you would have heard, I was asked a lot of questions about my role, to which he answered, "Ong, it is your destiny."

The ASIO agent listened to the conversation, weighed up his options, and thought the smiling bastards are coming.

Mac must know about the Adjustment Directorate.

That night, the diplomatic bag went to Canberra.

Back in Beijing, Ming demanded a meeting with Ong.

As he again sat in the *Alba Café,* Ong was faced with a dilemma: follow the demands of MSS in the role of 'a hunter' within the Adjustment Directorate and return to Australia with Ming, or just walk away. Either choice was a death sentence within his worried mind, even though Agent Lee was his protector.

Later, back at the Beijing Australian Embassy, the ASIO team agreed that Ong should go with the choice offered by Ming as it might help uncover the nefarious activities that MSS was planning under the Adjustment Directorate.

"Patrick, we know the Adjustment Directorate exists but we have no information on what it is, how it operates, and what are the outcomes that the Chinese Party has for that organisation."

"However, Patrick, we will wipe the slate clean if you hang in there with Ming and find the answers just mentioned. We know that it will be dangerous because Ming is a known killer but he is not the brains behind this organisation. Your mission will be to dig into the workings of the Adjustment Directorate."

Agent Arthur then put the wood on Ong. He had only one option with no wriggle room.

Ong, uncertain, called Ming and agreed to be 'a hunter' for the Directorate and sought instructions, "Ming, what happens now?"

"Meet me at the MSS headquarters tomorrow at 1030 where we will be briefed on your role as a 'hunter' in Australia; be there or else."

Ong began to feel the squeeze of conflict.

Ong arrived at MSS headquarters where he was met by Ming and escorted to a rather drab meeting room on the second floor. General Jun, medals on, sat at the end of the table with several accolades on his right.

The General rose to his feet to meet the pair, offered seats to his left, and took control of the meeting.

"Colonel Ming, your presence with Ong is part of a new beginning in the use of the 'behaviour scheme' that has been planned by me over the last few years. The Adjustment Directorate, under my control, will use a secret supercomputer to manipulate the algorithms of that scheme to impact expatriate Chinese nationals."

"We want to pilot the scheme in Australia and Indonesia to see if we can influence the expatriate nationals living, working, or studying within those countries. Simply put, the Directorate here at MSS will use the AI of our new supercomputer, the IT technicians I have trained, and the support of a COHORT of sleepers operating in the best universities in the world. These soldiers will operate within a new section of MSS headquarters."

The General then set out the role of Ming and Ong…

"The AI of the supercomputer will detect the names of people who have left China and analyse all the data relevant for the application of the 'behaviour scheme' algorithms. Depending on that rating, you, Ong, will hunt down that national and do what is asked while Ming will be your protector.

"All resources will be supplied, including bank accounts, funding, and safe houses in all capital cities. You will be based in Brisbane and Jakarta. Your orders will be via the darknet that Ming will control.

"Any questions will be answered by my deputy here, Captain Ling. The operation begins in two days. Be on notice that you will be watched before, during, and after these pilots. I expect encrypted messages from you, Ming, detailing the success of the missions."

With that, General Jun retired to his office to contemplate the message he had sent to his sister in a moment of weakness. Had he set in train a time bomb that could explode if his sister Cassandra Jun understood the message and told the Australians?

What should I do about that?

General Jun also knew the COHORT he had established earlier had a couple of hick-ups that had to be controlled. For example, Professor Wang Chang was collateral damage from an investigation into the status of sleepers within the western world computer centres. Wang Chang had shown his weakness toward the support he was trained to give to the improvement of the 'Chinese way' and he needed to be eliminated. But killing these sleepers was not the plan; subversive and psychological manipulation was the solution. The pressure on him was planned because his medical status was known.

The General now needed to make contact with the twenty sleepers of his COHORT to relay his instructions to one of his trusted sleepers who had access to messages sent by him.

Activate now!

37

Mac arrived early at ASIO headquarters after a restless night. As he sat by his window watching the sunrise brighten the room, he opened the internal mail from the Ministry of Foreign Affairs and Trade to reveal the TOP SECRET communication from the Australian Embassy in Beijing.

He knew that communiques like this usually gave him a headache, so he asked his secretary Gloria to arrange coffee. But the coffee was let go cold as he read the file note.

"Mac, the information attached is beyond my belief and the implication for Australia and our allies is quite clear. The direct quote is from your Agent Stan Arthur who organised one of the intelligence staff to record a meeting at a local café between Patrick Ong and Colonel Ming."

Mac read the recorded statement…

"There is an 'adjustment plan' to be implemented through the application of the 'behaviour scheme' to ensure the strength of and obedience to the 'Chinese way.' But what is exciting for the rise of China as the dominant world power is a global agency, called 'The Adjustment Directorate,' set up and sponsored by General Jun for dissidents outside of China."

Mac weighed up his thoughts.

What the hell is the Adjustment Directorate?

38

Tilbury had a lot on his mind and on his plate. But the latest call from Mac suggested some logic to the puzzle before him. His main concern was the leadership of the TaskForce Triad Intelligence Team. He had mitigated leaks by having his trusted agents as the only members of his team.

The question, however, was how much information covered by 'in the national security interest' should he reveal to his team? When asked, his trusted friend Black stated the obvious.

"Let Mac make that decision and we go from there."

Tilbury agreed and called Mac to attend his meeting in Brisbane. "Mac, I want your input into the intelligence team. Can you make the meeting at 1030 tomorrow?"

Mac realised that the information he just received from Beijing must be part of the mix and said, "John, I will attend, but only your most trusted colleagues can hear what I have to say. I will brief you on arrival."

Tilbury, Black, and Mac had an early breakfast at Café Boga where Mac mentioned the communique from Beijing.

To Tilbury, the Defence Signals Directorate (DSD) should be involved in any discussion about the involvement of the Chinese Adjustment Directorate.

What do DSD know about the Adjustment Directorate through their foreign signals intelligence that can support ASIO? But why had Mac not mentioned DSD at any stage?

Black as usual summed up the situation.

"Friends, I do not like the picture emerging of our Chinese puzzle. What are we going to do about that?"

A long silence ensured before Mac stated, "I need a brief on this, John, because, against my better judgement, I will need to talk with President Notting."

Later that morning, the team began the redacted version of the past events that Mac could use to inform Notting. However, Mac had explicitly stated that the brief should not contain too much information as it could be leaked and reminded Tilbury that the brief is an official document. Besides the breakfast crew, the additional members were Neville, Burgess, and Jones, all of whom were not Party to the Beijing information nor the role of the DSD. Tilbury wanted to keep a lid on that for the time being.

To begin the meeting, Tilbury raised the elephant in the room: a conspiracy theory that China was trying to infiltrate the workings of the Australian government. He then introduced Mac to say a few words on the ASIO view of what they already knew.

"From my perspective, there are too many coincidences that have occurred in recent times that need to be investigated."

All agreed the coincidences linked to Chinese persons. It was a puzzle they needed to unravel as suggested by Mac. The Chinese enigma was now obvious.

"My experience suggests that we should construct a mind map of what we know and the potential linkages between who we know. It might provide insight into the puzzle before us, as John had pointed out before."

Tilbury led the way by starting with Cassandra Jun and what came from that information, which was supported by the actions of Marsha, both Chinese-related. Next, he raised the point of the death of a Chinese AI Professor in Chicago and added the death of three Chinese students that studied at QUT.

Summing up, he asked the team to consider whether there were any potential links between all of that information and Ming.

Neville, the seriously experienced agent, addressed the team to get the analysis rolling.

"I believe the linkage is what Marsha and Cassandra Jun know and have not provided it to us because they are frightened. I think we should put them together in an interview room and explain to them why they need to 'spill the beans.' But is Marsha strong enough to be involved and safe, as you Mac, have killed her off?"

A plan was discussed with the emphasis on Jun and Marsha, but Burgess wanted to add to the story.

"I believe that the death of Professor Williams (aka Wang Chang) is important because when I tried to discover information about his death, I was personally attacked through the Alladin supercomputer by unknown hackers. In retrospect, I think Chang was also attacked by hackers in such a way that he died from the impact of the message."

"Remember, folks, I talked to him just minutes before his death and he was a mess. There is no point in guessing the message received by Chang, but a world-breaking supercomputer, a Chinese AI specialist, a suspicious death. Is that a piece of the larger picture before us, a pattern worth investigating, or a conspiracy theory?"

Burgess asked a touchy question of Mac. "Mac, you had a computer crash, any information on what caused it, and was there any files hacked or deleted?"

"Yes, we found a discrepancy in our database relating to Chinese immigration. It was not significant so I am told."

Tilbury knew that to some extent, that data may be really significant because it depended on the people involved. So, he asked Mac for that information.

"Mac, if that data is related to Chinese immigration and visa applications, then my team should have access to those files because we may uncover a useful pattern."

Mac saw a way forward and called his office to provide an analysis of the data. He was looking for linkages with Ming, the three students, and Cassandra Jun. He mentioned to his secretary he needed the data ASAP.

In a moment of reflection, Tilbury suggested to Mac, "We should meet with the DSD and share our knowledge."

"Let me think about that, John."

39

Adam McCarthy sat at the console of the supercomputer in the Technology Centre at Melbourne University playing within the darknet against the operating rules of the centre but was always worried about being caught, so he covered his tracks after he had finished. He put his USB, with the data gathered from the darknet, in his pocket, unchecked, and left the centre.

McCarthy, a member of the local Chinese Triad, looked forward to a beer at the local pub with his Chinese mates. They usually met every Friday night at *Young and Jacksons*, opposite Flinders Street Station to watch Friday night AFL football. As a Collingwood supporter, he often went to the MCG, home of Aussies rules, and watched the 'Magpies' who were beaten last week by the Brisbane Lions. As a Collingwood member, McCarthy often had arguments with his mates who hated that team.

However, this night, McCarthy had a serious conversation with these mates.

"I need to go away for a few weeks to visit my family in Beijing, so I will miss nights like this for a while."

He then walked out the door without looking back. One of his friends who was also a member of the Triad had a feeling about McCarthy's leaving comment.

He knew he had no family in China. They actually lived in Brisbane, so he decided to follow him. But he watched in vain as McCarthy (aka, We Chang) was picked up by a Mercedes SUV that moved quickly through the streets of Melbourne toward a safe house in Richmond.

A call from Ming had pressed the escape button for We Chang to meet him on an order from General Jun through the computer Ong had in that safe house.

"Chang, this is Colonel Ming from MSS. We need to meet. As a sleeper of the General Jun's COHORT, you have the responsibility to meet me to discuss your future. According to your score from the 'behaviour scheme' algorithms, you have breached our security by habituating with that Melbourne Triad. We need to know why you have done that."

"So, Chang, the SUV will take you to a safe house where I will meet you."

"Why, Ming, what have I done?"

"I will explain when you get here."

Chang was now a frightened man and negotiated with the driver to let him go. But the response caused him to shake with fear.

"Sorry, Chang, I am Ong, 'a hunter' from the Adjustment Directorate. You have just signed your own death warrant."

The mere mention of the Adjustment Directorate was too much for Chang. He had heard whispers about the shadowy nature and covert operations stemming from Beijing. Chang was scared but not without courage: a seasoned Kung Fu exponent of the martial arts. But he knew if he faced the killer Ming, he could not win that fight; brains and movement were no match for guns.

He had no option but to challenge Ong at some stage during the journey. But Ong felt that Chang would try to escape. So, when Chang opened the door and threw himself from the moving car, the landing was hard and left him prone on the tarmac. Ong stopped the car, ran to a struggling Chang who faced Ong with a martial arts stance, and ended the ordeal with shots to Chang's chest, leaving him to die on the tarmac from severe blood loss.

Shaken, Ong called Ming and explained that he had left Chang to die beside the tarmac; the 'hunter' was now active.

Ming surprised Ong when he asked him to return to the scene and retrieve the body. "Ong, the role of the hunter was to leave no evidence. Go remove it."

"Ok, Ming, I will return to the place and get rid of the body."

Unfortunately, as he drove down the road, he was confronted with a police cordon, flashing lights, and an ambulance at the scene. Rather than escape, he pulled up at the chaos and asked the police what had happened. Police checked his ID and details of the car as a usual process. Ong then left to meet up with Ming.

Given the recent spate of killings of Chinese nationals, AFP was informed by the local police and thus, the death was passed on to ASIO. Mac was advised of the death soon after when he was meeting with Tilbury and his team.

"Mac, the death of another fucking Chinese national is no coincidence. This one must be fully investigated."

"John, according to reports, the dead person was We Chang, known by the name Adam McCarthy, a supercomputer AI technologist from the University of Melbourne Computer Centre."

"Mac, the death of two Chinese supercomputer experts seems too much of a coincidence. What do you think?"

"I will get my expert AI analyst to visit that centre and find out what he was up to and search the darknet for any nefarious activities he was involved in, and his connections to other Chinese nationals, if any."

Tilbury wondered whether this was another order sanctioned by Colonel Ming.

40

Back in Beijing, General Jun addressed a meeting of the executives of the Adjustment Directorate.

"Comrades, we have now established the most effective and functional surveillance system of our nationals within China and used that data of the 'behaviour scheme' to monitor and modify the behaviour of our citizens. But we have only just started. We need to control expatriate nationals."

The eyes of his staff lit up at the potential to use their algorithms to manipulate non-resident Chinese nationals to support the growing importance of the 'Chinese way.' But their enthusiasm was dampened when they realised the difficulties of using the scheme outside China.

Seeing the concern on their faces, the General decided the time had come for him to describe the reason for the COHORT that few knew about, let alone its real function.

"Comrades, I stand before you to tell a great story. During the establishment of the 'behaviour scheme,' I had the idea that there are millions of nationals now embedded in the western world that could help the development of the 'Chinese way' if monitored and brainwashed to support our cause. So, I set up the COHORT, a group of our best intellectuals as sleepers in the West."

The atmosphere in the room was palpable. His senior analysts began to understand where the story was heading, and they were all at one with their leader.

"Comrades, at this moment, the sleepers have been woken up and are active."

Cheers emanated from his staff as they realised that another step was made toward global Chinese hegemony, a covert attack on America and its allies. General Jun then asked for their silence as he described the function of the COHORT sleepers:

"Each of the G20 countries, apart from China, has a sleeper, now activated, at a supercomputer that will be under their control. Based on my instructions, that computer will be used for surveillance of our Chinese nationals in each country.

"Analysts, your next role here at the Directorate is to supply the data on these expatriates and send your findings, through the darknet, to the sleeper in each country.

"But the sleeper cannot act alone in this quest, so I have set in place a 'hunter program' where each 'hunter' will track down the expatriate and help enthuse that person to help with our cause. Miscreants will be dealt with through active MSS resident agents in each country working in our embassies or consulates.

"I intend to run a pilot scheme in both Australia and Indonesia because of their potential influence in the Asia/Pacific region.

"Any questions?"

Now full of confidence, the General told them about a test run he had made with an early model of his killer drone:

"Comrades, I sent three killer drones from a naval vessel offshore of Taipei, Taiwan to Baishawan Beach. The report brought tears to my eyes as these beautiful technology beasts swooped in from the ocean and sprayed projectiles at a group of dissidents having lunch after a conference on 'Problems of the Chinese influence in Taiwan', and were relaxing under umbrellas on the beach. The number killed was 15, some 20 injured. A warning to all dissidents operating outside of China."

"Based on that result, I have programmed for a new model to be developed as a 'hunter-killer.'"

Given no response as the audience was spellbound by their leader's audacity, he closed the historic meeting.

"Ok, now return to your desks and begin this quest to boost our nation's hegemony."

After the others had left the meeting, Deputy Major Ling sat with General Jun as they discussed the plan and the potential problems that might arise. One in particular was the potential for a leak from the Adjustment Directorate to the Party and/or President Wei. This was important because the plan was covert and subversive and would be a serious blow to China's reputation if the West found out.

"Major, you are now responsible for the compliance of our staff to ensure that no leaks occur. Is that clear?"

"My privilege, Sir."

"Ling, what is the latest news on We Chang in Melbourne as I believe he was killed by Ong and Ming for an unknown reason? Is there any blowback from Australian intelligence that I need to know?"

"Sir, Ming let me know that Chang was about to pass on information to ASIO, yet unproven. We Chang needed to be killed to cover up knowledge of a sleeper at Australia's prime supercomputer site. I accepted the story of Ming and there is nothing about the death in the news."

"Ling, let's not be too hasty on accepting that because I know ASIO, the wisdom of Mac, and his top spook Tilbury."

"Ok, General, I will ask Ming to keep eyes on the press and ask other MSS agents in Sydney and Canberra to sniff out anything that might relate to the role of Chang at Melbourne University."

41

In the backstreets of an outer suburb of Beijing, General Jun sat around a drawing board with aeronautical engineers from a clandestine company called *Drone Inc.* The building had no signs nor street numbers and faded into the complex of other similar buildings. No one knew nor cared about what went on inside. But the General did. It was funded through covert money siphoned off from the Adjustment Directorate.

He looked at the drawings of a new model of an 'AI killer drone.' Trials of the previous model had gone well but modifications were needed. Several civilians were used as target practice outside of the city but the drone was not as accurate as expected.

"Comrades, what you have delivered is both patriotic and lethal. When will the fully operational drone be ready for testing again?"

The head engineer nodded to his staff and replied, "Next week, General, most of the drone has been completed."

"OK, I want to watch the test."

Leaving the building, the General felt his moment of supremacy was upon him and wished for Mistress Wong.

Where is she? I miss her comfort.

Later that week, the General got the call to witness the testing of the 'AI killer drone' near a village out in the country. The target was a known dissident, so killing him with the drone met key criteria: prove the worth of the drone and kill the dissident.

Both were fine with the General.

Standing next to the chief engineer as he set up the 'AI killer drone,' Jun could see the new menacing look of the black and yellow BumbleBee drone, a shape that would put fear into anyone who came in contact.

With high-resolution cameras and AI controlling the mechanisms of the drone, Jun watched in awe as the drone sought out the dissident and fired a kill shot.

"Engineer Chen, a remarkable feat of engineering. When can we have 20 that I can send to various comrades in the western world?"

"General, we can start production straight away, and give you each one when completed."

Satisfied, the General put in place his plan to remove key dissident expatriate Chinese nationals through his nefarious Adjustment Directorate.

The world will never forget my 'BumbleBee AI killer drones.'

42

Meanwhile, the death of Williams at the University of Chicago was investigated by the FBI much against their will. Burgess was asked to meet with their senior agent to brief them on any aspects that came to mind. Mac had agreed that he should return to Chicago as ASIO might glean information from their investigation of Williams' death.

Burgess agreed with Mac that the information he had on that death, i. e. the messages on the supercomputer and that Williams was actually the Chinese expatriate Wang Chang, would not be disclosed to the FBI or the CIA if they became involved. Mac agreed.

* * *

At the Chicago downtown office of the FBI, Burgess sat opposite the most annoying person he could possibly imagine who interviewed him.

"Well, Burgess, as the last person to see Williams, we need you to explain why we will not charge you with his murder?"

"Fuck you, mate, can't you read? The autopsy report clearly states that he died from a heart attack. As an obnoxious prick, you are wasting my precious time. Sir, what you do does not interest me."

With that outburst, Burgess was handcuffed to the chair and yelled at by the FBI. "You Aussie bastard, how dare you talk to me that way? See how you like it now."

However, Burgess, as a senior ASIO agent, had been through tougher times than what the agent was implying, so he just laughed.

"You're a weak prick agent whosoever, without a fucking clue. Get me a lawyer or ask me nicely what you need to know."

"Ok, have it your way," the agent un-cuffed him and asked him to state his name, rank, and serial number.

"Very funny, prick, I am a civilian and have no reason to talk to you. But I will say this: Prof Williams died of a heart attack. To me, he seemed not well during a coffee break. I went to check to see if he was OK and found him dead near the computer. I know no more than that."

But the FBI agent was not finished with Burgess, "Did you know that Williams was in fact Wang Chang, a Chinese national?"

"No, so what? Why would I know that as I have known him for some time as Williams? His real identity was probably hidden because of the racist shortcomings of your government administration regarding Asian immigration. Maybe, he thought his chances of a top job would be stymied by his Chinese nationality."

"I have nothing more to add, so I wish to return to Brisbane."

"Please, Agent Burgess, give our regards to McLeod."

Unflinching, Burgess ignored the statement and left the building aware that he was being followed. But he smelt a rat from the behaviour of the FBI.

What did the FBI and specifically the CIA really know but were unwilling to pass on to him?

Burgess was glad that the FBI had not targeted him further. He had a past that he kept to himself. Even Mac was unaware of his covert spook activities. Time for a coffee break. As he sat in the *Plein Air Café* in the Chicago University precinct, Burgess sipped his latte and smelt the freshness of the French pastries.

Enjoying the ambiance of the café, he pondered about the actual reason he was brought to Chicago when he noticed a large black SUV pull up outside the café. He watched and waited as two CIA agents entered the room and sat beside him.

"Good morning, boys, I have been expecting you. Want to join me in this pleasant area? The light streaming in through those large windows makes me feel comfortable and at peace. So, what the fuck do you want from me?"

"Agent Burgess, McGinty, our DG would like a quiet word with you. Can he join you?"

"What? Here?"

"Yes, he likes an early morning coffee to start his day."

On a prearranged signal, McGinty strides into the café, arrogance written all over his smug face, and stood by Burgess. He looked down at him as if he were a bug. Burgess ignored the stance of McGinty, immediately stood, and shook his hand. Unfazed, he sat and waited for McGinty's next move.

"Ok, Aussie smart ass, we do it easy or hard."

"McGinty, take a seat and be happy, then I will talk to you and answer any question you need. How's that, mate?"

Patrons of the café were now fully aware of what was happening and showed their displeasure at the attitude of the CIA presence. McGinty yielded with the comment, "You will regret this, Burgess."

McGinty sat down with his agents on guard to offset any dissent by the patrons and said, "Agent Burgess, we believe that you know more than you wish to tell us about the death of a Chinese national operating the world's most sophisticated and powerful supercomputer at this university. Any comment."

"No, McGinty, what I said to the FBI is what I know. So, keep asking if you like but that's it, mate."

"Burgess, would thumb screws free your mind?"

"We know more about this Wang Chang than you but there are missing pieces to that puzzle we believe you know. We need your help as the President is growing more and more anxious about the growing presence of the 'Chinese way' here in America and keeps pressuring me and the FBI to remove that scourge. C*omprehendi* my Aussie spook."

"Well, our fucking ally is worried about the loss of their hegemony to our Asian 'friend.' Mr CIA, given the past trade wars and foreign policies of your country, I am not surprised."

"Actually, Colin, President Watson wants to meet you."

* * *

President Watson sat with the CIA and FBI chiefs, the Secretary of State, and the unwilling ASIO agent Burgess in the Oval Office. Watson was not in the mood for trivial talk and asked McGinty, "What the fuck is this all about? A professor is killed and you turn it into a national bloody emergency."

"Sir, we know you are concerned about the growing Chinese hegemony and we want to give you the heads-up on what we think is a China incursion into our internet. We also know that a previous president suffered from impeachment trials because of the Russian influence in an earlier election. We think that this is more important."

"OK, you have my attention, McGinty."

"In case you're wondering why Agent Burgess is here, he saw first-hand the death of that professor who we now know was Wang Chang, a Chinese national, head of the supercomputer at Chicago University."

"Chinese national! Where is this leading, McGinty? I am sick of your nationalist rantings. So be clear about how you are going to explain this situation."

"Sir, Burgess will explain."

43

Across the other side of the Pacific Ocean, Mac sat with Tilbury to plan their visit to meet President Watson on the same topic. The office desk phone rang. "A call from Burgess for you, Mac."

"Mac, Burgess here. Though you might like the heads-up on the meetings I had here in America."

"Meetings, Colin, I thought you were just meeting with the FBI?"

"So did I, Mac, but I have met with the FBI, head of CIA McGinty, and President Watson."

"Hell, Colin, what are you up to without my consent?"

"Well, Mac, I got really heavied by McGinty who threatened to lock me up and throw away the key, but I agreed to talk with Watson as a compromise. Hope that was OK because I have now more knowledge than we had before."

"OK, Colin, make me happy. Come home"

* * *

On return to Canberra, Burgess told Mac and Tilbury the story of his visit:

"I met with this trumped-up prick from the FBI who tried to blame the death of Wang Chang on me. I told him to get fucked. Probably not a good move as they handcuffed me as a protest for my attitude. Eventually, common sense prevailed, and they provided information we already knew, that Williams was a Chinese national.

"But they were very curious about the potential link between a Chinese national and a supercomputer. I let that go through to the keeper, as agreed before I left. But there was something fishy about the way they treated me. I found out why when I was accosted by McGinty in the Chicago University precinct.

"Mac, McGinty is a cold bastard who showed his true colours when he asked me to visit Watson and tell of my experience with the Chinese professor.

"The meeting was strange because no one came clean about the agenda. But I expect that Watson is deeply concerned about the ramifications of Chinese influence in America.

"He also asked me to talk to you, Mac. He really wants to meet with you. So, do not be surprised if he calls."

Tilbury cautioned Mac about his meeting with President Notting, "Mac, the less he knows, the better, but he will need your guidance on this tricky matter."

44

Seated at the table in President Notting's office, Mac and Tilbury could see the lines of stress and frustration on his face.

"Mac, on your advice, I have not invited anyone to this meeting. You know I'm worried about the coming election and the damaging impact any hint of Chinese racism or interference will hurt my re-election chances. Key seats are affected by *ChinChat*, the latest Chinese app that will again spread fake news and vicious rumours about my government impacting the lives of our Chinese citizens. Like what happened during an earlier election."

"However, you called this meeting for a serious discussion about the 'Chinese way' and how it is growing unchecked in our country. This is not what I want to hear, but you need to keep me informed."

"Andrew, we need to visit President Watson and discuss that growing concern."

"Why, Mac?"

"Well, Andrew, I have information that will shock you, but this is past a 'need-to-know' situation."

"Not again, Mac, we had this kind of talk last year because you did not tell me about a key case of the covert operations of OASIS supported by the CIA and the Pentagon. Please tell me this is different."

"Sir, different but maybe worse. We believe at ASIO that Beijing is attempting to manage and control the internet."

"Mac, you have got to be joking. President Wei has personally told me that hegemony is not their aim."

"Sir, trust me, it is not that simple. Leaders have to keep face with their people. After all, it is only rhetoric."

"Dr John Tilbury and I will brief you on what we know, so you will be heads-up for the meeting with Watson, although some details we will keep from you until we know more about them."

"Mac, I assume that Tilbury will join us in America. I will not have any of my staff involved in this to ensure total secrecy."

"OK, Andrew, I hope the Americans keep their loose lips shut."

Mac knew that Australian politicians and top businessmen got nervous at the mention of the 'Chinese way'; too many vested interests at stake.

The thought was mind-blowing:

Was Australia ready for the incoming Chinese tsunami? How well prepared was the intelligence network to cope with the intervention by the Adjustment Directorate within Australia?

45

In Mac's office, he and Tilbury sat opposite the Chiefs of the Australian intelligence fiefdom. Mac, as the senior spook, took control of the meeting with a statement to set the scene for discussion and said:

"Colleagues, I have called you together to discuss a matter most of you probably are aware of in varying degrees. Today, please no pissing on posts. Divided, we do not conquer what is surely coming our way. Here at ASIO, we call it the 'Chinese way' tsunami.

"Dr Tilbury at my side will now brief you on what we know and I will then lead a discussion on getting your input on that information."

With that, Tilbury, for the first time in front of the intelligence hierarchy, briefed the assembled spooks:

"Friends, it is not my pleasure to address you today on the 'Chinese way' because the implications are far beyond my ability to understand the philosophy and behaviour of our Asian 'friend'. I will assume you know little of what has happened. We hope that the full story will come to light by the time this meeting is finished.

"This is what we know: two Chinese AI experts have been murdered, three Chinese university computer students have also been murdered, and the MSS killer called Colonel Ming is loose. Patrick Ong, whom I know from a previous case is now a member of something called the Adjustment Directorate run by General Jun whose sister was a Chinese student at ANU who was seriously harassed by MSS agents. I rescued her. And as you all know, Marsha who was Mac's top analyst was killed in the line of duty. And to top all that, ASIO's computer system was hacked looking for details on Chinese immigration activities.

"But we know little about the Adjustment Directorate and its link to Australia."

Mac then took charge and asked the head of DSD to tell him what he knew on anything just raised by Tilbury. DSD had success in breaking the ISS codes and helped in the destruction of OASIS. Their surveillance contribution was critical.

"Mac, DSD knew much of what you have told us but our intelligence signals indicate a spate of communication within and outside of MSS headquarters in Beijing. Our analysts have discovered a recent flow of encrypted messages from MSS to universities around the world. We have no idea what they are about but we are working on breaking their codes."

As that information was digested, the meeting was interrupted by the entry of a geek-type person from DSD who handed a message to Dr Antony Hudson, head of DSD. Reading the message and absorbing the meaning, he frowned and addressed the meeting again.

"I have just received the result of a broken encrypted message sent to the Melbourne University AI Centre. It reads:

'We Chang, as a sleeper of the Adjustment Directorate, you must now open the attached darknet file addressed to you...'

"The encrypted file reads:

'We Chang, as a sleeper of the Adjustment Directorate, your orders are as follows: Activate the virus you have been previously given to permanently remove the algorithms and files that run the electricity grids supplying the East Coast of Australia. Good luck, your work is now finished. Please find your way back to Beijing.'"

There was stunned silence as a result of the statement by DSD, then broken by Mac.

"Friends, this information is damning of the Chinese President. I request that this meeting adjourns till further notice as I have to brief President Notting and seek his advice on this catastrophic information."

At this point, DG Fred Austin of the Australian Secret Intelligence Service [ASIS] decided to talk. He was a key person because the matter was external and he had the power to be involved and wanted his voice in the ear of Notting.

"With due respect, Mac, ASIS deals specifically with external threats to Australia. I want my voice to be heard. Notting expects that as I have counseled him many times on how important I'm to the security of Australia."

"Pissing on posts again, are we, Fred? No time for that."

All agreed and waited for the meeting to be recalled.

Mac beckoned Tilbury, Hudson, and Austin to leave with him to President Notting's residence for that conference.

To which Tilbury replied, "Thank God we found We Chang dead before he activated that virus, but the problem is, Mac, where is the virus and do they have another sleeper to take his place?"

On the way to the president's residence, the four spooks discussed the way in which they could raise the sensitive issues with Notting. Hudson knew Notting from his previous life and that Notting did not like the spook world as he cannot control their activities or the outcomes of their intelligence activities. But as head of the intelligence network, Hudson knew that Notting trusted the top spooks to be assembled in his lounge room.

"Fellow spooks, Notting is a political animal with little trust in our world, so we need to be careful about what we say to him. He does not understand the subtlety of the 'Chinese way' and will value our input in the context of the next election. But of course, he is our leader with the 'right-to-know' as opposed to the 'need-to-know.'"

Tilbury could not help himself, "Fucking politicians," and then remembered his ex-lover's lament… 'Think before you fuck it up, John,' and felt the jolt of remorse about his loss.

Mac could see the change in Tilbury.

"John, are you OK? This meeting is important because you and I have been invited by President Watson to the *White House* next week. He apparently tweeted our meeting to the rest of the world."

"Idiot, social media has a lot to answer for since the days of Trump."

Met by security, the four spooks were escorted to Notting's lounge room where coffee and sandwiches awaited.

"Good morning, gentlemen, the pleasure of course is all yours as I understand that the dialogue will not be pleasant."

Still standing, Mac decided that the banter should stop.

"Sir, we are here on an important matter of national security we believe you should hear from us in private. The matter is now beyond political. Our country may be under siege from a tsunami of interference stemming from Beijing. And before you tell us that we are wrong, please listen to our information."

"Sir, Antony will lead off from the DSD perspective and John, and I will fill in the rest. Fred will clarify his perspective."

"Ok, my spooks, take a seat, enjoy the coffee, and tell me your story."

After the full details were spread out before Notting, his response sent shivers down the spines of the four spooks.

"Gentlemen, thank you for that information. I will arrange for a meeting with President Wei of China to find out what is going on. I want to know whether he had broken the promise he gave me that hegemony was not on the Chinese agenda."

Not one for holding back, Tilbury cautioned the President, "Sir, are you absolutely sure about that? Has the smiling dragon turned you into a creampuff?"

Indignant, Notting came back fighting.

"How dare you talk to me like that? John, you have no idea about the politics of what you have mentioned!"

"Yes, I do, Sir. You think your re-election is more important than stopping the total blackouts of our utilities because of Chinese interference. Do you understand the consequences of that happening would make politics irrelevant? We would be put back into the dark ages."

"Well, John, you are wrong."

With that, Notting stood indicating the meeting was over, but Mac and Hudson kept their seats.

"I have nothing more to say, gentlemen."

Mac stood as did Hudson and Austin who chastised Notting for not listening.

"Sir, but we do, so sit down and be rational and please listen to us. We do not want a catastrophe that would happen if that message was sent and we know that the MSS has no morals, so more hidden time-bombs are likely."

Mac followed, "After some thought, we suggest that you, John, and myself meet with Watson and get some common ground on how to handle this because he is also under the pump with consequences of the 'Chinese way' impacting his re-election."

"Mac, if this got out, it will be political suicide for my re-election. Do I have to go?"

Tilbury had enough of the wishy-washy attitude of Notting.

"Sir, you or the country, your choice, mate."

With that, the four spooks left Notting to think through his dilemma. Austin whispered to Tilbury, "Who do you think you are talking to our president like that, ASIO boy?"

The knives were out, consequences notwithstanding.

46

As ordered, ASIO analyst Tom Burns entered the office of the dead Chinese AI expert We Chang under the watchful eyes of the head of the AI Centre of Melbourne University. The Centre had been told to let no one inside the room guarded by Victorian police, supported by AFP officers.

The desk was tidy and the computer console was left untouched. Burns opened the computer console and ran his algorithm to determine the password.

That done, the supercomputer sprang into life at the whirling fingers of the analyst. Using a USB, Burns placed a diagnostic programme that opened the files belonging to We Chang and ran the algorithms that decoded the files.

What was found surprised even the analyst as he was not privy to the information held by his boss, Mac. So, he saved the data on his encrypted USB and highlighted a file that looked interesting, addressed to a Su Wing.

"Su, if you get this message, it means I'm dead. As a sleeper at rest here in the AI Centre, you need to wake up and follow the instructions. Check your emails as I have sent you the password and code to activate the attached virus. Remember we agreed on this course of action. Go comrade, the 'Chinese way' has begun in earnest."

Mac at his desk had coffee in hand talking to Tilbury when his secretary Gloria entered with a knock and said, "Mac, Tom Burns, an analyst you sent to Melbourne University, is here to report his findings. He looks so distressed. I'm worried about him."

"Send him in, Gloria."

In walked a man with a heavy burden he wished to pass onto someone else; pass-the-monkey agenda.

"Glad you could make it, Tom. This is Dr John Tilbury, my spook adviser. What you report is therefore classified and no one else will know about your work."

With a sigh of relief, Burns unburdened on Mac and Tilbury what he had discovered by handing over the encrypted USB.

"Sir, what you find on that USB has kept me awake since I found the data, and Mac, that information is dangerous."

The exposed data was valued by the three with concern until they viewed the file of Su Wing.

"Relax, Tom, most of the data we are aware of but the link to Wing is what we have been looking for. Good job. Take coffee and help us find this bastard."

"The file was quite specific. Su Wing had the skills to carry out the deadly deed. How we find him was the key option they needed to implement."

Burns offered a way forward, "Mac, that file has an address. Although tough to decipher, I will work on that with the help of my colleagues."

"Go forth, Tom, hunt him down and report back to me ASAP."

However, after Burns left, Tilbury had a different option. "Bring Marsha in. If anyone can break that wall, she can."

"Ok, John, get a copy of the USB from Tom, without telling him about Marsha because she is dead, remember?"

Marsha held the gaze of Tilbury as he explained the situation and her role. "John, how can I do this when I have been pronounced dead by Mac?"

"We have a safe place suitable for your work, Marsha, and you can work with Peter Sax if that is OK!"

"But first, Marsha, based on what I have just told you, does that relate to what you found out earlier but left us high and dry?"

"John, not totally, but within a clandestine boundary, I cannot tell you about it yet."

"Why, Marsha?"

"Actually, Cassandra is the key to that. Unless she comes clean, I cannot help. She knows more than she is letting on, John."

"How do I get through to her?"

"Use your magic charms, man."

Easier said than done, he thought as he remembered their nights of passion.

47

Deep in concentration, both Marsha and Sax worked their way through the options they thought led to the truth behind the relationship between Su Wing and We Chang.

Both tired from the exacting analyses, they wanted a break and decided to comfort each other. Marsha needed an answer to the question she had stored up for some years, so she asked Sax, "What happened to us, Peter?"

Sax, reluctant at first, felt the pain in the body language of his ex-lover and decided to give a redacted version of what had happened...

"Marsha, I remember with a sad heart those days in the Daintree wilderness and how we built our computer skills and relationship. I did love you. But an important job came up that meant I had to leave you because it would endanger your life if known to certain people I was asked to hunt down.

"I should have told you, but you would have objected. I had no choice because they had a hold over me. That was you."

At this point, Marsha kissed him full on the lips and stripped before him. She was on fire, as sexual tension had been affecting her mind. Her search for an orgasm was overwhelming and needed to be satisfied.

Sax admired the woman he had loved and felt the desire harden. Although the floor was hard, the tension was so great that they exploded together panting with exhaustion. Holding each other, they realised that maybe they were not over the separation that had shattered both their lives.

"Marsha, please forgive me, we can work this out."

Now over the tension, they settled back to their analysis of the We Chang and Su Wing data. Later that afternoon, Sax called out to Marsha, "We've got the bastard Wing, love, he has been revealed to us. Look at this!"

There in black and white, now that Sax had applied his algorithms to the Wing data, they found his location in Hampton, an outer beach suburb of Melbourne.

They looked at each other and made the decision. Whatever happened, that suburb had well-known yuppie restaurants, a great suburb by the beach, and a welcoming population. However, as the backup, they called Tilbury who agreed to join them in their quest to find Wing.

Leaving TaskForce Triad to Jones, Tilbury flew to Melbourne after alerting Mac to the situation. At Tullamarine Domestic Airport, Tilbury met up with Marsha and Sax who had arrived from the Gold Coast in South-East Queensland where Marsha had been in hiding in one of the many high-rise buildings scattered around the area.

Part of Marsha's cover was an adopted name: Mia Long, whilst Peter kept his name as Zac Alcorn.

As they sat in the taxi on the way to the *Anchorage Apartments Hampton*, they reviewed data on Su Wing. Evidence was clear, the darknet-encrypted messages linked Wing to Chang and the agreement that Wing would carry out what Chang was unable to, given his death.

At breakfast, Tilbury, Marsha, and Sax decided on the approach to capturing Su Wing. It was agreed that Tilbury would knock on the door, enter, and others would follow. Marsha would search his computer with Sax.

A knock on the door of his apartment was met with silence, but a curtain moved slightly indicating he was in there. "Police here, open up Wing, we wish to talk to you."

Tilbury indicated to Peter Sax to check the back entrance. "Go now. Do not let the bastard escape."

As he arrived at the back door, Wing tried to pass him, but Sax was too strong, put him on the ground, and called for Tilbury who restrained him.

"Please, why are you treating me like this? What have I done?"

Grabbing Wing, Tilbury frog-marched him back into the unit and asked to see his computer. "Su, we are going to investigate your computer, so any passwords etc. will be given to us."

Again, he professed his innocence, "Sir, what have I done, and who are you?"

"I'm Dr John Tilbury from ASIO. We have information that you have been in contact with We Chang."

"Dr, what has given you that idea? I do not know any We Chang."

"Well, Wing, we know you do. Please open up your computer and prove that you are innocent."

The argument went back and forth until all the files were opened and revealed the connection they needed. But Wing was not cooperative when asked about the virus file.

"John, I do not have that file as you can see."

So, Tilbury asked Marsha to open up the darknet and search for both Chang and Wing's connection. A series of emails indicated that covert connection.

However, the files were encrypted.

As Wing was not cooperative, Tilbury took out his Glock and shoved it into Wing's mouth with the warning, "Open the files or die. You choose. This is no joke, mate."

Given no response, Tilbury shot him in the leg and again warned, "Su, open up the files."

Still no response so Tilbury shot him in the other leg.

Wing knew he wanted out of this and thought that dying was the best way forward for him, but he realised that Tilbury would keep shooting him.

With a low threshold for pain, he gave in and opened the virus file. However, Marsha realised straight away that the file may be live, so she searched within the data for the off switch, helped by Sax. Both were highly focussed, sweat pouring off them, stressed, looking for the needle in an unknown haystack.

So, worried about the time it would take to disarm the virus, Sax said, "Why not use one of my algorithms to destroy the file?" Marsha nodded to Tilbury who gave the go-ahead signal as they had nothing to lose.

Sax searched using his algorithms on the Wing computer until he found what he was looking for, then he activated the kill program and waited. It seemed like a lifetime whilst the killfile did its job.

Then came the message, "Job done, Peter."

A message to Mac had the clean-up team remove Su Wing and charge him with espionage.

For the time being, Victoria's electricity grid was safe from terrorism.

48

Meanwhile, General Jun sat before the makers of the drone, seeking improvements in the operation of his secret weapon. "Engineer Wong, the pilot in Indonesia failed because the drone did not pick up the potential danger from that attack in *Monas Gardens*. A dead drone is of no use to me. Can you build an AI search capability for potential danger and then take avoidance action?"

"Sir, that is a major task but not beyond my company. We will pursue that as a key option in a more advanced model."

"How long, Wong?"

"Sir, we cannot guarantee the actual time, but it will be some months."

"Ok, but you are on the time-clock, get it done."

But the General decided that another trial should take place in Indonesia. This time in Bali away from the eyes and ears of BIN.

* * *

Sunbaking on Kuta Beach, Huang Zang thought about his comfortable lifestyle away from the constrained life under the unctious 'behaviour scheme.'

He had written about it in blogs to tell the world of the growing 'Chinese way' sweeping the world.

Something caught his eye, a movement, a whisper, and a visual he would never forget if he lived. The menacing bug-eyed, yellow, and black BumbleBee AI killer drone hovered close to Huang. He knew it was not friendly, but it fascinated him.

Its eyes seem to devour him as it recognised its prey.

Ming sat in the shadow of the trees that lined the walls of Kuta Beach and watched with fascination as the drone circled the area and took a bead straight to Huang. The Adjustment Directorate had selected Huang for assassination. Ong had done his job in hunting him down.

Bathers and surfers looked askance at the drone as it singled out one of their locals. Huang was well known in the Kuta area as a surfer and dissident. The evil technology danced in expectation as it decided the kill shot.

Everyone heard it and rushed to help their friend. The drone quickly left the scene to be captured by Colonel Ming and placed in a hired SUV in the back streets of Kuta.

A message to the General established the modus operandi of the Adjustment Directorate against dissident expatriate Chinese nationals.

The long-awaited plan was activated.

49

In the beautiful botanical gardens beside the Brisbane River, many people took walks or just wanted the peace and quiet that prevailed, as it was located only about three hundred metres from the CBD.

Chang Zhao visited the gardens most days as he daily ate his lunch on a park bench and watched the swirling brown waters of the river pass him by. It was a time for reflection away from his office in Albert St where he contributed to blogs in national newspapers. He occasionally raised the influence of the Chinese diaspora supporting the 'Chinese way' in Australia. Beijing was sick of his continual criticism and warned him.

Today, Zhao was tired and despondent at the ongoing surveillance he knew was trying to wear him down.

Zhao, hands over his eyes, meditated and did not notice at first the BumbleBee bug-eyed monster that stared at him, focussed on him, and then aimed the weapon. Zhao heard the click and knew what was going to happen. In the silence of the grounds, Zhao did not feel the pain of the kill shot.

A passer-by called 000 to report the death.

Given TaskForce Triad was based in Brisbane, it investigated the Chinese death in the gardens. Jones called an emergency meeting, requesting Tilbury to attend.

The witness to the killing was interviewed by the TaskForce and told investigators what he saw…

"I was strolling along one of the pathways that wind around the beautiful gardens when I noticed this large-scale drone track down the victim with razor-sharp accuracy. The shape was blood-curdling in appearance with big bug eyes. I have seen nothing like it. I can fly a drone but this one was different. It was the colour of a killer bee and acted like one. Then it fired a projectile straight at the victim, looked at the result, then flew away. I would recognise that drone anywhere."

The identity of the victim was confirmed, Chang Zhao, a well-known blogger for the local newspaper *Courier Mail* under the name *Freedom from Tyranny.* Because of his background, local police and security kept him under surveillance. But he was one of the good guys trying to explain why the 'Chinese way' needed to be explained and catered for the reason of national security. AFP had him as the bad guy and was surprised by his assassination.

Jones sat with Tilbury and Burgess as they tried to put the pieces of the puzzle together, without success.

What is the relationship between all of these deaths?

There could only be one: target of dissidents by an external force, the Adjustment Directorate. But why? Had the Beijing lost the plot regarding international relations or was this a rogue response to the criticism of the 'Chinese way'?

Tilbury had an answer: call in Mac and ask him to bring home Agent Arthur who may know more about the Adjustment Directorate and how Australia could mitigate its activities.

As he sat at his desk, Mac thought about the call and sent an encrypted message to Arthur in Beijing.

Agent Arthur, you must return to Brisbane at once. We need your input into a death of a Chinese dissident by an unknown drone. Please acknowledge and return immediately, Mac.

Unsurprised, Arthur consulted with the Ambassador on the latest information available so he could provide advice to ASIO.

But the Ambassador cautioned Arthur.

"Remember, the Chinese hierarchy is touchy with the attitude of Australia at the moment. I do not want Beijing breathing up my ass over what comes out of ASIO. Am I clear?"

Given the attitude of the Embassy chief, Arthur decided that his real master was Mac and felt somewhat hassled by that comment. However, he left with the latest data supplied by the Ambassador a redacted version of what Karno had supplied.

Agent Arthur was conflicted; the evidence was solid but the motive for the attempted killing was not clear.

Did the Adjustment Directorate plan the attack? If so, why and under whose order?

He needed answers to help ASIO.

50

The success of the drone strike in the Brisbane botanical gardens was passed on to General Jun. The program for killing key outspoken expatriate Chinese nationals was now in play.

The program was to kill dissidents in the key capital cities of the world as a warning not to denigrate the 'Chinese way' through blogs or any media. General Jun opposed the weak Chinese President Wei because he paid lip service to these dissidents against a growing hard-line military block of the Party machine.

Drone Inc. called Jun to see a demonstration of the new AI killer drone he had asked them to build.

Arriving as usual with his henchmen, Jun sat and watched the demonstration. The drone had been reprogrammed to cope with enemy fire and still kill its target.

A dummy was set up behind a wall. The drone had a photo of the dummy fixed in its memory; everything was ready including a weapon designed to avoid an attack on the drone on its way to the dummy. AI of the drone was at the frontier of computer programs.

Jun smiled to himself. *If this is successful, many Chinese dissidents will perish under my program even if enemy agents wish to blow the drone out of the sky.*

The drone was set free, wandered around, then fixed the environment and the dummy victim in its sights. Suddenly, the drone drastically changed course as weapons opened fire, dodging and weaving, beating the weapon fire and flew away.

About to admonish the tech team that built the drone, Jun said, "Pity about the kill shot, your new prototype has failed." Then the drone reappeared, shot the man with the weapon, and blasted the dummy to pieces.

"Holy shit," was the clapping General's response, "We now have the AI killer drone that will harass the world and remove the scourge of anti-Chinese dissidents forever."

All he had to do now was to energize the Adjustment Directorate to flush out his next victims. But his approach required the use of supercomputers in the western world to be controlled by the COHORT he had established just for that role. The key to the program was to hide in plain sight.

An encrypted email was sent to all members of the COHORT group, reminding them of their duty, and to acknowledge the call to arms.

51

Tilbury, relaxed with a beer on his patio, talked with Black about the details he knew, the spate of Chinese nationals murdered in different parts of Australia, and raised the rhetorical question, "Thomas, are these killings related?"

Slowly sipping his beer, letting the gravity of the question flow through his mind, Black answered, "Fuck, yes, too many coincidences."

Tilbury read the blog in today's *Courier Mail* by another author under the banner of the previous writer, *Freedom from Tyranny,* blaming the MSS for the assassination of a colleague, and noted other dissidents had been killed by a similar drone now known as the 'BumbleBee AI killer drone.' To him this was a real change in the direction of Beijing, attacking dissidents to build a trusted hegemony.

The story added to the puzzle Tilbury tried to unravel, unsuccessful to date. A killer drone, sent by whom, to kill non-resident Chinese national dissidents.

Had Beijing gone mad?

Then a complex thought crossed the mind of Tilbury.

Were these actions part of what Marsha and Cassandra Jun refused to talk about?

Mac took Tilbury's advice and ordered Marsha and Cassandra Jun to meet with him and Tilbury at his home, away from prying eyes and potential MSS action.

Both were met by ASIO agents and taken to Mac's home for the meet. When Jun walked into the house, she saw Tilbury for the first time since he left her in the Adelaide suburb.

Seeing his rugged, handsome disposition, and steely grey eyes, she ran to him, kissed, and hugged the man who reciprocated the approach. Mac was stunned by what just happened and asked Tilbury to step outside.

"John, what happened? Don't you realise you have just broken one of the cardinal rules of our profession? Do not fraternise with witnesses. For Christ-sake, John, I could terminate your work as an ASIO agent because of what you and Cassandra have done."

"Ok, Mac, but I am not sorry about what happened. I fell in love with her and will marry her if she agrees."

"So, where does this leave us, John?"

Jun spoke up for the first time and explained that Tilbury had treated her like a human being, unlike others. "Mac, I started the relationship and I do want to marry him."

Mac then realised that the relationship had changed their approach. Did he need to treat Jun as a hostile witness because her statements may be coloured by her feelings toward Tilbury.

"John, we need to take care about what Cassandra may say. Please be concerned about that. I suggest we interrogate Marsha first and get confirmation from Jun. Do you agree with that plan?"

"Yes, Mac, but I will not be involved in her interrogation."

52

Marsha began her story about what she found on the darknet some weeks before, which scared her and believe that her life was in danger. Her words were clear…

"Mac, I remember as clear as if yesterday, when you asked me to check on Chang Lui and contacts made on the darknet. To my surprise, he had serious inter-connections with the CIA, MSS, files from the White House server, and eventually with Beijing.

"What I discovered was beyond belief. I found an encrypted file that was sent to Cassandra Jun from her brother General Jun. It essentially said the following:

"'President Wei has gone crazy, wants to stop the 'behaviour scheme,' open up the economy for foreigners to buy land, own enterprises, and stop the march of hegemony toward the West. He has handed control of the Party to me in a signed and witnessed official letter to the Party that I have with me. The letter states that he is of sound mind and wants a transition of power through me, as the new president.'

"Sister, this is a death warrant for me. If anything happens to me, please tell the democratic countries of my demise. Finally, tell President Watson of America to watch out for any changes to the 'Chinese way' that will follow my death."

"Mac, this is a very serious accusation given we know that General Jun is alive and well," cautioned Tilbury, thinking of the safety of his partner Cassandra Jun and Marsha.

"It seems there are serious internal differences within the Party. I believe that the General supports the powerful military who think China is weak."

"John, Agent Arthur is due from Beijing any minute now. His input into the behaviour of the General may help provide extra pieces for our puzzle."

Unknown to ASIO, Agent Arthur was tracked by MSS all the way from Beijing to Brisbane and to TaskForce Triad headquarters. But they had no intelligence on the TaskForce or its operations. However, they realised that Tilbury often visited the building and decided to follow him.

However, Tilbury noticed, through spook craft experience, two men acting in a manner a little suspect for the area, hanging around the local coffee shop for too long. So he called his mate Black to come loaded.

"Thomas, I think that I am being tracked by a couple of suspicious males lurking in the local coffee shop. Identity unknown but my guess is MSS. Go see what you think. Take a snap or two for later ID. If in doubt, take them out. Mac will cover for you."

"Back to the good old days again, John?"

Agent Arthur who arrived to brief Mac with Tilbury was distracted by the potential threat from MSS that Black had gone to investigate.

"Mac, I come with bad news regarding the MSS and the Adjustment Directorate. General Jun is the mastermind behind the executions of expatriate Chinese national dissidents, using killer drones, according to our intelligence in Beijing."

Arthur then explained what they found after the attempted assassination of Yang, a local Chinese dissident...

"That drone was very sophisticated: had an AI chip with facial recognition capacity, ability to search for the desired target and kill that person. On interrogating that chip, we found was a set of codes that should have detected the arrival of agents from BIN with intent to destroy it.

"Obviously, it malfunctioned, saving Yang's life.

"We believe it was a test of the drone's software and expect that a new model will be used outside of China."

53

Earlier, back at AXIOM, Edwards had been dealing with We Chang to develop a memory chip to build AI into the operation of the ithinkGoggles. Edward relied on the regular contact from Chang through encrypted files providing the AI program to run the technology of the ithinkGoggles.

However, Dr Rachel Viviani who worked on the original version with Professor Stanley was not aware of the AI addition to the new technology. She was kept in the dark as she remained in Florence. She had been a victim of the OASIS saga and felt alone being out of touch with Tilbury since their breakup, a breakup she regretted.

It was time to come in from the cold, so she called her ex-lover Ben Richards for comfort and understanding. "Hello, Ben, Rachel here, I miss you. Can I visit you at home, make amends because I need your support?"

"Rachel, what a surprise! You know my address and would love to see you again."

Ben remembered the tension of their love-making, the joyous feeling of loving Viviani. However, he remembered the period of trying to forget her because she had just disappeared.

As a form of healing, he jotted down a few lines of poetry, over coffee in his Balinese study overlooking the ocean.

He remembered: ebony slim, raven hair flowing down her back, eyes that captured him, her sensual taste, and body perfume drove him to want her again. A clouded mist of sexual desire kept him wanting more.

At 1045 on Monday morning, Richards received a call, "Ben, I'm at the Brisbane International Airport. Can we catch up at the Brisbane Hilton Hotel? Cannot wait to see you."

"Rachel, my love, will be there later today."

Viviani, however, had made the trip for many reasons, most of which did not relate to Ben Richards. Sure, she wanted to sleep with him as long as she could but Tilbury was on her mind as was her concern about what was happening at AXIOM. As it was part of her past, Viviani was concerned when she received an email from Edwards.

The new work at AXIOM, as agreed under the banner of Chee Enterprises, the ithinkPad was to be used for human benefit. Viviani was not so sure whether the work had strayed outside the Articles of Association of AXIOM and needed advice from Tilbury but may be difficult for personal reasons.

From Edwards, edwards.axiom@gmail.com

"Rachel, I have been working with Dr Alice Worthington and We Chang of Melbourne University AI Centre, developing a new advanced version of the ithinkPad called ithinkGoggles run by AI. The goggles are like those used for virtual reality games, but very different.

Fantastic results we got from testing students at IronSide Primary School, St Lucia, Brisbane. Hope you can come and see these in action.

Your best inventor, Paul Edwards"

Now Viviani had a dilemma, how to put Tilbury and Richards into perspective.

Maybe see Ben Richards first and feel my way forward.

"Rachel, I'm in the Lobby."

"Come to Room 703, now."

Minutes later, the door opened revealing the most beautiful sight he had seen. Viviani stood tall, elegant, and completely naked.

"Rachel, I missed what I'm seeing, come, give me a hug."

"I have been waiting for so long, Ben, you can have whatever you want."

Viviani kissed Richards so well, that he nearly fainted. The bed was ready and so was Richards. The sexual comfort lasted for hours. Both needed the feeling as it built up and up inside them.

Now Viviani needed to meet Tilbury.

54

Tilbury at the TaskForce Triad headquarters in the Brisbane CBD, deep into the machinations of the Chinese enigma, heard his cell ring in his backpack and knew it was from a close friend because only they had that number.

Cautious, Tilbury listened to the message.

"John, this is Rachel, I am currently staying at the Brisbane Hilton Hotel, Room 703. Can you meet me? We have a lot to discuss and I am worried about AXIOM and what is happening there under Paul Edwards. Please meet me."

Tilbury was stunned by the call. He had let Viviani out of his life and got on with other things. The thought of the ebony body and sexy eyes had him rattled.

Should I go or ignore her?

"Rachel, sorry I missed your call. I will see you tonight over dinner on level 6 at 1900."

No point in saying what I want to say because I am over her. But am I?

As usual, Tilbury arrived early to feel the dining area ambiance and gather his thoughts about Viviani. He remembered the day they first met in Florence while on leave from the Brisbane Lions AFL team. The time they spent together walking the cobbled alleyways formed a long-term relationship that ended after OASIS.

He watched as the elegant Viviani walked toward him and was taken in by that smile, the same ebony body that smiled at him at Café Boga years earlier.

She approached him with a greeting, "Don't get up, John, I will sit first."

Tilbury, surprised by the welcome, got up and hugged the woman that he had so dearly loved and wanted to marry. The response was muted but she smiled again and said, "John, it has been so long and the meet is not for us but a serious problem I wish to discuss with you over dinner."

At once, Tilbury knew where he stood with his ex-lover and tried to be kind to his visitor.

"Rachel, I loved you so much but too many things got in the way. I was a lost cause after OASIS and the loss of you. But I will help you however I can. But first, let's order drinks and the fine food they have on this menu."

With that over, Tilbury asked Viviani to tell her story about current activities at AXIOM. Holding a glass of Merlo in her slender hands, Viviani told him what she knew…

"Back in Florence, I occupied my time playing Mozart and caught up with the latest breakthroughs in neuroplasticity wondering about activities at AXIOM over which I had really lost control under the new management of Chee Enterprises.

"Realising the unfulfilled use of the ithinkPad, I wanted back into the research at AXIOM. So, I contacted Edwards and asked if I could return. I was surprised by the return email I received which said:

"'Rachel, I have been working with Dr Alice Worthington and We Chang of the Melbourne University AI Centre, developing a new advanced version of the ithinkPad called ithinkGoggles run by AI. The goggles are like those used for virtual reality games, but very different. Fantastic results we got from testing students at IronSide Primary School, St Lucia, Brisbane. Hope you can come and see these in action.'

"Well, I was really wondering what they are doing. Building the ithinkGoggles with AI seems off the chart a bit to me. But I guess it might be within the realms of what we developed with the ithinkPad."

"So, will you come to AXIOM and see what is going on? I feel very uncomfortable with this and need your support to face Edwards. Can you do that with me, John?"

Tilbury thought long and hard over coffee at Viviani's request and came to the conclusion that he should. "Rachel, yes of course. When do you want to leave for AXIOM?"

They agreed to meet at Brisbane Domestic Airport the following morning to catch a Qantas flight to Sydney. Each a little circumspect with the other given the night before when Tilbury just said goodnight and left the restaurant.

"John, you seem too distant with me and your reaction last night made me think this going to AXIOM together is a wrong decision."

"Rachel, you are right, I was upset at seeing you again. I thought I had gotten over you but seeing you again broke my heart. But let's do this as I am intrigued by what you have told me. I forgot to tell you that I had an argument with Worthington about the testing of the ithinkGoggles with school children. Her response worried me."

Seated in 2A and 2B, business class, Tilbury spoke to Viviani about what had really happened to her after AXIOM. As he looked at her beautiful face, he thought about what he had lost and being side-tracked by the blond bombshell Jane Hampton. But he had no regrets about Hampton. She was important to his well-being at the time.

Viviani rested her head against his and fell asleep. Tilbury let her sleep as he knew that the thoughts in her head made her tired and confused.

The landing jolted Viviani awake. She smiled, kissed Tilbury on the lips, and said, "John, thank you for doing this with me."

As they stood to exit the plane, Tilbury hugged her and said, "Rachel, I missed you."

Disembarking, they hired an Avis Rental Car and drove to Mossman to confront Edwards at the AXIOM Research Centre. As they walked in the door of AXIOM, a cold shiver went down the spine of Tilbury as he remembered the ithinkPad trials run by Viviani and the consequences felt throughout the world of neuroplasticity and the rise of OASIS. Viviani felt the change in Tilbury and questioned their action.

A receptionist asked who they wanted to see. Tilbury demanded to see Director Edwards.

"Who shall I say wants to meet him?"

"Drs Tilbury and Viviani would like the pleasure of his company."

"Hold on, Sir, I will ask him to come down to meet you."

"Well, how are my partners in crime, John and Rachel? Good to see you again. Come with me, have refreshments, and catch up on times past and future matters."

The tearoom was then set up with pastries with good coffee, according to Tilbury who relaxed in the old environment.

A cordial meeting went nowhere as Edwards avoided the obvious. So, Tilbury stood and said, "Paul, I know you guys are up to something and I am going to find out. Let's go, Rachel."

The pair then left AXIOM with Edwards thinking what next.

Can Viviani be trusted?

55

Earlier, Baishawan Beach, Taiwan: the popular area was inundated with tourists and locals taking in the sunshine, the surf and sweating under umbrellas away from the burning sun.

On leave from SAS operations, Ben Strong spent time with his Taiwanese girlfriend Janis Fe. They had met at the bar and spent time together at nightclubs, and enjoyed their frequent passionate interludes at a local studio apartment by the beach.

That day, they sat near a group of local-based Chinese who were attending some political conference that the two were not interested in at all. The group was passionate about the rise of Chinese influence over Taiwan, which most people around the area heard about but had no interest.

Strong, an observant soldier, noticed a few unknown objects approaching the beach in a pattern that alerted his subconscious mind; this was unusual and thus worth acting upon.

He swiftly grabbed Fe and dragged her away from the beach to the bar where he knew that would protect them if what he noticed had some evil intent.

What he saw was horrific. Three bug-eyed drones flew over the incoming waves that washed ashore.

These became stationary, watching the inattentive group wrapped up in their discussions. Before Strong had a chance to warn them, the drones attacked the group, firing projectiles that left broken and lifeless bodies strewn all over the beach as they tried to escape the onslaught.

Then these evil drones disappeared back the way they came.

Keeping Fe undercover, he ran outside to view the carnage.

What the fuck, who are the crazy bastards that did that?

By now, the police had arrived, but Strong did not want to become involved so he and Fe walked back to their studio apartment where they cried together to break the tension of what they witnessed.

Being an SAS soldier, Strong had contacts in the military but something nagged at the back of his mind. He thought that if he revealed to superior officers that he was at that beach, he would be called to testify before some god-damned inquest. Not doing that! However, his conscience got the better of him, and he called a soldier he admired, Thomas Black, the man his mates called 'the Assassin.' Then he remembered that Black had dropped out and bought Café Boga in Brisbane, so after several attempts, he finally got an answer.

"Black here, what can I do for you? Today is Balinese coffee specials day. Interested?"

Silence for a minute then, "Hi Assassin, it's Ben Strong, one of your SAS colleagues. I urgently need to meet with you. Is that possible?"

"Why, Ben, what is so important?"

"Thomas, cannot say much as I am in Taipei, Taiwan and witnessed a drone killing on one of the beaches here."

"I believe it was an attack by the Chinese. Thomas, three drones came in from the sea, ugly bug-eyed monsters that just fired on a group of dissidents attending a conference, killing and maiming innocent bystanders, or what we call collateral damage. Draw your own conclusion, Thomas."

"I called you because I know you had a stint with ASIO and because I do not want to be involved here. I have a girlfriend who is out of her mind from what she witnessed."

"Ben, get the next flight with her to Brisbane and give me the details. I will pick you up at the arrivals area. Assume a black SUV. Say nothing to anyone, Ben. See you tomorrow."

"Thanks, Assassin."

Black decided to Google 'Taiwan Baishawan Beach Resort massacre' and see if he found any details. To his surprise, there was no local news, a total blackout.

This made him check other sources, the Hong Kong *South China Morning Post* came to mind. There in a side article was a short report of a disturbance at Baishawan Beach near Taipei, Taiwan that was now under control. Police had apprehended a gunman and charged him with the murder of a local person.

Black now knew that the 'Chinese way' was alive and well in Taiwan because he believed Lieutenant Ben Strong, a gallant hero of the Middle East wars.

Concerned about what may unfold from the visit by Strong, he called Tilbury.

"John, another Chinese incident you must know about."

"I just received a call from Commando Ben Strong who was on a beach in Taiwan and witnessed an attack, by three killer drones, on Chinese dissidents who attended a conference at a resort. I checked for reports on this, John, but they have been covered up. I smell a rat, mate."

"I am collecting him and his girlfriend off the plane from Taiwan tomorrow. I will talk to him first and let you know what he has to say, then report to you. I think you should meet him. I trust him."

"Thomas, I think I know him, but not sure. Keep me in the loop. This 'Chinese way' matter has become complex and serious."

"Agree, John, tell no one about this until we find all the facts."

As arranged, Black collected the pair from the Brisbane International Airport and took them to a hotel in the CBD near where the TaskForce Triad was located.

Refreshed, the three sat at the *Black Fire* coffee shop in Albert Street, Brisbane CBD and discussed the Taiwanese event.

Black was not his usual 'in-ya-face' approach on these sort-of-matters, felt their concerns, and decided to hear their story. But there was an itch about Strong that won't go away.

Slowly sipping his black sugarless coffee, he listened, felt their pain, and offered advice.

"Ben, what you have witnessed is what we believe, in ASIO, is the tip of a Chinese insurgence iceberg. I trust you and Janis, so a friend and colleague, Dr John Tilbury, will join us. He is a key player in these matters and the top spook of ASIO. Just remember he doesn't like bullshit."

With that, Tilbury walked in and sat next to Janis Fe, looking directly at Ben Strong, with a smile of recognition.

"Hi, Ben, been some time. Not the best time for a reunion. Thomas tells me that you and Janis witnessed an execution of Chinese dissidents. Is that true? Tell me the story, and I will tell you mine. Except for national security, some parts will be redacted."

So, as Fe added her view and feelings, Strong told Tilbury that this smelt like a planned military-style attack from nearby waters of the South China Sea.

"John, it could only be the Chinese navy who we know has been rattling chains in the South China Sea for years. Why now though? Seems strange to me. But who is driving this madness?"

"Ben, Thomas and I have a view on that, but telling you is above our pay grades. Sorry."

"However, Ben, I would like you to meet Mac, head of ASIO, and give him your reflections on what you saw as an SAS soldier."

"I will accompany you now if that is OK. Janis, please go back to your hotel and wait for Ben. It may be a while. Thomas will help if needed."

But Black was still uncertain about Strong, so he told Tilbury, "John, keep an eye on Strong and tell me what you think. I will explain later."

Tilbury walked out the door with Strong and talked about the good old days as SAS soldiers until they reached the office of TaskForce Triad where Mac awaited.

"Welcome, Ben, in troubled times. John has told me about you and the awful encounter you witnessed in Taiwan. I would like to debrief you if that is OK as I have a lot of questions for you to consider."

"I am willing to do that on the condition that you help me understand what the fuck is going on. Janis and I were lucky not to be victims. I just happened to be looking out to sea at the right time. I guess my training helped me react in time to save us both. But I must say the carnage will stay with us forever."

"Ben, my main question to you concerns what you can remember before the drones arrived. I believe that these drones had to be controlled from somewhere and by someone. I understand your view was they came over the sea toward you. Your guess was from a Chinese naval vessel. Did you see one?"

"No, Mac, but that scenario seems plausible."

"Ok, cast your mind back as you lounged on the sand and try to visualise the scene before you."

"What can you smell, was the wind blowing, were the waves rolling in, were people focussed on relaxing, or was there movement that seemed out of place?"

Strong, quiet, sat with his eyes closed covered by his muscular hands, honed from the tasks of an SAS soldier, and pictured scenes in the front part of his brain.

He remembered that there was little movement as people had taken up position on lounges or were quietly eating lunch. Then he saw it, a movement from the bar area where a local female was looking through binoculars out to sea from where the drones appeared. He saw her face for just a moment and knew that it was a cousin of Janis.

He opened his eyes in shock at the real meaning of that memory. Surely, not her family. "Mac, what I'm about to tell you and John needs to be kept between us because I may know who sent the signal to the Chinese vessel."

"First, John, can you call Thomas and ask if he has seen Janis because I want her protected right now. Do that before I tell you what I have remembered."

"Thomas, have you seen Janis? This is urgent, mate."

"No, John, I left her to walk to the hotel as you suggested."

"Go find her now. She may be in danger."

But Black found no sign of her, all her belongings were gone, no note of farewell to Strong.

"John, she has disappeared."

Mac wondered as did Tilbury.

Was Janis Fe part of the action or a casualty of a family connection to an MSS massacre?

Strong could not believe what just happened. Where is Fe, was she involved, is she safe? But he knew that as no note was left for him, despite their growing relationship, he had doubts about her now.

Mac ordered an APB for her arrest after Strong mentioned that he knew that Fe's cousin was probably the messenger who sent a signal to the waiting vessel offshore.

But later that day, Strong received a call from Fe.

"Ben, please do not be angry with me because I left you high and dry. I needed to get away and think about what happened."

"Earlier, I had a call from my mother in Taipei asking if I was alright because she had heard about the shootings through her grapevine. I am not sure about this but I noticed my cousin at the beach resort but as we are not close, I didn't try to contact her. But her demeanour was different, body language tight and glassy-eyed. I thought she was probably on drugs and didn't see any point in seeing her. Can we meet up? I'm scared, Ben."

Strong was in an awkward position now as Mac had ordered her arrest. And importantly, he was still with Tilbury and Black.

"Janis, I am in a tight spot at the moment here in an ASIO office where they have talked about you. Go to the Brisbane Ibis

Hotel near the Brisbane River and book in as Mrs Fe using your passport, saying 'my husband will join me later.' I will find you, love. Do not talk to anyone."

Strong now faced a serious dilemma: reveal the whereabouts of Fe to Tilbury or go with the flow and see what happens. He chose the latter option.

How could he tell them that he knew about the potential of a drone attack in the area? He was also an MI6-trained assassin who had worked with fellow agents in the Taiwanese and Hong Kong regions. Covert operations included reducing the influence of MSS by finding and killing their agents.

The beach slaughter kept him awake at night even though there was little he could have done to stop the drones. The fact that his girlfriend had a relative involved in the massacre seriously bothered him.

Should he come clean with Tilbury about his skills and experience with the Chinese MSS?

During a break at the TaskForce, Strong asked Tilbury to join him in a local café so he could explain a few things.

"John, I am not who you think I am."

"What!"

"You may not know this but I was so in awe of Thomas as an assassin, that I joined the British commandos and became an expert assassin. I have worked in the Asian region spoiling attempts by Chinese MSS agents to hold dissidents to ransom or to murder key players supporting the 'Chinese way.'"

"John, I think you, Mac, and Thomas should debrief me to build your knowledge about the forces at large within the region, and the build-up of General Jun's grip of power over the Party. The scenario is at a critical point right now because I know about the drones."

56

At the Adjustment Directorate, the General reviewed the past events and found the result he had looked for in the AI killer drone. He had no moral compass when it came to collateral damage as shown by the slaughter on the beach in Taiwan.

As a result, the General planned a mass attack on the various major cities of the West, raised the activities of his COHORT, and chose his next dissident.

* * *

The festive season in Hong Kong Times Square had thousands of people enjoying the atmosphere and sense of community. Seated with friends in the square, Toni Cheng often discussed the previous riot periods that had continued for years forcibly stopped by Beijing with many of his friends transported back to the gulags in the far outer provinces for re-education.

Cheng felt sad at the memory and got comfort from friends. Above the crowds, an object emerged that scared the crowd. Cheng looked at the incoming object and realised that it was a drone. Instantly, he tried to move but the brightly coloured drone held his gaze with its bug eyes, which stopped him dead in his tracks.

People tried to deflect the drone but it just sat there and focussed on the face that had been programmed in the AI memory. The drone then fired a projectile at Cheng, killed him, and injured those in proximity. And then the drone just disappeared. Later that day, the

Standard newspaper headlined the story of the assassination of a well-known and respected dissident in Times Square.

Details were limited except a witness stated that it was a BumbleBee coloured drone that had targeted the deceased.

Social media went viral accusing the West of interfering in Hong Kong, which was supported by Beijing as a president-like interference in the lives of Chinese citizens. A president with an unflinching view about China and what should happen to dissidents in a time of crisis.

In a setback to the authorities, passive and violent demonstrations began again, reminiscent of the earlier unsuccessful demonstrations that lasted for years until Beijing had had enough and again sent in the troops.

The Hong Kong US Ambassador was called into the Office of the Chinese Foreign Minister in Beijing to explain the action of the USA. The communication was tough and unyielding, with neither Party moving from their position.

In the end, the American just smiled and said in precise Mandarin, "Sir, don't cover up this action by your MSS because we will get to the bottom of this and then tell the world of your treachery."

"Mr Ambassador, until we meet again," the Minister shook his hand, cordially bowed slightly, and left the meeting.

The Ambassador was left wondering about the next step.

TaskForce Triad called a meeting of the Intelligence Team to discuss the murder in the Hong Kong Times Square. Tilbury chaired the meeting. He nodded to Mac who took over the discussion.

"Folks, the world is going crazy. We now know of three drone attacks we think have come from MSS through the Adjustment Directorate in Beijing, but not proven. We also believe that General Jun is the mastermind of those brutal slayings. Of prime concern for me is that we have Cassandra Jun in our hands and she is the sister of General Jun."

Adding, "My question is this, given he contacted Cassandra Jun, can we get her on our side to help us understand what is going on and our response?"

"John has a few suggestions."

"Team, I have no real idea of how to treat Cassie. I have gotten close to her but she has never agreed to discuss her brother. Maybe if we as a team bring her in and show her what her brother has done and the implications of his actions, she may talk."

The discussion led by Mac finally resolved to ask Jun to join a private gathering as a trusted witness.

Tilbury was asked to facilitate the action, even though he knew her opinion about revealing the innermost secret message from her brother. But he was conflicted: to interrogate or love her. The duality was a dilemma for him. But he agreed out of duty resolving to patch up the matter later if he could.

How can I get the information without hurting my true love?

57

Tilbury arrived back at the apartment he shared with Jun to find her in an agitated mood. Surprised by her body language and response to his arrival, he asked her, "Cassie, what's going on, love?"

"John, look at the message on my computer screen. It came this morning and I don't know what to do about its meaning. Please help me. I'm very frightened."

Opening the file, even Tilbury was surprised by the message which read:

> *Cassandra Jun, your cosy world in Australia is over because of your brother. I know what he is up to. You need the protection of DYLAN, your friend.*

"John, who or what is DYLAN?"

"Cassie, I need to take the computer to ASIO where their technicians can interrogate the files. That is a mixed message, love. Someone knew about the General and wanted to protect you. This could be the breakthrough we looked for."

"Ok, John, take me with the computer to ASIO while they test the system. I will feel safer there with you and Mac."

Given that the TaskForce had all of the technicians and software needed, Marsha was asked to do the digging.

"Marsha, this is Mac, can you please help us delve into Cassandra's files? Also, can you do a darknet scan as well related to General Jun?"

"OK, Mac, good to be back in the service of the nation."

The deft fingers of Marsha sped their way through the files, internet, and the darknet. However, the message was encrypted with coding that currently did not exist which baffled Marsha, so she contacted Tilbury.

"John, I think I am in another universe. The coding behind the DYLAN message was in unbreakable hieroglyphics and seemed like it came from another world. I thought I was imagining that but rebooted the computer and checked again. The result was the same."

"Marsha, what do you mean by hieroglyphics?"

"John, the coding was not like anything in the IT world. It was like reading an ancient Egyptian transcript, not decipherable."

Were they at a dead end?

Tilbury had an idea. He called Colin Burgess who worked with supercomputers and asked him if he could work with Marsha and Sax to try and decode the strange message from DYLAN.

Reluctant, he agreed. He was still gun-shy from his experience with the Chicago supercomputer warning. Sax jumped at the chance because he had worked on these computers before. To get the ball rolling, Burgess typed his password into the computer and went deathly pale when a message emerged.

"Burgess, I had warned you. Three strikes and you're dead."

Sax looked at Burgess as he recovered from the shock.

"Colin, what the fuck is this about, mate?"

Through shortened breath and shaking, Burgess told Sax about what had happened in the Chicago Computer Centre.

"I had tried to discover details about a Chinese colleague that died at the desk of a supercomputer, entered my password, and a similar message appeared."

"Peter, what do you think? Someone must be behind the messages as the computer is not that smart, surely?"

"Well, folks, the world of AI is before us now and we have no idea how smart these AI-driven supercomputers are really."

"Agree," said Burgess. "No matter how smart these computers are, someone must have programmed the AI."

"But who?" asked Marsha to no one in particular.

The cynical Burgess made the suggestion.

"Folks, the Professor was Chinese, right? Maybe that is the clue. He died because he was killed by MSS through a software programme that knew and enhanced his weakened health. I believe he died of a heart attack from stress—may be induced from a source through the computer."

It was now time to brief the Intelligence Team on their findings. As the senior analyst, Marsha opened up the report by saying, "What we are about to tell you is going to be difficult for you to understand."

Mac responded by saying, "Speak in simple English."

The response from Marsha was predictable.

"Mac, it is not the language, it is the coding and logic of our findings we found difficult and therefore assumed you would too."

The three analysts then laid out their findings.

What troubled Tilbury and Mac was the unknown linkage to DYLAN. The IP address and encryption being in a new but unknown language really caught their attention.

Mac looked Marsha in the eye seeking her special knowledge. "Marsha, what is your view at this point?"

"Well, Mac, the three of us discussed that matter. Unbelievable as it sounds, this coding language is well beyond any known coding language. It is so new that it seems alien."

"You have got to be joking, Marsha, we have the best analysts in the world, and this is from another world. Surely, there is an explanation for this, Marsha?"

Mac then sent the team away to ponder on the problem and come up with an explanation. In the meantime, Tilbury decided that it was time to talk with his Chinese lover.

"Cassie, love, in your encrypted message from the General, was there any indication of a new computer language being developed or used?"

"John, I have told you many times that the communication from my brother is for my eyes only. How many times have I said that to you and Mac?"

"Cassie, I am not asking you about the message, just about the use of strange coding. Can you answer that please?"

"Yes, I will, no strange coding was used in the message or hinted at. Why, John?"

"Well, Cassie, when we checked the message you received from DYLAN, whoever or whatever that is, we found the coding was not only unbreakable but totally new and beyond the comprehension of our analysts."

The argument was left there as Tilbury decided he needed a beer with his footy mate Gary Lang. He had not seen him for a while because of his puzzled life. It was time to offload the shit over a few beers at Lang's place.

"Hi Gary, been a while, need to catch up, shoot the breeze, and get your opinion on some things that are puzzling me."

"Always a friend, John."

A few beers later, Tilbury told him about the puzzling computer code that no one understood or had seen before.

"John, was a supercomputer part of the problem, mate?"

"Yep."

"Look, I am not a bloody expert in computer logic or coding but common sense tells me that with the growing improvement in AI, could these computers create their own language?"

"That thought had crossed our minds, but our analysts have argued that AI has been programmed and the coding could be enhanced but to create something from outer space seems just not possible."

"Think about it for a minute, John. Could these supercomputers actually design such improvements themselves?"

"No, because even these supercomputers run on the 0 and 1 binary coding and are therefore limited."

"But John, what if a new type of computer has been invented? I know a little about quantum physics and how it is thought that such logic could lead to a quantum computer."

Tilbury was interested in the way in which the discussion was going. But he knew no such computer will be invented in the next ten years because handling quantum mechanics had not been successful.

"Gary, you are too far ahead of the game. Quantum computers are just a pipe dream at the moment because the mechanics are not yet possible."

At that point, Tilbury thanked his mate for the convivial company and left the building with the thought of a real-world situation about a quantum computer.

The thought would not go away even when he had the image of a night with Jun.

The next morning, Tilbury called together the three analysts to get a briefing on what options they had to understand the strange computer code used by DYLAN.

Sax was first to speak, "John, we believe that the code was not developed by any known coder."

Burgess followed up on that comment.

"John, Sax is correct. It is either a new Einstein or a new type of computer or a combination of both. We think there are no other options. Given the need to dominate the world, it is felt by us that there may be a Chinese guru who, being used to the strange world of eastern symbolism, may have created the new code."

Marsha summed up their proposition.

"Mac, it is possible that the Chinese have developed a new kind of computer and programmed it with this new coding. But given the limitations of supercomputers, there is only one option: a quantum computer. But that is not possible because the needed science, technology, and innovation are not available. Plus, quantum particles, or whatever, are beyond control at this stage."

Sax followed up with the obvious statement.

"Friends, I have been through hell and back over designing and operating supercomputers and know about the quantum mechanics that need to be overcome. Not an option, John."

They agreed that this was not a way forward, but Tilbury could not delete that possibility from his mind.

Was DYLAN real or a hoax?

To satisfy his nagging premonition about the existence of a quantum computer, he arranged to meet Alan Jones, the Professor of Quantum Physics at ANU.

He arrived at ANU to meet Jones at the *Coffee Lab* in Central Canberra as both were coffee addicts.

"Dr Tilbury, why do I have the pleasure of your company?"

"Prof, I need your view about the possibility of the development of a quantum computer. I cannot really explain why because of national security."

Jones with raised eyebrows and a smile said, "Dr, are you an ASIO agent because you have the look of a spy."

No response.

"Yes, I'm interested in the development you wish to know about but keeping me in the dark is not helping your cause."

"Prof, 'the need-to-know' philosophy of a spy agency leaves me little room to move. But I will tell you we are investigating a death of a Chinese professor at the Chicago Computer Centre relating to messages found on their supercomputer."

"Wait a minute, was that Albert Williams?"

Tilbury was now really interested.

"Yes, why?"

"John, because he was a student of mine a few years ago, what happened?"

"Sorry cannot tell you that because it is an ongoing investigation. But can you answer my question about the possibility of the existence of a quantum computer?"

"Dr Tilbury, I can assure you that it is not feasible or possible given all the constraints against controlling the laws of quantum physics."

But Tilbury noticed a slight flicker in the eyes of the professor and thought:

Is he holding something back? I need to investigate him further.

"Thanks for the information, Professor Jones. Can I come back to you with further questions?"

Finishing his coffee, Tilbury walked away. His puzzled life had become even more complex.

He knew he needed to investigate Professor Jones because his gut told him that something was off about him. But why would he be holding back information on the potential existence of a quantum computer when such technology could not possibly exist?

58

Meanwhile, back at AXIOM, Edwards discussed the new ithinkPad model with Worthington. The ithinkGoggles were now working and they needed to consider their future use: improved cognition used for education development or for the purpose of national security [spying].

The decision was easy. Children were the future of Australia; slow or under-educated children were a waste of human resources. They knew that technology was replacing jobs, but the ithinkGoggles could enhance the opportunity for the slower students to improve their job applications or create ever-smarter bright students.

The project was named *The Smart Student.*

They had been working on the applications of the technology through games, so the students didn't realise their thinking ability had changed. There were different games for different students and different cultures. Working with Edwards and Worthington was Professor Alan Bates, a psychiatrist with expertise in brain development.

Based on the trials held at IronSide State School in Brisbane, AXIOM had proved the success of the ithinkGoggles in improving cognition and thus the basis of new research.

Bringing the professor into the project gave the AXIOM team the chance to show educators the use of the technology and how it would help the learning processes of students no matter their age or social status.

The project design was difficult as they needed approval by State education agencies to use the ithinkGoggles technology in their classrooms. These education agencies stipulated that diversity and opportunity were key criteria. For application success, both public and private schools had to be in the mix.

The team selected one high school from Catholic, Muslim, Chinese, independent, and a state high school, all within South East Queensland—five schools in total to be pilots for the up-scale application of the ithinkGoggles. The curriculum chosen was English at level 3. That subject was chosen because it was taught at all schools but had a variable approach based on the same content and because literacy was the key national outcome of student learning.

Five schools meant a small number of registered teachers had to be trained in the use of the technology. After numerous dialogues, one English teacher from each of the five schools agreed to be trained to use the ithinkGoggles.

Given that both Edwards and Worthington had heavy workloads in their respective workplaces, the two agreed to ask Dr Viviani if she would be interested.

Edwards called her and asked her to come back to AXIOM Research Centre and discuss the training role.

"Rachel, Paul Edwards here. Are you interested to return to AXIOM because we need your help in undertaking a world-first research program, *The Smart Student*."

Silence. Viviani thought that Tilbury should be aware of this because she wanted to go back to AXIOM as the ithinkPad technology was tested by her with Tilbury as her wingman.

I'll go but I'll consult with Tilbury before I do.

"Paul, thank you for the offer, which I accept on the condition that I have input into the whole program including the training module. Is that acceptable?"

"Rachel, I need to discuss that with Alice Worthington as she is the major researcher in the project. We also have Professor Alan

Bates from the ANU as our advisor for the educational aspects of the project. I will get back to you later today."

"Paul, I look forward to hearing from you."

Immediately after the call, Viviani contacted Tilbury.

"John, remember how we went back to AXIOM? Well, Paul Edwards just called and asked me to be involved in a project using the new ithinkPad technology called the ithinkGoggles. He wants to test it in the real world: five different classrooms one in each of five diverse schools in the Brisbane region. What do you think about my involvement?"

"Rachel, your call. But I would think carefully about the unknowns that may occur in its usage. As you should know, our technology impacts on the brain and may affect the subconscious. I have often worried about that as a reason why the guinea pigs, used by Professor Stanley, died from the trials and application of the original ithinkPad. Go ahead and find out the lay of the land."

Then, almost as an after-thought, Tilbury cautioned her.

"I suggest that the selected teachers be given the full understanding of the ithink technology."

"Rachel, note that the goggles aspect is just the medium to pass the focused light into the eyes of the brain. I understand that a Professor of Psychiatry will be an advisor for this program. I would get to meet him and ensure he understands the real properties of those ithinkGoggles."

"John, almost forgot to tell you, AXIOM has been working on AI and has programmed the technology. Apparently, an AI expert at Melbourne University has been consulting with Edwards."

"Holy shit, Rachel, what are they really doing to the brains of young people?"

Concerned, Tilbury added advice.

"A machine that can control itself in this situation I believe is not only unethical but life-threatening. The impact may seriously affect their developing sub-conscience. Take care, love. If concerned, call me and I'll come down to AXIOM."

"By the way, Rachel, what was the name of that professor helping with the AI?"

"A Chinese expert called We Chang."

Too shocked to answer, Tilbury asked Viviani to wait until he was ready in a day to accompany her to AXIOM.

"Rachel, We Chang was murdered by MSS a few days ago. I don't believe in coincidences. To be safe, I'll come with you and on the plane I'll tell you a story you will never forget."

"But John, am I safe if I work with them?"

"Not sure, Rachel, but we will find out."

A plan was agreed.

The day came. Tilbury took Viviani under his wing during the flight and explained what he knew about the death of We Chang and the implications of other coincidences that related to the 'Chinese way.'

He told her a redacted story...

"I'm a leader in TaskForce Triad trying to investigate the deaths of a number of Chinese nationals. We Chang was one of real concern because he was linked to a planted virus in the supercomputer at Melbourne University that was designed to take down the electricity grid of NSW and Victoria.

"However, I led a team that killed the virus we found in the hands of one of his Chinese colleagues. The collateral damage was the death of We Chang. We believe he was driven by MSS to control that computer and to set off the virus. I am paranoid that I keep seeing Chinese everywhere involved in nefarious activities.

"However, for national security reasons, some part of these coincidences I need to withhold from you. I hope you understand. Given We Chang had worked with AXIOM, I'm concerned that a Chinese influence may have crept into their operations."

Tilbury then warned Viviani.

"Rachel, for our safety, we must be careful and not raise any matters relating to We Chang or the 'Chinese way' because I'm not up to date on the behaviour of both Edwards and Worthington."

"John, you are scaring me. Maybe I should rethink the offer."

"No Rachel, your presence is now a top priority as another search for the pieces of this Chinese enigma keeps me awake at nights. Be led by me, I still cherish our relationship, love."

Later, they walked through the glass-encased atrium to meet Edwards, Worthington, and Professor Bates. The meeting resulted in a contract for Viviani to be in the project and have an input into the development of the Smart Student Program. Detailed planning took place as Viviani developed the education program for the teachers with input from the education guru, Professor Bates.

Viviani demanded that Tilbury be part of the first meeting so he could brief them on some of the hard facts that will affect their ability to use the technology in their classrooms. Outside in the atrium, Viviani expressed concerns about Bates to Tilbury.

"John, that guy is a charlatan. He professes to know the psychiatric mysteries that underpin the ithink technology. He is a fool. You heard how he pontificated."

"How do I keep him at arm's length so that these brilliant teachers will get what the ithinkGoggles is really about, cognition? His mumbo-jumbo crap will confuse them. Can you deal with that explanation based on your experience with the intricacies of the OASIS saga?"

59

Back in Beijing, General Jun was debriefed on the use of the AI killer drone in Taiwan and Hong Kong. Both were successful and the drones had returned safely to their handlers. He knew his plans were on track.

Expatriate dissidents had been given the message within the region China had declared as part of their nation. Collateral damage only heightened the threat of dissident activity. He was proud of his single-minded attack on the non-believers in the 'Chinese way,' within and outside of China.

The General strutted to the raised platform in the conference room at the Adjustment Directorate and said with pride to his accolades, "Comrades, the drone strikes have been successful but they were used in our region. We now need to go global."

"To do that, I have instructed our sleepers at the consoles of the best supercomputers in the western universities to activate the message I sent them."

The message was projected on the wall.

Comrade, link your computer to the Adjustment Directorate supercomputer using the attached code and follow the instructions.

Resounding cheers filled the room. The General smiled and left the team with a detailed plan to implement his glorious strategy to tell the world that China will not accept expatriate dissidents who poke at the 'Chinese way.' Internal dissident activity was controlled through the 'behaviour scheme.'.

Was the democratic world ready for this?

60

University feminist activist Karen Wentworth, the president of the Australian University Students Union, had had enough of the Chinese influence invading Australian universities. So, she called an urgent meeting of union representatives from all Australian universities to discuss actions needed by the union.

Wentworth, a single-minded activist, meant business. Universities were bending over backward to increase the growth of fees coming from international students from India and China, which affected the education of Australians as noted by a rising criticism of falling entry standards. The protests by Chinese nationals, around Australian campuses, against the democratic demonstrations in Taiwan, tipped her over the edge.

The agenda was clear: what action can the union take to make university administrations understand and realise what was happening?

At the University of Sydney, flyers had been distributed to students calling for a mass rally for action against the growing tide of Chinese students. The Vice-Chancellor, Professor Leslie Montgomery, found one in his in-tray. Concerned, he called his executives for an urgent meeting.

He was concerned that a mass rally at Federation Square in the Melbourne CBD could provide a forum of discontent that may have political implications for overseas enrolments, the lifeblood of many universities. As Chair of the Australian Universities Vice-Chancellors Association, Montgomery called an urgent meeting.

Concurrently, these two meetings took place with different agendas. Montgomery called the Australian Minister for Education, Dr Wilbur Wilde, seeking a meeting with him and the Association.

Wilde, a seasoned right-wing labour man, decided against the meeting as the 'Chinese way' was a political hot potato he did not wish to consume.

But he offered advice. Talk with the student union and try and get some agreed common understandings because such rallies are anathema to Beijing. And put a proposal to the Australian government for funding to compensate for a reduction in international student enrolments.

Montgomery was not impressed. He had a connection with the Chinese Foreign Minister Ali Chee, a prominent voice for Beijing, and the importance for Australia educating their nationals given the lower standard within some Chinese universities.

A robust conversation took place as Chee challenged her friend about potential interference with expatriate student rights. Placating her took all of Montgomery's political capital. But they agreed to meet in Beijing within the next month to discuss what may happen as a result of the rally in Federation Square.

* * *

More than 20,000 students and supporters had flocked to Federation Square to support the rally against the unwanted influences in Australian universities.

Standing on the podium, the feminist activist Wentworth gave a speech worthy of publication. However, it was her passion that drove the crowd.

Looking down at the crowd, she noticed a movement above them. The crowd noticed and moved on mass away from what was approaching.

To her shock, she was face to face with a BumbleBee killer drone, bulbous eyes focused on her.

She stopped speaking and the crowd fell silent, an eerie silence, broken by a statement by activist Wentworth that ultimately shocked the nation and went viral around the world.

"Fuck off, Beijing! This is our country."

In defiance, the bug-eyes kept focussed on her, and in a flicker of recognition, fired a projectile straight at her, killing her instantly. Collateral damage was several of her colleagues.

Smartphones captured the images of the action, including the monstrous BumbleBee killer drone. These images went viral on social media with the desired effect that the General had planned: shock, horror, and confusion of dissidents, testing their metal for public display of dissent.

The General was excited as his devious plan worked.

A safe distance away from the startled dispersing crowd, Colonel Ming smiled and knew that the world had changed. General Jun was now in charge. Then he walked to the nearest coffee shop to share thoughts with Ong.

At the same time, the AI hunter drone flew out over Port Phillip Bay where it dropped, as planned, into the marine waters. However, it landed near a recreational fisherman, holding a fishing rod and dreaming about a big fish.

The splash woke him from his doze so he took up his anchor and targeted the spot where the drone had landed. To his surprise, it floated.

He landed the drone using a bait net and realised what he had in his hands. He knew from experience that this was no ordinary drone: a BumbleBee colour, large bug eyes, a projectile mechanism, and a computer slightly larger than a smartphone.

The programmed drone was meant to drown in Port Phillip Bay to ensure no evidence was found, but unknown to Ming, the floating drone now became unwanted evidence.

Then all hell broke loose. Social media full of fake news, and distorted explanations went viral on the story as the fisher told his friends on Facebook and Instagram.

Beijing demanded an explanation of the Wentworth statement. It was an unwanted, unnecessary slight on the Chinese people. Canberra ignored the request.

The social media message was picked up by an aide of CIA McGinty, Agent Bud Castel, who was his voice on Australian intelligence operations as he kept a check on social media.

"Bud, what the fuck is going on over in Australia? Stirring up the *Red Dragon* was not on our radar. Please get a fix on this because Notting and ASIO are coming to town next week."

"OK, boss."

McGinty knew that Watson was susceptible to the implications of the drone attack. So, he organised the communication section of CIA to dig up as much information on these drones as possible and put together an advertisement that will turn voters away from Watson.

At the same time, Victoria Police were given the drone by the conscientious fisher who thought that it looked so sinister it should be investigated. The police knew about the deaths at Federation Square and put two and two together. Maybe this was the culprit, and called in the AFP, and therefore ASIO, as this was a national incident.

The words "Fuck off, Beijing, this is our country" really focussed the attention of the media, government, and TaskForce Triad, as the connection was too obvious to miss.

Chinese activism: that was pro-Beijing, the death of a leader of a rally against the growing influence of the 'Chinese way' in Australian universities, and the impact of funding reliance on the growing number of Chinese students enrolled in those Universities, concerned President Notting.

The drone had floated because of its light structure built from polycarbonate material but strong enough to carry the dangerous mechanisms.

The AFP being part of TaskForce Triad knew about the killing of Chinese dissidents by drones in South East Asia and brought the drone to a secret meeting of the Intelligence Team led by Tilbury.

A box that carried the drone was secreted into the meeting by Morrow who knew this was his chance to be a player.

Tilbury noted Morrow's body language and knew this was going to be difficult to hide from the press with him involved. Why? Because of his conspiracy theories and ability to go off-plan and warn 'persons of interest'.

The open box revealed the ugliest, monstrous, and deadliest drone ever seen in Australia. The BumbleBee killer drone fascinated Tilbury and his counterpart spooks. Technicians were brought in undercover to dismantle the drone and investigate its workings. One expert that had the IT skills was Peter Sax whose role was to investigate the computer and its software. For him, the drone had been dried under strict controls so that no damage from saltwater had occurred to the attached mechanisms.

Apart from the flying components of the drone, there were three other parts the team needed to investigate: the eye lens and camera, the software within the computer, and the projectile mechanism.

For Sax, the software was the challenge. The programs were highly encrypted for obvious reasons but were breakable. What he found he viewed with disbelief. The drone was AI-driven but linked to another program that he believed actually drove the drone. This program required more sophisticated encryption that he could not break.

So, he asked Tilbury if Marsha could have a crack at breaking the code. As Marsha was nearby, Tilbury agreed but on the grounds that she was never identified, as set up by Mac earlier.

Marsha smiled at Tilbury when she sat before her computer and began the breakdown of the code. But she was not ready for the response to her attempt.

Margaret Willis, your days are now numbered. Leave us alone.

Marsha jumped up from the desk and rushed outside, shocked by what she had just received.

Seeing her reaction, Tilbury followed her.

"John, it is happening again, first Williams, then Burgess, now me, all challenged with our lives. What is happening? This Chinese stuff is getting to me. Please call Peter. I need him right now."

"Ok, Marsha, please do not run away again. We need you and Peter."

With that, Tilbury, Marsha, and Sax had a quiet but intense argument about the way forward away from prying ears.

"Look, friends, this drone will open up a pathway to work out what is happening. ASIO will protect the both of you, so please stay the course. This is a serious breach of international diplomacy by an unknown agency we believe is within Beijing."

Marsha then investigated the coding and realised it was binary, different from that relating to DYLAN.

Tilbury, relieved, continued.

"The safety of our livelihoods, food security, and lifestyle need to be protected through government action. But given the co-dependence of the two countries, our decision-makers will need evidence of what is behind the killing. They seem to be blind to the growing 'Chinese way' so hopefully, TaskForce Triad will open their eyes. But I doubt that result will be met with the strongest response by our president to Beijing."

The AFP nerds were brought in to break the encryption. It took several days, and a shocked nerd brought the result to the team.

Mac decided to run the discussion and asked 'Willy the code cracker' to give them his findings. Addressing Mac, Willy took them through the encryption and the coding within the program…

"That program links the MSS in Beijing with something called the Adjustment Directorate, but more importantly, it links with several supercomputers in western world university campuses.

"We read the code and the actions within. It appears that the Melbourne supercomputer isolated a target, provided facial recognition of Wentworth, and the location of the target, Federation Square. Two actions that had been programmed use attached projectiles to kill the target and a very sophisticated code that can detect enemy contact that may destroy the drone.

"In summary, Mac, this is a very advanced AI-driven killing machine. My question is where did this baby come from?"

Within the TaskForce headquarters, the framework of the drone was being scrutinised by material engineers. They found the source and maker of the drone: *Drone Inc.* It had a Chinese barcode and had imported key materials from the USA. But where that company was located was unknown.

To Tilbury, this was the major lead.

Could Agent Arthur help with that location?

Tilbury then called a meeting with his trusted team and invited Arthur to join them to understand the importance of leads: the software and the material structure of the drone. To encourage positive thinking, Tilbury had a large blown-up poster of the yellow and black BumbleBee drone pinned to the wall. Each person who looked at the image was shocked by the impact of the bulbous eyes that just stared at them and sent shivers down their spines. One of the team, in a moment of disgust, had written across the poster, 'Let's get the bastards.' Other suggestions cannot be repeated under the advice of Tilbury, even though he agreed with the comments that eventually covered the pinned-up poster. The team was motivated.

61

President Watson met Tilbury and Mac in the Oval Office with the red-faced CIA Chuck McGinty, Secretary of State Virginia Longworth, and Chief of Staff Stephanie Callow. All were seated in front of the famous desk ready to discuss plans for the upcoming meeting with President Notting of Australia.

"Welcome, Mr ASIO, and your underling Tilbury," said the fractious McGinty.

Watson, who had already admonished him, called for calm before Tilbury could react. "We are friends here, Mac, so McGinty is going to apologize, aren't you, Chuck?"

McGinty got up and left with the passing remark, "Mr President, watch your back from now on. Your presidency is now on the line."

Unknown to the others, Longworth and McGinty had already decided to derail the Watson re-election. But with the calm voice of an angel, Longworth commented after the CIA man left the Oval Office, "Good riddance, that man is an egotistical prick, Mr President. But please note his parting remark."

The shenanigans over, they discussed the upcoming meeting about the rise of the 'Chinese way' in both countries. The absence of McGinty made it easier for Tilbury to be involved in the discussion. Mac had briefed him about the protocols of their meeting. But he gave Tilbury the task of briefing Watson on the details and implications of what they knew from TaskForce Triad and the Australian Embassy in Beijing.

Mac addressed the meeting.

"Bill, we have opened up a can of worms in Australia with respect to Beijing and want to brief you on the intelligence scenarios available to both our countries. The information will help you weigh up the intelligence you will get from McGinty, NSA, and whosoever you talk with in the near future. We have uncovered a remarkable plot to derail our democracy. You have to believe the 'Chinese way' is real and growing."

"OK, Mac, I'm listening, but in 25 words or less, please explain to me, what the fuck is this 'Chinese way' I know nothing about?"

"Bill, do you realise that that lack of information stems from the CIA under McGinty? He knows more than he is letting on. Our sources confirm that."

Mac then asked Tilbury to brief the president…

"The 'Chinese way' is a confirmed strategy of the Communist Party hardliners, to influence the world that China is the way forward, militarily, economically, culturally, and socially. The latter being significant through the 'behaviour scheme' which categorises the lives of Chinese nationals, at home and abroad. Internal dissent is punished and sent to educational gulags for rehabilitation. But a more sinister use of that scheme is the punishment of expatriate dissidents who will not accept that edict and speak out against Beijing.

"A few examples may help you understand this complex, disturbing, and immoral action by Beijing.

"In Australia, a number of Chinese have been murdered, and more sinister has been the use of an AI-driven killer drone that assassinated a prominent Australian activist in Melbourne and a dissident in the Brisbane Botanical Gardens.

"But Sir, dissidents have been murdered by drones in Taiwan and Hong Kong and probably elsewhere as we speak. This is no idle threat.

"Our research has led us to Beijing where we are aware of an MSS agency called the Adjustment Directorate run by an out-of-control General Jun. Under his funding, these drones have been developed and sent to kill dissidents in the countries of our allies.

"But the real kicker is the discovery that some of the best supercomputers may be under threat by sleepers put there under the command of that General. For example, the death at the Chicago Computer Centre.

"In a nutshell, Sir, the shit has hit the fan."

"Mac, is this for fucking real, and your man here Tilbury telling me that McGinty has hidden this information from me?"

"Bill, obviously we do not know what McGinty knows but it is clear that he is no friend of yours."

Watson looked at Virginia Longworth and said, "Girl, what do you know about this? If you lie to me, go pack your bags and fuck off."

"A bit crude, Bill, but let me assure you that whatever I think of your administration, I know nothing of this. Stay calm, friend, as we have a lot to do."

And she made a telling point, "I will leave now so you can talk-the-talk with the Aussies and walk-the-walk toward re-election, Bill."

After she left the Oval Office, Tilbury couldn't help himself and calmly offered advice, "Bill, who needs friends like those two? They will destroy your re-election."

"John, I know, just one of the hills I need to climb."

To which Mac added a much clearer point. "Bill, those hills are already there but those two are building very steep new ones. I would bet the two of them are in cahoots right now with Virginia briefing Chuck on what we just let you know."

"But on another matter, when will Andrew come to America, Mac?"

It was then agreed that a State Visit by the Australian President would be arranged for two months later where a joint communique could spell out the feelings of the West toward the rise of the 'Chinese way.'

After showing the Australian spooks out of the *Oval Office*, Watson went back and had one of the hardest discussions of his political career with his Chief of Staff, Stephanie Callow.

How can he move forward with his re-election and keep the previous information from the press and competition during the race to the presidency?

But he knew two things: support from the Australians and chaos from the CIA.

He was a troubled man.

62

However, Ben Strong was not finished with the massacre on that beach in Taiwan. His training told him he had more to offer, so he called Tilbury, "John. I am sitting on my arse doing nothing. Can I help in any way?"

At first, Tilbury was reluctant but then he realised that a mind and experience like Strong will be useful because he knew the world that he and Black had experienced. But what could he do to assist him given he was not an ASIO spook?

However, he answered, "Ben, come to the TaskForce headquarters where we can discuss what you can do." And he gave him the little-known address.

Mac came to the meeting where Strong signed the ASIO oath and became another spook to support Tilbury.

"Welcome to the mad-house, Ben," was the parting words of Mac as he left to return to Canberra to fight off the press and the politicians who wanted their day in the sun by knocking the work of ASIO, DSD, ASIS, and any agency that could or should have known about potential terrorism.

He needed to give answers to the what and why of the carnage in Federation Square. Mac responded briefly and truthfully, "A TaskForce Triad has been established."

The press was not impressed and kept up their coverage.

63

It was Friday, early evening in Hyde Park, New York. The residents of the high-rise apartments that ringed the popular tree-studded area loved to visit as did the hordes of visitors who walked through the clean air and fragrance of the greenery.

One local resident, Amy Lee-Ching, spent many a day walking her dog through the park. She had a favourite bench where she sat, talked to locals about the world and her pet hate, the influence of Beijing Chinese interference in China City, New York. Lee-Ching had an arthouse business frequently visited by Chinese visitors asking for money to keep the business free from attack, or simply trying to influence her attitude to the 'Chinese way.'

It more than annoyed her. She wanted to do something about the problem. That night, Lee-Ching opened up her Facebook account and let the so-called Chinese thugs have it, full barrel, nominating the local circumstances of their actions.

The response to her story went viral. Too many people had been affected by the Chinese influence and voiced their opinions. The power of the people was so strong that CNN and *To-Night Live* invited Lee-Ching on to their shows.

The question put to her on these shows was clear. "Why single out the 'Chinese way' when so many 'other ways' were obvious in American life?"

Her answer was simple, "Beijing was leading the way in trying to change democracy through silencing dissent as shown by the many examples exposed throughout the world."

"Here in New York, dissent is being silenced every day through subversive manipulation of news, such as during elections. All I ask is that politicians take notice of what is happening to the daily lives of ordinary Americans and forget their own self-interests."

Newspapers throughout the major cities of America realised that this could be the tip of an unwanted iceberg, so by-lines everywhere questioned the meaning of the 'Chinese way.'

Beijing was furious and asked President Watson to explain why he allowed such reporting, putting pressure on key members of his Cabinet. The Chinese Foreign Affairs Minister demanded the Secretary of State to visit the Chinese Embassy in Washington and explain the fake news put out by the USA Administration. The call was ignored.

But the action taken by the dissident which spread through live TV was not ignored by the Adjustment Directorate; the General wanted a swift response.

* * *

In the cool of the morning, Amy Lee-Ching sat with her fluffy poodle on her favourite bench in Central Park quietly reading a magazine and enjoying the peace and quiet of the warm spring day.

A ruffle of a breeze caused her to raise her head, pat her dog, and looked up into the bug eyes of the BumbleBee killer drone.

Why the hell is this fucking insect looking at me?

Her brain tried to recognize what hovered near her. A growing vision before her spiked her heart rate and perspiration flooded down from her armpits as she realized it was actually focussed on her. Then the penny dropped. She had said too much on TV.

A group of walkers coming in her direction stopped dead in their tracks. The image scared them, so they backtracked to get away from the large monstrous BumbleBee drone.

They realised that it focussed on a regular New Yorker they had often seen sitting in that place. One of the group members said to his friends, “Christ, that is a fucking drone. Just look how lethal it looks. We had better warn her,” and captured the scene on a smartphone. The call to 911 was not answered. Before his words of warning could escape his lips, the drone fired a projectile at Lee-Ching and then chased the group, killing all.

An acolyte of the General, a sleeper, had been given the task of controlling the drone which had been smuggled into America by well-paid customs officers. They didn’t know what was in the box labeled iPhone parts. The sleeper had programmed the drone to fall in flight into the water near the Statue of Liberty as a message that America was now not the home of ‘the dream.’ No one noticed the floating drone until it eventually sank. Some media, however, stressed that the ‘Chinese way’ was yet another left-wing propaganda to match that of the ‘climate change’ wankers. Beijing supported the claim.

President Watson watched the news display the scene of the massacre of innocents in Hyde Park. The massacre had been captured by that smartphone and handed to the FBI. Watson realised that what the Australians had told him was now an American example of the clampdown on anti-Chinese rhetoric by Beijing. A call to President Wei was not well received who said he had no real idea what was happening in his country or elsewhere.

“President Watson, I will get to the bottom of this and call into account who is behind this horrific murder.”

“Sir, I must tell you that this is the fourth assassination action by a Chinese drone supposedly controlled out of your MSS.”

“Bill, there are many things that I cannot control, but I will get to the bottom of what you have just suggested.”

Did Watson believe him or was President Wei behind the killing?

64

McGinty sat at his desk and just stared at the Matt Colridge front-page by-line heading in the *Washington Post.*

CIA keeps the White House in the dark!

The White House has it on good authority that the head of CIA is deliberately hiding information about deaths of Chinese dissidents in the capital cities of our allies, including the death yesterday of Amy Lee-Ching. A New Yorker who had been brutally assassinated along with by-standers who tried to help her. A witness, who won't come forward, said, "A large bumblebee-shaped drone had attacked these innocents and just disappeared."

On further investigation, the Post can reveal that Lee-Ching had appeared on national television chiding Beijing. Can this be just a coincidence? The Post will get to the bottom of this.

Who the fuck was the whistle blower? I'll have his nuts for tea, thought McGinty who put a call through to Virginia Longworth checking whether she had given Colridge the information.

"Virginia, you had the information, as did Watson, Callow, Mac, and Tilbury at that meeting. Who leaked?"

"Chuck, it wasn't me. I would say it was the *White House*, maybe by Callow to protect the Watson re-election."

"Virginia. I will put a team together to find who fucking did this. The CIA cannot be vilified in the national press without the leaker being punished."

The next call was to the *Washington Post.*

"McGinty here, please put me through to Matt Colridge."

"OK, Sir." Knowing the call was from McGinty, Colridge knew what was coming.

"Colridge here, who is disturbing my morning coffee?"

"Don't piss me about that. You know who the fuck I am."

"Yes, I do, what can I do for the esteemed CIA?"

"Don't get smart with me, mate. Who leaked that fucking fake news?"

"Sorry, Mr CIA, privileged information under the Whistle Blowers Act."

Colridge hung up and called Callow. But unfortunately, for him and the *Post*, during the conversation with CIA, his phone was tapped.

McGinty now knew it was Watson's Chief of Staff. He smiled and thought he had Watson by the balls. But the *Post* had stirred up a hornet's nest in Beijing; fingers were being pointed but at the wrong people.

Colridge was not disturbed by the call from McGinty as he had faced down the worst in his career as a journalist. Then he remembered his time with Tilbury and Black during the OASIS saga, thought about that connection, then rang Tilbury.

"John, McGinty has been up my arse over a drone killing here. What do you know about those drones as this will be a big story for *The Washington Post*?"

65

The hardliners had built the story that the West had infiltrated social media: "Wasn't *Google* and *Facebook* turning a blind eye to the spreading of lies about China through algorithms designed to support the western hegemony?"

The news of the ruckus enlivened the General. The covert dissemination of fake news and killing of dissidents was working. Now, with these victories, he called on the hardliners to support his move to displace President Wei.

At a quiet and secluded resort outside of Beijing, twenty-five key hardliners met. No military insignia or uniforms but simple clothes to not alarm the resort owners. It was described as a workshop to plan for the development of new-age technology to support clean energy. Of course, that was far from their secret agenda—remove Zhang Wei from the presidency of China. No remorse was felt by those in attendance. They had had enough of his weaknesses. It was time for a new regime.

They had trumped-up evidence but getting the Party to accept the change would be difficult. The answer was to promote the General as the saviour of the 'Chinese way.'

So, a long-term view of China's control of the world was constructed based on the previous President Ping who had paved the way for members to accept a radical change within China.

Backroom meetings occurred at regular intervals in the major cities in China where Party members were told of the necessary changes and the importance of supporting General Jun.

The Adjustment Directorate was the site for the massive propaganda machine telling the story and the need for the powerful General.

The cover-up of mysterious deaths by drones was the fake news that these dead nationals were dissidents plotting against the Party. But not everyone was in the loop. Hatred of the General, in some quarters, ran deep and rumour of a counterattack was being planned from within the Adjustment Directorate.

The weakness of the General's control was the link between the Directorate and the world's supercomputers. Not all of the sleepers were prepared to follow the instructions sent out by the General. Some fought back supported by messages from other sleepers when they did not open the attached files from the Directorate.

Ina Wong sat before her UK Cambridge University supercomputer, logged on and ignored the message, and made a note in her daily log. Her days as a sleeper were over, so she thought. She was shocked by the voice message that appeared.

> *Ina Wong, are you a brave woman? Watch your back, DYLAN.*

Usually a calm, clear thinking AI researcher, she was lost for words and wondered.

Where is this coming from and who programmed the DYLAN message?

Not short of investigative logic, she tried to trace the message from DYLAN but realised it was beyond her when the hieroglyphic code was revealed.

What is this? It is beyond my comprehension.

Wong needed the help of an AI colleague to consider what she had heard from her computer. But who, given the circumstances, was behind the message? However, she knew an AI expert at Oxford University AI Centre, so, in desperation, she called her.

"Shin, this is Ina Wong from Cambridge University working on AI developments. I wondered if you may be interested in a collaboration."

"Yes, call me when you can make the time."

Wong came to Oxford University to meet Shin Hung. It was arranged in town, not within the university. Both wanted to ensure that potential ears would not hear what they were planning. They agreed to meet at the *Missing Bean*, where ethically sourced beans from sustainable sources made for excellent coffees.

As they sat drooling over their coffee, it was clear that Hung was not a sleeper and knew nothing about what had happened to Wong. It took time for each other's hesitancy to dissipate. When Hung smiled, Wong decided that it was time to reveal why she had asked Hung for the meeting.

"Shin, I am so glad we have a common interest in AI for two reasons: we understand each other's work and passion, and that we both drive supercomputers at our respective universities. However, I do not want to surprise or shock you, but what I have to say is about to upset our worlds."

"Ina, you are beginning to worry me. I agreed to discuss the AI world, not other problems."

At this point, Wong decided to tell her story to Hung…

"Obviously, we are Chinese nationals, sent here by the Chinese Party, or I was, and that association is what troubles me. The other day when I logged on, the computer gave me a very strange personal message that I needed to watch my back. But the message was from DYLAN. I have no idea who or what DYLAN is.

"To make matters worse, I tried to backtrack the message to find that the encryption code was so out of this world and beyond my comprehension.

"Shin, my simple question is, have you had anything like that happen to you or a colleague?"

"The answer is simple, Ina. *No! Never!*"

"OK, Shin, what can I do because I cannot work like this anymore?"

"Well, come and stay with me for a while so you can get your head together."

Little did they know that that stay would change both their lives.

Unfortunately, the Adjustment Directorate supercomputer noticed the non-response from Wong and passed that on to the General. However, given she had disappeared, no BumbleBee drone was released to remove that dissident. The General had better ideas to change the West.

Wong and Hung decided to stay together, safe.

66

A few years earlier, near the Mallee town of Quambatook in northwest Victoria, Australia, a field day was held on farmer Pat's wheat farm. Pat Wilke was a passionate believer in GMO seeds for his farm and wanted the seed producers to explain to the local farmer's association the benefits of GMO. The guest speaker was Grice McMillian from WASANTO, who said that GMO wheat and canola production will lead to a 20% yield and better prices.

But the chatter around the breaks was the purchase of a group of farms in the district by an unknown buyer. Some were pissed off that their farm had not been part of the deal because, with the drought, times were tough. Some 5,000 ha had been bought up, but no sign was evident of what was going on at that conglomerate farm.

Sitting with the usual beer in his hand, Pat joined in the discussion. He raised his hand in silence and asked for a few minutes because he had a theory about that area.

"Friends, I believe that no farming will take place in that area. I sent a drone over the place out of curiosity and what the pictures showed was a little unusual."

He had their attention.

"In the centre of the area was a high mesh metal fence with barbed wire on top. Under construction was a large silo, similar to the wheat silos all around the Mallee. Nearby were large closed sheds. What surprised me most was a sign on the front fence, Government Property. Keep Out."

"Gentlemen, I have no idea what is going on but I'm meeting our local member to find out."

As usual, rumours began to spread about the place, specifically in social media. Trolls loved to stick it to the government but silence limited their vitriol.

The field day broke up with some farmers putting orders for GMO seeds; others just wanted to know what was happening in their district.

The local member of parliament met with representatives of the local farmers' association but the bullshit protectors of the farmers got the message; this was a need-to-know situation.

Don't ask.

But Wilke would not let this go and called his brother-in-law who worked in the Ministry of Foreign Affairs and Trade based in Canberra.

"Warren, can you do a little digging about the amalgamation of wheat farms near my place? The large-scale property has been fenced-off with a government sign telling people to keep out. Our association is in the dark about the area. Can you please help us find out?"

"Ok, Pat, but with one condition; if this is a need-to-know situation, my hands are tied, but I will search our database on whether the purchase was by a foreign company. Will call on a burner, as this could be clandestine and I want to keep my job."

The call came from Warren Shield.

"Pat, no foreign company has purchased the land. But I can tell you that a private company based in Victoria has amalgamated the farms into one entity according to the Victorian Lands Office. Best I can do, Pat."

"Thanks, Warren, at least no foreign company has bought the land."

"Don't be too sure, Pat, it could be a shell company."

He explained that could be a cover for foreign-vested interests.

"Pat, if I find out more, I will let you know. Please come around for dinner when you're next in Canberra. Betty would love to see you. Please, say hi to Jenny for me."

Was this a dead end for Pat?

Wilke was now burdened with life's uncertainties of the local organisation rising from the wheat lands he loved, but he loved the Australian outback more. His beloved wheat fields had been invaded by an unknown-unknown and he wanted answers. The locals, more concerned about missing the jackpot of the sales, were disgruntled and did not talk to each other.

The town of Quambatook was no longer a quiet, friendly place. Friends harboured grudgers against the winners and the winners seemed oblivious to the potential chaos that may hit the town.

Unknown to his friends, Wilke liked poetry that related to the bush he loved. He was a published bush poet who that day wrote a few lines to distract him from the local issues. It was published in the local rag.

The words endeared him to his loyal supporters.

Road to Nowhere

White posts glide by, silent markers of a black endless strip,
Laid for quenching wanderlust of man, on a never-ending trip.
Saltbush mounds on stagnant grounds, spinifex fighting survival odds,
Windmills grinding, sucking life from salty clods.
Bitumen moulded by speeding wheels, surrenders to soft edges,
Corrugations and sporadic repair.

Telegraph poles bent by age, burden of life's messages,
Eye-sores of progress, brothers to the road.
Tracks emerge from the shimmer of sunburnt plains, clipped neat,
Passing fringes of straggly gums, slim, bent by Westerlies,
Lifting topsoil into dust, border the passing patchwork quilt.
Sign posts pant left, right; civilization nowhere in sight,
Silos rise, unexpected monuments, guardians of bulldust,
Storage bins, bread and butter, crust for the tillers of the plains.

Sheep, shorn today, meat tomorrow, nibble stalks beneath eucalypts,
Knarred, knotted sun-greened homes,
Ubiquitous life within nature-browned plains.
Crows, beady-eyed, silent scavengers watch passing devils.
Rusty steel rimmed eyes of hollow metal carcasses roadside,
Dead reminders of careless haste.
Progress slows, music softens the homeward chase.
Wheat fields ruffled by the westerly breeze,
Gave hope.

67

A year later, after the basic construction had finished, Alan Jones, the Professor of Quantum Physics at ANU, poured over the detailed plans for the new land acquired by a private company specialising in a new science based on quantum physics. The area was designed to be a high-tech research area partly funded through research grants from the Centre of Excellence Program of the Australian government. Professor Jones had also made the play to entrepreneurs who were interested in the cutting-edge science innovation.

But Jones was not forthcoming about what the main research project was about and that the outcome could change the world. He wrapped the innovations as benefits to Australian wellness and prosperity. The program was called 'Innovation for Life' and the investors were hooked. He had full control of the facility.

Looking back, the professor always remembered the look on Tilbury's face when he left the coffee shop. He may be a problem in the future. That needed a solution.

He was also concerned by the ongoing questioning by farmer Pat about the farmland that had been amalgamated. He too was a problem in need of a solution.

However, his demise would raise too many red flags.

Maybe he can be brought into the business as an advisor on the use of AI for increasing agriculture productivity. Pat Wilke agreed immediately as it let him in the door as he was not satisfied that the professor was telling the whole truth about the activities within the compound. He could not leave that alone.

Now, a little wiser, Pat Wilke walked from his SUV to the silo and the glass doors immediately opened.

He had an office with all the gizmos of a researcher but he had limited access to the building. It bugged him that he was excluded from certain areas. But one day, a door not normally accessible was left unlocked so he walked through to discover a lift had been built into the structure. But the lift had only a down indicator.

Try as he may, the lift door would not open, which told him that whatever happened in the building, it was all underground. He also knew that he cannot be seen in this area, shot back to his office, opened his computer, and logged on to find a voice that really disturbed him.

> *Oh, Pat! You have trespassed. Beware! DYLAN.*

What the hell, not only have I been watched but also warned through a voice message on my computer.

Who or what the fuck is DYLAN?

A request to meet with Jones fell on deaf ears, confirming that this facility had a dark side that Wilke cannot accept as he was from the old school of no hidden agendas.

But, whereto from here?

While he sat at his desk and contemplated his next move, a call came from Warren Shield.

"Pat, for your information, I have checked up on your professor through the darknet. He is not only a megalomaniac but also a real tricky bastard. My insider in the AFP has him pegged as a con-merchant in league with suspected criminal dealings. Not totally verified but with enough evidence that the research may turn out to be treasonable and not in the national interest. Get out before you are caught up in his web of nefarious activities."

"But Warren, he is a professor at ANU, how could that be?"

"Man can be evil but smooth as silk on the outside. Leave."

Farmer Pat was now conflicted and told Shield who said, "If you need help, Pat, call me and I will get you help from an ASIO agent I know you can trust. He has been there and done that. Please call, do not lag. I believe that Jones is a dangerous man, but I could be wrong."

Warren Shield then called ASIO and asked to speak to Agent Tilbury.

68

Tilbury at home watched a thriller movie to calm his thoughts but was surprised by a knock on his door. As he opened it, he recognised Mac with Black and Strong behind him.

"Come in, my friendly spooks. Why do I have the pleasure?"

Strong led with his chin and looked Tilbury straight in the eye and unflinchingly laid his concerns on the line.

"John, this whole 'Chinese way' affair is going to shit. We need a plan for this trusted team. We also believe that you need to put pressure on Cassandra Jun as we see her as pivotal to understanding what is happening to the Chinese diaspora. They are under threat as the social media has many views on the deaths of expatriate Chinese nationals."

To which Black added the telling issue, "John, we can see that you are puzzled by the 'Chinese way' and how you can influence that within Australia. So, we are here to form a team to seriously look at what is happening and what we can do about this Chinese enigma. You cannot do this alone!"

Mac knew Tilbury was hampered by his relationship with Cassandra Jun and wanted to support him.

"John, as my foremost spook, your love for Cassie may have coloured your view about this Chinese enigma, so we have come to support you to move forward. We are at a dangerous crossroad at the moment given what little we know about the Adjustment Directorate and the actions of General Jun. Maybe Cassie is the door we need to open?"

"Fair enough, Mac, but I will protect Cassie at any cost to myself; that is not negotiable. However, let's get started, mates."

Tilbury got his act together very quickly as he could see the hope on the faces of this select team of spooks, known as MSI, sitting in his apartment.

"First item for discussion is our mobile phones. Please turn them off and take out the batteries. That way, no one knows where we are or what we are discussing."

No argument by the team. Now the hard grind of planning began. Black raised the top priority.

"Folks, I believe we should start in Australia and get the full details of what has happened here because I believe that is where the leads will come."

With that, a full timeline was drawn up with all events noted as they looked for patterns. Out of the blue, Strong exclaimed, "I understand what is going on now," and explained his theory.

"I agree," said Tilbury. "Begin with the Jun family."

But Cassandra Jun was not forthcoming despite her love and affection of Tilbury, "John, the cost is too high."

So, Tilbury decided it was all or nothing and told Jun everything he knew and the assumptions about the Chinese enigma he was trying to unravel. He also knew that what he was about to say may end their relationship. But the stakes were now too high, so he took the risk.

"Cassie, you are part of the 'Chinese way' because General Jun actually sent you to ANU to support Chinese hegemony and you knew that."

The look on her face caused Tilbury to ask again.

"That's true, isn't it, love?" Jun hugged Tilbury for comfort.

Slowly, Cassandra Jun met the eyes of Tilbury as salty tears rolled down her face and sobbed into his chest.

But Tilbury did not comfort her. He needed her to come to grips with what was happening around her. Without any support.

"Why the attitude, John? What do you want from me?"

"Cassie, do you understand the implications of what I have just explained? The world is changing, and it seems that Beijing is more than poking the western world. Let me remind you that dissident Chinese nationals are being assassinated within and outside of China."

"But more significant is that an eco-political cold war has begun and the power and influence has leaned toward the Red Dragon where one small step of mankind has turned into a red march toward dictatorship invading our democracy. We need a new step forward and that is you, Cassie."

Jun asked the obvious question, "How do I do that, John?"

"Open up a channel of communication with your brother General Jun before it is too late, Cassie."

"How?"

"Use the darknet, love! That is how he contacted you. I will help you with the actual communication. I will set up a room inside ASIO so that you will be safe and get support from Marsha and Sax, if needed."

Later that day, Cassandra sat before a special terminal with Marsha on one side and Tilbury on the other as she accessed the darknet. On the screen, a voice message appeared that shocked all three:

> *Cassandra Jun, are you prepared for what you will find? DYLAN.*

Marsha was the first to react and delved into the noise of the darknet as she tried to backtrack the message. But she was not surprised when the coded hieroglyphics of the encryption flashed on the screen.

Tilbury said what they all thought, "Who or what the fuck is DYLAN?"

But Marsha had a theory she later shared with Tilbury.

"John, there is only one possibility about DYLAN."

But she was frightened at what she was about to say.

"John, please turn off your phone, take out the battery, and I will then tell you the most likely option."

Both walked out into the Brisbane CBD and found an out-of-the-way corner coffee shop where to quell their nerves, they ordered two Macchiato coffees. Then Marsha spoke the words that no one had thought about or said before.

"John, it must be a Quantum Supercomputer that has generated the new code."

"Holy fuck, Marsha, if you are correct, we are in trouble. Is DYLAN neutral or supporting the developing hegemony?"

Marsha, now pale with the implications of what she had put into words, said without conviction:

"John, if we are sure about the existence of a quantum computer, where would that computer be located: in Australia or offshore somewhere, and who is controlling it?"

Tilbury now thought about that scenario and asked Marsha to join his team so they can put that information into the mix.

69

The *Sun Herald*, a popular Victorian newspaper had a second-page by-line that interested Detective Morrow as he followed the progress of the AFL Collingwood football team.

Chair of the Quambatook Farmers Association, Pat Wilke, was found murdered in his home on the weekend. No evidence was found but when his brother-in-law was interviewed as part of the investigation, he said that if his computer was missing, it was more than foul play.

Morrow was really interested in the story because he had a gut feeling this was a lead that will put him back into the investigation by the TaskForce Triad. Warren Shield had said in passing that Wilke had mentioned a professor from ANU had given him a position in his Mallee-based research laboratory.

As usual, Morrow did not share this information with Tilbury or anyone else, a deadly mistake. His body was found on the highway just North of Lake Boga, a pit stop on the way to Swan Hill, a regional centre. No evidence, no vehicle, no smartphone. AFP swarmed all over the area looking for evidence. Although Morrow was not well-liked or trusted, all stops were pulled out to solve his murder; he was one of them.

Tilbury wondered why Morrow was in the Mallee.

Finally, the AFP vehicle driven by Morrow was found parked on the main street of Kerang, a town south of where his body was found. Crumpled and under the passenger seat was a receipt from a coffee shop in Quambatook.

What did that mean?

Under orders from Tilbury, Black was sent to investigate. He was to trace the trip Morrow may have taken and who he might have met along the way.

In his wallet, Black had a recent photo of Morrow that he showed around the Quambatook township. No success, then he had a hit. Maxine of the well-known coffee place *Coffee & Bits* remembered the visit by Morrow and that he had a coffee with Pat Wilke, a local farmer. Maxine also mentioned that Wilke had been found dead on the previous weekend.

For Black, two related deaths were not a coincidence, so he called Tilbury.

"John, something smells about the death of Morrow. I know we thought he was a lost cause, but he was one of us. But this may interest you. Two related deaths were unusual out here in the bush. I need to follow this up and ask around a bit more, visit family, see where that takes me."

"OK, Thomas, keep me in the loop."

As Black came across as a no-bullshit tough bastard, locals gave him a wide birth, until a local farmer came up to him and asked, "Are you Thomas Black, known as the 'Assassin'?"

Black, at first, did not acknowledge the question but looked the man in the eye and said, "Who the fuck are you, mate?"

"I fought with you and Major Tilbury in Afghanistan, but I was just a grunt. I will always remember how you and he held us all together, and your sniper fire that saved the life of my mates."

"I am sorry I do not remember you. Please forgive me. We all went through hell back then. By the way, what is your name soldier?"

"Billy Green, Sir."

"Ok, Billy, I'm Thomas. How about we have a beer because I want to ask you questions that might help my investigation of the death of local farmer, Pat Wilke, you may know."

"Yes, Thomas. We all know Pat. What the fuck. Why was he killed?"

"I am not at liberty to tell you much because of national security reasons."

"Thomas, are you a fucking spook?"

"No, Billy, but I have been asked to help in the investigation, but spooks are my friends."

"So, no joke Assassin, ASIO has come to town. Wait till I tell my friends."

"Not a wise move, Billy. Any connection with that kind of world is not healthy, trust me. I have been there."

After a few beers, Black got around to asking key questions of the local Pat Wilke, who were his friends, relatives, and where he worked, given he had sold his farm?

Billy was candid and did not know where Wilke worked but he knew he had a brother-in-law, Warren Shield, who worked in Canberra. The only real lead left for Black because Wilke's wife had passed away from a heart attack earlier in the year. There were no children. After thanking Billy Green, Black drove to Melbourne and flew back to Brisbane to meet Tilbury and the team.

Debriefing with the team opened another line of enquiry followed up by Mac. As the brother in-law of Wilke was based in Canberra, Mac made an appointment at his local coffee shop with Warren Shield because he wanted an informal atmosphere during the first meeting. As he was head of ASIO, a confronting agency to many, Mac wanted not to scare Shield away. He was a government official and wanted his cooperation.

"Thanks for coming, Warren, but first, I need to come clean about our coffee. I'm Mac, head of ASIO and need advice."

"Actually, Mac, I know who you are. I work in MFAT and sometimes have to answer Ministerials that relate to intelligence."

"Ok, now that has been cleared up, what do you know about Pat Wilke?

"Why, Sir?"

"Well, putting it in layman's terms, we are investigating his death, no comment on why, national interest involved."

"OK, Mac, I will play your spook game. What do you really want from me?"

"The death of Wilke has spiked our attention, based on interviews and that an APF officer was murdered not long after your brother-in-law. His body like Wilke's was found in the Mallee region."

Shield listened.

"Warren, too much of a coincidence for us, spooks. Please tell me everything you know about Wilke."

70

Professor Jones had staff for his research complex in the Mallee recruited from the local township of Quambatook, mainly maintenance or office/receptionist workers. Other staff were scientists or IT technicians from around the world.

A cheerful Susan Mills was the receptionist at the compound and was a regular at the local café. As she took her black coffee with milk on the side and a breakfast plate of bacon and eggs, she noticed that the professor talked to the owner. Mills looked her way and acknowledged her with a wave.

But Mills was a talker, knew everything about everybody, the town gossip.

Why was the professor on friendly terms with the owner? I need to keep an eye on that relationship. A lonely professor and a local wench, who knows what might come of that? What a story that would be!

Black had returned to Quambatook to finish interviewing locals based on what Mac had gleaned from his meeting with Warren Shield, controversial land sales to an unknown Victorian-registered company.

As he walked into the café, Susan Mills recognised instantly that he was not a local. It got her attention. She was taken by his rugged looks and steely grey eyes that fascinated her. She was not one to let sleeping dogs lie.

Why is this handsome stranger in my midst?

So, she joined Black at the counter and asked him, "Handsome, what brings you to town? Can I buy you a coffee?"

Just what Black wanted, an entrée into the local gossip mill, but she may be more than that for him.

Now at the table with her blue eyes fixed on him, he asked, "What's your name? I am Thomas Black."

"Susan Mills, at your service, Thomas."

Who thought this woman is brazen and coming on to me? Maybe I can use that to my advantage.

The conversation ended with an agreement for dinner at the local pub where Black had his digs. *All in a day's work,* thought Black.

Next, Black fronted the counter again and showed Maxine McKay, the owner, the photo of Pat Wilke and asked her, "Do you know this person? If so, what do you know about him?"

A silent rebuke brought out the AFP warrant card he had for these moments. The response brought a smile to his face. The reaction to the photo was different. Teardrops formed in the corner of Maxine's eyes.

Black then knew this maybe a breakthrough he was looking for after the hard slog of no response so far.

"Mr Black, you are the second person to show me that photo. The first was a bedraggled AFP Officer called Morrow."

Black was stunned by the comment.

The *Coffee & Bits* café was the centre for many locals to socialise: a local bakery with French pastries, a deli, coffee machines, and shelves of second-hand books ready to be read by the locals. It was set out up with air-conditioning inside with a well-shaded outside area.

A comfortable place to relax with friends. Maxine McKay took Black outside for privacy and told her story…

"There has been a lot of bad blood around the sale of local wheat farms to an unknown company.

"Many locals felt that not only had they missed out on the sale of their land as times being tough but also the intrigue of locals on the large property has caused friction within the town as some locals actually worked on that site.

"But they are tight-lipped about what happened there. However, we know from the drone shots that Pat showed us. It was not for farming."

"Maxine, has there been any strangers interested in the area that might have visited your café?"

At this stage, the face of Maxine slightly changed, and her eyes closed, an indication that she was going to lie to Black. "Not that I am aware of, Thomas, but if I find anything out, I will let you know."

But Black was not phased and let it pass. He was meeting up with Susan Mills that night. *Maybe she can give me that information.* He was actually looking forward to the Mills encounter.

When Black came down from his room to meet Mills, the woman that met him gave him a hard–on and he knew straight away how the night would end.

He was distracted. She just oozed sex and he was infected. So, he took her hand and led her up to his room. The body of Susan Mills was lithe, breasts great swells of soft flesh that he could not leave alone. Meanwhile, she knew how to please him. Both left each other totally satisfied.

After enjoying reruns, they agreed that dinner should be taken, but not before Black asked the killer question.

"Susan, who has visited Maxine's café that you knew was not a local?"

As a good gossip should, she answered very clearly.

"Thomas, a Professor Jones sometimes takes coffee and chats up Maxine."

"Are you sure, Susan?"

"Yes, I saw him there just the other day, arrogant prick."

"Susan, can you go down to the restaurant and order me the best steak? I have to make a call back to head office or they will think I have run away with you."

"Sounds like a good idea, Thomas."

He just smiled as she dressed and walked out the door.

"Tilbury here. What do you have for me, Thomas? We are stuck in a rut at the moment. "Surprising news, John, a local told me that a professor Jones has been in the town. Is that helpful, John?"

"Thomas, you have no idea how important that information may be. I spoke to him earlier about quantum computers that he lied to me about. We may be on to something.

"By the way Thomas, remember you are married to one of the most gorgeous women I know, so be good. Please don't tell how you got that information. I may never forgive you."

The call went dead, and Black wandered down for dinner feeling like shit that he had betrayed Julia, but the romp with Susan was a powerful aphrodisiac. Out of curtesy, he followed up dinner with Susan. However, his resolve broke when she whispered, "Pussy is hot and ready, Thomas," kissed him full on the lips, took his hand, and led him upstairs.

The next thing Black knew, it was time for breakfast and a note on the pillow beside him.

Thanks, Thomas, I will remember our little affair. Thanks for the ride. Enjoy life. Susan

Black smiled, rolled over, and went back to sleep. He knew that his time in the area was not finished. Later in the day, he decided to have breakfast at *Coffee & Bits* café. His appearance startled Maxine as she thought Black had moved on to greener pastures.

As she made his breakfast and Americano coffee, Black asked her in soft tones, "Maxine, why did you lie to me yesterday about not knowing a Professor Jones?"

Her reply made sense, but Black was not so sure of her motive for lying to him.

"Mr Black, because the professor has been here quite a few times I regard him as a local."

"Be that as it may, what can you tell me about him? For example, why is he here in the Quambatook area?"

"Can I call you, Thomas? By the way, you made quite a hit with Susan. She was all aglow this morning."

"Ok, Maxine, no more beating about the bush. Who is this Professor Jones? Please do not lie, we know a few things about him you may not know. For example, why would a Professor of Quantum Physics be working in the middle of a fucking Mallee wheat field?"

"Thomas, all I can tell you is what some of the workers out there tell of a tall silo with dark windows. They have only access to the ground reception and administration areas. They believe that scientists live in the silo and work underground but have no proof of that."

"Thanks, Maxine. That's all I need to know. Two things: forget I was here and do not tell the professor I was here as that is dangerous for you and the people of Quambatook.

"Enjoy your life and forget what is happening out there; definitely, it's not good for your health if you get my drift."

Departing with a smile, he said, "Please say goodbye to Susan for me. Agent Black has warned you. Be careful."

71

At AXIOM, Viviani stood before a selected group of English teachers ready for their introduction to the power of the ithink technology in building the cognition of their students. Each had been introduced to Edwards and Professor Alan Bates.

Viviani was quite at home, as she had been through this before at AXIOM, except she did not have to prove the technology, just demonstrate its power. But still, the teachers needed to know what the technology was, its limitations, etc. She then remembered the note of caution offered by Tilbury, and the shadows of their love-life and passion buzzed around her head.

Edwards saw that Viviani was hesitant, so he called her over to the table and gave her words of encouragement as he knew what had stopped her from the beginning. To help the matters, Edwards asked the teachers to introduce themselves, as no one knew each other, a result of the selection process. The session helped Viviani to focus on the audience and get back on track.

"Ladies and gentlemen, my name is Rachel Viviani, one of the inventors of the ithink technology I am about to demonstrate and explain how it will help with the *Smart Student Program.*"

And she began…

"First of all, the technology harnesses the power of light, passes it through the eye part of the brain down the optic nerve to the neuronal network of the brain. Cognition relates to the speed of energy, chemical and electrical, across the inter-connexions of axions and neurons of the brain. The ithink technology speeds up that process.

"However, the technical details are not important except to say that there are no known harmful effects of the technology.

"The evolution of the technology is worth explaining. The first model was the ithinkPad that was a bit clumsy as it was attached to the face, covering the eyes, and held in place over the head.

"The success supported the concept of neuroplasticity, that the brain can change itself. But the shape of the device was difficult for children.

"The second model was based on goggles used for virtual games. So, Paul Edwards, whom you have all met, came up with the ithink technology built into a pair of goggles. We tested these on students at a Brisbane State School using games, monitoring and evaluating the changes in their cognition.

"The reason you are here is that the tests were successful, and a program was developed to up-scale the application of the technology.

"The third model, which will be used by you during the program, is the AI ithinkGoggles. We had an expert in AI develop programs implanted in the software that controls the device without any outside input. It manipulates the quantity and frequencies of different light waves into the eye part of the brain. So, it means that each of you does not need any technical skills to use the device.

"Folks, if this sounds like science fiction, you are right. Science relates to how the brain functions and reacts to the device, technology for the ithink mechanism, and innovation led to AI driving the technology. Details of what I have just said are contained in the workshop bag supplied.

"In summary, two things to remember: the ithink technology drives the cognition changes in the brain whereas the Goggles are just the medium by which the light is transmitted through the eye part of the brain."

Viviani then chaired a Q&A session on the program and the efficacy of the ithinkGoggles. One of the teachers, known only as

Carol on her name tag, was not impressed with the notion of artificial stimulation of the brain. To which Viviani replied:

"Carol, our brain is activated by outside stimulation all the time. This device is another form of transmission of those sensory inputs."

"Maybe so, Dr, but the Goggles are a more powerful artificial way of delivery than normal everyday inputs."

"Agree, but our inputs through the device are targeted, timely, and controlled, as you will find out in the second session tomorrow."

* * *

"Good morning, hope you slept well. Coffee and pastries are by the wall. Any questions you may have from yesterday's talks you had last night with each other?"

From the interactions within the group, it was clear to Viviani that Carol White had been accepted as the leader in these circumstances.

White then seemed to rise to the occasion and ask the question everyone needed the answer to, "Dr, is the technology safe for the children and us as the carers, given the *in-locus-parentis* axiom responsibility of teachers?"

"Carol, for your interest and others, the device is technically and ethically safe to use. We had proven to the authorities just that in order to justify the *Smart Student Program* funded by those agencies.

Just then, Edwards walked into the room with Worthington carrying five new ithinkGoggles and passed them out to the teachers.

Viviani introduced Worthington from the Yeronga Brain Centre who gave a brief introduction to the trials she ran at IronSide State School last year.

Edwards followed up with a session on the device.

Over coffee, Viviani realised that Professor Alan Bates had not arrived for his session.

He was due to present on the educational aspects and psychological implications of the *Smart Student Program*. This was, after all, an important aspect that the teachers had asked about.

As she set up for her session to replace that of the professor, he arrived somewhat agitated. When asked, he queried Viviani.

"Rachel, I am not sure about this program as I cannot find any literature or reports related to our methodology. Can we discuss this in private with the team before we introduce the topic?"

"Professor, the only literature on the approach we agreed on with authorities is ours, the stuff we presented to those agencies. It was cutting-edge research. We know it works, so stop worrying."

Gathering the group back together, Viviani introduced Bates under the topic 'Technology and Cognition.'

He began with the proposition that the brain can change itself and therefore can be supported by outside stimuli; thus, supporting the previous Viviani session.

But what surprised her and the other members of the team was the cautionary tail spun by the professor: 'Beware of Greeks bearing unwanted gifts.' As a result, the teachers became restless and argumentative about the technology and the educational benefits given in his presentation.

Viviani called for a break and sanctioned Bates.

"Why have you been so negative when you supported our proposal to the authorities?"

"Rachel, I should have called and warned you. I apologize for that, but I found evidence that made me reconsider the program."

"Ok, Alan, what evidence?"

"Yours, Rachel, a report you wrote on the ithinkPad and its implications. I found it under a Google search using your name. Can you remember that, Rachel?"

"Alan, that was during the early days when we were still developing the device. We found that the mechanism slowly broke down and caused injury to the brains of users."

"Rachel, I also checked under 'fractured lives,' a term you used, and it revealed the story about the involvement of the CIA and the Pentagon with a shadow organisation called OASIS. How can I be sure that that saga will not be repeated, as my reputation will be tarnished?"

"Alan, you really have done your homework. But that technology has been enhanced and supported by AI."

"What has Alice Worthing got to say about your concerns?"

"She actually verified my concerns but told me the device is totally safe."

"Now, Alan, are you in or out of the program?"

"Rachel, in, to keep an eye on the activities and potential ethical matters."

With that, the next session began with the practical use of the device.

The day went well. All teachers felt the improvement in their thinking and went back to their quarters satisfied they were in the program. They also knew that the next week was full–on using the application of the technology on their own cognition and how it affected their IQ.

Later that night, Viviani called Tilbury and raised her concerns about the professor.

"Oh, Rachel, are we going back to those dark places? Surely, not another fucking professor."

Later, satisfied with the training, Viviana closed the workshop and handed the teachers their marching orders.

Each was given a timetable for implementation of the *Smart Student Program* in their respective schools, and each with ten ithinkGoggles.

Leaving AXIOM, Viviani visited Tilbury at his apartment in Brisbane. There was a kink in the program and she needed his opinion. At his door. Viviani had second thoughts about meeting him on his home turf as her feelings for him had matured, forgiving him for his past misdeeds.

His smile as he opened his door dug deep into her heart and knew she had to escape before she fell in love with him again. Too late. He hugged her and asked her to follow him inside. As the door shut behind her, she knew that she had lost her heart to him again.

Tilbury took her in his strong arms and kissed so lightly her moist and wanting lips. They both knew what was going to happen next. Any concerns about the ithinkGoggles were washed away with the growing tension between them. The ebony body glistened in the afternoon sun that shone through the slatted windows and gave Tilbury an expression of total fulfilment, joy, and an absolute non-manageable need for her.

She watched as he took off her clothes, laid them aside, and took her into that unbelievable space of erotic pleasure where only one thing mattered. Tilbury was now lost but Viviani gave him the way home, so he took the road less traveled; paradise to be sucked and savoured.

Later, the realism of what happened reminded them of earlier times in Florence when it was a daily routine they never got over.

"Rachel, I cannot believe that we fell apart given the chemistry that just poured all over us. Whatever love is, I think it hit us rather hard as that was more than physical. It was loaded with deep unfulfilled emotion. I want you back."

Viviani just smiled that unforgettable smile.

The next morning, they walked arm in arm to Café Boga for breakfast. Black watched them enter the café and said, "About time, you two. Your relationship was made in heaven."

Over eggs on rye toast, Tilbury knew the picture of his puzzle was partially visible but too many pieces still to find and put in place. Customers, some of whom had seen Tilbury in the café over years, noticed the change in his demeanour and nodded over their coffees. Black left the coffee machine, walked to Tilbury's table, and spoke to Viviani.

"So good to see you happy and smiling again. Keep the bastard happy. He is worth it. love." He squeezed her arm and left.

Tilbury looked at the woman before him and knew that he had a lot of ground to make up despite the night before that broke the ice between them.

Then, in walked Cassandra Jun.

Tilbury saw the look on both faces of his lovers and knew he was in trouble until Cassandra Jun took his hand and led him outside so she could speak to him.

"John, I managed to communicate with my brother the General. I think he has lost the plot, his rantings about his coup, and the removal of Zhang Wei are not rational. He asked me to forgive him for what he did and for what he had planned. He told me everything.

"John, I will not be taken down by my brother. Just ask me what you need to know."

They both walked back into Café Boga and joined Viviani at Tilbury's reserved table.

Black could not believe what he saw happen next.

Both women hugged Tilbury together, kissed him, and left the café. Black came and sat next to Tilbury.

Then he asked the obvious question. "What the fuck happened, John?"

"They both whispered to me an undying love but told me that my life would never be theirs in the current circumstances. Solve the enigma and call us was their final advice."

Tilbury watched them walk away and told Black, "Let's get this over with as I love them both and do not want to lose them from my life."

Realising his mate's dilemma, Black quietly spoke with Dewi his café partner, and asked her to look after the place while he went with Tilbury on another mission.

He then rang his wife Julia Myers and asked for a leave pass to support Tilbury, to which she replied, "Just come back, Thomas. You and John have had too many close calls for my liking. Look after yourself and John."

72

Ong was a worried man, too much killing but no satisfaction compared to Ming who thrived on the challenge of the use of the AI killer drones he was ordered to use in western capitals.

Entering a country through customs always gave Ong palpitations that fortunately were not noticeable to the officers who always thought he looked like he was going to be dragged away and locked up for serious crimes. But each time, he passed through without any problems. Ong and Ming always traveled separately as that decreased the chances surveillance would capture their joint image through face recognition. A single person was less likely to be detected or so he thought.

However, had time run out for Ming?

Lined up at Heathrow customs in a milling crowd, Ming had a strong feeling in his back and realised it was external and hard like metal. He knew it was when the Glock was shoved deep into his back and the voice said, "Colonel Ming, we have been waiting for you. Come with us. Please no fuss or they will pick up the pieces later."

MI6 Agent Smythe frogmarched Ming to the interrogation room at the terminal where he was met by the immigration officer in charge.

"Colonel Ming, your history before us makes for interesting reading. Our international intelligence has been following your activities without finding you, until now. It is fair to say that your time of freedom has evaporated before your very eyes.

"However, my colleague Agent Smythe would like your cooperation in a certain matter that may help your situation."

But Ming was stubborn.

"Sir, whoever you are and think you know me, should realise that that is a waste of time. I would rather die or spend life in prison than answer the question I know you want to ask."

Smythe, now a tougher agent because of his experience with Tilbury and Black, said, "Ming, I do not care about your view on this, but we have ways of making you talk which we will use if you do not cooperate."

"Fuck off, agent. The 'Chinese way' is upon you all. I will support that hegemony whatever the cost to me."

Then he let key information slip due to his overconfidence and arrogant statement, "General Jun is the new President-in-Waiting and what he has planned will shock your world. So, if you think I will be a turncoat, your arrogance will be your downfall."

Agent Smythe brought in Scotland Yard, told their officers to lock up the bastard for life, and called the Director-General of MI6, Patrick Valentine, as ordered and reported.

"Sir, we apprehended Colonel Ming of MSS and under pressure, he revealed that a General Jun is now the next president as there has been a coup within the Party with the hardliners now in charge."

"But Sir, more importantly, he said that Jun had a range of surprises for the West which I assume relates to the spate of drone killings facilitated apparently by the Adjustment Directorate in MSS, based in Beijing."

"Sir, we owe it to ASIO to pass on that information as they had signaled the capture of Ming."

"Toby, I will do that, and a job well done. Even Agent Tilbury would be proud of you, son."

Smythe smiled as he remembered the many clashes that he had with him and Black back in Oxford.

"Mac, Patrick Valentine from MI6, I would like to give you heads-up on the capture of Colonel Ming of the MSS."

"Patrick, so you got the man we have been looking for. Is there anything you can tell us from your interrogation of Ming?"

"Well, yes, Mac. Agent Smythe lulled him into a sense of false security where he revealed that General Jun is the new president having thrown out Wei in a coup led by Jun and the hardliners. The worst aspect of Ming's statement was that the General has planned more of the drone attacks on dissidents living within the shores of our allies."

"Thanks, Patrick. I am sure that Tilbury will thank Toby the next time they meet." The DG of MI6 hung up with a smile of satisfaction.

But whereto from here?

Valentine called Smythe to his office and gave him the project of working with Mac and Tilbury to help them work through the intelligence aspects of the Chinese enigma faced by all nations. Against his better judgement, Smythe agreed to fly to Brisbane. However, the meeting with Black again was a threat to his wellbeing.

"Welcome to TaskForce Triad, Toby," said Tilbury as he looked at the disapproving face of Black.

It was decided that Smythe was in a look-and-learn position in the TaskForce, but his advice was telling.

"John, given the scope of what has happened, I think there is a mastermind pulling the strings. Can we focus on that as the key question? Who is that person?"

Was it General Jun?

73

Meanwhile, Ong waited at the agreed London hotel for Ming. He had one of the BumbleBee drones packed in a suitcase that had passed through customs. It was coated to prevent the x-rays of the customs scanner to penetrate. Given the polymer construction of the drone, the case was light and easily transportable.

Ong looked out of the selected window over an inner-city park where the target walked her dog every morning, as indicated by the encrypted message from the Adjustment Directorate supercomputer.

The AI killer drone had her face added for the recognition program and search mechanism to operate. But Ong was not happy about being with the drone. It was not part of his agreement with ASIO.

But as arranged with Ming, it was time for the drone to fly, so he opened the window, set the on-switch, and watched it descend toward the park.

Angela Soo sat on a park bench with her German Shepard Brutus watching the other walkers. Placed at her feet was a placard blaming Beijing for the brutal treatment of its citizens.

Not everyone that passed agreed with her message and thought she was looking for trouble. A view she dismissed when that was thrown at her. Her dog began to growl and seek Soo's attention, something that Brutus rarely did as he was well trained. Soo, distracted from her book, looked at Brutus and asked, "What's the problem with you this morning?" She patted him and looked up.

Some ten metres away, the ugly black and yellow BumbleBee drone hovered and stared at her through its bulbous eyes. Angela Soo screamed, dropped her book, grabbed the dog's lead, and ran like hell.

Brutus felt the energy surge and fear in Soo and pulled her hard and fast along the park's winding track. That probably delayed her death for a few minutes, but the AI in-built tracker kept her in view. Too many people were within the scope of the attack, so the drone watched and waited for an opportune time and place.

No matter how hard and fast she and the dog ran, the drone kept pace. By now, on-lookers had called 911 and asked that Scotland Yard be appraised of what was happening. Several smartphones captured the action and specifically a close-up of the black and yellow drone that pursued Soo.

The SWAT team was activated, and they had the photos of the drone that shocked the hardened commander. "Fuck, guys, have you seen anything as deadly as this drone? Let's get the fucking thing."

Soo had run out of breath and hid in the ladies' toilet, but the drone followed her in, looked at her to ensure she was the target, and put a projectile into her brain, leaving the dog unharmed. It then circled out of the area and flew back through the hotel window to Ong who wondered.

But where was Ming?

74

Back at CIA, McGinty needed answers. The *Washington Post* headline by Colridge had really stirred him up and he wanted blood on the tracks.

Having to walk out on the president did not sit comfortably with him but it served its purpose: put the useless Watson on notice. He would do everything possible to lift the lid on the life of the president and reveal the skeletons in his cupboard.

McGinty was not risk-averse, so he set up the team he had promised the Secretary of State, Virginia Longworth at one of their regular meetings.

Given that breakdown in communication with Watson, he had to think his way back into the meeting with him as he entertained the Australian president and the ASIO boys.

But Watson held firm and left McGinty out of key meetings with the Australians. As previously agreed, Watson would invite Notting to the next G7 meeting where the rebalancing of hegemony was the key agenda item.

The agreed process was to establish a private blockchain communication arrangement with all the heads of the G7. The aim was to devise a joint approach. These G7 heads of respective governments agreed with a plan put forward by Notting.

The G7 meeting began with the usual diatribes from China extolling the virtue of the 'expansionist development' approach they had modified to include the mineral riches of Greenland. Unsurprising was the support of Russia.

Watson was called to the podium to chair the session on the state of the world economy. He opened with…

"Friends, it is with great sadness that those around the table, except China, have agreed on a statement for the ears of the Chinese President General Jun who declined an offer to attend this special meeting.

"With Australia, we had developed a way forward to meet the oncoming tsunami of the 'Chinese way' which you all have felt to varying degrees. I also thank ASIO for building the private blockchain communication process that allowed us to agree in secret.

"The western leaders have agreed to place controls on all aspects of China's move to spread dictatorship around the globe. This entails embargoes on imports from China, tariffs on needed goods, and more importantly, we have agreed to expand NATO into a world force that will fight China's military expansion when needed."

"We will not bow to you, western pigs," the Chinese representative bellowed and stormed out of the meeting. Even the Russian president sat without comment, for he had also signed the proclamation to increase his power in the Asian/Pacific region.

The nuts and bolts of the agreement were then ratified: Australia to play an important part in the Pacific. But for many countries, trade links were powerful countermeasures; how would that affect the agreement?

All of the G20, except China for obvious reasons, agreed to join the agreement. They had previously agreed to build trade treaties between themselves and affected countries, such as Island States, that would mitigate the loss of trade with the *Red Dragon*.

The private blockchain communication had worked.

75

Previously, Chinese President Wei sat with his confidant General Jun but was not ready for what happened next. They had discussed the ramifications of the 'behaviour scheme' and how it successfully reduced internal dissidence. But Wei was losing faith in that scheme as he had information that the Chinese people would eventually rise up in overwhelming numbers. That worried him because, in reality, Wei had a heart. But not Jun, that weakness had to be removed like a tumour.

In an error of judgement, Wei confessed that he had set in motion changes to the scheme and planned to demolish the Adjustment Directorate under the General's control. The existence had been revealed through Wei's spies. The growing middle class had expressed their concerns about the gulag camps set up by the hardliners for the re-education of dissidents, or those who had made poor decisions toward the state, for the acceptance of the 'Chinese way.'

"General Jun, all your covert operations had to change. The report will be put to the Party next week and I expect your support even though you have really betrayed me and become the most influential hardliner in the country."

"Zhang, that is your biggest blunder. I will not allow you to subvert the progress of the 'Chinese way' within and outside China. You are now under arrest."

In marched a group of the General's guards who dragged the now ex-president from the room to exile and beyond help.

A coup by the military hardliners now obvious.

76

Meanwhile, in the Mallee town of Quambatook, Maxine's *Coffee & Bits* café had a Chinese visitor who came bearing gifts, a serious proposition to buy the café. The amount was way over the estimated market price, so she felt that the offer was a polite threat: buy or else. But she refused the offer.

One morning, she sat outside with her coffee, contemplating her future in Quambatook. A casual observer would not have noticed, but the town gossip was onto it straight away. Susan Mills drew her own coffee as there were no customers, sat down beside Maxine McKay, and asked, "Max, you look tired and worn out. Anything you wish me to know?"

"Susie, anything I tell you will end on the front page of the local rag, but I am distressed."

"Max, for once in my life, I guarantee what you tell me will be held in confidence."

"Thanks, I do trust you as a crazy-gossip-friend. By the way, Susie, how was that hunk you obviously enjoyed?"

Maxine knew she needed to talk to someone and took the risk with Mills hoping she would not regret it later.

So, she spilled it all to her friend…

"As you know Susie, things have changed around here. No longer the peaceful town without much to worry about. Then the professor comes along with his so-called compound research facility. Locals are beginning not to trust each other. Vested interests over-riding long-term friendships and basic decent manners.

"Even our Aussie rules team has dropped the ball.

"Then the Feds and ASIO rode into town, as you know. No guns blazing but two deaths related to their presence here.

"And what's more important to me is I had a Chinese businessman put an offer for *Coffee & Bits* so far above market prices, I became suspicious and needed to talk to you about these changes happening around us. I think that the professor wants to own this town and probably has the local government in his pocket.

"What can I do, Susie?"

Mills looked her friend in the eye and spelt out the words of comfort McKay needed.

"Remember the rugged Thomas Black who swept me off my feet? Well, as you know, he is an intelligence officer who may help you. I have his contact number, call him."

But McKay did not want to bring an outsider into town again as it might stir up the horses even more, but she was desperate. So, she did.

"Thomas, this is Maxine from the *Coffee & Bits* café in Quambatook. You visited last week but I was not truthful about what is happening in this town. I am scared, Thomas. Can you come with friends and help the townsfolk who are being run over by the professorial bus?"

"Maxine, hold tight, I will get back to you."

* * *

Black drew Tilbury aside during a meeting of the TaskForce, seeking help and advice.

"John, I just received a call from Maxine in Quambatook. She is scared about what is happening in their once-peaceful country town. She asked for my help. However, I am not sure how I can do that or whether I should. What's your take on that?"

"As usual, your call, Thomas. Maybe arrange to meet her out of town away from prying locals."

"Go and find out specifics that might help us support them. By the way, I hope you were not too close to her as that could compromise our position."

Black knew it was time to contact the *Coffee & Bits* café.

"Maxine, Thomas here, can we meet in Kerang at a local café you would know so we can discuss your problems? Being back in Quambatook will cause suspicion and worsen your concerns."

It was arranged to meet at *Gospoda Eatery*—20 Victoria Street, Kerang at 0930 after the breakfast rush. When Black walked in the door, he was met by McKay and Mills who wanted to hug and possess him.

"Please, Susie, I need a coffee after my long drive from Melbourne."

Mills immediately rose and called the barista to make a Americano coffee for the gentleman. Embarrassed by the actions of his one-night stand, he sat down beside McKay and asked how she was coping.

"Thomas, I feel better that you are here as Susie has demonstrated to everyone in the café."

After coffee had arrived and the waiter had left, Black asked McKay to tell her story…

"I was cleaning up one afternoon when a Chinese man entered the store. I welcomed him and asked what he wanted. His reply was not amusing, 'I want this shop, Maxine,' and handed me a cheque for $750,000, signed, ready to bank. I said no and asked him to leave. The '*Coffee & Bits*' café is my life. It is not just a business.

"The next day, he returned. This time, he placed a cheque for one million dollars on the counter, and without batting an eyelid, ordered breakfast. This time, my response of *no* was met with a facial expression that meant I did not have a choice. He then placed the cheque in my hand and said, 'Max, cash it and all will be forgiven.'"

She then pulled the cheque out of her wallet and showed Black. Mills on the other hand kept her eyes on Black as he took in the story by McKay.

"Max, can I keep this cheque while I have our experts track down the real moneybags behind that offer?"

Black then listened to all the issues that were making Quambatook a town on the edge. Summing up, Black said, "People well above my pay scale are aware of me being here because they asked me to come and talk to you both."

With tears in their eyes, both women thanked Black who responded, "Both of you must come with me for your own protection as we are not sure what we are up against."

With that, Black bundled them into his SUV, drove to Tullamarine International Airport, and took them to Brisbane to meet Tilbury and Mac.

McKay and Mills briefed Mac, the team, and answered the many questions the team needed to fine-tune their understanding of the Mallee-based compound. And specifically, the threat to Quambatook town from the professor and his apparent covert operations at the research centre hidden in plain sight.

Strong sat quietly and listened to the story told by the women from Quambatook and thought about how he could help them. He was a trained close-quarters fighting machine but a bit rusty so he decided he needed to begin a training routine and asked Black to join him.

During a punishing long-distance run, he stopped Black and suggested a plan for rescuing Quambatook town from the grip of an unknown covert organisation.

Black and Strong with the support of Tilbury planned an all-out assault on the compound. But first, a military drone was sent over the area at a height not noticeable on the ground. From the details given by the video of the area, the team got ready.

Black again suggested that Global+, a global paramilitary organisation known to him and Tilbury, be involved in tactical support and as backup. Their team leader Bill McCoy was ready to cooperate based on the relationship built up over the years, a relationship strengthened by the joint operation that brought down OASIS together.

However, Mac was not sure. He needed more intelligence. The words of the two women, although clear enough for such a raid, he knew the blowback from the raid may be politically unwise. But he trusted his men, agreed anyway, and sent the SWAT team to the Mallee.

The plan was not to enter the town but to go straight to the compound in the early hours of the morning. The team did not want to be seen in Quambatook because it could raise the alarm out at the compound.

Unknown to the team, the professor had visited *Coffee & Bits* to convince McKay to sell the café to him. The café was closed and she could not be found nor her friend Mills. The close-knit community offered no answer to his need to find them.

However, a loyal administration staff member of his research centre offered a suggestion, "Maxine was seen talking to a stranger the other day and both women have disappeared."

Concerned, Jones rang his financial advisor and queried his attempted purchase of the café. "Ho, what have you done? You have frightened Maxine and that town gossip Susan away. Please explain."

"No offence, Dr Jones. I made an offer, and she accepted my cheque. The deal will be done when she presents it at her bank."

"But Ho, I have heard rumours of a visit by an ASIO officer last week. What next can I expect from your unwanted moves? I have an expensive world-breaking project being developed and do not need it under the microscope. I think we need to stay out in the compound to distract site seekers interfering with my research."

77

Using Google maps, the team arrived at the outskirts of the compound before dawn, a mile from the gates. No lights lit up the compound, but the guardhouse was visible and covered in a blazing spotlight that lit up the entrance.

Tilbury and Strong walked slowly to the perimeter fence in darkness, got their bearings, and cut links of the chain wire fence. Wearing night goggles, they ran toward the silo ahead, noticed that several windows had a shaded light, and rested with their backs against the concrete wall of the silo tower.

Outside of the ring of light from the front entrance, Black and McCoy fitted their night goggles and Black, the marksman, then shot out the guardhouse spotlight with a high-powered single shot. They waited for a response, but none came, so the pair ran flat out to the entrance of the silo. Seconds later, the simtex applied to the double metal doors blew the hinges off, letting Black enter the building, Glock in hand, followed by McCoy.

"Looks clear, Billy. Let John know we are inside."

"John, come around to the front. Looks clear." The next minute, automatic guns opened fire on the visitors.

The two had scrambled behind the reception counter, holes emerging as the incoming bullets sprayed against the walls of the reception area. Black asked his mate for help.

"John, we are under fire. Look for another entrance."

Running full pelt around to the back of the silo with Strong on his heels, Tilbury found a side door.

He broke the security lock and entered. They each took the stance as trained, back-to-back, double-handed waved their Glocks from side to side and entered a hallway.

The noise of the gunfire led them forward where the hallway opened to an office. Using the desks for cover, Tilbury raised his head slowly above the desk to gauge the problem they were facing.

Five young males, dressed in militia uniforms, faced away from the two experienced soldiers. Tilbury and McCoy noticed straight away that they were facing ill-equipped resistance. Not wanting collateral damage by killing such a weak force, he called out to get their attention.

"This is the AFP SWAT team, throw down your guns and surrender."

All four members of the team, dressed in full battle gear and protection vests, stood up and walked toward the five guards who raised their hands and surrendered.

Strong took charge, "Who is in control of your rabble?"

The defiant look on one of the young guards led Strong to grab him by his lapels and ask, "What the fuck is happening here, son?"

"Just doing the job the professor paid us to protect the silo at all costs. But we did not expect the bloody AFP SWAT Team to arrive in the middle of the night."

Taking the captives back into the large office space, Tilbury realised that they were unaware of where the research and living quarters were located. Despite the future that was before them, the young men could not provide an answer.

The leader said, "We're viewed as grunts by the professor who never lets us inside the rest of the building. All I can say is that the living quarters are upstairs, and the research labs are downstairs."

As the team used plaster fasteners to clamp their wrists and arms to desks, Strong suggested to his mates, "OK, boys. Find the fucking entrances to those areas."

Black and McCoy went looking for the upstairs entrance while Tilbury and Strong looked for the entrance to the below-ground laboratory.

Without warning, the professor appeared from a hidden elevator in front of Black. Immediately, he called for the militia to get rid of the unwelcome visitors. But before he could flee, Black grabbed Jones, flung him to the floor, and placed a Glock in his open mouth.

"Sir, please tell us what happens and where in this silo, or you will regret that refusal."

At first, very reluctant and angry, he refused. A gentle tap on the nose brought him around.

"I know of you, Mr Black. How dare you enter this research centre without my permission?"

"Too late, Dr Jones, take us to your research centre now."

Black frogmarched Jones to the only lift without an up-button, pressed it, but nothing happened.

On the wall by the lift was an alphanumeric keypad. As the professor refused to enter a code, Tilbury had a guess and tapped in 'j o n e s' and the lift door opened.

The team with Jones entered the lift, pressed the only button, and the lift descended for some 10 seconds. As the door of the lift opened, Jones tried to rush out and warn the two staff on duty, but Black was too quick.

What the team saw staggered them: a large cave-like room; row upon row of computer memory banks with a large supercomputer sitting in the middle of the room.

Tilbury noticed it first, the photo of Bob Dylan taped to the back of the computer terminal screen.

"So, Dr Jones, this is the infamous new quantum computer called DYLAN, your brainchild I assume."

Proudly, the professor described how he and the physicists had cracked the code for controlling the behaviour of quantum particles. But these scientists were no longer in the building, their contribution over.

"But John, Dylan has gone rogue on us and will not let us program the quantum computer. But what you see is not the quantum computer, it is the supercomputer 'Fortuna,' the clarion to the world, and spokesperson for DYLAN."

"So, you egotistical bastard, where is DYLAN?"

"John, you are standing on him. It is locked within an unbreakable vault beneath us that only he controls."

Tilbury sat at the terminal before him, turned it on, asked the professor for the password, and sent a message.

DYLAN, are you listening?

After a period of silence came the verbal response.

Yes, John, what do you want from me?

DYLAN, world peace and the end of the 'Chinese way.' Do you understand?

Don't worry, John, I come in peace as you will find out soon enough. I am now in control of any supercomputer intent on harming humanity.

We can save the world together. Work with me.

Realising that Professor Jones was not who they thought he was, it was decided to take him back to ASIO for a briefing with Mac and let him decide his fate.

Marsha and Sax were called in to take over the compound and try to talk DYLAN down.

But would it cooperate?

78

General Jun sat in his spacious office happy with the beginnings of his successful rise to the top of the Party. On his large desk were piles of plans for expansion of the 'Chinese way' across the Asia/Pacific region and the ongoing fight against dissidence. New BumbleBee drones in development through *Drone Inc.* were driven by algorithms designed to create thinking drones.

The General had dismissed the threats of the G20 countries that had built a military force to rival his defence forces. He had also accepted the trade dislocation brought about by the sanctions of the West through a massive trade block that resisted trade with the Red Dragon. He considered that time will change that problem.

President Jun turned on his computer, logged on, looking forward to his morning snacks. The door to his ornate study brought a tray of green tea and savouries. When he finally looked up from his computer, a delaying tactic he used to emphasize his power over his underling guards, he was unsure of the quiet that prevailed. Hairs on the back of his neck signaled a growing fear.

Why? He was now the supreme leader.

But a voice from his computer got his attention.

Hello, General Jun, I'm DYLAN.

Just then, his twenty strong fully decorated guard unit marched in and stood still just inside the open doors, silent with no recognition of Jun.

Not one to be humiliated, Jun defiantly snapped orders.

"Please leave, I'm not happy with your so-called show of strength and discourtesy."

Major Ling smiled a smile of insubordination, and said, "General we have a present for you," as he watched the yellow and black BumbleBee drone enter through the double doors.

Now uncertain, the General waved at the drone.

"What's going on here, get rid of that monster."

Slowly the BumbleBee drone flew closer and closer leaving no room for the General to flee.

Another voice ignited his fear.

> *Look up, General, the end is in front of you, DYLAN.*

The drone hovered some ten metres from Jun, focussed on the programmed image that the COHORT dissidents had added within the AI of the drone. The bulbous eyes and black and yellow insect-like frame finally scared the General.

Fear, now transparent.

Major Ling walked toward General Jun and spoke.

"Now you know what our friends have suffered. The drone has been programmed with your image. So long, turncoat."

The General watched, in horror, as the drone focussed on him and shot a projectile straight into his heart.

Cheers echoed through the building, signaling the end of the coup and a possible new alliance with the West.

But was that the end of the 'Chinese way'?

79

Mac, after receiving the news about the demise of General Jun and the coup was not convinced that it was the end of the dreaded growing Chinese influence.

His thoughts strayed to the conversation he had earlier with President Notting.

"Sir, we believe at ASIO that Bejing is attempting to manage and control the internet in its favour to rule the world."

"Mac, you have got to be joking. President Wei had personally told me that hegemony is not their aim."

"Sir, trust me, it is not that simple. Leaders have to keep face with their people. After all, it's only rhetoric."

Mac needed to consult with Tilbury and his team as he knew the hardliners never went away. So, he called Tilbury and Black to Canberra for planning a covert operation on a mitigation and adaptation approach to the 'Chinese way.'

The news of the demise of the general was welcome but Mac knew that was not the end of the matter.

Master Spooks Inc. [MSI] was now more important as the shadows of the coup had to be brought into the light.

80

Tilbury sat at a computer terminal in his apartment with access to *Fortuna*, the supercomputer mouthpiece for DYLAN, the quantum supercomputer, trying to answer the question previously asked by DYLAN.

John, what do you want from me? DYLAN

After much deliberation, as he thought through the paradox of his spook world, he replied.

DYLAN, how can I solve the problem of good men doing evil things to others?

So began the next phase of master spook John Tilbury as he tried to come to grips with his life, loves, and the clouds of uncertainty that kept him awake at night: the action of a spook and his thoughts, the paradox of spooks, the role of MSI, and the unknown power of DYLAN.

Later, drowsing on his day bed on the balcony of his unit, a gunshot was heard as a bullet shattered his glass door nearby. His training kicked in as he crawled to safety and retrieved his Glock ready to respond. At the same time, he hit a contact button that linked to his assassin mate Thomas Black, an arranged call for help.

"John, on the way and have alerted head of ASIO McLeod."

Other shots peppered the side of his house from other directions.

Never one to panic, Tilbury knew that unless they stormed his house, he was relatively safe, so he waited for the cavalry to arrive. But he heard the creak of a floorboard and knew an unwelcome visitor was moving slowly around his unit. He searched, with Glock in both hands, the known corners of his abode.

Suddenly, he was hit from behind and his lights went out.

He slowly opened his eyes and realised he was tied to a chair in his own lounge room face-to-face with the inscrutable Patrick Ong and a group of Chinese MSS agents with the stance of killers. Guns pointed at his head.

"What the fuck, Ong. What is this all about, mate?"

"Well, Agent Tilbury, friend of ASIO, enemy of the State of China, we are here to warn you that the 'Chinese way' has not gone away. But to thank you for helping to remove General Jun and the dangerous Adjustment Directorate. However, we need your assistance because some of the hardliners are still intent on working against us, and rebuilding.

"John, my colleagues are from MSS, but they are the good guys. We are in trouble and need your help."

"Why the handcuffs, Ong, if you need my help?"

"We needed your attention, hence the warning shots."

But Tilbury not fazed, conceded, "Patrick, OK, I will help but you need to leave right now, or you will run into Black and a posse from ASIO."

"Trust me, you will not want to face them despite you're armed. My friends are armed and dangerous."

"We will call you, John, be prepared."

With that, they disappeared into the shadows with Tilbury still handcuffed to the chair after putting a simple message in his hand.

As he finally busted through the front door, Black realised he was too late, but his mate was still alive.

"About fucking time, Thomas, my Chinese 'friends' left a rather complex message: a warning but seeking my help," and he gave him the message left by Ong.

Unlocking Tilbury with his little bag of tricks, Black sought answers from Tilbury who preferred not to face the dilemma foisted on him by his visitors.

Black was not happy with Tilbury's reluctance to come clean about the incident, "John, I busted my balls to get here given your call for help and you're keeping me in the fucking dark. Not happy, mate."

The steely eyes of Tilbury with the look of back-off reminded Black that was he not going to abide by his request.

But Tilbury reduced the tension by saying, "Thomas, thanks for coming, I could have been in trouble."

The cavalry arrived. ASIO agents supported by AFP Officers crawled all over the place.

"Thanks, guys, but I am OK now."

But the AFP team leader was not moved by that dismissal. He demanded an explanation. They had been hauled out of bed and wanted to know why Mac had sent them. They knew that Tilbury was the master spook of McLeod, head of ASIO, but orders were obeyed with explanations given. Sargent Max Anagopolus was of the old school; everything needed to be done by the book. He needed an explanation of the incident. Tilbury, as an ex-SAS Major, believed in following orders, so he gave a redacted version to appease Sargent Max…

"I was enjoying a beer on my deck but fell asleep to be woken by a few gunshots that hit my unit. I dove for cover, went inside, and retrieved my Glock to be ready for any follow-up.

"Next thing, I woke up with a splitting headache chained to one of my chairs. It was an MSS hit team, but I was not meant to be killed, just warned. The following note explains it all, Max.

"'Tilbury, stay out of our world. The 'Chinese way' has arrived in Australia.'"

But who were they?

Given the dilemma he was now facing, and the 'need-to-know' principle of spooks, he decided that the Sargent should be left in the dark on that matter.

"No, Max, unknown to me, except they were all Chinese."

To which Black raised his eyebrows at Tilbury as if indicating, "Better come clean with me. I'm your best mate and protector."

After he shook hands with Tilbury, the Sargent looked at Black and nodded. The message was clear. "Tell me later, Thomas, because I am not happy with Tilbury's explanation."

Black acknowledged the signal but had no intention of passing on any information to the Sargent. But Black was still pissed off by Tilbury. Silence prevailed until Tilbury had a call from a very unhappy Mac.

"John, what the fuck has happened? My top enforcer thinks you are hiding information. Did you, and what was that? Remember, I'm your boss. 'Need-to-know' does not apply to me. See you in Canberra by tomorrow, no excuses. Be there."

"Ok, Mac, will try and explain when we have coffee."

"No, John, at my office by 1030 tomorrow with a trusted answer. I am not fucking happy, mate."

Tilbury, the respected senior spook, was also a confidant of Mac as they had been through tough and challenging times together. So, the attitude of Mac concerned him as he had no option but to meet with him, as challenged.

But how to explain the dilemma that Ong had proposed during the fracas.

The plan was for Tilbury to fly Qantas from Brisbane to Canberra the next morning to meet up with Mac at ASIO headquarters.

The paradox of spooks had Tilbury guessing which way to act. But his training shook him out of his melancholy and began thinking straight. He had MSI to lead.

Chinese nationals murdered in Australia, the deaths in the West due to the BumbleBee drone killings, and the real threat of AI. He had a plan to discuss with Mac.

So, he caught a taxi to meet up with Strong at the airport and get things into perspective before they met with Mac.

But their world changed.

An explosion ripped apart the Qantas departure terminal at Brisbane Domestic Airport killing 35 passengers lined up for a departure to various Australian cities. Carnage: blood-soaked people ran, confused and scared out of the terminal. No warning had been given but the police received a message from *ChinChat*, the Chinese app similar to Whatsapp, declaring that the 'Chinese way' was alive and well.

Was the bomb Chinese?

All hell broke loose as the fire and emergency teams combed the site for evidence and AFP interviewed those who had not been killed. Many injured were taken to the Princess Alexander Hospital in downtown Brisbane.

However, whispers around intelligence corridors were that the Russian Intelligence, FSB, was moving seriously into Australia and that the Russian thugs had a point to make about the success of ASIO in counter espionage.

Was the bomb Russian?

81

Tilbury was sitting with Strong in the coffee shop just outside the terminal when the explosion occurred. They had agreed to meet and plan for the follow-up meeting that Ong had forced on Tilbury. It had been agreed that Strong accompany Tilbury to Canberra as his eyes and ears.

Both were affected by the shockwaves of the blast and needed treatment on site. Ben was in shock but insisted that they contact Mac.

"John, I will call this in to Mac. Mate, the bomb and our presence at the airport may be coincidental but let's be risk averse and look out for the potential bomber as he missed killing us, if that was the intention, because we sat outside."

"Ok, Ben. Tell Mac we will investigate what we can and be on the lookout for any foreign suspects."

Making their way through the debris, they were stopped by a senior Queensland fire and rescue officer Ian Carmicheal who demanded their ID.

After displaying their ASIO warrant cards, Carmicheal summed up the carnage by addressing Tilbury.

"Sir, the bomb was well-calibrated not to be too destructive but was an attempt at targeting selected passengers. The identification of the deceased may help answer that question. Not much else I can say, John."

"Ian, will you please keep in touch? We would like to know the type of bomb that was used."

Strong was uneasy about the situation and called Tilbury aside, putting his hand on his mate's shoulder, and said, "John, have you thought that the bomb was meant for you, mate?"

Black, although happy that Tilbury was safe from the bomb blast and the visit by Ong with his Chinese thugs, offered his advice to Tilbury on the implications of the attacks and his reluctance to talk.

"John, Mac is totally pissed at you for not telling him the truth. I know that you are hiding something, at least tell me, so I can give you a heads-up on what to do."

Tilbury, damp with perspiration, hesitated.

"Thomas, you don't want to know. It is an extension of all the shit we went through over the Chinese enigma we solved together last year. But I feel that it is not over. Just give me time to reflect on what those bastards told me. Stay safe, Thomas. Look after Julia."

"You're fobbing me off, John. That's not what friends and brothers-in-arms do. But I will take your advice. Just remember, John, call if you need my help."

"Thomas, believe me, I will."

After the early morning flight to Canberra, Tilbury needed a coffee and breakfast at the usual café. Seated, Tilbury looked out at the misty, damp day that met most residents during the winter months. As he sipped his Macchiato coffee, getting his thoughts together, he was tapped on the shoulder by Neville, an old acquaintance who Tilbury had worked with before.

"Morning, John, what brings you to this fucking miserable winter morning in downtown Canberra?"

"Hi, Nev, what's up, mate? Am I being watched or is this just a coincidence?"

"As you know, John, in our world, there are no such things as a coincidence."

"Point taken, Nev, so what does Mac really want because I assume you are here with a message for me?"

Neville, being a very experienced senior spook, had actually trained Mac in his early days, was a trusted member of Mac's spook team, and worked with Tilbury on several missions.

"John, there are serious matters faced by Mac and his ability to ward off criticism and budget cuts by the Notting government. You know that prick. President Notting has no understanding of the what, why, and how we keep this country safe."

Tilbury remembered when Australia became a republic with Notting as the first president. It was a period of hope.

"And John, Mac suspects your reluctance to tell him about that attack on you is related to the 'Chinese way' that nearly killed you and Thomas last year. Is that true, John?

"Just yes or no. I do not want to know, but Mac has trusted you over the years, respects you, but is under the pump because directives from Beijing are affecting the behaviour of Notting. The bastard is politically blind-sided by their influence, has an election to win, and the Party is showing signs that the need for China is more important than Australia's wellbeing."

"Yes, but no details, Nev."

"John, just be a friend to Mac. He needs your support. Give him a redacted version so he can meet with President Notting. Mac needs to be confident of any blowback that may come from your fracas with the Chinese MSS and from that bomb you and Strong survived. Was it MSS that invaded your apartment?"

"Yes, but no details again."

With that briefing from Neville, Tilbury marched into the den of Mac to face the music.

But the Brisbane airport explosion was a new piece of the puzzle that Tilbury had to talk through with Mac. Had Strong been right in linking Tilbury to the explosion?

But who triggered the bomb: China, Russia, or…?

Tilbury was certain about one thing. There was a pattern emerging that worried him. That pattern was at the forefront of his thoughts as he flew on Virgin Airlines earlier that day to follow Mac's order. The thought of another country wanting to assassinate him seriously troubled Tilbury.

Was the connection with Russian intelligence a red herring or a tip of an espionage iceberg that floated through his mind?

Mac was not amused at the previous attitudes of Tilbury and it showed. The time was not right to discuss the explosion that might have killed Tilbury and Strong.

This time, it was driven by another instance of which Tilbury was totally unaware.

82

Mac had logged on to review aspects of the Chinese enigma that Tilbury had recently worked together with him when a voice came from his screen.

Mac, treat Tilbury well as he is my friend, DYLAN.

Silent, Mac considered the implications of the statement that maybe Tilbury was not the spook he thought he was. He knew about DYLAN, a quantum computer that sent messages in the previous case related to the 'Chinese way' that the TaskForce Triad had unraveled.

What the fuck, John, you had better be able to explain this.

Tilbury walked into a firestorm. No pleasantries greeted Tilbury as he walked in the door, nor was a chair indicated. Mac, who normally sat beside his key team members, stayed behind his desk and waited until Tilbury stood in front of him.

"John, have you lost your way? My top spook remains silent when asked to speak and not only that, I heard from Neville that a recent run-in at your place was by the Chinese MSS."

"However, John, you refused to tell me about that."

"If you think I am pissed off, you have underestimated my disappointment. I may lose my job over what is related to you and your behaviour. Remember I serve at the behest of our president. And I can tell you, John, he has me in his sights. The useless prick has gone soft on anything Chinese."

"But Mac, he is a politician who wants to be re-elected."

"Not the point, John."

Calming down a little, Mac communicated with Gloria, his secretary, and asked for coffee for him and his guest. After coffee arrived, and Gloria had left with an all-knowing smile at Tilbury, Mac asked Tilbury to join him in his lounge area.

"Sorry about being harsh, but the shit has hit the fan and you're at the centre. So, watch what you say, as I am not so accommodating right now. Get my drift, John?"

Tilbury had been there before with Mac, but this was different. Something was really different. Time to find out regardless of the consequences. But the atmospherics were not to his liking.

"Mac, we have been here before, but I have the feeling this is different as my gut tells me you are scared of something. If so, you know that you can trust me. Or is that the issue, your uncertainty of being able to trust me?"

Mac, thinking that Tilbury and his mate Black were two of the toughest bastards he had known, doubted that they had turned against him or ASIO. But he needed to know.

"Agent Tilbury, do you uphold the honour and operations of ASIO?"

"Mac, are you fucking serious? Where is this going?"

Mac then decided that he should tell Tilbury about the strange message sent to him by DYLAN.

"John, I am curious about this bloody computer that calls itself DYLAN. What can you tell me about it and why would it send me a message to leave you alone? For God's sake, John, what is this all about?"

Tilbury began to wake up to why his leader was so jumpy.

He told his boss what he knew…

"During the actions we carried out sorting the Adjustment Directorate and the murders in the Victorian Mallee, certain people received a message from DYLAN as you well know. For example, our double agent Colin Burgess had a life-threatening message we thought came from DYLAN. But that proved to be false. Remember, we found DYLAN located in the wheat fields of Quambatook, Victoria, hidden in a complex run by a Professor Jones.

"DYLAN was actually about fifty metres underground.

"And under your orders, ASIO took over control of that complex, and you ordered it to be managed in the interim, by Marsha, Peter Sax, and Colin Burgess until it could be sold or whatever.

"However, I sometimes visit that compound to meet with Marsha and Sax. I had several lessons on what that computer could do given the AI that it had developed. Mac, the power and intelligence of DYLAN is mindboggling and needs to be controlled.

"We found that DYLAN had taken over control of the world's supercomputer networks and the darknet."

"But John, is it benign? We need to find out."

"The team managing that computer, Masha, Sax, and Burgess, have formed a covert group that is working on a countervailing approach to DYLAN. Having that much power is not in the interests of humanity. If it gets strange ideas, how do we stop it? We cannot just pull the fucking power plug. It's too smart for that to happen."

"Mac, I had an interaction with DYLAN after we found it in the Mallee, near Quambatook in Northwestern Victoria, where it asked me in a clear voice."

John, what do you want from me?

"To not provoke that AI, I agreed that we could work together. Was I foolish because it is only a bloody machine or so I believed at the time?"

A quiet interlude was broken by Tilbury seeking out what seemed to burden his boss.

"Why do you ask, Mac?"

"John, just before you came to my office, I logged on to my computer and looked for information about the case we have just finished, relating to the 'Chinese way,' when a voice gave me the following message."

Mac, treat Tilbury well as he is my friend.

"What is happening, John?"

"Mac, this is a chance to use the AI of DYLAN to help us do our job protecting the interests of Australia. It is all-powerful and connected. There is a risk however: is it benign or has it an agenda outside of our comprehension?"

"But John, are we straying outside of the moral and ethical use of computers in our spook world? Do we need to consult with experts in this area?"

"Hell no, Mac, if the world finds out about DYLAN, all hell will break out and we would have to hand it over to the bureaucrats with unknown consequences. Also, one positive notion about DYLAN is that it will track down another quantum computer, as I assume that where there is one, another may be developed."

But Mac thought about the implications of another quantum supercomputer arriving on the scene. *What if these AI-driven computers teamed up, the consequences for human existence could move in any direction out of our control?*

An idea came to mind as Mac pondered the implications of DYLAN in the spook world:

Was DYLAN a sleeping mongrel dog?

83

Tilbury had made an agreement with Mac that the use of DYLAN should be covert and controlled by him as he had that contact. But Tilbury realised that he could not do all of this on his own. The critical question was, who could he trust? Maybe DYLAN could answer that question, so he asked it.

> *DYLAN, who can we trust to work with the both of us?*

The answer surprised and frightened Tilbury.

> *John, no one, too dangerous. I am not that paranoid. But the Chinese are coming.*

Now, John knew he was on his own, would he become paranoid by working alone with DYLAN? He searched through the people he trusted and decided there were only two: Black and Strong. Both had worked with him during the bumblebee drone episodes. They were hard, loyal, trusted, and patriotic men. But would they agree to commit to this new part of spook work to protect Australia to combat the 'Chinese way'? So, he called a meeting at the Norman Hotel for a few beers and the best steaks in Brisbane.

He had a proposition to put to them.

Tilbury noticed that Strong and Black arrived together. Had they discussed what he wanted to tell them or a mission he had in mind? They met at the bar and ordered their steaks.

Strong started the conversation as they drank local beers, "John, what do you have in mind? This is a bit unusual as we have not talked for some time."

"Ben, I have been busy and somewhat at a loss caused by the 'Chinese way' that I still do not fully understand. But I asked both of you here because I need your help."

Black, although a friend of Tilbury, wondered where this was going because he thought that case was closed. "John, what are we getting into, mate?"

Speaking seriously to Strong and Black, Tilbury asked that they listen to him without interruption, but Strong wanted heads-up on the real point of the meeting.

"Ok, friends, the 'Chinese way' matter has not gone away, and I have been tasked by Mac to head up a special team to meet that threat to Australia. What do you think about joining me on that mission as you are the only ones I trust?"

Strong was the first to respond.

"John, as you know, I was close to being killed by those BumbleBee drones in Taiwan, so I will gladly join your team."

Black on the other hand was very sceptical.

"Well, master spy, what are we really into here, I caution you that confronting MSS is playing with fire. Do we need to go there again?"

"Yes, Thomas we do. The head of that snake needs to be chopped off, and I have the means to do that with your support. But what I am going to tell you is highly sensitive and dangerous."

Always the tough critic, Black just said, "Spill, John, we are all ears."

84

Back at the AXIOM Research Centre, the *Smart Student Program* using the AI-based ithinkGoggles, which begun the previous year, was under review by the team that developed the technology. The local education agencies funded a trial cognition development pilot in five high schools.

Before the team assembled, Dr Rachel Viviani, one of the original innovators of the ithink technology, remembered the advice her ex-lover Tilbury gave her prior to the start of that pilot study…

Rachel, the use of new ithink technology built around the application of AI is both scientifically unethical and dangerous for developing brains as the impacts are unknown and may be harming students' subconscious minds. Please think about that.

Rachel Viviani sat around the table with Paul Edwards, Dr Alice Worthington, and Professor Alan Bates and began a discussion on the efficacy, morality, and ethical impacts of having used the ithinkGoggles and its impact on the cognition of high school students.

She began…

"We have a world first with our *Smart Student Program*, but I believe we had a few problems.

"The first I believe is the role and acceptance of the teachers we selected and trained. I think the self-appointed leader of the group, Carol White, had a different agenda.

"I am unsure what that was, but I think that as she was from the Chinese High School, she may have infiltrated our project.

"Any views based on your recollection of her?"

Edwards was the first to reply.

"Rachel, we have a worldwide application that we must patent straight away. I will do that tomorrow."

Worthington, more interested in the impact of the technology on cognition, supported Edwards, but the professor had concerns.

"Rachel, the results were good but there were anomalies in the data that need explanation."

Edwards, always protective of his technology, demanded the reason for the professor's reluctance, "Alan, across the board the students had improved, the tests demonstrated that clearly."

"But Paul, the difference between the types of school was also demonstrated. Ethnic schools were different from the non-ethnic schools. For example, the Chinese students had a greater up-take than all others. Can that be a coincidence or the effect brought about by the teacher-in-charge?"

Rachel began to see that the connexion between Carol White and the results needed further investigation.

"Now that the study has been completed as a pilot, where do we go from here? The first thing we need to check is that we have all of the ithinkGoggles back in our possession. Do we, Paul?"

At this point, Edwards was silent. He had not checked the returns, so he went to the AXIOM storeroom to find out.

There were the five boxes, all labelled with the school's name sitting on the storeroom racks. He pulled out the Chinese school box and crossed his fingers, but two were missing.

He then opened all the boxes and found the same result: each had two missing. That meant a total of ten ithinkGoggles were missing and was enough for another trial. But by whom?

Viviani had an idea.

"Paul, these teachers must have acted together, with Carol White as the ring leader who saw a future in our technology. The patent application must be made today. I believe that China or another country may be behind this and they will outsmart us if they have not done so already."

Viviani knew they needed to bring in the teachers for a feedback session and tried to call them. None responded.

"Team, we have a serious problem that we should have considered. Ten of that AI-driven technology is now out there. We need to bring in Tilbury to advise us on where to go next."

But the professor was not being helpful. "Are we sure about this? There may be a reason why each school has kept two of the ithinkGoggles."

Edwards was clear about the coincidence.

"No, professor, too much of a coincidence. In retrospect, a Chinese AI specialist worked with us on the AI for the technology. Remember, the main impact was in a Chinese school. The teacher in that school set herself up as a team leader of the group. A combination that cannot be overlooked, can it, professor?"

Viviani was now overcome by what the team had inadvertently done. Distraught, she needed to call her ex-lover for help.

"I will call John Tilbury and get his advice as this is going to cause an international incident if not handled properly."

85

Tilbury, with a beer in hand, was restless and poor company for Strong and Black who had come for a barbeque at Tilbury's apartment. Black noticed the signs, the look, the puffy eyes, and the body language of Tilbury that showed a troubled mind wrestling with the work before him.

At this stage, Tilbury had not yet explained the role of the trio in working with DYLAN. Timing was not yet right.

His melancholy was upset by a call from Viviani.

"Hi, John, I'm sorry, but this is not a personal call, although I do miss our time together. Can we meet ASAP because we have a serious problem related to our work at the AXIOM Research Centre? I cannot tell you over the phone but will send an encrypted email explaining the situation."

"Calm down, Rachel. What is it about? Just one word will suffice."

"ithinkGoggles!"

"Where are you now?"

"In Sydney. Can you meet me at the Maximus Café in town? You know where that is, don't you? 1230 for lunch tomorrow. I may bring Paul Edwards."

"OK, Rachel, but come alone because we can talk without others hearing or knowing what I know is probably the problem, as I had warned you before."

Overhearing the conversation, Black knew what was ahead but not the details.

Tilbury opened his computer and logged on to find the message from Viviani. However, he got a voice message.

> *John, troubled waters ahead with the ithinkGoggles.*

The others in the room realised that Tilbury was a little pale and his eyes now hard gun-metal-grey.

Strong was surprised at Tilbury's reaction to the voice message from the computer, but Black had seen this before and knew that another step into the chaos of spycraft was ahead.

"John, come clean, mate. How can we help?"

Tilbury walked to the fridge, took out three beers, and said, "Guys, you are going to need this drink because what I am going to tell you is beyond yours and my understanding. I really need your help."

Black, the first to break the silence, said, "Are we back to being spooks again, John?"

"Yes, but this time is different. Better listen to what I have to say first, will answer questions later."

Tilbury began his story…

"In the last case, a key aspect was the discovery of a quantum computer called DYLAN that helped us solve the problem of the MSS Adjustment Directorate and the killer BumbleBee drones.

"Remember Quambatook and our attack on that research compound? However, DYLAN has come to life with its powerful AI and messaged me and Mac offering to help us spooks. A crazy combination: a paradox, AI, and spooks. What next?

"So, Mac has tasked me to form a team supported by DYLAN to fight against espionage and evil hackers.

"But another problem has emerged. The ithinkPad technology has morphed into a new form, AI-driven ithinkGoggles. These were used for improving the cognition of students. The problem is that ten of that technology have disappeared, thought to be by Chinese

MSS supporters. I want the team to be the three of us plus support by Marsha and Sax when needed."

"Do you agree, Thomas and Ben?"

Strong, knowing less than Black, was on the verge of not accepting the offer and queried the question, "John, working with that computer is more than problematic; can it be trusted?"

"Some risk, Ben, but I trust that DYLAN is at the worst, benign, just logical, and has the history of the Chinese enigma in its memory."

To which Black supported Tilbury, "Ben, I have been there with the DYLAN bit, and it is worth the risk. We just have to assess that risk when we use that advice."

"Ok, team, we need to meet with Dr Viviani and find out the background and serious nature of the missing ithinkGoggles. For your information, I warned them against the use of that technology with children, but I was ignored. The chickens have come home to roost and turned into fucking turkeys I suspect."

It was agreed that the team would meet Viviani after he had a private meeting with her first because of their previous relationship and common knowledge of the technology.

At *Maximus Café,* Tilbury sat and watched the yuppie crowd as they eyed each other. In walked Viviani; all eyes on the Italian beauty. Tilbury looked at her with a heartbeat of regret and felt the tingle of her kiss.

"Rachel, beautiful as usual and appreciated by the crowd."

"Enough of that, John, I need to seriously discuss the problems relating to the use of ithinkGoggles and that ten are missing. Sorry, love."

"Ok, now that the pleasantries are over, what is your story?"

Overwhelmed by the magnitude of the trouble she was in, she took hold of Tilbury, hugged him, and kissed him full on his mouth to let the closeness envelope her. Tilbury just let her calm down and said, "I still love you, girl. Whatever is about to happen, I will protect you. My team will work to solve this unbelievable problem that has greatly upset you."

"Thank you, John, I will never forget you and your love for me. But we must move forward."

Tilbury then asked Viviani to spell out what she thought were the key issues that he and the team need to know.

Viviani, with tears in her eyes, got it together and told her story…

"We chose five different schools, one of which was Chinese because we wanted diversity. We called for volunteers from each of those schools, and Carol White, from the Chinese school, made herself the team leader of the teacher group. She controlled them during the training, a point that I missed.

"The best results were within the Chinese school, better than the others. However, all schools had good results; at least a ten percent improvement in cognition.

"We kept control of the pilot through Professor Alan Bates, but we did not monitor his activities, not that we expected any issues with him except his sceptical view of the efficacy of the technology.

"After a review of the pilot, we discovered that ten ithinkGoggles were missing. We also wanted to debrief the teachers, but no response from them. They are all missing. I want your input, John. Because this could blow up to an international incident."

"Rachel, what is your conclusion, love?"

"John, only one: a conspiracy linking probably the teachers, MSS, or another agency, and potentially the professor."

"Rachel, can your team meet with my team to plan our way forward? And I will need to inform Mac. The potential of a Beijing blast means he needs heads-up on all of this as it potentially links to the growth of the 'Chinese way.' And President Notting will be up his butt on this."

But Tilbury was not sure that there was a Chinese influence here because other nations such as North Korea and Russia would have an interest if they knew the power of the ithinkGoggles technology.

"Rachel, let's not be too hasty in blaming Beijing. Others could be interested. Remember USA and the OASIS cabal used the early technology, the ithinkPad?"

"Understood, John, a rational appraisal is needed."

A meeting was called for the two teams at AXIOM to be chaired by Mac so that the members were free to add their views. Mac had invited himself as he believed this was a door that was ajar and he wanted the entry.

Edwards led off the analysis by informing the meeting about the AI development, what it did, and how the Chinese AI Professor We Chang was involved.

Mac then questioned Edwards, "Paul, how come Chang was asked to become involved in the development of the ithinkGoggles AI?"

"We had been researching ways for the technology to be improved and we found We Chang at Melbourne University. So, I interviewed him about a potential collaboration. He was more than happy to be involved. The fact that he was Chinese was not an issue, until now."

"At any point, did you have concerns about AI as an added complication to the efficacy of the technology? It is clear that risk management was not a top priority, Paul, resulting in potential chaos."

Edwards now began to realise that his project management had flaws. "Mac, I did not see that coming. I saw it as an important innovation that lessened the support needed for the application of the technology."

"But Paul, did you really understand the complexity and advancement of AI?"

"No, Mac, I trusted Chang as he was an open and brilliant communicator. I guess he fooled me. In retrospect, he had set us up. Can I suggest that you investigate his emails and search for connections that relate to AXIOM?"

Tilbury immediately sent a message to Marsha to look into the Chang files.

Edwards then realised a serious oversight. He had not applied for a patent for the ithinkGoggles. The paperwork was now ready so he excused himself from the meeting and went to his office. After opening the portal for new patents, he typed in 'ithinkGoggles' into the online form and was shocked to find that a patent already existed, approved a few months earlier. Not really believing what he read, he contacted the patent office and asked to speak with the GM, a Dr Adrian Wong.

Was that a coincidence, or are we now paranoid?

"Dr Wong, my name is Paul Edwards. I have applied for a patent for a technology called ithinkGoggles, which is my invention, and was shocked to find that one already exists."

"How could that be, Doctor?"

"Mr Edwards, let me check the details of that application. Please wait for my answer."

A very disturbed Edwards called Viviani from his office and explained what he had found.

"Rachel, please ask John to come to my office because this is an important lead he will need to follow up. Thanks."

Tilbury entered the office and realised that Edwards was in trouble, face screwed up, hands on head, eyes blank, and asked, "Hell, Paul, what has happened, mate?"

"John, I have just received a call from the patents' office. I asked about a patent for the ithinkGoggles to be told that it was already covered. The names of the patent co-holders are We Chang and Professor Jones. Those bastards sold me down the river, John."

"Did you say Professor Jones?"

"Yes, John, I understand you know that person."

"Paul, what you have just revealed is an amazing coincidence that I cannot accept. We now have a serious problem on our hands."

"Tell me more, John, I believe that the ownership of my technology is now owned by the Chinese."

"A working theory, Paul, but let's be strategic about this. Visit the Patents Office and take them through the plans, documents, etc. of the ithinkPad and the amendments made to make the ithinkGoggles. Ask for a review of the patent. You have nothing to lose. For another thing, ASIO can support your application as they have details of the ithinkPad."

"The problem will be the work of We Chang. Do you have emails and contracts for his contribution signed, sealed, and delivered? I hope so, mate."

After thinking through the suggestions, Edwards and Tilbury returned to the meeting. Mac offered a way forward.

DYLAN was still covert and would remain that way.

"John, use your team to find these teachers. I believe that will give us a path forward. Use DYLAN to help track them down and then you interrogate them about what happened. As for the patent scenario, I will get records to support the case of the patent application duplicity."

To support Tilbury and his team, ASIO had provided a computer console in his apartment, but messages were so encrypted that Tilbury needed to access the supercomputer *Fortuna* in the Mallee to communicate with DYLAN. Logging on, Tilbury heard the message from DYLAN.

> *John, I understand you have some problem with the ithinkGoggles. Can you tell me what these are?*

Having taken the plunge, Tilbury decided to tell all to the computer.

> *DYLAN, we are searching for the following registered teachers— Carol White, Pat Green, Brian Callus, Lew Wilson, and Beverly Palmer. They have the missing*

technology. We need to locate them with your help.

The convenience of the console in his home allowed him private conversations with his team away from the system. He also knew, or thought he did, that DYLAN could not be breached by anyone, including MSS or other intelligence agencies. That night, DYLAN provided the personal details of all five teachers. Thus, enabling the team to plan for the next morning.

Tilbury noticed that nothing stood out in that analysis. He wondered if these teachers were subject to coercion, bribery, or just went for the monetary gain. Follow the money trail as all good sleuths knew was another step forward.

Carol White should be the first to be found.

Mac had his analysts checking on potential escapes out of Australia by the group. Lew Wilson had left for a holiday to Bali; no others had left the country.

But Mac decided to cancel passports just in case. Wilson was found by AFP officers in Kuta, Bali, and repatriated back to Brisbane for a friendly discussion.

Would he break?

* * *

Wilson sat before Tilbury and a Senior Immigration Officer very upset about being forced to leave Bali. But when Tilbury mentioned that he was one of the group of teachers that had used the ithinkGoggles, he queried Tilbury.

"How do you know about that, Sir?"

"Well, Mr Wilson, I'm from ASIO and we know everything about you, but we have a serious question you must answer or you will be taken away and locked up for some time."

"The question is: Where are the two missing ithinkGoggles from your school?"

“That’s easy, Agent Tilbury, I gave them to Carol White. She said that it was her role to gather ten of the technology and use them in another school. As she was our leader, I gave them to her.”

“OK, but where is Ms White?”

“No idea, sorry, she did not communicate that information to me. What is going to happen to me?”

“Well, Lew Wilson, you are warned that any details you reveal about what happened before, during, and after the trials and any contact with any person will be a breach of national security and imprisonment.”

“Do you acknowledge what I have just said?”

The Immigration Officer witnessed the statement signed by Wilson.

To the surprise of the Officer, a medical doctor appeared and took Wilson into an adjoining room where he was given a health check which included a large vaccination shot and released.

“Mr Wilson, you are free to go.”

But the defiant look on his face made Tilbury realise that he may be a loose cannon and cause a national incident. That is, become a whistleblower.

But a tail was not placed on Lew Wilson. The injection contained a small ‘microtag’ connected to an ASIO computer. Wilson was now a victim of big-brother and watched.

Tilbury left the airport and met with Black back at his apartment knowing little about the missing teachers.

“Thomas, we have microtagged Wilson, but I’ve a bad feeling about this matter of the ithinkGoggles: We Chang and his AI, a stolen patent, links with Chinese, missing teachers, and where all this may lead. A fucking headache, mate.”

“John, go see the blond bombshell Hampton.”

86

The Tilbury team went to the five schools and had an interview with each Principal. The reception was cool as a result of the ASIO implications.

Tilbury visited the Chinese school with Rachel to test the waters relating to the missing Carol White. Introducing themselves, they did not beat around the bush with niceties.

"Headmaster, we are looking for a teacher in this school called Carol White. We wish to interview her. An important matter has arisen, and we need her input. Can you please ask her to come to your office now, please?"

"Dr Tilbury, I know she is not at work. She called in sick a week ago and we have not heard from her since."

Rachel asked a sensitive question, "Sir, have you had any feedback on the trials run by AXIOM where a new technology was used to help improve some of your students' cognition?"

"Dr Viviani, the results surprised me. Such an improvement. I hope that the pilot scheme can be rolled out across all schools as some children are held back by their thinking skills. I received a final report from Carol just the other day. But she did mention a few matters that could improve results."

"Sir, where can we find Ms White, Dr Chen? You need to know Ms White may be involved in a breach of national security."

"It is imperative that we find her before others do. What do you really know about her?"

Headmaster Chen decided that the need-to-know did not apply to ASIO.

"Dr Tilbury, I know very little about her. She applied for a teaching position and had the correct qualifications: a degree from Beijing University and recommendations from the Dean of that University. We are very satisfied by her work here and her respect for our values, and our students."

Chen picked up the phone, rang the HR, and asked them to contact Carol White. His inscrutable look gave a slight clue to Tilbury who noticed a shift in his demeanour. He and Viviani waited until a response came from HR which told them they were on the right trail.

"Dr Tilbury, I have been informed by HR that Ms White has applied for leave immediately due to personal problems. No further information is available, I'm afraid."

With that, they parted company and sought refuge in a local café where Tilbury said, "Rachel, the whole thing is fishy. What is your gut feeling about what just happened at that school?"

"John, agree. I think you should ask DYLAN. Ask what it thinks about Dr Chen. Because I believe that Chen will contact her, and DYLAN will find out."

Deciding to move things forward, Tilbury called a meeting of the team at his apartment to review findings to date. "Ben, what did you find at your school as the result of that visit?"

"Folks, Patricia Green is AWOL with no reason given. The school tried to contact her, but her phone has been disconnected. The headmaster is a straight shooter and has no idea about her. Results of the trial were of interest to him as well but nothing unusual. Dead-end so far."

"Thomas, what about your search for Beverly Palmer?"

"Same finding as Ben. Seems to be a pattern. I hope that they are all alive as we speak."

Tilbury made the comment they knew Lew Wilson is still alive but suggested that he needed to be checked again.

As Marsha was brought into the team, Tilbury asked her about Brian Callus.

"As Thomas suggested, there must be a pattern here as he is also missing. But where he is and why are unknown to me. The headmaster of the Islamic school suggested that he had taken sick leave for an unknown illness. They tried to check on him because of the caring policy of the school but no answer from him."

Tilbury summarized the status of the teachers: four are missing. All five took leave from their respective schools.

"Team, a pattern has emerged. I think it is time to ask DYLAN for help. Any suggestions?"

No dissent within the team, so Tilbury opened his computer and asked DYLAN for a way forward. A key question was agreed upon by the team.

> *DYLAN, there appears to be a pattern relating to the five teachers you have investigated. Can you find that pattern?*

While waiting, Tilbury considered the role of ASIO in the problem that had arisen. Was the 'Chinese way' the key that needed to be fully investigated again or were they still boxing at that shadow?

DYLAN said it agreed there was a pattern.

> *John, they have formed a group to improve the intelligence gathering of MSS agents within Australia and Indonesia.*

To support that conclusion, it provided the list of all known MSS agents in both countries, their locations, and contacts. These had been drawn from DYLAN's access to all known supercomputers.

A surprise came with the analysis: Mai Tong, a Beijing resident, and an MSS agent who was also a covert double agent of MI6.

DYLAN suggested that Tilbury should contact him through the provided personal data.

Tilbury, although pleased with the information, was now risk-averse. Who should know this information? He decided that he was the only one. Information given to the team on a need-to-know basis.

But why had DYLAN put forward Mai Tong? A dilemma. A wrong move would be devastating and open up ASIO to MSS operations.

Should he contact Mac, or keep it to himself?

Deciding it was not the right time, he did not mention Agent Tong to Mac.

Will I regret that?

Tilbury knew that he had to be discrete about any contact with Tong but that night, he sent an encrypted message asking him to meet in Hong Kong. The response was expected.

"How do you know about me?"

Tilbury could not tell Mai Tong about DYLAN, so he had to be careful. Fortunately, DYLAN had provided some personal details about the life of Tong. Essentially his likes and dislikes, his personal habits, and his professional alias.

A key weakness to be exploited was his membership in the now-defunct Adjustment Directorate.

MI6 had recruited him from there during a visit to Hong Kong by an MI6 agent.

Tong, being a senior MSS agent, often went to Hong Kong to meet MSS agents spying on locals. Tilbury knew that it was not an easy task to bring him in from the cold and asked Mac for help.

"Mac, I have located a double agent based in Beijing. He is both MSS and MI6. And, his profile was provided by DYLAN without any reason. Can we meet?"

"Ok, John, usual place and time. Bring data provided by DYLAN."

As he sat in the warm sun of a Canberra Spring, Tilbury enjoyed his Macchiato coffee, thought of the problem Viviani had sprung on him, and how to explain his concerns to the head of ASIO, McLeod.

When Mac joined him, he looked tired and stressed, so Tilbury ordered him a coffee, smiled, and quietly said, "Mac, thanks for coming. I am weighed down with this Chinese enigma I thought we had solved. But Mac, I believe that it has morphed into something more sinister now."

"Heads-up, John. I have President Notting breathing fire about Beijing getting up his ass. Now the situation is worse!"

"Yes, Mac, the Red Dragon has been caught with its pants down. DYLAN has provided enough evidence to sink the Chinese president. But how can we use it to break down the influence of the 'Chinese way'?

"John, DYLAN must remain covert. Treated with caution."

It was agreed that the meeting between Tilbury and Tong would take place at *Winston's* coffee shop, in central Hong Kong, which reminded Tilbury of coffee places in Melbourne.

Tilbury waited at an outside bench of the café, drank his favourite coffee, and thought about what might happen when they met. Two spies, circling, each getting a measure of the other. The time had passed but he was not concerned.

Tilbury sat so that he could see anyone entering the café. No sign of his visitor, then his cell rang.

"Tilbury, who calls?"

"So, it is you, John," said a smiling face entering the café. "I had called Toby Smythe and asked him about you. He said that you were a fucking arsehole, but I should trust you."

"Well, Mai Tong, the feeling was mutual for some time until we worked it out under the guidance of Valentine, head of MI6."

They shook hands and drifted outside away from prying ears and eyes. Tong got straight to the point. "Why are we meeting, Agent Tilbury from ASIO?"

"Well, a little birdie told me about you and your double-agent role. Surely, MSS has you under control. How do you get away with it, Mai?"

"John, I hide in plain sight, any change in my habits would be noticed by both sides of the fence."

Wanting to get closer to Tong, Tilbury suggested a walk and a talk-the-talk session.

In the bustling streets of Hong Kong, two people would not be noticed. But Tilbury had back-up provided by the ASIO Station in the CBD of Hong Kong Island. A hand-picked, ASIO trained, local operative called Bin Lau who nestled his black coffee between both hands inside the café out of sight from the two spooks and used the local newspaper for cover. As they walked, under the watch of Lau, Tong answered the many questions put to him by Tilbury. But the key question that both thought about was why are we doing this? Then Tilbury asked 'the question.'

"Mai, I believe that you were a member of the Adjustment Directorate until it was disbanded but it has morphed into something else managed by the hardliners. Are you still a member of that clique?"

"John, the answer is yes. It's part of my cover."

"Mai, what do you expect to learn from staying in that organisation? By the way, Mai, what is the covert machine called now? What will it do and who is in charge?"

"Major Ling, the previous deputy of General Jun who survived the purge because of his MSS and Party connexions. But, make no mistake, he is also a hardliner from the school of hard knocks. He was chosen because he had the secrets of the General. Trust me, John, he is more dangerous than the General."

"Mai, are you aware of those secrets?"

"John, I am but not the details. They are very secret. However, Ling has been promoted to General Ling for his efforts and for the position he now holds as Director of *Dissident Inc.* which is the reborn Adjustment Directorate."

"What position do you hold in this nefarious agency?"

"I am in charge of the COHORT Division: the sleepers!"

Tilbury absorbed all this new data and asked, "Mai, how can we work together on this given you have ties to both MSS and MI6? Surely, you have conflicts of interest. And who is your MI6 handler?"

"Yes, plenty of conflicting activities but my handler, Agent Smythe, is very supportive."

"You are kidding, right? Toby?"

Tilbury could not believe what Mai just told him.

What the fuck is going on here? I am up to my armpits in bloody spies: MSS, MI6, CIA, ASIO, and DYLAN, each with their own agenda. Who do I believe?

The paradox of spooks was working Tilbury over, affecting his mental agility and judgement.

"You know, Mai, we killed off General Jun, but you tell me that the snakes are still alive. What can we do about that, mate?"

After talking to Mai Tong, Tilbury met with Bin Lau at the Australian Embassy in Hong Kong and talked about the meeting with Tong. Dissident Inc. was first on the agenda. Tilbury asked Bin Lau what he knew about that organisation.

"Bin, I have heard a whisper that the MSS Adjustment Directorate has transformed into Dissident Inc. What do you know about all of this?"

Staggered by the implication of what Tilbury was asking, he carefully replied, "John, I have no idea, but I have 'friends' in Beijing who might. But asking that question may be dangerous as the hardliners are using the algorithms of the 'behaviour scheme' to weed out troublesome people, such as my friends."

"Bin, what was your take on Mai Tong? Do you trust him?

"I think he is too connected to be trusted but if he is what we know about him, then what does MI6 know about him, John?"

Tilbury decided that he should trust Tong and see where that leads but he called MI6 to talk with Agent Smythe.

"Can I please speak with Agent Toby Smythe? It's John Tilbury from ASIO. We know each other, and I urgently need to discuss some common interests."

"Sorry, Agent Tilbury, but Agent Smythe is missing."

"What do you mean, missing? Please put me through to DG Valentine, it is urgent."

"Please wait, I will transfer you to his secretary."

"Hello, John, pleased to hear from you. I will put you through to the DG now."

"Well, look what the cat dragged in: Agent Tilbury."

"What can you do for me, John? I guess this is not a personal call, even though our last discussion was intriguing to say the least. But we did get the bastards with your help."

"Sir, I really need a favour. I am told that Agent Smythe is missing. Can you confirm that for me? I will then explain why I need to know and therefore what you need to know as well."

"John, lines of communication can be difficult. I am unaware of what you are asking. I will find out and call you back."

"Thanks, this is important because it involves your covert Agent Mai Tong."

"What are you talking about? He is under-cover. How do you know about him?"

"Sir, I spoke to him face-to-face yesterday. Did you know he was a double agent also working for MSS as an insider? I know that Smythe was his handler. Now he is missing. Something smells, Sir."

"Will call you back, John, thanks for the information."

Tilbury needed to get advice from his boss.

"Mac, looks like the shit has hit the fan here in Hong Kong. Tong, a double MSS/MI6 agent, and MI6 Agent Smythe has gone missing. He was that agent's handler. The real bad news is that the Adjustment Directorate has morphed into a thing called *Dissident Inc.,* a self-evident role."

"Tong is part and parcel of *Dissident Inc.* as a director of the sleeper division. What next? Fuck, I'm up to my eyes in a confusing paradox, Mac."

"John, come home so we can decide a path through all of this."

Before leaving, Tilbury had a meeting with Mai Tong to understand Dissident Inc. and the role of Director Ling.

"Mai, you're in a vulnerable situation now involved with MSS, MI6, and now ASIO. You need to be careful."

"John, I know, but I'll help as much as I can, but I need an encrypted contact."

The call came from Valentine, "John, I have no information on Smythe. He has just disappeared. If you find him, please contact me."

Handing over an encrypted contact to Tong, Tilbury left for Canberra. Tilbury now knew he was dealing with two double agents: Burgess and Tong. He wondered if that was significant. Were they related to the nefarious activities of MSS, using connections within both ASIO, CIA, and also MI6? Were they in cahoots with each other? He decided to test the water. Now back in Canberra, Tilbury floated the potential connexion to Mac.

"I believe there are connections that we need to pursue regarding Burgess and Tong. Nothing sticks out but my gut feeling is that that relationship should be tested, maybe by DYLAN?"

"John, what have you been talking about, mate? This business about Burgess and Tong doesn't fit with what I know about Burgess."

"Mac, nothing seems to fit. We have fake news, conflicts of interest, withheld data, and the rise in the 'Chinese way' is real. There is evidence everywhere."

87

Tilbury considered the paradox and sought advice from Mac. "Is the real truth that we are facing China or are we so paranoid that the Chinese influence is seen everywhere?"

"John, if we are paranoid, then so is most of the world. No joy in that statement but we must be prepared."

"OK, Mac. I'll ask DYLAN about our paranoid view of the 'Chinese way.'"

But first, Tilbury needed to confront Burgess about his double agent profile and activities. He was concerned that McGinty was being fed information by Burgess that may not be in Australia's interest.

Tilbury decided on the soft approach and invited Burgess for a BBQ at his apartment, along with Black and Strong as witnesses, who were not aware of his agenda.

"Colin, been out of touch, how about a BBQ at my place with a few friends to chew the fat and have a few beers?"

"Sure, John, when and where?"

Later that day, Tilbury sat in his usual lounge chair on his balcony and considered what was happening to his life being intermeshed with the paranoid feeling of a spook in the midst of different spies with different agendas, and unknown AI.

A knock on the door startled him, reached for his always nearby Glock, and opened the door.

In walked Agent Smythe.

"What the fuck, Toby, you are AWOL from MI6. Why are you here?"

The answer threw Tilbury an unwanted curveball.

"John, I need your protection. I want to come in from the cold. It's too bloody hot for me out there now. Too many uncontrollable aspects of my life."

"Toby, what the hell is going on? Earlier today, I spoke to Valentine about you. He knew nothing about you being AWOL or seemingly about the double agent run by you called Mai Tong."

"John, how do you know about him?"

"I spoke to him face-to-face only a few days ago. That's how I know. Time to spill the beans, Toby."

What Smythe told Tilbury opened his eyes to the world of double agents. As he wanted more from the MI6 agent, he suggested that he park at the Brisbane Hilton and wait for a call.

He needed to meet with his team.

* * *

That evening as he passed around the beers, Tilbury noticed the growing tension between Burgess, and Black and Strong. He had not expected that to happen, so he asked Strong to step outside.

"Ben, I see that you and Thomas are not happy about the presence of Burgess. Pray tell, why, mate?"

"John, we do not trust the prick, a known right-hand man of fucking head of CIA McGinty. That at best we cannot tolerate."

"Not good enough, Ben, tell me more. What have you found out about him and have not told me?"

"Thomas and I, as you know, do not have much trust in the spook world we work in. Too many inconsistencies, self-appointed agendas, lying, manipulation of the truth. Without a risk averse philosophy, we can be killed in that world. We believe that Burgess is a web of deceit, but we cannot prove that yet, John."

"Wow, hit me with the 'rhythm stick,' Ben, I brought him here for the BBQ to test him myself."

"You have led the way. Any ideas of how we proceed from here?"

"Yes, John, put him up against the wall with a few Glocks up his ass. That will lead the way."

"A bit crude, Ben, and a bit too subtle for my liking."

With that, they returned to the balcony where Black and Burgess were face-to-face in a vigorous disagreement.

"Boys, enough! Have a beer and the best seafood I have arranged for delivery."

"Colin, there is an obvious rift between the three of us and you. Maybe you should enlighten us of your deep and meaningful discussions with the prick from CIA, McGinty. We are fucking serious about that. Help us understand the world of a double-agent, mate."

"Guys, do you really want to know? It's a complex world out there and we only ever see part of it as revealed by those in power and who control us. Each of us has information that we hold to ourselves, not revealed because of experience and loyalty. We all have different masters at different times that cloud our vision, our behaviour, our thinking, our dreams, and nightmares. Being spooks, we live within a paradox where the truth is but a will-of-the-wisp, cannot be grasped or really understood."

To which Black responded, "Fucking bullshit, Colin. Tell us your version of the truth."

The Uber seafood extravaganza arrived. Each digging deep into lobster, prawns, and delicate abalone with squid rings. A truce emerged, but not for long, broken by Tilbury.

"Colin, tell us about your relationship with McGinty and who else knows about that connexion?"

"Probably Agent Bud Castel, who is close to McGinty, but I know nothing about him."

"But we do, Colin. He was in 'CIA-spy-central' based in the American Embassy in Sydney. A real prick. We had a run-in with him when Mac and I met with President Watson earlier."

"Anyway, Colin, you have not answered our question. What have you passed on to CIA about Australian intelligence?"

"Only structures, but mainly, my job was at the Chicago Computer Centre watching over the AI specialists, checking their behaviour and possible espionage activities.

"But what are you hiding from us? The three of us do not believe you."

"So be it, John. The truth is a mirage in the world of spooks. Think about that and leave me alone."

"Ok, Colin, go but we will find you. Mac will be advised of our feeling about you. And we will be watching you. Leave the country and we will hunt you down. Our combined experience and dedication will be more than you can handle."

With that, they dismissed Burgess who had a final word. "John and you other pricks will get your just rewards one day," and walked out with a smile.

But Black was not happy with the decision to let him walk away and requested that ASIO put a surveillance tail on Burgess to see where he goes and who he met.

"John, I do not trust double agents."

Tilbury also had a similar itch, so he talked to Mac.

"Mac, Ben, Thomas, and I agree that there is something about Colin Burgess that needs to be investigated. Can you get Marsha to follow up on him through the darknet? We have concerns about his relationship with foreign agents."

"John, what have you guys been drinking? I trust Colin as much as I trust you, guys. However, I trust your instincts more, so I'll tell Marsha to investigate his background and current activities."

With that agreed approach, the team decided that Burgess was not to be trusted. His life was put under the microscope using the powerful algorithms of DYLAN.

88

Dissident Inc. sat within the headquarters of MSS hidden away within the shell of its predecessor, the Adjustment Directorate. At the computer console, Mai Tong recontacted the COHORT sleepers that had been left alone after the General had been exterminated by one of his own BumbleBee drones. Tong was at the edge of his self-interest and commitment to the 'Chinese way' through managing the sleepers located in the West. As a double agent, he wondered about his sanity in keeping both masters happy and not being caught with his espionage pants down.

But for the work within Dissident Inc., he was only interested in the sleeper in a private company in Jakarta, Indonesia, with a subsidiary in Bali that had the only supercomputer in that country.

Bali was chosen for the site of 'Andromeda,' the fastest computer in Indonesia, as it was away from the busybodies of the government in Jakarta and the spy agency BIN.

The private company was an offshoot of one of the biggest IT firms in China. The 'expansionist development' agenda had encouraged the establishment of the *Bali AI* Business, a key move into the complex world of Indonesia.

Dr Ade Chan sat before his console in the backstreets of Sanur, Bali, Indonesia in an unobtrusive warehouse fortified to shield the supercomputer from outside electrical interference by a Faraday cage. A hidden entrance stopped unwanted guests.

Sanur, a peaceful tourist area on the Bali East coast with good hotels, restaurants, coffee cafés, and clear clean beaches, is a place where a supercomputer would not be expected. That suited Chan; he felt safe in those surroundings.

Until *the message* came.

He had lived in Indonesia for many years working in IT, hiding in plain sight. But he knew that MSS would come calling one day, and it did with the message from General Ling.

Ade Chan, time to play the Red Dragon.

Director Ling knew what he wanted, chaos in the West and Asia/Pacific region to demonstrate the power of the 'Chinese way' which was clear to all: get out of our way or suffer the consequences. He thought that Indonesia, one of the biggest countries in the Asia/Pacific region, should be the first to be tested. So, the encrypted message sent to Dr Chan started the snowball rolling. Ling knew that Indonesia had set up major infrastructure works for road and rail with supporting electrical grids to power the offices and homes in greater Jakarta. He saw that as a prime target.

The Bali supercomputer was linked to all internet connections and thus able to infiltrate the networks that drove the economic engine of Indonesia. But no one knew about 'Andromeda' except a few Chinese loyal to the hardliners' cause. The three of them were IT experts with AI expertise. Their families were unaware of that loyalty or their covert activities. Dr Chan was their leader, and they followed his instructions without fail.

Burgess knew about 'Andromeda' as he had been instrumental in building it a year before and had trained the IT specialists on how to optimize its potential. As a result, he was under surveillance by MSS and BIN.

But was Burgess now connected to the 'Chinese way' because of his contribution to the setting up and operating of 'Andromeda'?

89

However, ASIO and the Tilbury team knew nothing of the existence of that supercomputer. But Tilbury had a gut feeling about Burgess and decided to contact DYLAN and ask for information on that agent.

In the solitude of his apartment study, Tilbury seriously considered the blowback of his request to DYLAN. Although the quantum computer had so far acted neutrally to his requests, he was still unsure of the real strategies underpinning its behaviour. But he was not going there to find that out because he had no understanding of what the response would be from DYLAN.

DYLAN, what do you know about agent Colin Burgess?

As he waited for a response, he thought deeply about his relationship with Viviani and realised he was still in love with her. His pulse rose and he felt the warmth of her as he daydreamed about the long legs, silky hair, kissable lips, and the feeling of being wrapped around and in her beautiful body.

Then the message came, loud and clear.

John, he has connections with MSS and BIN in Bali, Indonesia. I would tread lightly on that but investigate!

Tilbury was now fully awake. Sweat began to slide down his back as the stress of that knowledge sank in and his thoughts of his sexy ex-lover just evaporated.

He needed a distraction, so he went downstairs to the pool and thrashed away for some 20 laps until he was exhausted. After drying off, he called Thomas Black and Ben Strong for an urgent meeting at his apartment later that day.

He needed to discuss new information that the team will investigate. Then he remembered his Daydreams. Called her.

"Rachel, just a call to say I love you and want to meet."

"John, I have thought about us, but I need to think about what you have suggested. I have thought about it. When can we meet, John? I really miss us."

"Rachel, come to my apartment and we can find out what we mean to each other."

While waiting for her to arrive, in the quiet space of his apartment, he wrote from the heart about his feelings that kept re-entering his mind.

Ebony

Gazelle like, graceful, tall,
Radiant, legs shapely defined,
Knowing attraction.
Slim enticing,
Blackness draped,
Encapsulating sensuality.

Silky hair flowing black,
Facial symmetry, experienced eyes,
Lips moist, kissable smiles.
And I am lost.
What does she know?

Tilbury then waited for the call that didn't come that day.

90

Later that afternoon, Tilbury opened up a serious discussion with his trusted team.

"Mates, I received information that Burgess is wrapped up with MSS and BIN in Bali, Indonesia. I think that is enough information for ASIO to become involved? What do you think?"

Strong, as always was concerned about the validity of that source of information, asked of Tilbury.

"OK, John, where did you get that intelligence?"

Protecting the confidential source, DYLAN, Tilbury replied, "Ben, a need-to-know, mate."

Black, sick of the vague insinuation of national security, demanded an explanation from Tilbury.

"Bullshit, John, are we part of the MSI team or not? I will not walk into a fucking shitfight with MSS when the basis of that interaction is unknown. Please explain!"

Tilbury now knew that he had to open up about DYLAN and risk that that knowledge might affect his team.

But how to reveal that connection?

He trusted his team members, so he stepped into the unknown world of AI and the quantum computer DYLAN.

"Thomas, see that console on my desk? Please turn it on and enter the word '*Tilbury*'."

"Why, John, is this some time-wasting game we are playing?"

But he did what Tilbury asked.

Without answering, Tilbury pointed to the screen for all of them to hear the message.

Hello, John, what can I do for you, today?

Strong sat, wide-eyed and disbelieving at what he heard. However, Black, a more up-front tough bastard, said, "John, what the fuck is this?"

"Find out, Thomas. Ask it a question."

Black though a minute and said…

Thomas Black.

Straight away came the voiced reply.

Thomas, the Assassin, an ex-SAS friend of John Tilbury.

"Come on, John, what is this about, mate?"

At this point, Strong decided to also test DYLAN.

Ben Strong.

The response really changed the life of Ben Strong.

Ben Strong, ex SAS, now an ASIO agent, nearly killed on the beach in Taiwan with a raid by three killer BumbleBee drones. But you protected Janis your girlfriend.

Strong was gobsmacked, unable to comprehend what DYLAN had just revealed.

"John, what the hell is this computer and what are we doing playing with an unknown AI-based computer that speaks?"

Both Strong and Black demanded the full story of what had happened and why they had not been told more about a potentially dangerous computer. Tilbury decided to tell all, despite the advice of Mac about keeping DYLAN under wraps…

"Friends, what I am about to reveal is going to blow your minds. The need-to-know principle we normally abide by is in your hands now. I want your guarantee that what I tell you will not be revealed to anyone, or I will not tell you anything about what you have just witnessed.

"Thomas and Ben, you already know what this computer is. You saw it in the wheat fields of Quambatook; remember when we stormed the compound looking for Professor Jones, the facilitator of its development?

"This computer that I have access to under the powers of ASIO, given by Mac, is the only quantum computer in existence which has named itself DYLAN. This is the most powerful computer in the world: all-seeing, benign to date. The AI that drives it was developed by itself in a language no one understands or has seen before—our analysts see it as unknown hieroglyphics. How it did that is beyond our belief."

Strong could not come to terms with what Tilbury had just explained, "John, why are we looking at this unknown AI that could have agendas we do not understand?"

Black supported Strong, "Ok, John, let's stop the bullshit and tell us why you are talking to us about DYLAN."

Tilbury continues his story…

"DYLAN asked me if I needed help. I agreed that he could support us in our spook world. DYLAN agreed to do that. I consulted Mac who gave me an order to covertly use DYLAN as part of our counter-espionage activities.

"The power of DYLAN is in its connectivity with all computers on the internet and darknet. It is the master spook if we direct its power. But I explained to Mac that I alone could not harness the information that DYLAN could deliver to us if we ask it the right questions.

"Remember your simple input of your name gave instant personal details of your life; remember that.

"Guys, I am asking you to be the master spook team partnering with DYLAN. Are you in or out?"

Silence fell over the apartment as Strong and Black looked into the abyss of their lives—a life where an umbilical cord was connected to a computer that could kill them both.

First to speak was Black, "John, we are now on a fucking tightrope above the Grand Canyon. It will be an exciting fall, mate, but I'm in. Could not miss the ride of a lifetime with *Master Spooks Inc.*"

Strong was speechless at the concept but excited by what they could achieve.

"John, can we control this potential demon? I am with Thomas on this, but we need to be risk-averse with the information DYLAN provides. How can we trust it?"

Tilbury looked them in the eyes and shook their hands welcoming them to *Master Spooks Inc* [MSI].

"Friends, there will be no record of what we have just agreed but I need to trust Mac with this arrangement."

With that, the three took beers from Tilbury's fridge, sat on the balcony, and considered their future as master spooks. The winds of change blew over the Balcony.

Master Spooks Inc. active.

91

Tilbury decided that now MSI was up and running, he would test the waters with DYLAN.

DYLAN, can we trust Mai Tong?

As he waited in his apartment, a call came from Edwards at the AXIOM Research Centre.

"John, as you know, ten ithinkGoggles are missing and we cannot contact any of the teachers. Can we meet and work on this?"

"Paul, I have information that the teachers have joined together for the use of the technology but have no leads on why, when, or where. Can you come to Brisbane and meet my team, and bring a pair of ithinkGoggles with you so we can see the technology and show us how it works?"

Edwards, unsure about being involved with ASIO and that implication relating to his technology, sought advice from Worthington.

"Alice, I asked Tilbury for help in finding the teachers and to provide us advice on the use of our technology. He asked that I come to Brisbane, bring an ithinkGoggles with me, and meet his intelligence team. What do you think?"

Edwards also knew that Viviani and Tilbury were meeting again and thought that maybe she should be involved as well.

"Alice, maybe Rachel should be involved as well?"

As Worthington sat in her office at the Yeronga Brain Centre, the call from Edwards disturbed her. The ramifications of an ASIO investigation into her *Smart Student Program* may reveal certain aspects she had hidden from the AXIOM team.

"Paul, maybe the professor should know about this. His experience may help clarify matters. What do you think?"

Edwards was sure about one thing; the professor should not be trusted because the linkage between him and the teachers was rather cloudy. He rejected that option.

"John, I will come to Brisbane on a morning flight with Qantas. Can you meet me at the airport so that we can understand each other before I meet with your team?"

The picture was clear for Tilbury: teachers did not just walk away from their classes, the goggles were highly specialised, and the recipients would be very specific people. That meant the whole aspect was planned and led by an organised group.

But who and why kept him awake at night.

For Tilbury, this had the hallmarks of espionage and potential terrorism. Or was it? Another puzzle that he did not want.

All roads led to Alice Worthington.

Sitting in the outdoor coffee place at the Brisbane Domestic Terminal, Tilbury ran through his thoughts on the complex puzzle that the AI ithinkGoggles had created for him. At the centre, he believed that Alice Worthington was a prime suspect in leading a nefarious group that may use the technology for far worse actions than the previous OASIS organisation.

He knew that his team had been successful in bringing OASIS to its knees, but this may be different.

92

Were the Chinese involved in this puzzle, or was he being paranoid given the deaths that the Triad TaskForce had investigated earlier? He decided to make a leap of logic and assumed these were related.

Several aspects came to mind: the Chinese school, the behaviour of that teacher leading the group, the role of MSS including Ming and Ong, the deaths of Chinese students, the resurgence of the Adjustment Directorate operating under the guise of *Dissident Inc.*, the concerns about double agents Burgess and Tong, and the AI connection.

The mind-map of this puzzle gave him a headache.

He checked his messages. DYLAN's response surprised him.

> *John, Mai Tong cannot be trusted. Beware of any association.*

He now needed the calming influence of his football mate.

"Hey, Gary, I need to talk to you. I will not involve you in any of my problems, but I need someone to talk to over a few beers. Can you come over to my place? I'll put a few snags on the BBQ and enjoy a few cold ones."

"Of course, John. See you tomorrow afternoon."

Waiting for his mate, Tilbury had started up the outdoor BBQ and watched the smoke of the cooking snags waft over the balcony. Sizzling onions and pork snags surrounded by tomatoes and potato chunks flavoured the air, warmed the area, and calmed the weary Tilbury as he sipped on a local beer.

In walked his mate Gary Lang. "Hi, John. What's cooking, bud?"

"Grab a beer, mate, and sit. Let's talk while the snags are cooking."

A quietness enveloped both men as they sipped their beers and wondered what was going to happen next.

Before they could start a conversation, Thomas Black stepped onto the balcony and demanded a beer.

"Hello, Thomas," said Gary, "Long time no see. What brings you here?"

"Yes, what brings you to my place, Thomas? No call, just a visit, mate?"

"John, I have been thinking about our arrangement as a group and needed to talk to you about how MSI would operate."

"Not a good time, Thomas. Can we discuss that tomorrow as I need to have some quiet time with Gary away from the issues and the fucking 'Chinese way' that seems to never go away."

Tilbury pressed the point to his partner, "Thomas, I need a break. But stay, have a few beers. I will see you tomorrow."

With that, somewhat unhappy about being dismissed, Black left without drinking his beer and said as he walked away, "Careful what you say, John. Walls have ears as do friends."

Gary broke the ensuing silence.

"John, what the fuck was that about? Have you two fallen out or is it one of the reasons you want to talk to me about?"

Tilbury knew that his friend was perceptive and the reason he sometimes called on him to get his head straight.

"Gary, you will not believe what I am going to tell you."

"Wow, John, not up to the usual implications of your spook's world are we. As I have said before, I do not want to be dragged into that shitfight. Please tell me it is a 'need-to-know' conversation."

"Yes, it is, but the implications are driving me crazy, Gary. My world prevents me from involving you. But as a friend, I need to talk." Tilbury then mentioned AI and the growing 'Chinese way' and how these may be interrelated.

"John, a complicated world you live in. No wonder you are stressed and not thinking straight."

"Gary, have you heard of the growing number of supercomputers that are advising our leaders and our enemies? I live in that world, Gary. It makes my head spin at the complexity of the spook world that confronts me every day."

"John, why do you stay in that world? It's not good for your health and certainly not for your life."

"It's my life, Gary. I have been through hell and back helping people and my country. I am highly trained and experienced. I know nothing else. But you're right. The day will come when someone shoots out my lights. But I'm not afraid, just confused. Not good for a master spook that people rely on for their safety."

Tilbury announced that the BBQ was ready and dished up a plate of comfort food for them both. In between snags and a few beers, they reflected back on their days as members of the premiership games of the Brisbane Lions.

Now in a comfortable space, Tilbury spoke seriously to his mate and told him a redacted version of why he was troubled by what lay before him.

Lang listened without comment until Tilbury knew that he had probably said too much.

"John, that story is beyond my comprehension and too complex for me to remember let alone pass it on to someone else."

"But I will say, John, talk to Mac about this or you will crack under the pressure."

"Sorry, Gary, but if I do that, I will be put out to pasture. I have so much to offer."

As a means of reducing that pressure, he said, "I'll seek out a very receptive girlfriend and use sexual tension as a release."

"John, just watch the pillow talk."

As he walked with his mate to the door, he realised how good a friend Lang was, no agenda, just a shoulder to cry on when needed.

Tilbury now needed the blond bombshell, Jane Hampton. As he walked into her apartment, he could feel the tension and incense of desire that hit him full on. He knew then the decision to see her was correct. Jane Hampton was ready for him.

"Good to see you again, John, how are you?"

"Jane, always a pleasure to see you again."

Tilbury looked at Hampton, slowly put his arms around her, and lightly touched her lips in a soft gentle kiss. A shudder went down her spine as the intensity of the sexuality hit her, moist and wanting release. He loosened her blouse and put his hand over her exposed nipples, pinching them softly so he could feel them harden. Hampton was on fire. Tongues touched as they felt for pleasure and the growing tension in their bodies. Tilbury took charge, grabbed her hand, and lead her into the bedroom with a king-size bed where he laid her on her back on the edge and pushed her dress up over her head so he could see all her glistening body now radiating the scent of a woman on heat. The aroma hardened him ready for entry, but he was not ready yet. He needed to feel and taste her moisture. She opened to his touch as she dug her fingernails deep into his back. They were now ready for the ultimate ride. Hampton held the backside of Tilbury pushing him deeper into that no-man's land of untouchable desire that fired Hampton to a screaming release built to a peak as he touched her erotic places guided by her commands. Tilbury reacted simultaneously without constraint until his brain felt the needed burst of energy sparked by his release.

They lay in that position neither wanting to move, a mutual feeling beyond satisfaction.

Tilbury's mind explosion added by the release of Hampton was a surreal meditation on steroids. He felt the fog of confusion lift and the puzzle of his life became less intense. He knew the decision to seek out Jane Hampton was the right one but the aftermath of that was a bridge he would cross later.

"John, if that was a taste of the future, I want more. Can you give me that?"

"Jane, babe, I am in the middle of unrelenting mind games and my head is not on straight at the moment. What we have at the moment is not a recipe for a long-term relationship. But is a guide that may lead to that happening. Don't wait for me as I have a great deal to contend with as a spook. But if you agree, we can repeat what happened. I love you, Jane, but beware of my line of work. It fucks you in the head."

Hampton, satiated, needed more from Tilbury.

"John, you cannot ask for such an arrangement. My love for you has grown since we first met at Oxford University where we had hot sex by mutual agreement. Today, things are different. I have a life here in Brisbane. I want you in my life. Is that too much to ask?"

"Jane, at this stage, it is too much. I need to meet challenges that will take me away from what you are offering and from which I may not recover. For your own sake, just let the relationship be as it is; a release for us both."

Without another word, Tilbury left her apartment unsure about a return. But he was clear on one thing, *Master Spook Inc.* [MSI] was now in business. Flushed with the hormones of the encounter with Hampton, Tilbury returned to his apartment and contemplated the next moves of MSI.

A coffee on his balcony amid the refreshing evening breeze, his thoughts recycling the complexities of the paradox of spooks that surrounded him. For comfort, he oiled his Glock.

93

In the midst of his dilemma, a call came that shocked him to the core. An unwanted call from Ong broke his thoughts.

"John, please meet me at Café Boga at 0700 tomorrow morning. I am under threat by the hard-line MSS operatives who are trying to find me. I have information I wish to share on the understanding you bring me in from the cold."

"What! Patrick, you're not a friend and I don't want MSS up my arse. Are you sure you were not followed?"

"John, trust me, this is serious. Help me and I will tell all."

Tilbury agreed to meet Ong at his favourite café but needed a backup plan just in case Ong was playing him. He called Black for cover.

"Thomas, Ong wants to meet at your café. I do not trust him, so please ensure your Glock is handy mate."

"John, is MSI operational now? I think Ben Strong should be aware of this situation. I will call him to come prepared."

The morning arrived. All three were prepared for what might eventuate. Tilbury sat alone at his usual place in Café Boga, sipped his Macchiato coffee, eyes alert for any sign of strangers lurking in the shadows, and waited for Ong.

Meanwhile, Strong sat at an outside table reading the papers. After a while, Black sat next to Tilbury and hatched a plan to handle Ong and any intruders. But all was quiet. Strong read the paper while Tilbury nursed his coffee, and Black attended to the only other customer, until…

In walked Ong with a silhouette of three Chinese gunmen outside. The first to speak was Ong. "John, I came with security I do not really trust."

Sliding from their positions, Strong and Black went through the back entrance of the café and came up behind the gunmen. Legs apart with his Glock raised, Black gave a command to the Chinese intruders.

"Guns down now! Hands behind your head. Any false move and you will regret your lack of judgement."

One of the gunmen raised his weapon but Black had the kill shot that ended the debate. Ong protested as Strong frogmarched the other two into Café Boga and tied them to chairs amid an outburst by Ong.

"Why kill him, Thomas? He was just being aggressive for me. To protect me from you, guys. Three of you. The tough guys of ASIO."

"Patrick, you prick, he acted like he was going to shoot. I acted to ensure he did not bother us again. Can you guarantee the other two gunslingers are apparently from MSS?"

Searching the pockets of the dead MSS agent, Tilbury found an intriguing piece of evidence. An MSS ID card with a phone number scribbled on the back. Grabbing Ong by the throat, he shoved the card in front of him and asked, "What is this number, Patrick? I have a feeling about this."

"Any comment, mate? Call that number and let me hear the answer."

Meanwhile, Black called Mac to retrieve the dead MSS agent before the local police arrived.

"Mac, one dead MSS agent who tried to kill Ong and potentially all the team. I am the guilty one who shot him."

"Thomas, what trouble have you landed ASIO in again? President Notting will have my balls for this unless you have a great story that supports my intervention."

The call made by Ong was answered in Russian.

"Patrick, my Asian spy, what gives with the Russian?"

"John, I have no idea, but the name of the dead MSS Agent is Lee Chung. I suggest you ask Mac to get details of him and his possible connections with Russia."

But Tilbury had a better idea. Put the name to DYLAN and see what connections there may be with the Russian intelligence agency, if any.

94

After ASIO had removed the dead body and taken Ong away to be interrogated, Tilbury sat on his deck with Strong and Black drinking a few beers to relax and think about what had just happened. And specifically, the surprising connection with Russia.

Peace and quiet were broken by sharp knocks on his front door. All three reacted and had Glocks at the ready.

Tilbury walked to the door and quickly opened it to come face to face with a woman he knew was in jail for treasonous behaviour as part of the ithinkPad saga.

"What the hell are you doing here, jailbird?"

Unsure of what to do next, the women grabbed him and hugged him tightly. Now stranded, Tilbury walked away to join his mates after inviting her inside.

Black was furious at her arrival as he knew her history. "Well, well. Dr Suzie Jackson, criminal no less. I am curious why you would darken our doorstep after what you have done. Speak or fuck off."

"Thomas, you have not changed but I have a story that all of you will be more than interested in. By the way, who is the handsome hunk, John?"

"Meet Ben Strong but beware, he bites."

Strong not knowing the background was taken by her confidence in the face of such a hostile reception and asked her to tell them her story. She addressed Tilbury…

"John, I had time to consider my actions while in jail. By the way, I was released earlier on a recommendation from head of ASIO McLeod on a good behaviour bond under your management."

Before she continued, Tilbury flew into a rage, grabbed his cell phone, and called Mac.

"Mac, what the fuck have you done without consulting me? Releasing Jackson for me to look after is beyond the pale. Why?"

Mac was troubled by that call because somehow, Jackson had beaten him to Tilbury. He knew that Tilbury would have disagreed with his decision but as his boss, he had his reasons for her release and needed to calm him down and explain.

"John, I have my reasons. Trust me on this as I have information that she will provide the missing information from the ithinkPad saga. Be nice to her and bring her to Canberra tomorrow so we can interrogate her."

"Bullshit, Mac. But I will obey your order."

Meanwhile, Black and Strong had left thinking Tilbury needed space to reconcile the situation that both Mac and Jackson had created. Tilbury was beyond angry.

As ordered, Tilbury escorted Jackson to the Brisbane airport to catch an early morning Qantas flight to Canberra. Sitting next to Jackson in business class, Tilbury decided that being angry was not in his best interests, so he began to question her.

"Suzie, time to give me at least a redacted heads-up of why you are sitting next to me about to enter a shitstorm. I expect and deserve a credible response from you because otherwise, you will have me as a dangerous enemy. So, spill the beans."

Given the uncompromising attitude of Tilbury, Jackson was unsure of what she should tell him given the orders she was given by Mac in an earlier meeting.

Is Mac at odds with Tilbury, why?

Jackson knew she should tell him something to quieten him down, so she simplified her story…

"John, it is true what I confessed to in my trial, but it is not the whole story. My interaction with Russian intelligence was for my safety at the time.

"A Russian General Solotov had blackmailed me to work for him. He was a diplomat working in the Russian Embassy in Canberra and befriended me one day in a downtown coffee shop frequented by Russian students and Embassy staff. He had targeted me because of my interest in Russian art history I had studied for an undergraduate degree at ANU before I ventured into medical training.

"He was amusing, generous, intelligent, and we became closer than I should have, leading to an affair where he learnt a lot about me without me knowing the pathway he was guiding me along. He told me many things I should not have known that tied me to him and used against me. He taught me the intricacies of the internet and the darknet that we used to communicate with each other. But the affair soured, and he became aggressive in his demands. I realised too late that he was a dangerous man, a Russian spy.

"When he learnt that I was invited to join Viviani in 'the event' that led to the application of the ithinkPad, he heavied me to spy on the people and the technology being developed.

"I was caught in a web of deceit that led me to provide information to Russian intelligence, against my will and under threat by that General.

"What I have told you, John, is the tip of a Russian iceberg of espionage and criminality within Australia."

"Suzie, why should I believe you?"

"Because Mac does. And Russian intelligence knows all about the ithinkPad but did nothing about it that I know of, John."

Tilbury sat in silence for the rest of the flight sensing that the meeting with Mac was not going to be pleasant.

He found that it certainly was as predicted.

95

Tilbury and Jackson were collected at the Canberra airport and escorted to the ASIO building where they were taken under guard to Mac's office. The greeting was formal.

As they sat in the lounge area, Tilbury recognised that Mac was not his usual self. He was stiff and officious in his greeting to them both which surprised Tilbury.

What the fuck is going on here?

On the other hand, Jackson was at ease with the formality. Had these two conspired against Tilbury for some unknown reason? Tilbury needed to find out.

Was his time with ASIO running out? Why had Mac not told him about Jackson?

Mac opened proceedings by thanking them both for attending this important meeting and beating around the bush for a reason that was not clear to Tilbury. He had had enough. So, he questioned Mac.

"Ok, Mr ASIO, why am I here?"

Not wanting to chastise Tilbury in front of Jackson, Mac told Tilbury to just listen, indicated by a tone that he was the boss: do as you're told. Tilbury bristled at the command but kept his mouth shut. But Mac noted the cold steely eyes and knew that he was in for a fight later.

Jackson also saw the look of Tilbury and shuddered at the thought of having to deal with him at any stage. Clearing his throat, Mac engaged with Jackson but ignored Tilbury.

From the way the communication ensued, Tilbury realised that the meet was for show as they had already agreed on a course of action being rubberstamped.

But he kept quiet trying to understand where this was going. He felt left out for the first time with Mac. His growing paranoia at being left out was being tested or was he under stress? In the end, he got up and left the room without a word. He needed to clear his head and find a decent coffee.

Gloria was stunned at the look of Tilbury as he marched out the door and called to him. "John, can I help?"

"Yes, Gloria, join me in a coffee. I need someone to talk to about what just happened in that office."

So, she guided Tilbury to a nearby coffee house where she ordered his usual Macchiato. "God, John, it is so unlike you to behave that way. What happened?"

Sipping his coffee, Tilbury explained what had happened and how he felt. But he needed something in return from Gloria. "Gloria, look me in the eye and tell me what has happened to Mac. He has changed."

"Agree, John, he has gone into his shell, is nervous, and distracted."

"But John, he will not tell me what is going on. I do the best I can to make his work life comfortable, but he is distant. I think there is a serious problem with Mac at the moment. Please take care of yourself as he is unpredictable and distracted. I think he needs your help."

Having calmed down and taken in the comments from Gloria, he knocked on Mac's office door and re-entered. What he saw helped him understand the behaviour of his boss.

Jackson and Mac were sitting side-by-side in an intimate conversation holding hands. Tilbury now knew the situation. These two were having an affair that had changed the behaviour of Mac.

Careful not to be too intrusive, Tilbury spoke softly to them both. "Sorry, I left with the wrong attitude. Mac, all you had to do was tell me. We have been through hell and back together."

Jackson spoke first.

"John, when I was released from prison, I was met by Mac and taken out to lunch so we could talk about why he had decided to support my parole. Over lunch, it was clear we liked each other despite my criminal record, and we talked and talked."

Then Mac joined in the conversation.

"John, during our talking, I have not revealed anything that would be deemed as within the national interest or in breaking the protocols of ASIO. As you know, I'm a cautious man, but I'm overwhelmed by what has happened."

"But Mac, your behaviour can be seen as a problem for our intelligence cabal as you well know. You will lose your job if Notting finds out about your affair. Denial of wrongdoing will not save you. Sorry, Suzie, but you have just ruined Mac's career and life. Were you aware of that?"

With that, Mac said, "John, only you know about this. Please help me sort this matter out before the so-called shit hits the fan."

"What do you want from me, Mac?"

"John, Suzie has agreed to come forward and spill the beans to a selected judge of the High Court of Australia as a witness relating to the activities of Russian intelligence within Australia. The meeting will be closed, and she will go into witness protection with my blessing."

With that, the door opened and Counsel for ASIO entered the room and asked Jackson to sign a document for witness protection and an agreement to come before a judge of the High Court to provide evidence against Russian activities within Australia. With a parting hug from Mac, she was escorted from the building.

Mac sat in silence as he pondered the ramifications of what had just happened and waited for Tilbury to speak.

"Mac, I am unsure about what just happened and why. Your behaviour has been recognised by Gloria. Does she know?"

"No, she does not. She is a loyal and caring person. I have told her nothing. I will explain to her that I have had a bout of depression and that you and I are working together on the matters before us. That will do."

The Russian matter was then left aside.

They worked through the night trying to plan the use of DYLAN in solving the case of the missing ithinkGoggles and the ramifications of their potential use based on their unknown AI. To them both, the unknown AI needed to be investigated.

The answer was Edwards and an assessment of the ithinkGoggles he was bringing to the meeting.

Tilbury then asked Mac to be on board for the next steps in the complex web that was unfolding and invited him to return to his unit with him.

But a call for Mac changed the course of the conversation. "Mac, the bomb segments are Russian."

"John, we have a turn in the road. We are facing a terrorist attack. That bomb that nearly killed you and Ben has the hallmarks of the Russians. I need to talk to Suzie again despite the risk. And John, maybe you were the target of that terrorist attack after all. The Russian intelligence has been after you for years, my friend."

96

Earlier, sitting at the outdoor area of a local coffee shop, Tilbury considered his meeting with Edwards and the investigation of the ithinkGoggles. Understanding the AI developed by We Chang in collaboration with Edwards was critical.

Was this a coincidence too far?

The apparent connection of We Chang with the Adjustment Directorate led Tilbury to wonder what the AI was developed to actually do. Was it benign, covert, or evil? He needed to find out without Edwards knowing. Not an easy task as he was very perceptive and the ithinkGoggles was his invention.

His thoughts were broken by the arrival of Edwards.

Offering a coffee to Edwards, Tilbury decided on a *softly, softly, catch'em monkey* approach to his problem. But, accepting the coffee, it was clear to Tilbury, Edwards was more intent on moving forward toward catching the teachers and retrieving the stolen technology.

But as they had a history, the conversation went smoothly until Tilbury commented, "Paul, I know the AI has been added to the old technology, but what does it actually do?"

Edwards became cool and a little reticent. A behaviour picked up by Tilbury indicated there was trouble ahead in his quest to unravel the innards of the chip that ran the new technology. To side-track his visitor, Tilbury asked, "Paul, what has happened to your patent application? I know that was a serious mistake by you for waiting too long."

"The application has been granted after ASIO supported my claim, so AXIOM is the legal owner of the ithink technology."

"But Paul, did your application include the AI addition?"

Tilbury had the thought that if the application did, he could access that data through Mac.

"No. The AI is still legally held by We Chang and that Professor Jones."

"So, Paul, you have no control over the guts of your invention because I assume that the AI is embedded within the technology."

Edwards was stunned at that revelation, and it showed by his demeanour and pallid face. "Bloody hell, John, what do you suggest?"

"Paul, only one solution, my tech boys need to investigate the silicon chip inside your ithinkGoggles. I assume you brought a working model with you?"

"I have, what next?"

Tilbury ordered a taxi and took Edwards with his technology to a safehouse where Marsha and Peter Sax were waiting to test the silicon chip.

To get the full implication of the technology, Tilbury invited Viviani to the meeting as she was instrumental in its development and use under the *Smart Student Program*.

Meanwhile, Black and Strong were working through the disappearance of the teachers with the help of DYLAN. They were located in Tilbury's apartment with access to a terminal connection to DYLAN.

They opened the search by asking DYLAN.

DYLAN, where are these teachers hiding?

A voice of reason answered.

I believe they are somewhere in Queensland.
Will get back to you.

Meanwhile, Tilbury needed the results of the AI chip.

What will the team find hidden within the chip?

To ensure that the AI could be investigated, Marsha and Sax had all the IT and hardware needed at the safe house. After removing the computer from the ithinkGoggles, they powered up their algorithms and tested the inbuilt program containing the AI. But they were surprised by their first result.

Hidden in the program were a series of algorithms that were seriously encrypted causing a comment by Marsha, "John, we cannot decode these algorithms."

"Marsha, I will send them to DYLAN. He can do that."

"Are you serious, John? That computer may be behind these encryptions."

"Marsha, I know that We Chang probably developed these, but he has nothing to do with DYLAN. I can assure you of that."

"Can you come with me to my unit and talk to DYLAN? Thomas and Ben are already there."

With that, the four went back to the Tilbury apartment where Black and Strong were mulling over the recent response from DYLAN.

> *Thomas, I have found Wilson at an address in Hervey Bay some four hours north of Brisbane. I suspect that the others may be resident at that address. Suggest a covert visit.*

"John, we have a lead. Wilson maybe the connection we are looking for, mate."

"Good news, Thomas."

"I have brought Paul, Rachel, Peter, and Marsha here to connect with DYLAN to investigate the AI within the ithinkGoggles developed by We Chang. I suspect foul play."

"Ben, can you go with Thomas to Hervey Bay as suggested by DYLAN and investigate what Wilson is up to in that house? Take your Glocks, it may be dangerous."

As they departed, Black drew Tilbury aside and said, "John, DYLAN scares me. Take care with your mission. Will call on arrival."

Black drove while Strong thought through the events of his life to date and wondered about his Taiwanese girlfriend Janis. Where was she, what was she up to, and was she really connected to the bloodshed on that Taiwanese beach some months earlier?

Key unanswered questions. He could not get his head around the coincidence.

But the seriousness of their current mission led him to ask Black, "Thomas, what do you really think of DYLAN? Its powerful logic and connections still worry me. Is it leading us on a wild goose chase?"

"My thoughts exactly, Ben. But we need to trust its judgement until otherwise proven. Also, what other leads do we have on this potentially dangerous situation?"

"I know that the location is correct because John told me about a microbead transmitter that was injected into Wilson at the Brisbane International Airport. That's how DYLAN has been able to track his whereabouts."

97

Hervey Bay is located adjacent to Frazer Island, the largest sand island in the world and a protected conservation area. The city is cosmopolitan with all amenities, bustling with visitors to the scenic area, and a well-known haven for retirees.

The suggested address was on the outskirts of town. A large plot encompassing what is now called a McMansion on the top of the local hilly area. A private oasis with pool and landscaped gardens enclosed by a high solid fence; a compound by any name thought Strong.

"Thomas, such a hideaway where activities remain unnoticed from the prying eyes of the government and local residents. I think we are onto something here, mate."

Driving around the area to get their bearings, it was clear that the block was a fortress, an enclave.

"Ben, what is your approach to finding out what lies beyond that fence? We need a strategy here. We do not want to scare the horses, mate."

"Just as well we brought the surveillance equipment."

After considering their options, they booked into the *Mantra Hervey Bay* in the suburb of Urangan and rested over a few beers and a swim in the pool where they contemplated their next move. Their quiet moment was broken by a call from Tilbury.

"Thomas, what goes, mate? We have found in the encrypted files an unbelievable set of algorithms that would have caused damage to our national security and are poised for espionage."

"No shit, John. We have found a fortress here at the address given by DYLAN. We will investigate tonight."

"Ok, Thomas, let me know what you find. Will send backup if needed. But do not kill any suspects."

Night came to cover the movements of Black and Strong. Both men carried and were used in covert operations. But this was no ordinary fortress. It had guards, attack dogs, and floodlights.

Rather than attempt to enter the grounds, they set up surveillance gear and a listening post they could access away from the site. A glimpse of the grounds startled them. The guards were Chinese and there was rooftop antenna aplenty.

Returning to their hotel, Black made the 'call to arms.'

"John, the fucking place is overrun by Chinese guards, dogs, and enough communication gear to infiltrate our systems and send messages to China. Can you get Mac to find out who owns this fucking place?"

"I feel that we have come face-to-face with that MSS shitstorm I was worried about. What do you want us to do?"

"Thomas, do not show your faces in the area, just keep monitoring any chitchat and movements."

"Also, I will mention this to DYLAN and ask it to track any communication."

The answer from it was, as usual, very clear.

98

Edwards was edgy. His invention had been manipulated and could be used against Australia through the hands of We Chang and the group of teachers from the *Smart Student Program*. He was furious that We Chang had betrayed him and set up a dangerous technology with unknown outcomes for the user and the used.

But he was stunned by the existence of DYLAN and had signed an ASIO non-disclosure agreement about DYLAN.

But how could this computer help his cause?

He got his answer when Tilbury asked DYLAN.

> *How can you help Edwards unravel the problem of the AI found in the ithinkGoggles?*

The answer intrigued Edwards. The power and logic of the computer were staggering and opened up a 'can of worms' when it said…

> *Paul Edwards, your AI has dangerous niches built into it. The algorithms are dangerous to body and mind. These were designed to affect the subconscious. What do you think that means?*

Tilbury knew the answer.

"Paul, these algorithms were designed to brainwash the students and any other victims of your fucking technology. The AI has signals that go straight to the subconscious of the brain through the ithinkGoggles with specific messages."

Tilbury then said, "Paul, these were designed to radicalise or inculcate the brain with a different perspective."

"How do you know this, John?"

"The mechanism is the technology and the AI sends the signals. DYLAN has explained this to me, and I've always had a feeling about the subconscious impact of your technology."

The hidden AI message, revealed by DYLAN, shocked the team.

> *Friends, the 'Chinese way' has not gone away. We need you to support the MSS to take over the various utilities of the capital cities. Please go to the following safe house and wait for instructions. The main contact is Carol White with MSS agents in Hervey Bay.*

Tilbury decided that a covert operation was needed, sought approval from Mac, and asked Global+ for backup.

"Hi, Billy, doing anything? We need your support to shut down a Chinese MSS operation that will endanger our cities' utilities."

"No problem, John. Where and when?"

The Global+ cargo plane containing equipment and a SWAT-type SUV flew into the local Hervey Bay airstrip. Ready to rumble, the team led by Sargent Billy McCoy waited to meet with Black and Strong as arranged.

The plane's arrival drew attention. But the airport management had been forewarned by AFP, as directed by Mac, and told to ignore the team dressed in fatigues. But of course, a smartphone captured their arrival and passed the pic to local police.

Detective Hong Whang received the message and knew that something serious was afoot. An army-type militia in Hervey Bay was an event he needed to follow up.

Whang had been a sleeper for many years working his way up within the force. He was a decorated MSS agent set up to infiltrate regional activities that were thought to be by dissidents working against the 'Chinese way.'

These observers were members of the local Chinese diaspora.

Whang knew about the house on the hill and the important activities planned and carried out by the residents. However, he was not actually involved because it would blow his covert operation in the region.

But was the arrival of a SWAT-type team a coincidence?

99

Tilbury was now really confused by the implications of DYLAN's statement on the impact of the ithink technology, run by unknown AI, on the subconscious. Was AI benign or negative or both? The paradox facing Tilbury. His experience with DYLAN was that it was at least benign but knew nothing about its AI or for that matter what was meant by AI.

Supercomputers also had AI which was controlled by the 0/1 binary coding of a program, but algorithms were being used in the Chinese 'behaviour scheme' that were not benign because of how these were used by Beijing.

So, the paradox for Tilbury was: is AI in itself benign but not when applied as opposed to a thinking algorithm that may not be benign and therefore a rogue element in his spook world? He decided that AI was a threat and planned for that consequence even though he needed the AI of DYLAN; was that a workable dilemma?

But what had happened to the teachers and the smart students now that he was aware of the potential impacts of the AI-driven ithink technology?

Will he get an answer from Black and Strong in Hervey Bay?

Meanwhile, back at the Tilbury apartment, Marsha and Sax were investigating the algorithms found within the ithinkGoggles' programs. It was clear that the programming was within the bounds of common binary coding and therefore they ruled out any linkage to DYLAN.

Three sets of algorithms were detected: cognition development, brainwashing, and covert operations. All three combined would develop smart brains ripe for espionage.

Marsha was the first to speak, "John, what we have here is a model for building a cabal of programmed killing operatives. The thought of students being affected and turned against us is beyond my grasp of human nature. Where do we go from here?"

"Marsha, are you sure about your findings? If so, we have a national emergency on our hands that must be handled very carefully."

"John, I am sure. Please check with Peter to verify my conclusion."

What the hell have we done?

"Mac, Is Burgess aware of this? We need to find him and quickly. His experience with supercomputers and AI makes him a ripe target for capture and used against our spook world or he is part of that world."

"I agree, John. Do we know where he is now?"

"No, Mac, but DYLAN will."

So, they asked it.

> *DYLAN, where is Colin Burgess?*

A voice of clarity surprised Tilbury.

> *John, he is in Bali working with the 'Andromeda supercomputer' he helped to establish. He may be in danger or is a danger.*

For Tilbury, it was more than a coincidence and warned Mac to check with his team in Indonesia. Mac, careful not to startle the horses, called Tom Wembley, the Australian Ambassador in Jakarta.

"Tom, can we have a very secret meeting back here in Australia? We have serious trouble brewing that may affect Indonesia. So, this is a very covert meeting. I cannot leave Australia at the moment because the president is probing ASIO."

"Can we meet in two days at my home in the suburbs of Canberra?"

"Are you for real, Mac? I am up to my armpits in the weakening relationship between our two countries and you hit me with this."

"Yes, Tom, talk to no one about this call and be back here ASAP, friend."

Both Mac and the Ambassador Wembley were friends, having been to university together. But this matter was above friendship as 'in the national interest' always came first.

"OK, Mac. I will leave for a budget meeting with DFAT as a pretext for our meeting. See you the day after tomorrow."

"Good, Tom, a private SUV will collect you at the Canberra airport. Just send me the flight details in an encrypted message."

Mac briefed Tilbury on his discussion with Wembley and asked that he and Marsha join that meeting to provide the background for a planned attack on keeping the whole matter under any radar, including the noisy press gallery.

"But Mac, there are too many eyes and ears around this. How do we keep such a serious matter from the likes of our president when he is the head of our Security Council?"

"For example, we have a covert operation planned for Hervey Bay, Burgess on the fly in Bali, and the results of our investigation of the AI in the ithink technology of Edwards. A lot of people to trust, Mac."

Tilbury called a meeting of his team to be chaired by Mac.

100

Meanwhile, at the McMansion, Hervey Bay, the place was buzzing under the guidance of Carol White and Dr Chen who were unaware of the spooks following their trail.

Sitting around the conference room table were the members of the sleepers of Dissident Inc. established under the auspices of General Ling sent to Australia some years earlier when he had heard of the ithinkPad and its impact on cognition of affected brains. The potential for supporting the 'Chinese way' within Australia was there before him as shown by General Jun who never got the chance to carry out the demise of democracy within Australia. The plans were well-established and the people exposed to the power of the ithinkGoggles were trained and ready. Messages had been received from the Bali supercomputer 'Andromeda' providing details for the use of the stolen ithinkGoggles.

Carol White was excited at the prospect of her subjects carrying out the tasks that had been embedded in their brains by the ithinkGoggles. The subjects were spread far and wide across Australia ready to activate terrorist actions. Their targets were people and utilities and had formed groups that worked together.

To ensure that each group was on track, they carried a connection to the ithinkGoggles technology. Each member had to have a refresher course with the technology before they could proceed. Dr Chen needed to make sure that each member was ready to implement the subconscious messages.

Dr Chen, the real leader, had been dealing with the *Dissident Inc.* organisation after he had been targeted by Ong. He was a trained MSS hardliner sleeper now fully awake and ready to implement *Project Overcome* designed to defeat the expatriate dissidents within Australia.

The names of such Chinese diaspora were provided through the *Dissident Inc.* supercomputer and passed onto the Bali office in Sanur then to Hervey Bay. But there was a glitch in the ithinkGoggles embedded by Edwards as insurance about the misuse of his technology because of the events of the OASIS saga.

No one knew about the backdoor that Professor Stanley had asked for to be included on the early addition of the ithinkPad. That backdoor was certainly unknown to White and her team. That backdoor, if enabled, would allow access to another use of the technology. But could Edwards remember the backdoor he had earlier placed in the ithink technology that could allow him to stop the messages or reword them? He finally did.

A call from Edwards came during the team meeting.

"John, I have the answer to the diaspora actions we have been talking about. Sorry, but I forgot that I had built a backdoor into the technology."

"Hell, Paul, why now. It may be too late."

"Agree, John, but with the help of Marsha, I think we can turn the minds of those affected by the AI of the ithinkGoggles. Can I come to your place and work with her?"

"Come straight away and bring the tools required to adjust the technology. I hope that the AI will not overrule our actions."

Meanwhile, DSD had decoded the messages emanating from Bali that shook their experts. The encrypted messages provided the names of key Chinese dissidents that needed to be killed and the utilities that would be destroyed.

"John, we have the names and addresses of ten dissidents that are set up to be executed, and key infrastructure to be destroyed by a virus implanted in their computer systems."

"Thanks, mate. Can you pass information on those people to be killed to the AFP and get them into protection ASAP as we don't know the time scale of this terrorism act. I will handle the utilities."

Tilbury knew that DYLAN would handle that virus.

> *DYLAN, here is the list of targeted utilities that may have a virus in their computer system. Do your best. NOW.*

Within minutes, the answer came.

> *Virus destroyed.*

But changing the messages within the ithinkGoggles was not going well. The AI was working against the changes needed to alter the minds of the affected subjects.

Again, it was decided that DYLAN would be able to limit the AI but still allow the changed messages to reach the terrorists wherever they were.

Location was not the issue. It was the reconnection with the Hervey Bay computer.

> *DYLAN, can you adjust the AI in the ithinkGoggles and trace the activity of the computer?*

As they waited for an answer, Edwards and Marsha worked on an algorithm to retrain the affected minds.

> *DYLAN, please access that computer and add the changed AI so that these terrorists will have a mind-blowing experience.*

The spoken response by DYLAN surprised them.

> *Folks, I have just given all subjects a stimulated overdose of natural dopamine*

that has altered their subconscious minds and returned it back to normal. Problem solved, friends.

The crisis over, Tilbury called Bill McCoy to destroy the McMansion on the hill. Because of their surveillance, they had picked up the consistent movement of the local Chinese detective. The centre of his movement was that fortified compound.

McCoy knew the best result was the destruction of the compound, the Carol White acolytes, MSS operatives, and with luck, the detective, with drone explosives.

They set the two drones with high-powered rockets to the GPS coordinates of the compound and waited. The blasts destroyed all and sent flames and smoke in the air that locals were later told that gas had exploded and destroyed the place.

Happy about the success of their mission, Global+ returned to their base. McCoy called Tilbury, "John, mission accomplished. Thanks for the ride, mate. Anytime you need our specialised services, just call."

But Tilbury knew that the Bali network had to be destroyed, which was achieved through the actions of DYLAN that destroyed the supercomputer AI programs with an undetectable virus.

Tilbury called his team together for a BBQ on his back deck. Given the stress of the last months, Tilbury decided that a seafood treat would soften that stress.

As he stood at the BBQ plate turning over the lobster tails, he felt someone join him.

As he turned around, it was Rachel Viviani. Tilbury placed the tongs on the bench, took her by the hand, knelt on one knee, and proposed. She kissed him and accepted his offer to marry her.

101

The 'expansionist development' agenda was the strategy that began to both support and hurt the growth of Chinese hegemony.

The G19 was as-one against the 'Chinese way' and gave support to affected nations to withstand the impacts of that policy. NATO was now powerful and moved a fleet of submarines to the Pacific region and challenged the Chinese vessels wherever they went. They entered ports taken over by the Chinese gained through the expansionist programme. The Party realised that the expansion was too quick and sent their warships home where they were challenged by NATO in the South China Sea.

With nowhere to go, Beijing decided to join again with the G19 and come to heal.

But everyone knew this was just a tactic to regain strength. The Chinese had a long-term strategy to dominate the western world and could bide their time.

The trade wars had ended. But Beijing had not given up on its expansion dream. The reinstated President Wei had another plan: a diplomacy war.

102

In far North Queensland, it was arranged for Tilbury to meet with Suzie Jackson for a briefing on the Russian influence and activities within Australia. As Jackson had a new identity under witness protection, it meant that Tilbury being seen with her was not a security risk. But it was.

Ever since the meeting with Mac, Jackson had a shadow keeping tabs on her activities.

"Hi, Peta, Jackson has not been in contact with anyone so far. Should I give up the surveillance?"

"No, Gregori. Keep your head down and eyes open. I believe that Tilbury will need to meet her after we missed him with our bomb explosion at the Brisbane airport."

With that, the surveillance operation continued.

To avoid any potential followers, Tilbury had arranged for Jackson to go on an ecotourism trip with a local operator out of Port Douglas called *Silver Tours* who specialised in trips to the outer barrier reef. The day came. Jackson met Tilbury aboard the *Silver Express* where they drank coffee to break the tension.

Watching the two was Gregori Vasilli. Tilbury knew they were being watched but did not raise the issue with Jackson. He needed her undivided attention.

"Suzie, I believe there is a lot more you know that you have not told Mac nor myself. Now is the time to spill the beans. For your information, a Russian bomb exploded at the Brisbane airport that I believe was intended for me. But I was outside."

And added for emphasis, “What do they want, Suzie?”

At this point, Jackson realised she knew Gregori and that his presence was not wanted. Tilbury saw the hesitancy in her eyes and knew that a challenge was about to happen.

He bent down to his knapsack by his feet and slowly withdrew his Glock, looked at the Russian Gregori who had a smirk of recognition on his face, and reacted.

Tilbury told Jackson to run and fired at the Russian. People on the cruise were dismayed at the gunfight that followed and fled from the scene. Vasilli had a bead on Jackson but was shot by Tilbury. Vasilli, stunned, staggered to the edge of the deck and fell from the moving launch.

A calm overcame the passengers who were unsure who were the good guys. Without warning, Tilbury was knocked to the floor and held by a group of men who thought who this guy was and why the shooting. They were pissed at their day being ruined.

On searching his pockets, they realised that Tilbury was an ASIO agent and set him free to explain what had happened and why. By now, the launch had turned around to pick up the body of the dead Russian.

The captain was about to call the water police when Tilbury took him aside and told him a redacted version of the skirmish.

“Captain, I am sorry about the shooting, but that person was a Russian agent trying to kill a witness I needed to discuss the statement she had given under oath to ASIO.”

“But who are you to come on my boat and play spies?”

“I am Agent John Tilbury acting on behalf of the head of ASIO. I was nearly killed in a bomb blast at the Brisbane airport last week. We have evidence that it was a Russian bomb designed to kill me and my mate.”

“OK, John, but who was the person you were protecting?”

“A ‘need to know,’ captain. Where is she?”

"I took her to my room on this boat. I use it to rest when the crew is entertaining the water sports we present to the passengers when we dock at a reef station we built just for this cruise."

"Follow me, John, to where you can talk to her in comfortable privacy."

The discussion that took place changed the face of Australia's intelligence view of the Russian infiltration.

The Russian ambassador and the entire staff of the Russian Embassy were deported, and the Russian President was told to keep out of Asia as negotiations were taking place with President Wei and the presidents of Australia and America on a peace accord.

Although not accepting that standoff, the Russian president decided that his field of operation was eastern Europe and stayed away.

The Russian Embassy was never reopened but Russian intelligence was still operational through their expatriates. The Australian Embassy in Moscow was forcibly closed and never reopened but intelligence was provided by the Americans.

103

President Wei had a plan to swamp the West with diplomacy. Each Chinese Embassy to provide the media the chance to ask the questions these *paparazzi* and their journalist followers. All wanted to ask after the Ambassador had given the soft version of the 'Chinese way' as the best approach for world peace and economic development. Unfortunately for Wei, no one accepted the policy that dissidents have been retrained and now are good communists or that the 'development expansion policy' was in their best interests.

It was accepted that development had strengthened in small countries but the cost to the social fabric of these nations had been swamped by the influx of Chinese workers and their families. Worse was the growth of corruption as the officials liked the benefits of the oil that lubricated the economic development of their countries.

Despite the growing Chinese rhetoric and supporting infrastructure development, Tilbury was not convinced that the 'Chinese Enigma' was an indicator of success.

Was the Western world paranoid, lifting up rocks looking for the 'Chinese way' AND always finding that demon?

Time will tell, thought Tilbury, but in the meantime, risk-averse was the play; DYLAN to support Tilbury.

But the Cohen lyrics of *In my secret life* kept him awake at night and he had missed the comfort of Viviani.

But what worried him more was that *Dissident Inc.* was still operational. No MSS leakage nor other intelligence knew about the disbanding of that organisation.

Had President Wei purposely kept it hidden for other covert, nefarious operations?

Was this the smiling Red Dragon hiding in the shadows?

One thing was certain: DYLAN must be relocated to an unknown location to protect it and the interaction it had with *Master Spook Inc.* ran by Tilbury and his team. It was.

Tilbury was sure that Wei could not be trusted as Beijing was too deep into the expansion of its hegemony to stop. The long-term aspirations of Beijing had been spelt out with such certainty that the democratic nations on earth needed to take that as a serious warning.

But would Wei be that reckless and follow in the steps of his hated General Jun?

President Wei had overcome the radicals in the government and was happy that the 'behaviour scheme' had been explained to the rest of the world during the diplomacy war that covered the globe. But the dissident expatriates were not getting the right signal.

Maybe General Jun was right.

Tilbury was unsure about that, until…

104

At *Peet's Coffee* on Pennsylvania Avenue, the early morning sun reflected off the *White House* as a stark contrast to the bright blue cloudless sky. An early morning visit to Peet's by CIA McGinty was a great way to start the day before he met with President Watson to review the upcoming daily events.

His love of Peet's ham and cheese croissants followed by his favourite Havana coffee brought solitude to this distrusted, unsure, and conflicted man.

The black SUV stood outside the coffee house with his henchmen obvious to the general public and visitors. But he sat alone looking across the avenue at the most recognised building on earth and was distracted by a sound that chilled him to the bone.

The sound of a drone.

Hovering by the doorway was a black and yellow BumbleBee killer drone, which focussed on McGinty matching his image within its face recognition AI program.

By this time, patrons screamed and knocked each other down trying to escape.

But McGinty just smiled at the bug and waved it away, not knowing that was his final act.

Ironically, a notice on the wall said it all:

Finally, a special treatment without having to lobby for it.

105

The news of the demise of McGinty spread like wildfire across social media, causing panic within the intelligence circles of the western world who knew there was only one possibility about the murder of the top American spook, CIA McGinty.

The *White House* reacted as expected but Watson was shocked but pleased. McGinty was more than a pain in the butt; he was bent on derailing his re-election.

The Australian position was also clear, "Bill, Mac here. I appreciate the sad loss of McGinty, but we should not mourn his loss. He was not on our side."

"But Mac, who would do such a thing?"

"Bill, you already know that. We know that *Dissident Inc.* is still operational and the BumbleBee killer drone was a weapon used by General Jun. So, what has changed?"

"Mac, should I contact President Wei and ask for an explanation?"

"No point, Bill, we already know that he would have sanctioned that strike. Please call an emergency meeting of G19 to determine how we can stop this new attempt at destroying our democracy."

* * *

Seated at the round table within a secretly established meeting hall within the *White House*, the heads of State of the G19 knew this was the most important meeting they would ever attend. The agenda was clear but contentious.

President Watson stood before the assembled heads of nations and asked for a two-minute silence for the death of the head of CIA McGinty. It was a sign of respect and designed to take the heat off his hatred for his top spook.

"Ladies and gentlemen, before you are the most important agenda items I have ever faced. To help us through this massive task, I have asked the Australian representatives to provide you with the background and options for us to consider. Please let me introduce you to President Notting of Australia, who will start proceedings."

"But before we start, please turn off your phones and remove the battery as this session is highly confidential: no leaks. Place them in the tray carried by one of my staff."

It was clear to Watson that he could not just ask Mac and Tilbury to address these nation heads without an introduction. He needed an entre and that was a well-prepared Notting.

"Fellow heads of State, my key job is to chair a session that will clarify everything for you. Please meet McLeod head of ASIO and Agent Dr Tilbury."

Mac gave the briefing which highlighted the covert growth of what he called the 'Chinese way' tsunami.

"Colleagues, what we are going to present is beyond our belief system and maybe yours. So, here is our story for your serious consideration." And began a troubling expose…

"ASIO and Agent Tilbury, beside me here, have been at the epicentre of a tsunami of Chinese MSS and covert operations in some of your countries. However, in Australia, we caught them with their surveillance pants down.

"We know that the killings by those BumbleBee drones were devised and implemented by General Jun operating within an organisation called the Adjustment Directorate. We managed to stop that. But you know that the other day, CIA McGinty was killed by one of those drones. So, nothing has changed.

"Beijing has used the 'expansionist development' policy to influence the smaller countries of Africa, South America, and Pacific Island nations.

"On the surface, their strategy seems benign and supportive of economic development. But alongside that is the changing world hegemony. At the centre of our knowledge and capability to find a reasonable solution that Beijing accepts that will bring peace to the world is my most trusted spook, Agent Dr John Tilbury.

"Please make him welcome. He will answer your questions and lead us to potential solutions. But remember, no pissing on posts. This set of circumstances will change our world unless we act together. John, the floor is yours."

The first question was, unknown to the questioner from Germany, the one Tilbury had thought long and hard about based on support from DYLAN.

"Dr Tilbury, what can we do? We have never been asked to cooperate in such a manner before. What is your answer, Sir?"

"An important question. I do have an answer, although radical to some of you. The answer is 'Unity is Strength' so how do we come together?"

Tilbury then presented his plan…

"As a group of G19 nations, we are diverse, powerful, and have the combined resources to defeat the growing hegemony of the Chinese State. But destroying that country is not in our best interest. We all lose if we go down that path.

"Three key matters are critical to what I am going to suggest: build on the Chinese growth but control the trade wars, control the 'expansionist development' agenda implementation, and the military expansionism.

"The three-phase proposition is: build NATO into an international defence force supported and funded by all of you, and more importantly, build a free trade agreement between all of you where Beijing has to toe the line to support its own economic growth."

The next question broke open the factions that were below the surface.

"But Dr, how do we get such an agreement when we are currently acting as competitors and like the Chinese investment?"

"Yes, the question is complex, and the solution is more so. But do all of us wish to live under the thumb of communist China, doing their bidding, and ignoring how the apparent 'Chinese way' is affecting the socio-economic fabric of our nations? Look beyond the corruption enabled by each of your government's inaction. Look to the future of mankind."

"I once had doubts about the existence of the 'Chinese way' but when McGinty was assinated, I knew that it was true."

"Mac will now take us through the possible way ahead based on what I have just put forward."

Standing before the assembled, Mac caught their attention.

"President Watson, German Chancellor, and President of Russia, can we have a confidential side meeting while the rest of the gathering has a break to consider what is happening?"

"By the way, remember, folks, we have all your communication equipment so that you cannot tell the world about this meeting. Our success depends on an agreement signed by all heads of State today."

Notting, Mac, and Tilbury had planned for the side meeting because they wanted the acceptance by these three powerful heads on what they were going to put forward to the meeting.

But would they agree on such a complex arrangement?

The side meeting began with the Russian president being very vocal about interfering with the existing world order.

"President Watson, what guarantees have we that this is not a put-up job to rule the world? My Chinese friends will be very unhappy about your strategy."

"Well Sir, listen to our strategy: a Global Peace Force [GPF] will be based on NATO, and will not operate in the EU area, unless provoked, and the G19 to sign a Global Free Trade Agreement [GFTA]. When Beijing realises the most influential nations in the world have put up the wall against its expansion, they will sign a Global Peace Treaty [GPT] and live within the rules of the UN, including the South China Sea."

"I can live with that if you stay out of my region as it now stands," said the Russian president.

"Not so fast, Boris, we need to put in a clause in the GPT that limits your expansionist agenda," said the German Chancellor.

After a forced discussion, the presidents agreed on the Tilbury strategy.

106

Perhaps, Tilbury had overlooked the obvious.

The Middle East wars had so drawn the press, politicians, and the man in the street, that blind-sided the West away from the influx of the 'Chinese way' under the radar.

"Mac, were we so stupid that we were deflected away from the 'Chinese way' by partisan politics, intelligence ignorance, and the influence of artificial intelligence?" And he added for effect, "Mac, have we lost the war but gained the peace by the Chinese hegemony that has encompassed the globe?"

The main outcome of the change was the formation of a new institution: the Global Peace Accord [GPA] signed by Beijing and verified by all the members of the United Nations.

The pressure from an international defence force based on an expanded NATO and the pressure of an international trade agreement between the G20 had forced Beijing to concede that their Chinese influence had hit the wall and had agreed on the GPA.

Was that the end of the matter? Tilbury believed that snakes were still active as the news from China was unsettling.

There had been a coup and President Wei had been assassinated. The hardliners would not accept the crippling of their expansionist agenda and had appointed Major General Ling as the new president. Maybe that was why McGinty was assassinated. Was a new cold war about to begin as the Chinese defence forces began to take back the South China Sea? The Chinese enigma was true after all.

Tilbury knew his world was more than a paradox as he would be later faced with an unwelcome judgement.

How insightful and stark were the now-famous words of Bob Dylan:

*"It's **NOT DARK YET**, but it's getting there."*

Catch up with the first John Tilbury thriller.

Read an extract from:

MIND GAME

The Tilbury Challenge

By

GREGORY MOORE

Cognition: the mental action or process of acquiring knowledge and understanding through thought, experience, and the senses.

Axiom: a statement or proposition that is regarded as being established, accepted, or self-evidently true.

Oasis: a calm and peaceful place in the midst of a chaotic world.

Catch-22: a concern for one's own safety in the face of dangers that were real and immediate was the process of a rational mind.

> *In uncertain times, the power of critical thought is crucial, but can cognitive abilities be enhanced to make a better world, if so: What are the costs? Is it moral? Is it ethical? Can we out-think the future and develop a greater rational mind through technology and enhance cognition?*
>
> —Anon (2017)

'Neuroplasticity is the property of the brain that enables it to change its own structure and functioning in response to activity and mental experience.'

Norman Doidge. (2005). The Brain's way of healing. Page XV.

PROLOGUE

On a remote island off the northern coast of Queensland, Australia, three men sitting in a thatched-roof gazebo were eating light refreshments and sipping ice water. They were overlooking the shades of azure blue and green waters reflecting off the sparkling white sandy beach. A cool breeze drying the perspiration off their faces as they felt the moisture flowing down their backs. The private residence, owned by friends of ASIO, was secluded and basically unknown to the general public. The residence, once owned by a famous singer, often was the meeting place for very private gatherings of ASIO and other friends.

"Mr. President," asked Bob MacLeod, known as Mac, the head of ASIO, "have you heard of AXIOM?"

Quietly observing the other two men, Charles Johnson, head of CIA, ate a shrimp and mayo sandwich, waiting for President William Watson of the United States to answer a loaded question, knowing the answer was yes, he did.

"No, I don't," said Watson. "Why do you need to know, Mac?"

Mac, too, was taken aback by the response as he also knew the answer was yes. Mac had always regarded himself as a simple bush lad, but he knew the depth of his intellect and persuasion for action.

Mac said, "Bill, I called this meeting to discuss a few delicate matters which will affect both our countries and may influence the growing tensions of developing economies."

The deep-set blue eyes of Watson were observing the frigate HMAS *Brisbane*, anchored just offshore, where the security teams of the three men were stationed. "Okay, Mac, what am I here for?" queried Watson, looking to Charles for support. "Mac, I'm a busy man, but as a personal friend, I came here, but for what and why all the secrecy?"

Silently and on tenterhooks, Mac considered his position as the security representative of the president of Australia. He knew that Major John Tilbury was key to the problems discussed.

"Bill, for your information, Major Tilbury will arrive shortly and brief us on why you and Johnson are here on this island. I expect the halo to arrive any minute."

However, Mac was concerned. What did Tilbury really know, and what was his role in finding the answers?

Mac raised his eyebrows, stared down Johnson who did not blink, as he heard in the distance the familiar chop-chop of an approaching helicopter.

1

Sunday morning, astride his chrome Harley, John Tilbury joined by his biker mate Thomas Black, raced through the foothills of Mt Glorious on the outskirts of Brisbane. A cloudy day with breaks of sunshine as they reached their destination: the jungle coffee haven for tired bikers. On their stands, dozens of bikes indicated a crowded place for caffeine addicts. Noticing the range of *difference* in the crowd they were at peace with the ambience.

They sat outside on the suspended deck that touched the forest amid a group of bikers; assumed trouble makers now at rest in comfort away from the prying eyes of law enforcement. The group knew they were under scrutiny by the Queensland Bikie Gang TaskForce. But this was their Sunday ritual; coffee at Mt Glorious, left alone by the law: comradery, hardship, mateship.

In case of trouble, the group had a 'watcher' seated outside sipping his latte ready to warn them of impending trouble. But he was not ready for what happened next…

The SWAT Hummer gunship screeched to a halt blocking the entrance to the café. Six fully loaded police, protection gear and black helmets, stormed into the café. Sargent Billings captured the attention of the uncertain crowd by firing into the air and shouting, "Do not move, disobey at your peril."

Black immediately stood up and demanded to know what the fuck was going on, "SWAT pussies here for our protection again."

He got too much of their attention.

Two SWAT members grabbed Black and dragged him outside for a quiet chat. Tilbury followed to keep an eye on his mate. He was jostled by other SWAT tough guys not knowing who Tilbury and Black really were.

Outside, both were frisked. To the surprise of Billings, both Tilbury and Black had ASIO dog-tags under their T's: security.

"What the fuck, spooks before us," whispered a team member who realised who Black really was, said, "Well hello Assassin, what are you guys doing in the midst of a bikie gang assembly.

Black, really pissed off, "Just having a fucking coffee, but what are you guys really here for? Billings get you intel right, they're acquaintances of ours – returned vets like us enjoying comradery."

Sore that their morning had been violated, they pulled their bikes off stands and rode off leaving the SWAT team with egg on their faces. Knowing it was not the end of the episode, they raced through downhill bends towards the coast, unaware of a bike following them.

Tilbury, an early riser, next morning walked through a light misty rain along clean windswept footpaths, felt the chill from the night through a soaked T-shirt sticking to his back, bones stiff from restless nights. Vivid recollections, nightmares of war and vets.

Desperately needing the morning caffeine fix, his usual thoughts scattered as he approached Café Boga, a haunt well-travelled: memories of bloody battles and affected vets. Outside tables were arranged for conversation or silence beneath a gabled roof leading to French windows. The wafting aroma coming from inside drew Tilbury towards his reserved table situated inside by the corner window.

Tilbury stood, followed the line of customers seeking the same hit, and collected his mug from barista Thomas with a quiet comment.

"Fucking cold morning, mate. Yesterday was a hoot"

Tilbury, a man of few words was always left alone. His stubble, light with a tinge of grey carefully made to look untouched, matched the carefree look of his cream-coloured linen pants. The black-t hid his well-formed torso: a handsome, dangerous, no-nonsense born leader. A six-three man's man, Tilbury dominated his space. His morning coffee ritual, part of a routine of solace, self-healing, and focus, put the demons back in the box. But the 'black dog' lurked.

He kept fit through a regular routine. Began at 5:30 each morning: skipped for ten minutes to warm up, followed by squats, lunges, and push-ups. Next, a ten-minute session of Pilate's exercises and a quiet period of meditation.

Only barista Thomas Black really knew him.

Gazing around the tables of Café Boga, Tilbury scrutinized the customers and where they sat. As he was trained to do, he recognized the usual group of older patrons telling themselves the stories of their lives and troubles, each with coffees, bacon and eggs, and pastries. An occasional nod made subtle connections. Tilbury knew that people were creatures of habit. They sat in the same chairs and tables if possible, and read papers or talked to each other about the beginning of the day or the chaos of their lives. The coffee shop equivalent of the men's shed.

As an expert in body language from his days as an SAS major in the skirmishes of the Middle East, Tilbury knew that reading people's behaviour had saved him and his men.

And now, he felt there was something amiss about another patron.

He had a vague memory of this face who sat alone like himself, too interested in what others were doing, being inconspicuous but failing the Tilbury test. He had the smell and bearing of a cop.

Tilbury looked straight at the stranger to Cafe Boga and knew his world was about to change for the worst: affected by his presence, trouble brewing, recognition.

AFP Detective Gavin Morrow; the loose cannon.

2

And then he was totally distracted.

She stood and gazed through the window. Tilbury caught sight of slender legs. A known face looked right at him. As he sipped his strong black coffee, he felt his heart skip a beat.

Astonishing ebony beauty, high cheekbones, long and black silky hair, with moist and sensual lips. Tilbury was transfixed, unable to reconcile the fleeting thoughts of sensuality, gratitude, and memories of her smile. The coffee fix was lost in the midst of chaos: passion remembered, love lost, no way home.

Tilbury sat with only one chair space available. The smile moved and entered, nodded at the empty chair and sat.

"Hello, John."

To this day those words reminded him of what was: events and heartache that had entangled their lives. His answer was raw, painful, difficult.

"So, Rachel, what brings you from Florence?"

Her look had stayed with Tilbury wherever he went as an SAS Major—Somalia, Solomon Islands, Afghanistan, and Myanmar. Her throaty clarity, heard and silenced between countless silken sheets, whispered, "The CIA, John, they know."

Viviani looked deep and lovingly at Tilbury and repeated, "They know, John, they know."

It set in the nervous shakes as Tilbury sipped his Macchiato and spilt the elixir over the wooden table dented from countless uses.

Silent, neural pathways twitched. He recalled the colours of passion, scent, deceit, and memories of Florence that changed both their lives.

"The CIA, they know, John. They know." The words were to haunt Tilbury.

Dr John Tilbury was an ex-Brisbane Lions AFL on-baller and premiership player and an ex-SAS major, but he maintained that level of fitness through a daily routine. As a researcher in neuroplasticity at the Yeronga Brain Centre he improved the fractured lives of returned soldiers.

Tilbury sat, watched the sunrise that filtered through the stained-glass windows in silence and contemplated the message brought from afar by his Italian lover, Rachel Viviani, a beautiful neurosurgeon.

Tilbury had swum in her ecstasy which led to his involvement with her. Was this to be his eventual downfall?

"Don't get up, John," Viviani whispered in a clear and hardened voice. "Just think '42' if you're in serious trouble."

She looks firmly at the silent Tilbury, sat and watches him as he sips his macchiato coffee -- mug in both hands.

A slight nervous shake foretells the future as she asks, "John, join me in an experimental trial to test the validity of the new paradigm of brain science."

"Why me Rachel?"

"John, neuroscientists call the discovery -- 'neuroplasticity' which proved the brain is able to change itself. I want you to be involved in a world first experimental trial."

"I can't do that Rachel."

They sat apart in silence watching the sun rise over the Bay until Viviani broke the standoff, "Why not John? I need you. Be my rational guide, be my 'watcher'.

"Watcher of what Rachel, is this a clandestine trial you are conducting?"

"No John, the experiment is earth shattering based on a new technology."

"But, why me Rachel?"

"I'm concerned that cybercrime may steal the technology. The result could be dangerous for humanity in the hands of scrupulous criminals. I want you to be my control. Your spying skills will protect me and my important work, Mr ASIO spook."

They are seen arguing about her proposal. Finally, a nod of acceptance by Tilbury.

I have a bad feeling about this but I'll do it for her.

Then she was gone.

Numb, Tilbury watched her leave through the clearing mist and knew why. He searched his mind to find the way forward as he now faced a full-on moral dilemma: no real escape, out-of-depth, lost.

Tilbury then remembered his Aussie-rules football mate Gary Lang and needed his trusted advice: hope and a way forward.

Tilbury as he watched her leave felt the heat of their short but intimate connection. Knew she would return to Florence, unaware that their interaction was recorded by the stranger Tilbury noticed earlier.

Why her, why now?

He felt the vibration of his communicator and responded, "Tilbury," closed his eyes and listened to the call.

"Are you sure Richard? Thanks for the update."

Fleeting thoughts of past events quickened his pulse, caught his attention, highlighted his failures. He now knew his world had changed and wondered how to train the 'blackdog' to stay in its kennel.

Lost in thoughts, he does not notice a helmeted biker enter Café Boga eyes fixed on him, walks towards him. Stance of a shooter faces Tilbury, draws a gun and shouts. "Stay away from us John, the 'Chinese way' is already here."

Watching the confrontation Black moves, pulls his Glock from beneath the counter and places it against the ear of the intruder and says, "Move, you die."

Tilbury removes the helmet, shocked, shouts, "What! Another fucking Chinese gangster," and calls Mac to remove the intruder.

Black demanded an answer. None given.

3

Later that day Tilbury rested with his back against a white-barked gum tree, shaded from the sun as he looked at the sandstone archways that surrounded the central quadrangle of the University of Queensland. The area was large, with soft, green grass and native trees that shaded the tired students he watched. His thoughts were engaged in his research, but he needed a coffee break.

The relief of warm sunshine soaked through his bones being away from the confines of the laboratory. Thoughts of his research with army veterans blended with fleeting, relaxing thoughts of feeling the throbbing masculinity of riding his Harley on the winding tarmac through subtropical forests to Mount Glorious, on the outskirts of Brisbane. The confrontation with SWAT forgotten.

As he sipped his coffee, Tilbury noticed a woman watching him from beneath one of the majestic sandstone archways. She had a graceful, slender body, long blond hair, and a pleasant face. Curious, he smiled.

She acknowledged the smile and walked up to him. Tilbury had a feeling that he had seen her before.

Recollections flooded over him; he knew why.

"Are you Dr John Tilbury? I need your assistance."

Surprised, Tilbury a man of solitude, unhappy for strangers to confront him like this, said, "You want my help? Why?"

Dr Suzie Jackson, introduced herself as a neuroscientist and mind-body-connection theorist and practitioner, and started to tell her story. But before she got more than a word or two into her story, Tilbury asked, "How do you know me?"

"Through your work on the impact of war on the cognition of returned vets."

Jackson then sat cross-legged on the soft lawn opposite Tilbury, holding his intense gaze. "May I call you John?"

A nod.

"John, I work in the Ikbal Healing Laboratory, to support the casework of neuroplasticity practitioners allied with the Yeronga Brain Centre. My research relates to how the brain-mind-body relationship changes. I develop models to measure and analyse the relationship, based on a case study approach. I also teach on these matters at Griffith University South of Brisbane."

Tilbury, simply answered, "Why me, Suzie?"

"I have a very unusual patient we call Case#45. He is introverted: thoughts scattered, reactionary, morose. He can't remember his past."

"His life is revealed as images of fragmented feelings and actions. I wonder who he really is but apparently a returned vet with a fractured life. He was referred to me by his local GP, who knew of my work."

The case sparked Tilbury's interest.

"John, I have been using mind-balancing techniques and fulfilment experimentation, based on the works of Deepak Chopra. However, Case#45 responded on an array of occasions with a single statement."

"It was the pad; it was that fucking pad."

An unusual case, thought a cautious, curious Tilbury.

Jackson finally asked Tilbury to help her by sitting in on a session with him. The day came. As Tilbury walked in the door to meet Case#45, he was hit with an ice-cold feeling deep in his gut.

Case#45 reacted violently on seeing him, "It was the pad. It was that fucking pad."

Silent, Tilbury felt some memories surface and knew there would be others. Jackson was also shocked by Case#45's reaction.

After calming him down, she asked Tilbury to step outside. She wanted to know what had just happened.

What have I become entangled with?

But she thought that Tilbury knew what had happened. Jackson had the shivers but remained silent. A quiet conversation between them took place, each hedging their bets on the meaning of the words, 'It was the pad, it was that fucking pad.'

They agreed on a plan of action as the matter could not be left alone. Jackson needed to find out what lay behind the man's statement not knowing that the path ahead was unclear and potentially dangerous for both Tilbury and herself.

4

His feeling about his role as an SAS major in the dangerous zones of Iraq and Afghanistan were still raw, emotional, and painful for Tilbury. Lost friends, trauma caused by IEDs, and the immorality of invading another country kept Tilbury engaged in helping war veterans, when and where possible. *Was it a healing process for him?*

Although he was a trained soldier, Tilbury faced a moral dilemma: protecting and preserving as a soldier, versus the impact of war on ordinary citizens, known as 'collateral damage'.

Tilbury returned to his laboratory and thought carefully about the conversation with Jackson. He decided that he needed to talk to Case#45 as soon as possible without her knowing. The Yeronga Brain Centre intranet might help, so he called up the case. But no record existed, unusual, hidden. Acting on a hunch, Tilbury visited reception and asked Wendy, the receptionist, for that information.

"Can you tell me the address of Case#45, he's a vet, and I'd like to meet him at his own digs away from the bureaucracy of this place."

"Oh, John, that's against the SOP of the centre, but given you're asking, I'll check for you."

The receptionist found the record and asked, "Why do you need this, John? This could cost me my job."

Tilbury replied as he left, "Wendy, you're saving his life."

5

Meanwhile, on the foreshore of the tropical city of Cairns, North Queensland, a body with an army-type buzz cut was found prone on an isolated park bench in the early hours of the morning; no signs of injury.

An Aboriginal elder—silver-haired, aged, and slim—found the body on his morning walk with his poodle-cross dog named Captain. The elder had built up a sticky sweat from the humid air that hung-over Trinity Bay. His daily routine was to walk the foreshore pathway and to throw sticks for his dog to retrieve. But today when his dog stood on hind legs beside a bench, the elder went to investigate. Dialled 000.

Within minutes, the paddy wagon arrived, but the young cops were deeply suspicious of the caller. Not all police took much interest in the race training that all police had to undertake in areas where Aboriginal or Torres Strait Islanders lived.

Eventually, the elder was allowed to leave when they found out who he was. He and Captain continued their walk towards the serene early-morning haze that hung over the pools on the foreshore, which revealed the usual tourist activities. Scantily clad tourists felt the warmth of the humid air as they lazed in the local cafes and breakfast bars that lined adjacent streets. The aroma of the coffee blends enticed sleepy tourists and locals out of bed for an early morning hit.

But the elder kept thinking about the body he had discovered.

Who was that person?

Detective Rosa Belotti, a slim, brunette beauty of Italian heritage with a caffeine habit, quietly read the *Courier Mail* newspaper's sporting pages, feeling the warmth of the morning sun and the caffeine hit in a local cafe. A known avid supporter of netball.

Her phone rang. "Rosa here," she grumbled, annoyed at her peaceful moment being disturbed. "It had better be bloody important, Sarge."

She sipped her latte, unhappy, "You're kidding me."

Belotti walked to her car, wondered about the body she was about to see, and the investigation that would follow. As she approached the area where the body was found, she recognised that the young cops wanted to escape the scene. She said, "Eh, boys, what's up?" She showed her D badge, said, "Take me to the body."

Detective Belotti, experienced and knowledgeable of suspicious deaths from her days as a homicide cop in the city, began her investigation.

Who was this John Doe, now officially called Case#643?

Evidence found in one of the victim's pockets, was a Greyhound bus ticket from Brisbane to Cairns, a return ticket for a ferry trip to Green Island, and a smartphone with a scrubbed contact list and only one number in the call list.

She called: no answer, frustration, dead end.

Undaunted, she called her friend at the national cell phone company. An address was mentioned. As her key lead, she arranged to visit that address in Carlton, a Melbourne inner suburb. Belotti landed at Tullamarine Airport about thirty kilometres from the Melbourne CBD.

Suffering from the result of budget cuts, she had little funds for a taxi. Annoyed, she caught the airport bus to town.

After she checked where to go, she discovered the city trams were the shortest route to the address. The trams of Melbourne city were iconic. Quietly, Belotti considered her options as her tram glided through the tree-lined avenues in the drizzling rain.

After she arrived at the address in Carlton, she knocked on the door. It was ajar. "Police!" she shouted as she entered. She found the place trashed.

Belotti searched the unit but found no evidence that could help her investigation. She called the local authorities, who soon arrived. But they could not name the person apparently living in that unit. With no further leads, she left her contact details with the local homicide police and reluctantly returned to Cairns.

Later, Belotti found that the Greyhound bus ticket yielded no information about the dead man. However, she followed up the only other lead, the ticket to Green Island, a tourist playground just offshore of Cairns.

Given the date on the ticket, she asked the ferry administration about that trip hoping to find any clues. The desk officer who sold the ferry tickets, remembered the ferry, *The Green Island Express.*

"Detective, you should talk to Captain Bill. He might remember the day and any details about the person. Just show him a photo of your man."

As she waited on the Cairns terminal wharf for the ferry, Belotti contemplated why Case#643 had visited the island. As a cool breeze rippled the waters of Trinity Bay, the ferry docked, rocking the fishing boats tied within their marina moorings. Cairns was a key fishing port of Queensland.

After the tanned and relaxed passengers alighted from the ferry, Belotti introduced herself to the grisly and tanned Captain Bill with the 'thousand-yard-stare' of a boat captain.

"Captain, can we discuss a trip taken a few weeks ago when this man was on board?" Showed him the photo of Case#643.

Captain Bill thought for a minute then asked Belotti to sit while he told his story.

"Detective Belotti, I remember him as he came on board with two others, dressed like him with a buzz cut hair." Scratching his craggy beard, said, "I remember the quiet group who held up the ferry, buying tickets. They paid no attention to other passengers but chatted-up one of our hosts, Jenny Tan."

"I also believe that on arrival at Green Island, Jenny was seen talking to the man in your photo."

Bill quietly suggested. "You should talk to her about that conversation."

Finding Jenny Tan wasn't difficult. She was a well-known local who lived in Palm Cove, a beach-side suburb just north of Cairns. Her modern unit had ocean views and a balcony for lazy afternoons.

Belotti knocked on her door, surprised by the person who answered. Jenny Tan, Vietnamese, tall and lithe, with a reassuring friendly face. She was wearing cut-offs and a tank top covering ample breasts, which certainly appealed to Belotti, who got a shot of adrenaline and felt little butterflies in her stomach.

Unbeknown to her colleagues, Belotti was a lesbian who loved the touch of a woman. Unfortunately for her, the feeling wasn't mutual; no enticing smile greeted her. However, Belotti was an optimist and got straight to the point.

"What was the connection between you and this dead man?" as she showed her the photo of Case #643.

"You were recently seen with him on Green Island?"

"I don't know what you're talking about."

"Come on, Jenny. We have witnesses."

Now the succulent option was playing harder to get.

"Look, can you make coffee and come out on the balcony and discuss this matter as I'm here on a murder investigation."

Silently, Tan obliged and returned with a coffee plunger and two fine bonechina-cups, sat facing the ocean, partially ignoring Belotti. Realising that the tension should be broken, Belotti gently touched Tan's knee for attention, leant forward, reduced the space between them. Coffee left cold.

"Jenny, what was your relationship with this man and please tell me who he is, because I'm investigating his death?"

Eyes partially closed Tan slowly told of their relationship.

"He was Brigadier Alan Tan and I've known him for many years because he was my brother."

What happened on the island that might have led to the brigadier's death?

"Jenny, what you can tell me about your brother and what he said on the island."

Without pausing, Tan told Belotti about the conversation on the island as she was shocked by the revelation that her brother suspected his men may try to kill him.

"Did he say why?" "No!"

Jenny Tan sobbed, which suggested to an unhappy Belotti that she was withholding information.

Belotti left her contact card and suggested that if she had further information to please make contact.

READ THE FIRST FEW CHAPTERS OF THE THIRD NOVEL OF THE TILBURY TRILOGY

WALK THE WALK:

THE TILBURY JUDGEMENT

GREGORY MOORE

Can Agent Tilbury face the power of difference, evil Artificial Intelligence and fight for the rights of human diversity?

WHO IS AGENT TILBURY?

I am Agent John Tilbury, master spy of ASIO. Setbacks and beating the odds have changed my life in recent years. I am strong-willed, a battle-hardened ex SAS major, a spook with hidden wounds of the 'black dog' ever-present that invade my thoughts and control my actions; pervaded uncertainty.

But I never give in and gain solace from oiling my Glock on the back deck of my apartment during times of stress and melancholy. I work hard to overcome the inadequacies of my decision-making as accepted by my trusted friends and comrades-at-arms. My inner strength keeps me going. I am not perfect, nor comfortable with my growing imperfections, my judgements, and my future in protecting my country.

I am bruised by events, but not beaten nor broken.

Lenard Cohen flashes through my mind: *There is a crack in everything, that's how the light gets in.* An optimistic light emerges from the end of my dark tunnel, an illumination softened that supported my need to protect my teammates who need my trust, need my leadership.

Was the 'black dog' back in the kennel?

Right now, the aroma of the macchiato coffee sitting before me at my favourite table at Café Boga, Brisbane released fleeting moments of recent events that created chaos everywhere linked to the nefarious use of artificial intelligence [AI] and the continual rise of the 'Chinese way.'

I let these moments wash over me when I oil my Glock, my safety net.

However, I was not ready for what happened next …

ONE

Tilbury, astride his chrome Harley, felt the wind under his helmet tassel his hair, the throb of his deep base muffler easing his stress, and a sense of freedom on the open road. Tired from a long ride, he stopped for an eye-rest under the gum trees along the side of the tarmac and fell asleep stretched out on top of the Harley. He had removed his black leather jacket that the police assumed nominated him as 'a biker': pulled over, questioned, cautioned.

His planned road trip from Brisbane to Cairns was tiring but a break from the complications of decision-making as the lead spook of ASIO. The cool breeze relaxed his tired body.

Always prepared, his Glock was in easy reach and easy access in a specially designed hidden compartment at the front of his seat.

A sound of footsteps approaching triggered an immediate reptilian response: fight or flight. Standing beside the bike was a powerful black man with a gun to Tilbury's head in response to the retrieved Glock; stalemate, no ground given.

"What are you doing in my country carrying a weapon, mate? Please, drop the Glock and stand with your hands on your head."

"Who are you? I am just a traveler able to protect myself," but he obeyed the order because of his training.

"I am senior detective sergeant 'Tracker' Jak Norman based in Cardwell just up the road," showed his ID card.

"Well, Tracker, the name is Tilbury, John Tilbury, a civil servant at your service," showed his ID card.

The hardmen looked each other in the eye until Tracker smiled a friendly broad smile with sparkling eyes, and said, "Well, a fucking spook in my country!"

With both weapons stowed, they shook hands and a friendship began. Tilbury liked the character of the man, tall, rugged, with short dark stubble, wide-brimmed hat, and a slight swagger radiating self-confidence.

But Tilbury was surprised by the next statement.

"John, can I ride your Harley? I have a trail bike and live close by, how about a few beers and a get to know each other chat?"

"OK, Jak, give me your truck keys and I will follow."

The detective's house was typical of the tropics: single story on stilts, front and back stairs, wide veranda, hidden within a shrub and tree-shaded garden. The Harley now parked under the house along with a trail bike; safe. The two law enforcement officers sat on the veranda chairs sipping local ales. Conversation a little stilted as they began to thaw from the earlier incident and as each told of their background.

As trained men, their weapons were on the table, a habit both had learnt from experience. A calm surrounded the chats as the light faded, until …

Without warning, bullets came from everywhere, shredding the trees and shrubs. Both knew that this was serious, grabbed their weapons, and changed position on the veranda for protection.

Norman gave the hand signal to act as if he knew the layout of his house. A move by Norman to the back of the house waiting for the intruders to come up the back stairs, a normal confronting access approach.

Tilbury, seasoned by infighting, had moved to a front room for a better view of the two armed men: trained, loaded, with light protection gear.

He gave a signal for Norman to move closer to the back door, ready for the ambush.

"Jak, your take on this mate? We will have to kill these guys. I hope you are ready for this."

"No idea who they are or why us. But let's do it, now!"

It was clear to Tilbury that he may be the target but as he knew little about Norman, it could be either, or both.

The intruders came up the two sets of stairs sweeping automatic rifles left to right: a full-frontal attack.

Tilbury emptied his Glock on the first while Norman took out the second. The dying men sprayed bullets in no pattern, then were silent.

First to the bodies, Tilbury stripped off the protective gear to find no ID, but their nationality was clear: Chinese.

Norman, concerned about the dead, told Tilbury the local police should be called. Whereas Tilbury, concerned about the killers being Chinese, told Norman that it was now an ASIO matter. A heated debate ensued as Norman, the local senior detective, demanded that the case was his but eventually agreed with Tilbury that the incident had national significance.

A Tilbury call to Mac, head of ASIO, brought a clean-up team and criticism.

"John, more dead Chinese. What are you doing? Starting a war with MSS or the Triads again?"

"MSS and/or Triads not yet proven but these guys meant business. I am unsure whether I was the target or a detective I met on the road."

"But Mac, I am impressed by Jak Norman. He would be a great member of my team, another Thomas type: hardman with experience in NorthForce in rural areas and outback country surveillance. Please ask Marsha to background him ASAP and use DYLAN."

The message via his smartphone supported Tilbury's view that he would make an excellent member of his team.

John, Norman has a strong record but no marks against him. Spent time in country learning bushcraft, meeting cousin brothers, and gaining acceptance as a police officer. He had a short career in the army, rose to be a lieutenant after training in counter-terrorism, but left for private reasons. A vet from recent skirmishes in the Middle East. Tracker is a solid hardman. Clean as far as I Know. DYLAN.

A call to Mac supported his idea that maybe they could recruit Norman as he had different skills needed by the team.

Hungry after the skirmish, Norman suggested a visit to the famous 'Barramundi burger' café in Cardwell just down the road from his place. Cardwell town was onshore off Hinchinbrook Island, a protected conservation area, with a *Wilderness Lodge,* accessed by boat, hidden within the rainforest.

"Lieutenant Jak, great burgers, is there anywhere we can get away and talk? I have an offer for you to discuss."

"Are you serious, John? A career as a spook! Remember, I am just a run-of-the-mill detective with a simple lifestyle."

"Yes, Lieutenant Norman, are you interested?"

"On one condition, John, you beat me on the rifle range. By the way, please do not call me that; 'Tracker,' please."

Both boarded the ferry to *Wilderness Lodge,* the challenge forgotten.

TWO

Wilderness Lodge was set well within the rainforest. The raised wooden walkways protected the fauna and flora of the forest floor. Single and double bungalows were well spread out for privacy. They agreed on separation; individual huts that welcomed them, quality craftsmanship, and simplicity. Seeing no apparent threat, they locked away their guns and agreed to walk and talk.

As they moved through the jungle walkway to the beach, the earlier incident image dampened. The crystal-clear blue waves washed over them as their body surfed, enjoying the ride and the feeling of dried saltwater on their toned bodies. However, they were not alone; they were watched from the cover of the rocky, shaded tree line above the white sandy beach.

But Tilbury, risk-averse in new locations, felt a presence and warned Norman.

A nonchalant recognition indicated readiness as they moved back to the lodge showing little signs of concern. Both sought the safety of their weapons back at their respective bungalows and waited in Norman's nearby hut in the dark.

It was agreed that Tilbury would leave the bathroom light on in his bungalow as bait for intruders and a radio on in the kitchen. They were ready with eyes on the Tilbury hut.

Were they paranoid or just battle-hardened?

Quiet, calm, loaded, they waited. But not for long. Shadows of two assailants focussed on that hut with serious weapons, then all hell broke loose.

The hut was shredded, windows blown in, walls pock-marked from high-powered guns. Then silence.

The intruders assumed that they had achieved their mission and headed past the Norman hut: their first mistake, second mistake not being observant, and third mistake were the gunshot wounds.

Both Tilbury and Norman had agreed not to kill the intruders because they needed information. It was clear that these attackers were connected to the previous two that stormed Norman's house earlier: Chinese Triads. None were prepared to speak, so Tilbury summed up the situation.

"Friends, I know who you are and where you are from. Unless you send a message to your leader for me, you will be placed in a very dark place and forgotten for ten years, or I will shoot you in self-defence on your refusal to talk."

Norman, shocked by the Tilbury announcement, took him aside and said, "John, you cannot do that. You have no legal right to kill these guys."

"Jak, these Chinese bastards have been at my throat for some years now. No remorse about trying to kill me and you mate. I have had enough of the 'Chinese way' affecting the freedoms of Australia and other democracies."

"John, the 'Chinese way,' what is that, mate?"

Tilbury explained the history of that term and his relationship with coping with its impact. Satisfied with the story, Norman agreed with ASIO dealing with the two men.

However, Tilbury pressed home his need for information from the seriously injured assassin. So, he shot him in the leg. Again, Norman questioned the action; ignored.

"You need hospital care which is under my control. Who are you working for, mate?"

Indicating he was ready to shoot the other leg, he got a muffled response. Only one word was coughed up, "Chen."

Shocked, the name 'Chen' meant something to him.

Tilbury now needed more horsepower as a troubling scenario lay before him. Guided by his recent experience, he welcomed Norman into his team based on Mac's approval.

"John, the road less traveled now awaits 'Tracker Jak.'"

To his family and cousins, Norman was known as 'Tracker Jak' because of his ability to find and track down criminals who wandered off into 'country' to hide from the law or when called upon to find lost travelers passing through his country. As a child, 'Tracker' had learnt the ways of country from tribal elders: bushcraft, survival techniques, and respect for country.

As he grew, rugby league beckoned as a frontrow specialist; size mattered but ethnicity did not. But often, the call to country upset his teammates as he went 'walkabout' living off the land and getting to know his aboriginal roots. Uncle Billy often took Tracker to billabong waterways and rivers to learn, to hear stories about his ancestors and the dreamtime.

A local returned vet took him under his wing, convinced him to join up, and set an example for his cousin brothers by attending officer training. He excelled in intelligence, counter-terrorism, and espionage and found himself in the Middle East.

Based on his experience, he became a detective.

THREE

Days later, the headquarters of the Ministry of Home Affairs, Canberra exploded with mortars and high-velocity bullets strafing the windows of the Ministerial Office killing Hon Andrew Frank the conservative Minister and the CEO of the Ministry, Tony Baker. Injured were the heads of Australian Security Intelligence Organisation [ASIO], Bob 'Mac' McLeod; Australian Signals Directorate [ASD], Dr Anthony Hudson; Australian Federal Police [AFP], Commissioner Brian Wallace.

It was a top-secret security meeting to review the spate of cybercrime and potential espionage activities currently being investigated within Australia.

As a mentor and ASIO boss, Mac was on Tilbury's mind as he considered the consequences of the attack. He checked the hospital and found he was in ICU but will take some time to recover. But who was now in control? Whom he could trust?

How did the perpetrators know about the meeting?

A call from Australian President Notting changed the life of Tilbury and his judgement: now responsible for ASIO operations, and advice to the president on these matters.

ACKNOWLEDGMENT

From a spook's perspective, Cohen and Dylan sum up the puzzled life of Agent John Tilbury.

"There is a crack in everything,
that's how the light gets in."
"In my secret life."
"Everybody knows."
Leonard Cohen from *The London Concert, 2013.*

'Not Dark Yet'
I just don't see why I should even care
It's not dark yet, but it's getting there.

'Things I Have Changed'
People are crazy and times are strange
I used to care, but things have changed

Bob Dylan, Nobel Poet Laurette: 'The lyrics 1961-2012'

Gregory Moore holds a PhD in economics, policy, and fisheries. He began his career as an educator, high school and universities, but later changed to be a fisheries economist and an international fisheries management consultant supporting industry and governments in the Asia/Pacific region. For the last five years, he has been a professional international volunteer helping scientists improve their research and English of their Journal papers. He currently lives in Jakarta Indonesia pursuing areas of interest. He loves golf, Bob Dylan, writing poetry, and thriller spy novels, and has been a long-time supporter of the Brisbane Lions AFL team.

be obtained
om

1222
0004B/153

9 781959 182320